We sell radical new literature in paperback and e-book format, catching the authors in their most creative period; when their ideas are fresh and innovative.

If you're tired of reading wilting novels churned out by so-called famous authors or previously incoherent people famed for something else...
Welcome to **Bastard Books**.

For more stirring titles visit our on-line shop at:

bastardbooks.com

All our featured books have a brutally honest *Bastard Books* review and reader reviews are included as we receive them. We let you download the first chapter (sometimes more) of every book so you can see before you buy. You can either buy paperback copies of the novels via our secure server or, for a discounted price; they can be downloaded onto your PC, Pocket Computer or Rocketebook.

You are welcome to review any of the books and by optionally including your email address you can share your thoughts with other readers.

THE ANNUNCIATION OF THE STARBORN

BERNADETTE DANAHER

Bastard Books

BASTARD BOOKS
(A division of Usualready Enterprises Ltd.)

Published in Great Britain by:
Bastard Books
85 Clifton Hill,
London, NW8 OJN.

A CIP catalogue record for this book is
available from the British Library

PUBLISHERS NOTE

This is a work of fiction. Names, characters places, and incidents either are the product of the author's imagination or are used fictitiously, and any resemblance to actual persons, living or dead, events, or locales is entirely coincidental.

ISBN 1-84346-030-0

For my family and friends

especially Pat
whose support has been incalculable

and Bob
who always believed

THE PROLOGUE

I HAVE SINNED.

It is only now, in this stinking cell that I shall not leave alive, that I can look back and see the magnitude of my folly. To all creatures before death, they say, comes a final clarity of vision. I have it now in full measure. Would that I had never been born.

You do not understand, I see. How should you? You are not one of us. Your people have not the Old Speech, the Spell Speech. Nevertheless I shall use it. Though here in this accursed place it can be no more than sounds that echo from the walls, every creature should die with their own language in their ears. Perhaps before the end you will cry out in yours, calling on the Mother… I shall not call on Her. For such as I, who have forfeited everything, there can be no mercy. Those gifted as I have been gifted have the power to make an end, and I have made my choice. Even my unborn will die with me. Not for her the shame of daughterhood to me.

When did it all begin? Perhaps even the Wise could not say. Since the Beginning ours had been a world… well, not at peace perhaps, but with its own kind of order. Now all that is over. I think that this is the beginning of the End, though I shall not live to see it. Others have said that it surely began on the night that one of the stars fell from heaven, plunging into the heart of the great forest of Three Stars – all know that this is an omen, and for whom should it be more significant than for us, the Daughters of the Stars? I did not see it, and I do not know. Perhaps beyond the Endless Ocean that truth will be revealed among all others… if I am permitted to journey thither. I think that for me there will be only eternal darkness. I have earned it. I have sinned.

Why are you here? In what way have you offended, to be flung here bloody and broken and left to die, with the black pain-sweat rank on you? I can hear your voice, but there is no answer in me: only the void in which my guilt screams that there is no forgiveness possible. In my pride and folly I have sold our salvation to purchase ruin. I have betrayed the Holy One. I have sinned.

Time creeps and crawls like a crippled thing here. I know from your breathing when you are wakeful and when the darkness claims you. If it mattered I could end your suffering, but there will be no pity for those who remain when we have gone… one day the last star will go out, and perhaps then my shame will go with it. Until then there is only the waiting.

I have sinned.

1.

Insignificant, it was, in stellar terms; for aeons it had wandered through the icy reaches of the system orbiting its star, a black and lifeless hunk of rock and ice with neither beauty nor purpose. That was not to say that it had no significance, nor that its existence was meaningless. Its wandering was followed. It could not be influenced, but the action of the solar winds could possibly serve to change the course of fate.

Thus it was that – after millennia had passed – it finally came within the gravitational field of one of the worlds which circled its sun. Its momentum could not save it from capture. Swiftly it was dragged planetward, its ice melting in the friction of the atmosphere, its rock glowing brightly in the heat and trailing a fiery tail of burning particles. It was not large enough to pose any threat to life on the planet to which it fell, weighing at most a couple of pounds by the time it ploughed into the soil.

But with it, came the madness.

She lifted her head, and looked out of the window. The night sky was clear and cloudless, and there was no wind. It was impossible that anyone should gaze on the glory of stars outside without being moved to wonder; she, as one of the Daughters of the Stars, felt her whole being lift towards them in worship. At any time and any season the night sky was a marvel; but in winter, when the air was as clear as glass and sharp as a knife, the staggering beauty of the spiral galaxy which filled half of the sky was almost beyond belief. The stars pulsed with light like jewels spilled on velvet, in every shade from pure white to pale blue or soft rose, crowded and glorious and endlessly wonderful.

She stood up, and extended her arms forward and down, exposing the wrists in reverence. "Praise Shieih, all you assembled stars! Rejoice in Her, arch of midnight!" Indeed it was a privilege beyond the telling to be a Daughter of the Great Goddess. The starlight poured through the window on to her long blonde hair and soft fur, gleamed in the triangular amber eyes. She was a Skair, a member of the race who lived to worship the Goddess who had created them, and although all Skaira were regarded with the reverence that was their due, they were a part of the natural order. Their divine origins did not protect them from the stresses and strains of everyday life; and Lidan was hungry.

It was time to hunt. Her empty stomachs growled. On such a night the scent would lie well, but sounds would carry. She would have to be very wary on the trail: the snap of a breaking twig would alert her prey. Sometimes it was easier on windy nights, when the motion and sounds all around masked her own – she knew where the deer came to drink at the pool, and had made kills there. Not often, for that would drive away the visitors, who were quite astute enough to weigh up the risks. But she had come insensibly to rely upon it if her luck failed elsewhere, and she knew that it was becoming urgent that she kill soon. For half a cycle she had eaten cereal and fruit foods, and that sufficed for a while – but like all her people she could not survive without blood. It was part of her heritage, the bequest of her leonine forebears: she and all of hers were hunters, who must regularly bring down and eat their prey in the eternal cycle of life.

The pool, then; it was not far away. She lowered her arms, and began to stretch away the stiffness of her evening nap. This was quite a protracted business, and had to be done carefully. Hunting was not a sport for her; she would go hungry if it failed. Therefore it behoved her to loosen up as methodically and thoroughly as any athlete, and she went about it with her usual care. Her coat was looking a little dull, she thought critically, running a hand down her flank: perhaps she would take a small flask of scented oil with her, and if the Good Goddess favoured her and she was successful at the pool, she could bathe there after she had eaten her fill. When her other preparations were done, she combed and braided her long hair – Skaira usually wore their hair loose whilst at home, but this could easily become a liability during hunting, being far too prone to becoming entangled in undergrowth or twigs. Finally and most importantly she examined her claws. They could be sharper (her route would take her quite close to her favourite stropping-tree, and she would pause there) but they were clean enough. Her finger-claws were always immaculate, though she checked them too as a matter of course. It was the work of a moment to buckle her hunting-knife in its leather sheath, and she was ready. She considered taking the oil, but decided to leave it for another day.

She stepped out of the hut and paused for a moment, surveying the scene that spread out before her. As far as the eye could see, there was forest – except away towards the West, where a formidable range of mountains reared into the sky. They dwarfed this little hillock into insignificance, but she found no fault with it for that: it was her home, and she was comfortable here. Many of her people would not have been so comfortable. Her own mother would have turned from it in disgust. She was well aware that she would not readily, if ever, be forgiven for walking away from the prospect of a life high in the hierarchy of the Palace, but whenever she thought of her decision her conclusions were always the same. She could not have stayed there. The routine, the dreary necessity of protocol and politicking, would have suffocated her. Instead of the life to which she had been born, one at the heart of power, she had chosen one of almost complete isolation on the hill in the forest, within sight of the Holy Mountain of Vanreil, and had never repented her choice. Many of her people did choose to live thus, as "out-lairers", and she rarely missed company. She had her books, the bulky volumes of the Law, which were an engrossing study, and the mere business of keeping herself alive took up much of her time. Fortunately, Skaira had an extremely strong resistance to cold; in the winter her golden coat grew thick, but her naked upper half seldom felt the need of a covering. The hut where she had chosen to live was small and simple, built chiefly of blocks of unshaped stone held together by rough mortar. It had only two rooms, the smaller of which was floored with stone and served as a storage area. There was nothing but a square of hide to drop across the window to keep out the worst of the draughts, with a second and larger to cover the door. Basic it might be, but it kept the rain from her while she slept, and boasted a couple of items of rough wooden furniture and a shelf to keep her precious books away from gnawing insects. With these humble luxuries Lidan the Skair was well content.

The night air called her, and the dull ache of hunger filled her belly. Involuntarily she glanced upwards, wordlessly commending her quest to the Mother of All, Shieih of tooth and claw. The stars glittered in silence as she padded down the hillside and passed under the shadow of the trees, becoming herself a shadow that moved on soundless paws.

Presently the scent of water on the breeze warned her that her destination was not far away. She knew that on one side of the pool there was a stand of reeds, and a deer-track ran alongside it. For obvious reasons she very rarely used this, but tonight it would serve her. She changed course slightly to come downwind of it, and slowed her already cautious pace. There was no scent yet of prey, but it was a rare night when nothing came to drink; and for her purposes it did not have to be anything large. A fat yearling, still carrying the bulk of his autumn feeding – her mouth watered.

She found a comfortable enough spot hidden among the reeds, and slid down into a position which left her nose directly in line with a tunnel among the undergrowth which had probably been made by some small rodent. It served now as a funnel, bringing scent directly to her from the deer-track. Now nothing would serve but patience, and of that she had more than enough.

Time passed. The stars wheeled silently above her, and she lay without movement, listening intently. Most warm-blooded creatures would have become intensely chilled during the wait, but the Skair core of sorcery rendered them almost indifferent to cold. At one point she heard a large beast come down to drink, but it came to a point almost opposite her own, and she had weighed up her chances of success and found them poor. She would make too much noise leaving the reeds on such a still night as this, and then there was the water to cross: admittedly it was not wide, the matter of a couple of leaps, but that would give the animal on the far bank ample warning of her presence and probably more than enough time to make its escape.

The middle of the night was well past when the first eddy of the scent for which she waited came to her damp sensitive nostrils. Her pulse jumped but not a muscle of her body moved. After a moment she opened her mouth to allow the scent to reach the sensory cells on the roof of her mouth, which gave her more information. A female beast, alone – the Skair's eyes narrowed and she inhaled again. No young at foot – not that that would matter, a fawn would be old enough to fend for itself by now, but earlier in the year the presence of a dependant would have rendered the hind ineligible to her as prey. Excitement rose in her. Saliva ran in her mouth, and her tongue ran around the sharp teeth as though already tasting blood. As stealthily as clouds her quarters gathered under her, the great paw-claws sliding from their housings and digging into the reeds beneath her for maximum traction. Her left hand silently unfastened the thongs securing her knife. She pushed her nose gently into the rodent-tunnel, monitoring the strengthening smell; now her ears could pick up the hesitant hoof-falls. Close, but not close enough yet. Her pulse hammered. The sounds grew louder, the smell stronger: now there was warmth in it. Every instinct in her body screamed at her to leap, but she waited – waited – waited –

Like a furry projectile she hurtled out of the reed bed, taking the deer totally by surprise. She struck it on the left side, and her weight bowled it over. The silent night was split by the hind's bawl of terror, and there was a sickening moment of struggling and confusion in the tangled undergrowth when the Skair could not get a grip on the horns. Like all of her kind, she aimed to bring death as quickly as possible; this was best accomplished in the dark by getting hold of the head and sinking the knife into the great artery that pulsed under the jaw. She preferred to get a horn-grip when dealing with deer – it immobilised a weapon and guided her own strike. Tonight, however, she was uncharacteristically slow about it. Snarling with frustration at her own clumsiness, her nose full of the scent of hot bloody hide, she sank her claws deep into the struggling animal, dropping her head and using her teeth as she fought for a grip on the thrashing antlers. A male would have been easier to deal with – they grew far larger horns. It was a minute or two, but seemed like hours, before she got a satisfactory hold. With a huge effort she wrenched the tossing head back, heaved up her own weight and thrust the knife into the stretched neck. The hot jet of blood took her in the face, and she snapped at it eagerly. The fatal blow delivered, the hind's struggles instantly weakened and soon ended altogether. Gratefully the Skair straightened up, raising her bloody hands skywards: "From Thy hand, O Mother! All thanks!" It was traditional, and quite automatic, but still heartfelt, as were the quieter words she murmured to the still-warm body beneath her as she bent to it again. It had lost its life so that hers might continue, and there was a debt of thanks owing to it also. That paid, she put her mouth to the knife-wound and began drinking the blood which was leaking sluggishly from it.

The small wind that precedes dawn had begun to blow before she stood up again, and her movements were slow and ponderous from the weight of meat she had eaten. A Skair's body contained several stomachs and allowed her to consume a vast amount of food at a single meal, which would be gradually digested over several days. Lidan had fed to satiation, and by the time she left the remnants of the carcass she wanted nothing more than an extremely thorough wash followed by an extremely long sleep. Yawning, she ambled towards the pool. Briefly she paused to inspect a particular tree at its brink for scent-marks, but there had been no visitors. Rubbing her sticky forequarter contentedly against the rough bark before turning to leave her own signature on it, she idly watched the wet mud seep up between her bloody talons. Around her the birds were beginning to wake; from one or two trees there came sleepy trills and chirps. The water was deliciously cold and clear, and with her usual disregard for the shocking chill of it against her body, she leaped in and threw herself flat, allowing the blood and bits of flesh to float away from her on the current. All Skaira could swim after a fashion, though the construction of their bodies made them clumsy in water and few achieved much skill at it. Presently she picked a twig from an overhanging bush and carefully cleaned her teeth with it; and once assured that she was thoroughly clean, she waded out of the pool again and shook herself on the bank. Twisting the long golden head-hair into a rough plait squeezed most of the water out of it – she would comb it properly later. She lifted her head and studied the sky. Dawn was indeed not far off.

Afterwards, she could never have said what prompted her to turn again and look back at the pool. But for the tentative notes of birdsong, there was total silence in the wood. And yet –

She turned. Although daybreak was near, the sky above was still quite dark, though the stars had a pale and weary look. But the pool was suddenly a mirror reflecting a glory of colour. All the tints of the rainbow refracted from the unquiet water, shimmering and breaking against the surrounding trees.

The Skair had far too intimate an acquaintance with sorcery to doubt what she was seeing. Her meal forgotten as completely as her dripping and dishevelled state, she sank into a crouch and extended her arms forward with the wrists exposed. Her head was bowed. "Your Daughter hears, O Divine One. Work Your will with me!"

"Greetings, Lidan my Daughter." Was the voice in the air or in her head? She would never know; only that afterwards she could never describe any quality of it.

"You have a task to perform, one that has waited for many years. The time is right. The first blow has been struck. Now it is your destiny that awaits you."

"My destiny, Firstborn?" She struggled with shock. "You know I am yours to command."

"I do not command you. The world has need of you, but you have the right to refuse. What awaits you must be accepted freely or not at all."

"Then I accept."

"Softly, softly." The voice was threaded with amusement. *"This is no game, Lidan my beloved one. Hear what must be done before you commit yourself."*

"I need nothing save to know that I do Your will," she said steadily, "but what you wish me to know, I will hear."

There was a slight pause. The Skair waited without impatience, raising her head slightly to gaze at the shimmering pool. The shifting, glittering light reflected in the tawny eyes, waking a faint green radiance behind the amber.

"You were drawn here for a purpose, my Daughter. Long ago, the forebear of your Line gave birth to a daughter in the dwelling you call home. My hand was on her, though she was to remain hidden from the sight of others. You have heard the tale of how she disappeared from the Shrine, to be seen no more. Her name was Tharien, Princess of Skaira. Her daughter was Shirah the Golden, Tan'arnah of whom the songs were written.

"Tharien it was who brought from another world the bracelet which you inherited. It belonged to a girl-child of that place, who so loved others that she gave her life for them. As a reward, the girl-child was reborn, as daughter to Tharien and fallow-sister to Rethan who ascended the Divan Throne when her mother's span was done. Rethan never knew what had become of her mother, nor that Shirah was her sister, though the two were close all their lives.

"The tale of this is long, and only a part of a story which has been unfolding for more years than life has taken to unfold upon this planet. Others have had their part in it. But now the tale is coming to its climax, and great danger is upon this world. You have been fortunate in that your foremother's blood drew you back to the place of her birthing. The world outside has changed, and war stalks Kerriel. To prevent it, it is foretold that the Starborn shall bring the Starborn. Only one not of this world can save it. You are Starborn, descendant

of the blood of another world. It is your task to bring the Starborn in whose hands the fate of the world rests."

Lidan swallowed. It was too much to take in. She was aware of course that she was descended from First Priestess Shirah – but not that Shirah had been a fallow-born daughter of Princess Tharien, whose mysterious disappearance was one of the legends of their world. She glanced down in awe at the silver circlet around her wrist; a trace of engraving on it had been almost obliterated by the passage of years. Her mother had given it to her on the day she came of age, explaining that it was an heirloom of her House. Nothing had been said about the engraving – the little of it that could still be seen on the plain, narrow bangle appeared to be lettering in an unknown language. It was more than likely that the meaning, like its history, had become lost in the mists of years. The stuff of another world, the property of the legendary Tharien!

"I hear You, Mother Shieih. I shall do whatever is in my power."

"It will take power greater than yours to cross the bridge between the stars. Trust me that it can be done, and that you will have all the powers you need."

"And – the Starborn? She knows of our need? She has great powers?"

"He, not she – and he knows nothing of us. His world has not yet discovered that others than themselves inhabit the universe. And he has no powers, not as you would define them. His power lies in what he is, not what he can do."

"A male?" Lidan could not hide her shock. Her ears twitched upright, and her amber eyes opened wide in astonishment. "And knows nothing? How shall I approach him?"

"The way will be made clear. He honours his Goddess often, and it is appropriate that you should meet with him in such circumstances."

If the revelation of her royal origins had amazed the Skair, this second fairly stunned her. To 'honour the Goddess' was to share body pleasures with another, to have sex with them. Such a privilege was forever lost to Skaira, who were born carrying their fertile eggs. "Mother Shieih – I heard you aright?" she said faintly. "I am to honour You with the Starborn?"

"The way will be made clear. You will cross the bridge between the stars, and take on a form that will be acceptable to him."

The concept was still too much to grasp. Without even knowing that she was doing so, certainly never thinking that the action might be disrespectful, the Skair sat down and put her head in her hands. She felt slightly dizzy, and concentrated on taking deep breaths to steady herself.

"How can this be possible?" she said almost inaudibly. To couple with a male – she had never considered such a thing. Why should she have done? No Skair had done so since their Creation, when they had lost all the pains and pleasures that belong to two-sexed creatures. They had been compensated – amply compensated: the life of one of the Daughters of the Stars was filled and overfilled with wonder. But it was told that the first generation, those who knew what they had lost, had mourned in their hearts nevertheless…

"To the gods all things are possible. But your consent is everything. There can be no force in this matter."

"But – it is necessary?" Lidan struggled to still her hurrying thoughts. Skaira were not shielded from the realities of sex just because these did not apply to them:

Shieih was the Goddess of blood and birthing, and for two-sexed creatures, sex was a part of Her worship. She found herself thinking irrelevantly of the day that the subject had been brought up for the first time in Training School; many of the cubs had already been exposed to the matter, but some were encountering it for the first time. When the facts of the act had been explained, there had been an explosion of giggles. It seemed such an absurd thing to want to do! It still seemed rather strange even now, though she was assured that the process was enjoyable. Skaira of childbearing age experienced erotically pleasurable dreams, usually heralding the onset of pregnancy; their brains retained the capacity for sexual sensation, even though they had no males to provide the stimulus.

"It is appropriate. There are few ways of achieving one-ness with another living soul, and the act of love is one of the greatest of those few. To bring him you must become one with him. Therefore, it is appropriate."

"But-" the Skair said at last, troubled, "Mother Shieih, what if he should not desire me? No-one can be forced to honour You against their will. It would be filth beyond imagining."

"He will desire you. I have breathed upon you, I Shieih of the dark hours. No-one whom you wish to lay with will deny you. And you will know what you must do, and desire him equally."

There was a pause. Lidan tried desperately to imagine what it would be like to be sexually irresistible, and failed. Finally, "If it must be done, Divine Mother, I will do it. But what if I do not know him when I see him?"

"There is no danger of that. Your body will know him. Nevertheless, to set your mind at ease, look into the pool."

Half in fear and half in fascination, the Skair leaned forward and peered into the iridescent water. Deep in the shifting, shimmering depths she saw a shape take form. Like a Venel or a Manyé, he stood upright on two legs. He was tall, though slender compared to a male Venel; his arms and hands were not unlike her own, though his legs were more Venel – the shape of the shoes he wore hid any details of the feet. She looked with close attention at his face. The shape was roughly oval, though his jaw was slightly square. There was no suggestion of the heavy teeth of a Skair, which made the lower half of his face appear a little narrow to her. His hair was dark, and cropped close to his head. It was the eyes that really startled her: they were unlike any on Kerriel, being oval and white with greenish discs in the centre. She was unable to read his expression with any certainty, but he seemed to be frowning in concentration. After a couple of moments' close observation she realised with an illogical sense of shock what he was doing.

"He is Dancer-born! Is he high in the service of his God?"

"They do not worship their God in the dance on his world. Dancing is his trade."

"His trade!" Lidan stared. "But… that is not…" She struggled to articulate a concept that lay so close to the heart of her civilisation that she had never heard it put into words. Finally it emerged as almost a wail of protest: "Such gifts are God-given. They should be given back to the Giver!"

"And so they are, though he would not think of it in that way. He and his kind give pleasure to many, and earn their bread thus. It is a calling which demands much."

There was another pause. She watched the Starborn in silence, appreciating the suppleness of his body. Dancer-born and trained Skair Priestesses would not have scorned the grace and certainty of his movements, whatever their significance. His clothes were a little strange to her – no race on Kerriel wore garments which hugged their legs in that way. He was clad all in black, which made him look more than a little sinister; the loose garment which covered his chest and spread out as wings to his wrists was of some strange fine fabric that glittered like fish-scales. A broad scatter of green gems fell from the right shoulder across the centre of it, and more sparkled down near the hems of his leg-coverings. He paused at that moment, and the frown gave way to a smile of unexpected warmth. He spoke to someone out of her view – there was no sound, but she saw his lips move – and took from the unknown companion an intricate crown, partly a mask, which he put on. Dark green and silver, the front of it covered well over half of his face, and increased the sinister look a hundredfold. His eyes glittered evilly through it. By the Eye! Lidan almost recoiled. Surely there had been some mistake?

"He plays a part only. It need not trouble you."

The Skair did not know whether to be disappointed or relieved when the picture faded. She became aware again of the forest surrounding her, the world that had gone to the brink of war without her knowledge. Of how much else had she been ignorant, isolated here in the Forest of Three Stars? What was happening out there, and into what would she bring the unsuspecting Starborn?

"A great evil has been unleashed upon the world, one long foretold. It must be dealt with, and soon. Therefore you must return to your home and rest, and at twilight tomorrow I will open the bridge between the stars, and send you forth."

Twilight tomorrow! And how could she possibly rest, with such a prospect before her? Nevertheless, the Goddess must be obeyed. The Skair bowed with great reverence to the pool.

"As you command, Divine Mother."

"Go with my blessing. At tomorrow's end I shall come to you again." The water gave out one final burst of radiance and became normal again, reflecting only the pale dawn sky now visible beyond the trees on its banks.

Lidan rose stiffly, conscious again of her full stomach and the limbs cramped from too-long immobility. Could it have been a dream? But she knew that it had not been. The entire episode had had a knife-edged clarity more real than any waking experience she had ever had. Till tomorrow, then. A day, and a night, and another day, and then she would leave the only world she had ever known and journey to another, and to an experience she could never have dreamed of. Marvellous were the ways of the Goddess!

In deep thought she went back to the hill she had made her home. Around her the woods were silent, without even the movement of birds. The very stillness made her hackles itch. Something was terribly wrong. Even the birds knew it. And it was up to her – all up to her, to bring the one who could set matters right again.

It seemed long before she was pacing up her hill again. At the crest she turned and looked out over the forest. An uneasy wind tossed the trees. Cloud had come up to sully the early morning sky. It would be a dismal day: she could smell rain coming before long. She had had her orders, though. To rest, and sleep – though how could she possibly sleep? Sighing, she went inside the hut. Her things were there, and she looked around at them with a new intensity before settling herself on the low pallet on which she slept. Her stomachs gurgled peacefully in the quiet. A pile of greenery served her as a pillow, and she rubbed her cheek against it, releasing the familiar pungent fragrance. It was oddly comforting. She closed her eyes, preparing for hours of restlessness, trying to free her mind from its dozens of emotions and images.

When she woke again, a day and a night and another day had passed. It was close to sunset. After a heavy meal, Skaira often did sleep for very long periods, but not usually for quite this long; although such a stretch of time would normally have left her feeling muzzy, she woke feeling much refreshed. She stood up, instantly aware that she stood on the threshold of great events. This in mind, it seemed even more important than usual that she should make careful preparations. She went outside, and after evacuating her body wastes she drank a little water from the spring, groomed herself and performed her stretching routine, gazing out steadily across the darkening woods. She did not pray: where was the need? Ordinarily she would have done, the first part of the night was for prayer to the Goddess of the Twilight, but this was not a night like any other.

At last her preparations were complete. She went to the very crest of the hill and turned again to face Vanreil. The cool night wind lifted her now unbound hair and brought many scents to her idly dilating nostrils. The rain had passed, and the dimming sky was rosy and dappled with cloud. Even the grass beneath her paws glimmered with raindrops and smelled fresh and clean. She found herself wondering what the Starborn's world would be like: certainly it would be strange, surely it would be beautiful. But how could any world possibly be as beautiful as this?

The swift passage of a shooting star distracted her momentarily. Already the first and brightest stars were glittering on the heavens. Twilight, the holiest time for Skaira all over the world. When she looked around again, there had been a change. In the nest of boulders with which the hill was crested, there was a gap that had not been there before. She caught her breath. Slowly she padded towards it. Inside there was nothing but blackness; no smell, even, to guide her. There was not even an echo to the sound of her soft nervous growl.

She looked around her once more, drinking in the beauty, the familiarity and the peace. It did not seem possible that it could be in so much danger. And yet unless she was successful in her task, it was all doomed. Summoning all her courage, and inhaling as if she were diving into deep water, she stepped forward into the blackness.

There was an instant's total silence; then her senses gave a long-drawn-out scream as they began to change. Bone and blood and flesh shrieked as if she were being rent asunder, but there was nothing in her that was capable of crying out. Time lost meaning. There was nothing holding her here except her own will, but that was iron. Everything must be lost; everything must change but the Self. Momentarily she heard a murmur that spoke of rest, and it took almost all of that iron to turn away from it. The waves of the Endless Ocean receded and were gone.

She had work to do, and she was gold in the crucible, a sword in the flames, a soul suspended in eternity. She set her teeth, and they were strange and blunt. The air her lungs sucked in suddenly was muddy with the strange sickly smell that was unknown on a world that had never conceived of the internal combustion engine. She had arrived. Shadows cloaked the corner where she found herself. There was no activity near. A frantic glance downward showed her a body she did not recognise as her own. There was no leisure to examine it, however. She had no way of telling how much time she had to play with, and the sooner she was launched on her task the less time she would have to dwell on her own stifled terror.

An onlooker would have seen nothing but an ordinary woman emerging from the shadowy corner. She stepped forward into the light with great caution, her gait far more careful than would have been normally accounted for by the height of the heels on her shoes. Without even knowing that she did so, she growled nervously again: the sound was absurdly thin and reedy to her ears. She opened her mouth slightly, trying in vain to improve a sense of smell that suddenly seemed utterly inadequate. Even her hearing was dulled, and she could not move her ears to improve it. A moment's panic at the spindly legs on which she must stalk about filled her, but when she could learn not to think of what she was doing they seemed to manage well enough. Ahead of her she could see lights, astonishingly bright, and what seemed to her a vast crowd of beings whose strangeness made her shudder inwardly with fear, revulsion and bewilderment. People. *His* people. His world. She drew a hand out of the pocket of the garment she found herself wearing: thin and weak, with blunt, fixed nails, it was clutching a small square of thick paper with black marks on it. She saw a man walking past her take out a small, flat folded receptacle from some inner recess of his clothes and remove from it several of these pieces of paper, handing one to each of his companions. She would follow him and copy what he did to get inside. The crowd were all heading in one direction, towards a huge building. That must be where she too must go. Where *he* would be waiting…

She took a deep breath, and walked forward.

2

Brendan got out of the worst of the crush at last, and breathed deeply of the cool night air. The first night of December 1998, and they had just finished a run of sell-out shows at the prestigious Kings Hall Arena. It was something to be truly proud of – something they could never have dreamed of when they set out, drawn like moths to an arc light by the daring and brilliance and magnetism of Adrian Connor.

'Riverdance' had opened the way, and 'Lord of the Dance' and other such shows had followed it. Irish-born Adrian too had dreamed the dream, believed that he had the genius to excel them all. A career in dance had been the last thing in Brendan Doyle's mind, until one night he had encountered Adrian in a Dublin bar. A slight, fiery-haired young dancer from County Kildare, Connor had already had the gist of his plans worked out, needed only a willing listener to pour out his heart to; they already knew one another slightly, having met several times at various Feiseanna, and fell readily into conversation. The love of music and dance that lay at the core of his hearer had caught fire like dry tinder, flaring into an answering passion. They had talked until the long-suffering proprietor closed the doors behind them, had walked through the city streets trading ideas in a fast and furious flow, until the grey dawn found them exhausted, exhilarated and committed. The combination of their united talent and creative fire had soon found them backers in the business world, and from there events had gathered momentum with terrifying speed. Now all the hard work, the sweat and suffering, was paying off. Brendan didn't need to look back to know that the maestro of it all was still engulfed by fans clamouring for an autograph, a touch, a word. It was the same everywhere, but he didn't grudge him that: the concept of the show had been Adrian's in the first place, and if he was now receiving a possibly unequal share of the glory, he still worked bloody hard for it. (He made sure everyone else worked bloody hard too, but they had to expect that: it had been made plain from the outset that those who wouldn't slog wouldn't survive.) And the slog had its rewards, quite apart from their burgeoning bank balances and the daily homage of their audiences. Oh, yes. He scribbled his autograph across a programme and smiled his thanks for yet another burst of praise. The adulation was becoming familiar now, but it was impossible not to be warmed by it even so. And it was from this that he was in the habit of reaping the rewards that were happily inaccessible to the Inland Revenue.

His requirements in this respect were reasonably moderate. He wasn't into excesses, wanting dozens of girls orbiting him at every turn. Not that he would have minded accommodating dozens of girls if they'd happened to feel like swarming over him, but he was content enough to deal with them singly, preferably in his room after a show, as a prelude to taking them to bed. It wasn't a "just get something wearing a bra" compulsion; some nights Lady Luck deserted him, and if that happened he was quite happy to socialise with the rest of the gang in the bar of whatever hotel they were sharing.

The level of the success he enjoyed would have made it impossible for him to be unaware that he was considered a handsome man. Nevertheless, his appearance was not that of someone who paid overmuch attention to his own good looks. He was casual in black denim, his dark hair damp with sweat from his work on stage; the finely modelled bones of his face, coupled with the sensual mouth and slightly swarthy skin, proclaimed his Celtic ancestry. His jaw was slightly square, with a firm chin that could be obstinate; a ready twinkle lingered in the hazel eyes. As he spoke to those who had waited so patiently for the chance to meet him, his voice was soft, its Irish accent pronounced. No matter how tired he might be, he always did make time for the show's fans. He would have been other than human if he hadn't enjoyed the praise, and he knew that even a few words were sometimes inexpressibly precious – even now it sometimes astonished and humbled him to find what a devoted following the show attracted.

It was relatively rare for him to be able to single out a prospective conquest in the initial hubbub outside the stage door, and this night's crowd had been no exception. He'd come in for rather more than his usual share of congratulation and felt it well earned. Strange how on some nights there just seemed to be an extra sparkle: perhaps it was the 'last night' surge, but tonight he really had been on top form. He always put heart and soul into his performances, but tonight he seemed to have been on fire. Even Adrian had commented on it, had had to exert himself to the limit of his own immense talent to retain his dominance of the stage. Between the two of them they had lifted the entire cast, and given a show that had been truly the best they'd ever done. Now there was the pleasant afterglow of accomplishment, and he was in the mood for a special end to the evening.

He wasn't sure what made him look in her direction: he thought afterwards that it had been her stillness. In that entire milling crowd she alone was totally silent, totally motionless. When their eyes met he experienced a slight sense of shock. Although she was still several yards away from him, he had the strangest impression of staring into depth. Her eyes were fixed on him with an unwavering intensity. She made no move towards him, simply stood there and watched his every move. Even as he signed programmes for others and replied to their comments on the show he was aware of her gaze. Without making it too obvious, he gently negotiated a way through the thinning crowd towards where she stood waiting.

Reaching her, he stood for a moment in uncharacteristic hesitation. He was conscious of an immediate physical attraction, but there was nothing in her face to tell him what she wanted – no request for an autograph, no attempt to comment on the show. Only the deep brown eyes looking directly into his, and again the sense of depth, like wells of shadow.

"Can I help you?" he asked softly, for want of any other way to open a conversation. Perhaps she was shy; although 'shy' was not one of the terms that would have sprung to mind if he had been asked to give an instant appraisal of her. In the general way of things he would have thought such a stare a little ill mannered, but something about the quality of it made him discount the possibility. The brown eyes opened a little wider.

"I would like to meet with you somewhere quieter than this. Would it be possible?" The voice was deeper than he'd expected, the pronunciation carefully precise and oddly accentless. His pulse quickened. There was no suggestion of coquetry in her face, but it was impossible to miss the opportunity.

"Of course." He told her the name of the hotel nearby where they were staying, gave her the directions on how to find it, and glanced at his watch before adding, "I'll meet you in the foyer at – say, five to?"
She nodded assent, not taking her eyes from his to consult any watch of her own. Her expression still had not changed. A couple of the rest of the cast near enough to catch the gist of the brief exchange winked at each other.

There were still others hoping for his attention, however, and he turned to them good-naturedly. As he moved away he glanced back once at her. She still had not stirred, but stood there looking after him. When they could do so without being overheard, his colleagues dug him in the ribs and made vulgar gestures and ruder comments, to which he responded with unimpaired good humour. Eventually they were out, heading across the car park. He felt the familiar surge of adrenaline dispelling the weariness in his body. There was no telling how the evening would end: that was always the way. Sometimes a girl would be in his room and between the sheets in less than thirty seconds, other times he'd have the fun of trying to talk her out of her clothes. Sometimes he didn't succeed in getting more than a kiss, and sometimes he didn't even get that much. It made the encounter more of a challenge. His lean face wore its devastatingly attractive grin as he sauntered to the waiting coach. Tonight he was feeling lucky.

She came in quietly out of the night, and he moved to greet her at once. Brunette, probably in her early thirties, in a white blouse and long black satin skirt. It was hard to get an accurate estimation of her figure, she was wearing a loose jacket of black leather that draped in graceful folds, but she wasn't painfully thin like so many of the fashionable women he'd encountered. He asked whether she'd like a drink in the bar or would prefer the privacy of his room, and she indicated the latter. This seemed hopeful, but her reply held no undertones, and he didn't make the mistake of reading too much into it. There was still a long way to go before bed.

A few minutes later they were in his room, and he took her jacket and waved her amiably to a seat on the sofa. She looked slightly nervous now, almost as if caught where she had no right to be. Also as if she half expected to be assaulted on the spot by the Lord of the Sidhe, crown and all. Expected – or hoped? He was quite familiar by now with the fact that his on-stage persona was intensely sexually attractive to women. Several times he'd started off in full costume to be obliging, and ended up with only the masked crown. It wasn't a practice he was particularly fond of: perhaps it was a consequence of the hours of hard work he'd put into becoming an evil personality when wearing that mask, but sex involving it was never quite the friendly, playful affair it usually was when he was plain Brendan Doyle.

"Now, would you like a drink?" A harmless enough opening gambit, and alcohol was a powerful weapon in his armoury. He had no intention of making any woman too drunk to resist him, but a drink or two often lowered female resistance to his Irish charm. She accepted a fruit juice, rather to his disappointment, and continued to watch him rather anxiously as he moved to the fridge and took one out for her. A little gentle small-talk, genuinely meant to put her more at ease with him, elicited the information that she was from the North, down specially for the show, and staying with friends locally. He sat down beside her on the sofa, and they talked for a while about the performance at the Arena. He was now in an excellent position to look down the low-cut front of her blouse, and was conscious of an immediate and surprisingly strong physical reaction. For all her shyness (she still hadn't got around to telling him her name), she didn't seem aware of just how inviting were those warm curves. He could see the edge of the bra underneath, a tantalising glimpse of lace, and he clenched his fingers around the glass in his hand. He'd never resorted to force, had no intention of doing it now, but he wanted this one very badly. A pity she hadn't been one of the meet-you-in-the-bed type: he was conscious that one wrong move would scare her away like a rabbit.

And yet – would it? He'd become adept at reading female body language, and the signals she was sending out were quite unequivocal. Her body was turned towards his, even though most of the time her face was shyly averted. She evidently didn't mind the fact that he could see straight down the front of her blouse and for a good way east of her cleavage. Was she a virgin? he speculated. Not likely. Apart from being as rare as unicorns, virgins of her age were usually smart enough to avoid being found in the hotel rooms of single (or indeed married) men, as this was likely to have terminal consequences for their virginity. He'd already checked for warning signs on the third finger of her left hand, but no ring twinkled there. So – not engaged or married; probably not a virgin. Not a slut, or she would be making far bolder eye contact with him. Shy, yes – but that body language…

He took a deep breath. There was no easy way to tell this one he wanted to see her naked on his bed. A kiss, however, would tell him a great deal – if he could get one in…

Afterwards he thought it was like taking candy from a baby, the way he got her into his arms. Although he began with the most gentle of kisses, her lips parted for his tongue, and he saw no reason to resist the invitation. Not reacting like a virgin. She whimpered low in her throat, and the tension in his crotch redoubled. Controlling himself hard, he strayed kisses down the side of her jaw, nibbled her earlobe, and began to work his way down her neck. In the meantime, his hands were stroking down her back, her sides, and her flanks. As if accidentally, one presently brushed her breast. He tensed, half expecting a defensive recoil: this was one of the key points in the will-she won't-she game. No recoil came, only a sharp inhalation that had a tremor in it. She had no way of seeing the gleam that came and went in his hazel eyes as he registered that reaction. He was not surprised when there was no resistance to his exploring hand as he finally slipped it into her blouse, cupping the roundness of her breast in his palm. She was rigid with anticipation, and abruptly gave a convulsive shudder. He paused, letting the tension build, then slowly slid his fingers on to her warm skin. As he did so he brought his mouth back to hers, half stifling the moans as she arched backwards, pressing her flesh against his hand. Willing? He thought. She was bloody *dying* for it.

From this point onwards he preferred a different setting, one more conducive to the removing of clothes. He began to tease her other breast while he bit gently at her neck and jaw. "Shall we find somewhere a bit more comfortable to continue this?" he breathed in her ear. With a sound like a sob, she nodded. Home and dry, he thought.

He helped her to her feet, partly because it was the polite thing to do and partly because it gave him his first chance to pull her body against him. She returned his kisses with a passion he would not have suspected from his first assessment of her, straining herself against him as though starved for human contact. *Definitely* not a virgin. He indicated the door to his bedroom and she moved towards it as if in a daze, he following close behind.

What followed was an experience quite unlike any he had ever had before. He had never encountered such a mixture of eagerness and innocence, shyness and honesty. She vibrated to his lightest touch like a harp, and as he slowly stripped the clothes from her body, he struggled to control the craving she aroused in him. He took some pride in being as much of an artist in bed as he was on stage, and he took his time. For this one it had to be something very special, and he used every skill learned in a hundred casual encounters, every touch, every whisper, every caress. There was no reason to hurry when every moment was such exquisite torment. The bed was a tangle of sheets, their bodies slippery with each other's sweat, when he could finally wait no longer. After torturing her with the possibility half a dozen times, he moved his weight forward with aching deliberation. She opened to him totally as he pinned her to the bed and began to thrust. Her eyes were closed, but he was not deceived by her silence; the body beneath his was incurved, waiting, each surge bringing her closer to the edge. Experience had taught him how to wait, but the pressure was becoming hard to bear. Suddenly her eyes flicked open, fastening on his face with a look of complete panic. *Now!* He let go, gave himself up to the fire. It swelled out of his groin, and for one instant of blind terror he thought it was going to kill him. Then he was past caring. He began slamming into her with every ounce of the passion he'd contained since first getting his hands on her, and the shreds of him that could still hear anything listened to her stifling her screams against the side of his jaw as she burned in the identical ecstasy. It went on and on, longer than it had ever done for him with anyone else, until his heart pounded in his chest and the sweat ran down the sides of his face, and the movements of his body became less and less co-ordinated as he fought to give them both every possible second of this paralysing pleasure.

Slowly the flames receded. He came back to reality, and the discovery that she was crying. That, too, had happened before, though not often: and he was reassured by her response to his newly gentle kisses that it was not from distress. He took his weight off her, and drew her into his arms, where she spent the few hot tears on his chest and presently quietened.

After a while: "Thank you," she said in a low voice. He kissed her forehead, and replied softly, "It was a pleasure." She was gazing up at him, a strangely intent look: her eyes travelled over every feature of his face as if trying to memorise it. He wondered if she was hoping for a repeat performance – another day he might have had the energy to oblige her with one, but on top of his exertions on stage at the Arena, his body was now completely exhausted. When he didn't say anything more, she put her head back down on his arm and began to nuzzle his chest. It was not unpleasant to lie there relaxed, feeling the warmth of her breath gently stirring the rough hairs. After what had passed, he would have liked to be able to talk to her – most women enjoyed that, and she was due some sort of recognition for the pleasure they had shared – but it felt strange that even now he didn't know her name. Presently, not knowing quite why he did so, he put out a hand and switched off the bedside lamp, and it was most peculiar how the entire scene changed. The curtains were open, and moonlight streamed in to cast a swathe of silver across the bed. He had not noticed before that she was wearing perfume; he could smell it now, and it was like none he had ever encountered before. The scent was oddly cool and pure, like snow or starlight – he must be mistaken, there must be an ioniser at work in the room somewhere. She continued to explore his chest, rubbing it softly with her nose and licking it occasionally; it came to him that it was like being cuddled up to by a cat. He would not have been entirely surprised if she had started to purr. He chuckled sleepily at the thought, and she looked up at him without raising her head. In the shadow her eyes were very dark, darker than midnight, deeper than wells where the sun never shines.

He turned his head presently to look out of the window at the moon, which stood in the sky like a silver searchlight. He could never remember seeing it quite so big and brilliant before. The sky behind it was the deepest imaginable blue, strangely untouched by the inescapable glare of the city's streetlights. He found himself thinking nostalgically of the village where he had been born, out in the harsh beauty of County Clare, where the sky and the sea and the mountains left one exposed to the gaze of God. It was a Spartan life compared to that he now enjoyed, but his roots were there, his home was there, and even if he never went back again it would always be a part of him. The music to which he danced, the steps he performed, were part of his heritage. It was wonderful to travel, to see the world and reap the rewards of the life he had chosen; but sometimes, just sometimes, he found himself absurdly homesick.

-Hell's bells! What had put him into this mood all of a sudden? A brilliant performance on stage and a beautiful woman in his bed, what else could he want? (Was she beautiful? He found himself unable to answer the odd question. Probably not. But she had been quite irresistible.) Did he want her to just walk out of his life like all the rest? It was all he'd expected, probably all that she'd expected once she realised where the encounter was leading. She was old enough to understand the rules of the game. Nevertheless, the thought of sleeping in a bed now empty of her presence was suddenly frighteningly lonely. How old was he, three years of age, wanting something to cuddle up to in the dark? But he wanted her; the spell was still strong. Perhaps they could share a shower… He couldn't be as tired as he'd thought. Outside the stars pulsed with light. He stood up, went to the en-suite bathroom and switched on the shower. She was still in the bed, watching him with those dark eyes. For an instant before he switched on a table-lamp, he could have sworn that they reflected the moonlight with a suggestion of green. No, nonsense. He tested the water, brought out the shower-gel. Sometimes it was amazing what you could get up to in a shower-cubicle with a good handful of gel. A surprisingly feline smile dawned on her face when she realised what he had in mind. With equally feline grace she slithered out of the bed and crossed the room towards him. He felt desire surge up in him again as he watched her move naked in the low light. God, she was unbelievable… He opened the shower door and stepped inside. She followed him in. The water hammered on their bodies, on sliding muscles and wet naked skin. He pinned her against the tiles and had her again, groaning with every thrust. The rush of the water was like thunder across them both, the violence of their coupling like lightning across the face of the storm.

And beyond that, there was nothing.

3

Lidan was the first to wake. She surged upright with a sound midway between a gasp and a snarl, and stared around her with almost dazed eyes. Her own dwelling – at that moment she could have hugged every stone of it. Her own hill (blessed be every blade of grass growing there!), her own world again! And her own body –

She paused at that, and looked downwards. Her hands ran thoughtfully over her lower parts. The memories were sharp as knives. She shuddered. Automatically her top lip lifted, baring her teeth. The thick fur of her hackles shifted. To feel such sensations as part of everyday life – how could it be borne? Was it thus for the other races of her world, and if so how did such things possibly fit in to an existence that could be called normal? Images flashed through her mind, sending shiver after shiver through her pelt. The heat, the closeness, the needing worse than the craving for blood; the way he had touched her, the things he had done to her!

It was with something close to horror that she stared down at the unconscious human sprawled beside her. Removed from his own world, and the proximity of others of his kind, he looked more peculiar than ever. When she too had worn that form, the strangeness had not been anything like as obvious; it had even seemed quite natural after a while to walk on two legs. As Shieih had promised, she had felt desire for him. Now it seemed utterly beyond belief that she had done and felt such things – the very thought of it repelled her. She was relieved beyond words by the return to her own place and her own body. And yet – and yet…

The experience had awakened instincts and emotions that had slumbered within her people for uncounted generations. By all the teachings she had grown up with, however, these were holy things, not to be spurned on account of their unfamiliarity. All the mental habits of her training in the Law urged her to rearrange her mind into order, to analyse and isolate her experience as a past event. It refused to be obliging in this respect. Against her expectation, even against her will, what had happened to her had changed her fundamentally, in ways of which she was not in control. Her tail twitched angrily. This was not how things should be. She was an adult; she should be able to cope. It was *his* fault. She looked again, almost resentfully, at Brendan. Why could he not have been hasty, crude, intent only on taking his own pleasure? Why had he had to do …all those other things that had awakened these unwanted feelings within her? She could have drawn him into the trap like any other prey, and felt no more remorse. Now it was all so complicated, and the situation was fraught enough without additional complexities. However, the innate and merciless passion for justice that had driven her into the service of the Law rose up in his defence. However she might with hindsight wish things otherwise, he could not possibly be blamed for what he had done, the care he had taken to ensure that the pleasures of the experience should not be only on his side. Almost apologetically, she touched the curly hair on his chest. She felt obscurely older and richer for the experience, if considerably less well-ordered in mind; and for all that she could not wish for a repeat of it, it had left her with a strange sense of affection for her partner in it, no matter how peculiar he looked. A sudden thought struck her, and she almost managed to smile at it: she was the only Skair in their history to have experienced the *Xiaihih*, the first sexual encounter. Among the Venelai it was an occasion of rejoicing, celebrated thereafter in much the same way as a birthday. She too must henceforth mark the date of the last day of Hanh'ara. As though there were any danger that she might possibly forget it! By the One!

Curiosity surfaced. There was one sense she had not been able to use to its fullest capacity when she was in that strange, weak body he had thought so attractive. She leaned over and began smelling him carefully. Very strange. As well as the drenching odour of shower-gel and chemical-saturated water, she could smell his sex-scent quite distinctly, and she shook her head over it, wrinkling her nose so that her teeth showed again. Now she had returned to her own form, those formerly intoxicating pheromones had no other effect on her than to bring her close to sneezing. Human noses were shockingly inefficient – she had only been able to detect a fraction of this even when she was in bed with him. Idly she wondered what his flesh would taste like. With some difficulty she refrained from inquisitively licking him: an incautious rasp from a Skair's tongue was capable of tearing the top layer of his skin off, and that would not be the best way to introduce herself.

But – what to do now? She had brought him successfully from his own world, but she had no idea what she had to do with him in hers. Nor had she any idea of what to say to him when he awoke. It was probable that he was going to be rather upset, to put it at its mildest estimate. The fact that his kind believed themselves alone in the Universe certainly was not going to help matters. He would have no experience in dealing with anything other than his own people, and the difference between them would be even greater in his eyes than in hers. What would he think about her? What would he feel when he knew the trick that had been played on him? Would he recoil from her in disgust? Illogically, the thought hurt and angered her. Perhaps she had better not tell him the truth about that. But should she begin their dealings on this world with a lie, even a lie of silence? There was no untruth in Shieih. Her daughters should not deal in lies, no matter for what motives. He would have to know, even if he hated her for it.

Heavy-hearted and anxious, she rose stealthily from the bed, managing to avoid disturbing his sleep. She had no way of knowing in what way sorcery of this magnitude might affect him. It had left her with a headache, and she went to the shelf where she kept her few utensils. There were a range of jars there containing various substances, and after fetching water in a wooden bowl from the spring outside she added a couple of drops from one of the jars to it. It made the water taste metallic, but it took effect very quickly. She put the bowl down and rubbed her eyes, waiting for the pressure behind them to subside. The chaos of worries, memories and conflicting emotions in her head was very hard to bear. Her training in the Law had honed a natural habit of calm, orderly thought: now she could not quiet herself enough to consider anything logically. She stared unseeingly at the remainder of the water. There was so much she did not know, even the simplest things – she did not even know what the Starborn needed for food! Suppose the water, even, acted on him like a poison? She could try to cure a headache and end up killing him! What if humans needed some substance, as

Skaira needed blood, for their very survival? In circumstances of such danger as now threatened, how would she feed him? How would she protect him? What would happen to him if something happened to her? 'Shieih will look after him,' she thought, and took some comfort from that conviction. Skaira had to take the chances of everyday life, and she had gone into this of her own free will: her survival had not been guaranteed. But surely he would be guarded and guided, the innocent who had been involved without his consent, without even being consulted.

Yes. There was the rub. She turned around and looked at him. It went against every tenet of the Law. He would be justified in feeling great resentment. She would have to be prepared for that. The fact that she had been obeying orders was no excuse. She had kidnapped the creature of another world and brought him into danger, and she was guilty of a grave crime in so doing.

Yet what choice had she had? It was fated to be so. That did not make it fair. Life rarely was fair, and it was a cub's cry that it should be. If she had had the time again she would still have done as she had done. She could only do her best now to ensure that he took no harm from his enforced visit to her world. What he had to do there was still hidden from her. No doubt Shieih would reveal it in Her own good time. In the meantime, she had to wait until the Starborn awoke and deal with the first problem, his reaction. It was difficult to admit even to herself how apprehensive she was. She sank to the floor beside the bed and looked at him more closely, getting used again to the shape of his face. "Bren-dan." The ineradicable Skair guttural rolled the R into a low growl. "Brren-dan Doyl." The tentatively uttered sounds brought back the shocking, utterly alien and threatening environment of the concert hall, the noise and the lights and the pandemonium of the humans around her. Her hearts speeded up again with remembered fear. She had copied the actions of other humans entering the hall, and had gravitated with them towards the inevitable merchandise stalls. A glance had shown that among the goods offered for sale there had been strange, brightly-coloured books, utterly unlike any she had ever seen before, that set her shivering with awe as she looked at the pictures they contained. Such realistic images – what an artist must have painted them! There were several pinned up to display their contents, and one of the pictures had been of a head, partially turned in profile, wearing an intricate crown and mask of green and silver… Her already hurried heartbeat had quickened still further. She had already discovered that the clothes in which she had found herself had pockets containing coins. She hadn't had any idea of their value but there had been sufficient to buy one of the books; she had even had some handed back to her, though they had gone with the clothes (and the book) when she returned to Kerriel. A pity; she would have liked to have kept them. It was hardly worth pining over now, however: what were coins and books when she had the Starborn himself, breathing and real on her bed?

She shivered. On her bed – as she had been on his… She had watched every movement he made on stage, marvelling at the grace and strength he had shown. He stood out among his fellow dancers for her like a cut gem among pebbles. It was easy enough to follow the tale they portrayed, Good versus Evil; he played the king of a magical folk, who kidnapped a mortal girl and took her away to captivity in his own kingdom. The hero had to come in pursuit, engage him in mortal combat and defeat him to rescue the heroine. It had not been so easy, in her anxious state, to sit still when he was apparently destroyed by the red-headed hero, as Evil should be. It had been difficult to remain motionless in her seat while the one on whom the fate of her world depended was struck down before her eyes; for all her struggles for self-control, she had growled softly and continuously, the sound fortunately drowned by the music. His triumphant foe had never dreamed that a pair of hostile and unforgiving eyes had watched him from then on; but had Brendan not reappeared, none the worse for his well-earned fate, to accept the applause of the audience at the end of the performance, Adrian would not have survived the evening. All had been well however; to her indescribable relief, he had emerged from the wings with the rest of the cast. He was even smiling, evidently bearing his erstwhile enemy no malice for having supposedly killed him ten minutes earlier, and her murderous thoughts of vengeance had died. The show ended, she had walked out with the crowd, and gone to wait with others for the dancers to appear. It had seemed a long wait, perhaps because she was keyed up to such a pitch of nerves. Many had wanted to speak to the man who had portrayed the hero, but he was of no interest to her. She had waited, and waited – and then, at last, *he* appeared, and her heart had given a sickening lurch. How was she supposed to attract his attention in such a crowd? And what if (Shieih pardon her for doubting!) he took no notice of her? There were so many females, and doubtless he could take his choice…

"Bren-dan." She had whispered the name, half fearing that her hunger would show too nakedly if she spoke it aloud. He had stopped to talk with anyone who spoke to him, writing something in their books. She clutched hers, wondering at the significance of this act; but in the event, she had not even remembered to proffer it. Close up, the effect of his masculinity was redoubled. A human nose was nothing like as acute as a Skair's, but she could still detect the intriguingly male scent of his body. Feelings she had never before experienced surged through her. She had shivered inside with panic and excitement, but a predator learned early to control external reactions. She must not alarm her prey… She'd found the mysterious symbols that comprised his name, written below the picture in her book over which she had pored with such fearful fascination once in the haven of her allotted seat. The woman in the seat next to hers had said the name to her partner, pointing to his picture in her copy of the book: Lidan's acute ear had fastened thankfully on the pronunciation. She could understand spoken English, but written was simply a blur of symbols. That said, she could have reproduced every letter printed in the programme faithfully even now if required to do so – for a Skair's phenomenal memory that was not difficult. She could even have put many of them into the order in which she had read them, even without having any idea of the meaning of the words she would be forming. A part of her mind mourned for the Artisans who would have taken such joy in poring over the book.

This train of thought took her to what her fellow-Skaira would make of him. The first term which sprang to mind when she imagined a disclosure of what he had done to her was the Kerriel equivalent of "mincemeat". Mother Shieih! How could she explain it? What would they think? She could not imagine even trying to conceal from others of her own kind what had happened. Could their quest be accomplished without coming into contact with other Skaira? That would perhaps be the safest course, but she had no way of knowing if it would be possible. Many of her sisters would listen to the story with reverence, and act accordingly – but there was no doubt that some would not be able to choke down the simple fact that a male had copulated with a Daughter of the Stars. Certainly more than a few would never be able to forgive either of them for what they had done. 'O Mother Shieih!' she moaned silently to herself. 'Guard me, guide me!'

At that moment a sudden movement from the bed both distracted her from her worries and doubled her anxiety. The Starborn was waking up.

4

"Hell's bells!" He started to sit up, but abandoned the effort with a groan. What had he been drinking the night before? He'd never woken with such a blinding, nauseous headache in his life. After a moment he relaxed with his hands pressed to his face. Thank God, no show this evening: he'd never have been able to make it – and for sure if he'd been mad enough to go on a bender of this magnitude, somebody would see to it that Adrian got to know... Oh, there were times when they all got paralytic, but not when there was a show scheduled. That wasn't the behaviour of a professional, and he knew it. It was unlikely in the extreme that even if he was ever insane enough to wipe himself out of a performance he'd be kicked out of the show – not that he'd ever consider doing such an irresponsible, idiotic thing; that wasn't what worried him. What really was worrying him was that he couldn't remember drinking anything last night. Glucose water, yes, a couple of glasses to fuel his energy levels on stage and quench the thirst generated under the cruel heat of the lighting system on his black clothing. Had some fool put something in it? Could he possibly have been drugged without knowing it? Surely not, the taste was far too weak to conceal any other. But he hadn't had anything else. Some of the others had gone off to party, but he hadn't gone with them. He'd been looking forward to a drink with the girl –

The girl! His eyes flew open. He took his hands away from his face to look around for her. Almost in the same instant, but too late, he registered the acute peculiarity of the bed he was lying on. His next discovery wiped it completely from his mind. For one appalled instant he stared up into the amber eyes staring down at him, then in a single movement which owed absolutely nothing to conscious thought, he slammed all his limbs down and heaved himself back away from whatever it was. The wall brought him up short, and it was doubly unfortunate that the first part of him to hit it was his head. On top of the pain already pulsing in it, this was the final straw. He slumped down and was ignominiously sick, for a couple of moments too overcome by his physical misery to even remember the existence of the hallucination in the room with him.

He was to be reminded of it very shortly, however. A hand awkwardly touched his shoulder, and its fellow placed a wooden bowl in front of him. Hands that had slots where the fingernails should be... He heaved over the bowl, but his stomach had not had much in it to begin with and that little had already been brought up. Some minutes passed before he was able to stop retching and reach shakily for the smaller bowl of water set down beside him. He rinsed, spat, and swallowed a mouthful, which immediately came up again. A second mouthful stayed down, although the taste was most peculiar. The blazing agony between his eyes was starting to diminish. He concentrated on breathing. God Almighty, he *had* been drugged. What had they given him? He had to get help. Get to a hospital – inform the police... some bastard-!

"Do you feel any better now?" It was even affecting his hearing. No human voice could sound like that. It was feminine – female, anyway – but there was an impossible resonance to it. It was almost like a light growl! He drank a little more water, trying to control his panic. None of this was real. Drug-induced hallucinations were realistic, or so he'd heard. It couldn't get more realistic than this.

There was no help for it. He looked up again. She was still there, and still looking like that. He willed her to go away, because she didn't exist. Somebody had put something in his drink and now he was seeing a woman with a lion's body where her lower half should be. Her eyes were a lion's eyes, triangular and tawny. She had whiskers. She had little round lion-ears sticking out of her head, higher than human ears would be. Her nose was broad and flat, and the end was pink and moist. And between her parted lips… He put a hand across his eyes, partly to block out the light that was cutting into his brain like red-hot knives, and partly to hide her while he got a grip on the situation. She wasn't there. She didn't exist. It was nothing to worry about – if he could only get to a hospital they'd make her go away…

"Help me," he whispered. Surely somebody would hear. He'd have shouted it aloud if he hadn't feared the noise would collapse his skull. "For Christ's sake help me!"

It was inevitable that Lidan should misunderstand his words. She had no way of knowing that he was not talking to her at all. The fear in his voice was very evident to her, however: every animal she had ever killed had had that note in its screams.

"Do not be afraid," she said soothingly, "you are quite safe." She looked at him anxiously. The changes in his scents told her that he was in a state of acute shock, and she had no way of knowing how resistant his kind were to that kind of physiological stress. A human body was horribly weak, and she knew that some mammals were so susceptible to the strain of being caught that they died without a fatal wound on them…

There was no help for it: this degree of fear could not be good for him. And she could tell from his breath that he was still feeling extremely nauseous. Living alone as she did, she had to be her own pharmacist when necessary and she had the means to hand to help him. She went again to the shelf where she kept her remedies, and selected carefully. It would be wise to keep the dose as small as possible – she would risk about a quarter of what would be suitable for herself. She measured the medicines into a bowl, stirred it and offered it to him, along with a small spoon.

His hand dragged down across his facc, and he stared at her with a mixture of resignation and fascinated horror. Whatever he might have expected from a figment of a drug-induced hallucination, feeding him wasn't part of it. Perhaps she'd turn into a bubble and float away in a moment or so. He took the utensils from her warily, deciding that since none of this was happening anyway he might as well play along with it. He looked at the spoon, then at the bowl (both made of polished wood), and sniffed the contents. It was nothing noxious, merely small quantity of what looked like blue jam. He dipped a spoonful, sniffed again and tasted it cautiously. It might look like jam, but its extremely sweet taste reminded him faintly of something he hadn't tasted for years – white chocolate. In the circumstances he would not have said that white chocolate was the best thing for a sick stomach, but the effect of this stuff was immediate. He ate a larger spoonful. No point in having a horrible hallucination when he had the option of improving it a bit.

His companion watched him approvingly, and with some relief. He did not seem to react badly to the medicine; indeed his colour was improving already. The pupils of his eyes dilated a little as the tiny amount of *vhi'the* he was inadvertently inhaling reached his brain and began to relax him.

"Would you like something to eat?" she asked, more to start a conversation than in any real expectation that he would be hungry. She was not surprised when he refused the offer. He would undoubtedly be wise to allow his stomach to rest for a while before putting any food in it.

"But thanks anyway," he added politely. "I know you're not real, but it was nice of you to ask."

Not real? She blinked at him. This was one reaction she had not been prepared for. Why did he think she was not real?

"Of course I am real," she said in some puzzlement.

"Well you would say that, wouldn't you?" he pointed out. "I mean, you probably think you are."

"I know that I am," she replied. "You can see me."

"Of course you're not. There aren't any such things as – as – as whatever you are."

"There are many of us. We are called Skaira. This is our world, not yours. I have brought you here." Best to make a clean breast of it straight away. She was surprised, and more than a little worried, by how calmly he accepted it, with a "Well that explains it." Admittedly the drug she had given him should be working already – it was very quick acting – but unless she had grievously misjudged the dosage, it should not have made him this nonchalant about the change in his circumstances. Admittedly she had no way of knowing if his kind were all remarkably placid by nature, but she still felt that something was not quite right. She did not exactly want him to be angry, but she was more than slightly perplexed by his equanimity. How could she get through to him?

There was a way. She hesitated for a long moment. He was not of her world. He was here without his consent. This was not something to be done lightly, even with the agreement of the other. But she had to reach him. This strange indifference of his could be infinitely dangerous.

Slowly, reluctantly, she reached out to him. His otherness, now, was frightening. This would be worse, far more deeply intimate, than merely sharing his bed – and that had been unnerving enough… She touched his forehead, and spoke words in the Old Speech.

For them both, pain. A rending of reality. A trail of stars spanning unimaginable distances. And then the knowing: a world so different from your own that the otherness is an unendurable agony. Continents you will never know, seas full of life you will never see, a sun whose rays illuminate a world to which you do not belong. Machines that clang and rush and stink, oceans whose waters have the stench of a life-threat beyond the imagination, buildings that come between the earth and the light like the end of existence. And a green world of sensuality and savagery, the stark necessity of the killing, the intoxication of the stars: forever a paradox between the joy of the hunt and the guilt of death, in a body that must drink blood in order to survive. Then suddenly, for her, the experience of his realisation of the truth. Not a scream, for he was beyond the relief of screaming at that moment. Loneliness beyond loneliness, the loss of everything that had ever been his reality. Utter horror. Fear, swamping him like the night; and anger greater than any he had ever known, a rage that measured the confines of his powerlessness like a newly-caught tiger roaring in its cage.

All sorcery contains danger. Lidan retained enough control to wrench them both back from the point where the mental fusion would have become so total that neither of them would ever have been able to become completely separate again. For her, accustomed to sorcery, and already aware what was happening, the effect was dreadful enough. Mind-touching was very rare in their society, but like all other juveniles she had been taught the way of doing it by an older and more experienced Skair at the Training School. Perhaps a little naïvely, she had not expected the contact with a human brain to be so very much different. Now she discovered that her brief experience in his world had done nothing like enough to prepare her for the horror of knowing his world as he knew it, for looking out of a pair of eyes so utterly different from her own. She recoiled from him, striking out bare-clawed at the air without even knowing that she was doing so; her hackles were erect, she spat and hissed, she dragged her face along the wall of the hut in a vain attempt to give herself a more bearable pain than the memories of that filthy world of his.

Brendan emerged from it almost mad with terror and fury. There was no comfortable denial possible now. He flung himself into the nearest corner, cradling his head, trying to blot out the pictures. He wasn't on Earth any more – he was on some unknown world millions of miles away from his home, with no way of getting back again. He was in the power of some murderous misbegotten alien being, who'd abducted him for her own purposes. Abducted him! And – Christ Almighty! – he'd fucked an *alien*...

His body shuddered uncontrollably, gripping itself into a tightly foetal position. If the medicine the Skair had given him hadn't begun to have an effect on his system already, he might have become hysterical. At that moment a single touch from her would have put his very sanity at risk; at the very least he would have attacked her, however suicidal such a reaction might have been. It did not arise, however; she still crouched beside the bed where he had lain, watching him with those intent, inhuman amber eyes. She was panting slightly, and a bead of blood trickled down the side of her face where she'd grazed it on the wall.

"Why? Why? What the fuck are you?" The words emerged muffled. He could hardly control his breathing enough to get them out.

"Because it was necessary." She hated the memories that were now polluting her brain; she hated the situation that had made it necessary for her to have brought him here at all; she hated herself for having done this to him; she hated him for the

waves of panic and rage that were beating out of him. "This world is in danger – and you are the only one who can save it."
"Fuck your world! Take me back to mine!"
"I cannot," she said shortly.
"What the hell do you mean, you can't!" He sat up and glared at her. "You bloody brought me here, didn't you?"
"You know that I did. And when you have done what is needed, I shall take you back again."
"What are you talking about? What have I got to do? And who the hell gave you the right to make me do anything anyway?"

With an effort, she controlled herself. Few Skaira had ever been spoken to in such a way, but he had every right to be angry with her. (A corner of her mind acknowledged and forced down the illogical irritation that his speech habit of contraction caused her: Skaira never contracted words, taught from cubhood that anything worth saying was worth saying correctly.) "I am sorry," she said quietly. "Sometimes there is no 'right'. There is only necessity."

For a minute or two longer he looked at her. The total unreadability of her face was appalling. Its points of resemblance to that of a human rather emphasised than softened its alienness. He dropped his head into his hands.
"Go away," he said. "For a few minutes, just – go away."

She paused for a moment. Then, without a word, she rose and went out of the hut.

He did not hear her go, but he knew that she had gone. For perhaps twenty breaths he sat unmoving, feeling his hands shaking. His entire body began shuddering again. Then, with an almost explosive movement, he straightened up. He began looking around the single room, taking in the details of its poverty. The bed, no more than a pallet with greenstuff for a mattress and a couple of simple woven blankets for covers. What appeared to be a large rug, the bare earth floor's only covering, made from various unidentifiable but beautiful pelts roughly sewn together. A shelf lined with jars of what looked like pottery ware, and another crowded with – books? Rising to stand on wobbly legs, he walked over and selected one. The cover felt like some kind of thick material, the pages almost like some kind of thin leather. He opened it. The text stared up at him. Not English; just line on line of graceful, flowing marks that looked to have been made with a crude writing instrument. Among the pottery jars he saw one that had several feathers resting upright in it. Quill pens. He threw the book on to the floor and opened another and another, frantically, uselessly. All the same. He buried his face in his hands again and whimpered like a terrified animal. The sound was horrifying in the silence.

After a while he picked up the book and put it back on the shelf, not even understanding why he did so. He wanted something, anything, to do with his hands. He picked up the jars and looked at them. Hand cast, he judged, and hand decorated. Although simple in design, they were not crude. The sides of several were painted with geometric patterns; others decorated with designs dug into the wet clay like seagulls' tracks in sand. Some were sealed with what looked like wax. One held what was undoubtedly perfume – the faintly resinous smell wafted from it.

The being alone was helping, a little. Having something to do was helping too. But he was not going to be able to stay alone here indefinitely. Sooner or later, she – the creature – was going to come back in. He began to shake again at the thought.

After perhaps half an hour, she returned.

Moving with the same easy, soundless stride, she came through the doorway and stopped. He was back in his corner by then, unable to make himself sit on the bed. She lay down, and looked silently at the wall opposite her.

"I can not blame you for hating me," she said quietly, at last. "I can not even ask you to forgive me. But this world needs you – and for the thousands who are at risk, I must ask that you help us."

He didn't answer for a moment or two. His panic, which had resurged on seeing her again, began subsiding a little, but his brain was still churning. It was almost impossible for him to connect this horrible hybrid creature with the woman he had supposedly taken to his bed: his stomach heaved when he thought about it. Underlying and exacerbating the horror of his position, trapped and helpless millions of miles from his home, was the appalling knowledge that he had unknowingly broken one of the most ancient taboos of humanity. His soul shuddered from the realisation. An animal – an *alien* animal… Even the almost human-looking parts of her were different: the hair that cascaded down her back was honey blonde, the same colour as the silky fur of her lower parts. Her skin appeared almost velvety. And there was nothing remotely human about the tawny eyes that were turned towards him with an intensity that was now appallingly recognisable as the stare of a predator.

"It was you all the time." His mouth was dry with disgust.

"Yes." Of what use to lie, even if she had wanted to? He turned his face to the wall. His silence was more eloquent than any words could have been.

"There was no other way. I am sorry."

"So am I," he answered bitterly, not looking round. "Sorry you never gave me a choice about it."

"You have a choice." She turned her head and stared out of the door, at the trees bending in the wind. Terrifying as the risk was, it was not right that he should not be told the truth. "Consent is everything. If you truly will not help us, I cannot force you. You have the choice to walk out of that doorway and find yourself back in your own world. All you have to do then is to forget us."

"Why didn't you just ask?" he said furiously, clenching his fists with helpless rage. He'd been deceived, used, trapped, and was sickened to his guts at the realisation and the method. "You should have asked. Not just bloody kidnapped me and dumped me here, and then told me I had the option of walking out on you if I wanted!"

It was true enough. She had already acknowledged, sitting outside all this while, that she was handling this dreadfully. And she had already admitted to herself that his resentment was justified; but still his accusation stung.

"How could I have asked you?" she snapped. "Would you have believed me if I had told you the truth? When I was in your human shape I had no powers beyond your own. In all that matters I *was* a human. I could not have touched your mind as I did just now. You will never know how terrified I was by my limitations! But I had my orders. You were the one, and this was the only way I could bring you. Were it your world in peril, would you hesitate?"

There was a long pause. He glared at her for a while, trying to find some way of denying it; then, reluctant honesty prevailing, he lowered his gaze and made a slight gesture of defeat. After a time, feeling the question still hang unanswered, "I suppose not," he admitted dully. Then, more harshly, "Well, what do you want me to do?"

"I will be honest with you – I do not know as yet. No doubt it will be made clear."

He muttered something that did not sound complimentary, but did not pursue the issue. She watched him sitting, clearly trying to reassemble the pieces of his world, staring in frowning silence at the white knuckles of his hands clasped across his knees. After a while he stood up. Very slowly, he made himself walk towards her. It was no more than a few paces, but each one clearly took an enormous effort of will. She rose, her human upper half rearing back gracefully as her forepaws braced under her for the lift, and turned around to face him full on, so that there should be no evasion, no possibility of pretence. Though he could have no way of knowing it, it was a posture that Skaira seldom adopted with each other except in the most serious situations; it was one of the preludes to fighting. It could also, however, be meant to indicate that there was total openness offered to the other party, and it was in this spirit, arms hanging loosely at her sides, that she adopted it.

They halted at arm's length from each other, and stood looking silently into each other's eyes. Fear and anger still urged him to lash out at something, but some quality in her stillness told him that she would accept the blow without any attempt at retaliation, and that knowledge made it impossible for him to do it. He could not make himself hit her. The fact that she was probably capable of killing him with very little effort had almost nothing to do with it; if she were telling the truth – and as yet he had no reason to doubt it – he could probably have used her like a punch-bag without reprisal, but that was not what held his hand. Wasn't it true that in the same circumstances, he would have done exactly the same as she had? He had no justification for taking out his resentment on her. At last, very slowly and warily, he reached out and touched her shoulder. His fingers were still shaking a little, and momentarily reluctant to touch her velvety skin, but it was something he needed to do. She stood quietly, permitting him to do what he would; she evidently understood that he was trying to come to terms with the situation in his own way. He gingerly took hold of a tress of the blonde hair – even that was slightly coarser than normal human hair. A very faint, wry shadow of his infectious grin softened his mouth. "'Take what you want, says God, and pay for it'," he quoted. "I suppose this is where I have to pay up."

She stared up into his face: he was not much taller than she, and still seemed very vulnerable even though he was now doing his best to hide it. "I am truly sorry that I could not give you a choice. But you can still go home. I would not blame you if you did. This is not your world."

He turned, and looked out of the door. Another world; he could still barely believe it. And yet there could not be any denial of it now. He was awake. He was in danger. And he could still choose to walk away.

A part of him – the very large part that was still shaking with shock – wanted to do just that. What did this world's problems have to do with him? What did he know about it anyway? And most importantly of all, what did he know about this creature standing beside him, who had kidnapped him for some purpose of her own?

She was honest. She'd given him the option of just walking away – she hadn't had to tell him that. She was brave. It must have taken some courage to go to another world and do what she had. And she needed him. Was that enough? She said he was the one who could help – the only one. What man could walk away from a plea like that? Didn't everyone long to be a hero?

It'd make a change from being the villain every night, he thought wryly. But he noted she'd said 'can'. Not 'will'. There was no certainty of his succeeding – and somehow he suspected that the price of failure would be high. He had a healthy interest in his own survival, and it might be wise to weigh up the risks before he put his neck in the noose. He wondered briefly what was happening back on Earth. Assuming their times were parallel – a dangerous assumption, but his body clock told him it was about mid-morning – they would have discovered him missing by now. He would have been missed at breakfast; probably one or two of his friends had gone up to tip him out of bed, and found him not in it. The panic was probably still fairly low-key. He could imagine Adrian simmering. There would be an account of the fact that he hadn't gone to bed alone – well, that wouldn't occasion any comment. They'd probably assume he'd taken her home, and stayed for a repeat performance. They'd be waiting for him to walk in to a broadside. Well, it looked like they were in for a long wait.

He glanced back at his companion. She had remained silent, allowing him to make his own decision. It came to him that she was either very strong or very proud, and possibly both: if she were telling the truth, it must be hard to resist the temptation to beg for help. But for whatever reason, she wasn't pressurising him. He was even gradually beginning to get used to the strange leonine face. "Explain one thing to me. Exactly whose idea was it to bring me here?"

For all its strangeness, he could still read the hesitation as she debated her reply. She wouldn't lie to him, but she had to frame it in a way he would understand. Finally, "I do not know how you would put it – do you have a god on your world?"

He frowned. "Are you trying to tell me a god told you to kidnap me?" There was suspicion under the words. Not his God, who was back on Earth – well, maybe not, wasn't God supposed to be omnipresent, but how could he be sure what deity the people on this world worshipped? And whilst he firmly believed in the faith in which he had been brought up, how strong were the chances of divine rescue if everything suddenly went wrong? He was no saint; he suspected that modern-day miracles would be rather out of the frame for the likes of him.

"Not a god. A goddess. Shieih, the Firstborn. She is the Mother, the source of life. She rules all that is female and fertile on this world. We – the Skaira – we are Her daughters. She came to me and told me what I must do. It was by Her power that I came to your world and took your shape. I could not have done it alone."

Resisting the urge to demand resentfully what the hell gave any bloody goddess the right to organise his life for him – Lidan evidently considered that might was right in that respect – Brendan considered this cautiously. It didn't sound too threatening. As long as they didn't expect *him* to start worshipping any goddesses…

"Didn't your husband object? Or don't you have a husband?"

"There are no male Skaira. We are all female, born carrying the next generation. That is why we are free to devote ourselves to Shieih."

He whistled softly. Asexual reproduction! It was an old enough joke that there was only one thing women really needed men for that couldn't be taken care of by a lawn mower and a vibrator. It seemed that on this world all they needed were the last two. Redundancy by evolution! No wonder all the men had died out.

"The other races have menfolk," added Lidan, evidently not wishing him to feel too left out. He turned around and looked at her. Why should he feel so surprised?

"*Other* races?" he asked. "Just how many of you are there?"

"Only three," she replied a little indignantly. "There are the Venelai, the Birdpeople. They look a little like you, but they are bigger, and they have heads like birds. Then there are the Manyei, the dwellers in the forest. They are smaller than you, and thinner, and they have legs like a deer's. They eat no meat and harm no-one."

"And who's in charge?" Very warily now – suppose the Skaira were the bottom link in the power chain? How would that affect his chances?

"In charge?" She pondered the question. "Well, the Venelai have an Emperor. He is in charge of his subject kings. The Skaira have a Princess, to whom we owe obedience. The Manyei – well, I do not think the Manyei have anyone in authority over them. They do not think in that way."

"So who's more important – the Emperor or the Princess? Who gives who orders, if it comes to the crunch?"

At this point he got his first demonstration of a Skair equivalent of a smile. The eyes warmed the way a human's did, but the movement of the mouth was strange: it would not have been difficult to make it into a stifled yawn. The tip of her rough pink tongue rested on her lower teeth. "By the One! It would be a brave Emperor who gave orders to any Skair! But there again, it would be a strange Princess who gave orders to an Emperor! The only Skair who could exert authority over the Horned Throne would be the First Priestess, and that only on religious matters. If the First Priestess speaks, she does so with the voice of Shieih. The Emperor would be insane not to give her a hearing."

Brendan nodded. He was beginning to get the shreds of a picture, although he wouldn't take any bets on its accuracy.

"Right. Now for the important bit. What, or who, am I supposed to save the world from?"

Her smile faded.

"I have told you truly – I do not know yet. Shieih said that there may be war, but she did not say between whom. I would imagine that the Venelai have had a falling-out; it happens. They are a quarrelsome folk sometimes."

"And I'm supposed to intervene in a war?" His voice rose incredulously.

“I do not *know*,” she repeated crossly. Her tail twitched: like any animal’s, it was an accurate guide to her moods. “It may be, it may not be. We must perhaps try to prevent it beginning.”
“Sounds sensible,” he commented drily. “You know something? You’ve told me about your people, you’ve told me about your world – but you still haven’t told me your name.”
The great amber eyes blinked at him, opening wide in evident surprise.
“Have I not? By the One! I am Lidan, Lidan eré Gisar. Yours I know. Bren-dan Doyle.” She pronounced the name with careful pride, and frowned as almost in spite of himself a faint grin touched the corners of his mouth. “What, have I said it wrongly?”
“Not exactly wrong. I just haven’t heard it said quite that way before.”
“Then you should have a more sensible name. Bren-dan! Have all your people such strange names?”
“Some have worse,” he replied, wondering what she’d make of his sister Fionnhuala’s. – “It’s a Celtic name. Very old.”
“Kel-tic. That is your people? Bren-dan the Kelti?” She blinked. Was it, could it be, a coincidence that the word *Kl’thi’* in the Old Speech signified ‘without consent’?
“Celt,” he corrected.
“Kelt.” She hesitated. Perhaps the resemblance was just an uncanny coincidence. Perhaps it wasn’t. “I like Kelti better. I think that is what I shall call you. It is easier than Bren-dan, anyway.” She nodded at him. “Well met, Starborn Kelti.”
“I like my real name,” he said. His chin had come up. Adrian would have recognised the stubborn look instantly. “Names matter to me.”
“Of course,” she said at once. “You must think me very discourteous. Do not think it is merely that I do not like your odd name! Whether I like it or not, names are not to be – thrown hither and thither, especially in these circumstances. I do not know how it is on your world, but I think it best we do not reveal yours to others here. Your real name, I mean. There is power in names.”
“You never told me yours, when you were on Earth. Was that why?”
“Certainly. I could not lie, but who is to say what powers might have been listening? It was best to say nothing. And you did not ask,” she added matter-of-factly.
“No. I had other things on my mind,” he admitted with a twinkle, and was amused to see the Skair go slightly pink. She took an interest in her paws rearranging themselves.
“I think that, too, should be forgotten,” she said awkwardly. “Or at least – not talked of openly.”
“I won’t if you don’t want me to. But I won’t forget it.” His smile became wry. An encounter that had landed him in this predicament would hardly slip out of his memory!
“No, nor I,” she muttered to herself, turning aside to hide her growing embarrassment. That much was certain. How could she possibly forget it? Especially when there was so much still in view to remind her – it did not seem to have occurred to him that he was still stark naked. This in itself did not bother her: on Kerriel immodesty lay in behaviour, not in lack of clothing. But the memories

were too close to the surface for her to look on him without remembering too easily much that she found it hard to be comfortable with. He evidently found nothing discomforting in the remembrance, but then he had done such things many times. At least he seemed to have begun coming to terms with her own part in it; she sensed a relaxation, a palpable lightening, since she'd hurled the truth at him that when on his world she had effectively been a human.

Conversation lapsed for a while, but it was a moderately comfortable silence. She busied herself with a little tidying up, largely to give him time to himself. He occupied this with looking out over the forest again, trying to pin down in what way it looked 'alien'. It extended as far as the eye could see, right away to where it blurred into distance and the horizon, except where it gave way to the foothills of what was evidently the start of a vast mountain range that spread away towards the north. The vista was not as strange as he would have expected, given the fact that he was in a completely different world, but he would not have needed to be told that it was not European woodland. There was a difference in the shapes, in the movement of the branches in the wind, even in the colours of the mountains beyond them. Very subtle; he would have been hard put to define any of them. He wondered whether it was some difference in the quality of the sunlight that filtered down between the drifting clouds that trailed their vast slow shadows across the hills. But there was definitely something. And what creatures lived there? Nothing he was going to recognise. It might be as well if he didn't get any ideas about going for a stroll on his own until he had a bit of experience with the local flora and fauna. He wondered what was going on on Earth now. The panic would be increasing. He wondered how long it would be before they got the police involved, and thought with a pang that he wasn't being very fair to his companions. He turned around and looked at the Skair who was now busy rearranging the greenery of the bed. "You meant it when you said you can take me back again if I want you to? You're not just saying it to make me feel better?"

"At any time you desire it," she said steadily.

"And to any time I want?"

"To the moment we left your world. The fabric of your time must not be broken. That is one of the rules of sorcery: the pieces must fit together afterwards."

"Sounds fair enough." He allowed himself a little malicious enjoyment of the thought of Adrian's gathering temper, now that he had the option of tinkering with time and putting it all right again. That was – assuming everything went according to plan and he survived whatever was waiting for him. But if it didn't, if somehow Lidan couldn't get him back, he wasn't going to be in a position to care much about the mystery he'd left on Earth. He'd never see Earth again. He thought about his family. It wouldn't be long before somebody got on to them. That bothered him much more. They'd be worried sick. What would become of them if he never returned? They would never know what had happened to him. There would be the hours, days, months becoming years of wondering and worrying, listening to every footstep and hoping at every knock on the door, every ring of the phone. If only there was some way he could contact them and spare them that – send a letter, let them know how much he loved them, even if he never saw them again. How inadequately we share our feelings, he thought sombrely. We never act as if there might not be a chance to say everything that matters before the end.

"Lidan." It was worth asking. "Is there any way I could get a message back to my world?"

She looked up in surprise. "A message?"

"Yes. Not much. Just to my family – in case I don't make it. It's not fair that they don't know what happened."

She considered, frowning. It was a reasonable enough request, and it raised him in her estimation that he should take thought for his family's suffering; but in the circumstances she wondered what he could possibly say that would be believed. Still, it was not for her to say what he should or should not write. Writing materials were not a problem. She had spare leaves of paper in the back of one of her books where she had made notes on points she wished to discuss with Argan the Law-Wise on her next visit to Vanreil. It was the work of a moment to tear out one of the soft leaves. Ink was also to hand, a little pot of dark plant dye. The pen was more of a problem – as it was a quill, it had to be dipped every few letters. He knelt beside the low table and stared down at the paper. There was so much he wanted to say, and at that moment the words would not come. It was impossible to tell them the truth of what had happened to him. Whatever he sent would inevitably end up in the hands of the Gardai if he never returned, and he had no wish to be posthumously written off as a crank. 'Kidnapped by an alien'! For a moment or two he hesitated, revolving in his mind various implausible explanations of where he might possibly have disappeared to that would spare his parents worry. None were adequate to the situation. No, he could not tell them anything. Only that though he... should he tell them they'd never see him again? He stared down at his fingers clenched around the quill, and tried to fight down the superstitious fear that writing it might make it come true. Finally he put down that they were not to worry about him, that he was well, and safe, and that he loved them. At least part of it would be true – the part that mattered... Once he'd mastered the trick of using the quill, it was soon written. The words looked pitifully inadequate. Not much recompense for all the love they'd lavished on him, but he knew how proud they'd been of him. At least it would be better than nothing, if not much. The soft vellum would surprise them, so would the strange ink, but his writing should still be reasonably recognisable to them. He was careful to make his signature at the bottom as close to normal as he could with the quill. His mind ached momentarily from the conception of two strands of time unravelling on his world; if he returned safely what would happen to the letter? Would it arrive anyway, to be dismissed as some strange hoax – or would the fact of his return twist reality so that he had no longer left, and therefore it had never been written? And if that happened, where would it go instead? He said nothing as he handed the page to Lidan. She wrapped the leaf around a small stone and tied it with some kind of stringy creeper; then went outside, breathed on it and hurled it skywards. At the same moment she said something, words in a harsh tongue that made his ears ache, and he had the briefest impression of a hole in the sky into which the missile vanished. The suddenness of it was frightening.

"Where has it gone?" he asked, realising too late and with a spasm of absurd panic that he hadn't put any address on it, and visualising it smacking down in the

shower cubicle of his hotel. God alone knew where it would end up if it did; probably in the nearest dustbin when the maid cleaned the room out…
"Where you wished it to go," she answered, not turning around. He supposed there was some reasonable explanation, but at that moment he didn't feel up to asking for one. Not much demand for postmen around here, then. The act had brought back his feeling of isolation, and fear hurried in on its heels. The Skair suddenly looked horribly alien again. What was he doing here, in this world he didn't belong to?

She looked around at him then as if sensing his feelings; perhaps she could sense them. "You are still tired. You should sleep, and when you wake we will eat. And when the evening comes we will go out and see what there is to be seen in the world."
"Go out when it's getting dark?"
"I know that it may be difficult for you. But until we know more of what is going on I do not wish to go far and I do not wish to travel in daylight when there are too many eyes. We will be safest in the dusk. I will look after you." She turned and came back to him, and in an unexpected gesture put her hands a little tentatively on to his shoulders. Her wide amber eyes met his with the fearless honesty of a cat's. For a moment he stiffened again, but didn't repulse her. "Do not worry, Kelti. We are both beneath the wings of Shieih."

Though that idea didn't exactly reassure him as she probably intended, she was right; he did feel unexpectedly weary. The bed looked inviting, and the thought of food later on was pleasant. Not just now, though he drank some water before he lay down. She lay in the doorway, looking out, arms folded and eyes alert. There were several woven blankets on the bed and he wrapped himself in one, more for the feeling of it than the need of warmth – it was surprisingly warm in the hut, even without the covering dropped across the doorway. It felt strange to rest his head against foliage, and he put a fold of cloth across it to make it feel a little more familiar. If he curled up and closed his eyes he could make it all go away; and he had not felt so defenceless and alone for many years. He needed very badly to forget for a while; and the combination of the *vhi'the* and his own tiredness were enough to conquer his fears, at least for the moment.

He slept.

5

Blue shadows were deepening among the trees before the Skair judged it safe to leave the hut. It had been a long, quiet day. Brendan had slept until around mid-day and woken feeling considerably better. He then had to ask about going to the toilet, and discovered rather to his relief that the Skair shared human ideals of cleanliness. There was a cleft in the rocks behind the hut which ran down to an underground course of the stream which also fed the spring further up, and body wastes were passed into it and thus hygienically disposed of. There was plenty of vegetation for use as toilet paper when required, which was another relief. It was a little disconcerting to be accompanied to the toilet site, and a little embarrassing to discover that the Skaira had an animal's matter-of-fact attitude to bodily functions: they were no more shy about evacuating the body than filling it, and Lidan was clearly surprised by his discomfort at her presence. She had only accompanied him to keep watch for any unforeseen threat, and it was a stroke of inspiration on her part to turn her back.

That accomplished, he discovered that his nausea had passed, and that he was hungry. Here he had his second check. It would not have occurred to him that his fairly moderate consumption of coffee constituted an addiction, but it was certainly something he was going to miss. He was careful to keep most of his intake to decaffeinated, so the withdrawal from caffeine was not going to be overmuch of a problem. But the simple fact of not having a cup with what amounted to breakfast was an early signal of the sort of minor shock he was going to have to get used to. The food itself was not as much of an ordeal as he had feared it might be. Lidan was not hungry yet and needed nothing, but she had no difficulty in providing a fair meal for him. The small annexe to the living quarters of the hut contained a number of containers, some of pottery and a few of wickerwork, and several shelves of what appeared to be different varieties of fruit. Much of what she laid out on a wooden platter for his approval was selected from these, together with small palm-sized cakes of cereal dotted with nuts and bound together with something that tasted like honey. It was no surprise that nothing was recognisable, but nothing was repulsive to the eye either. He tried most of the things, and most of them were reasonably palatable. The cereal cakes were sweeter than he preferred, but they were filling. He enjoyed one sort of fruit more than all the rest, one that looked a little like a small fat pear and tasted rather like vintage cognac. To wash it down, she provided him with a drinking vessel that appeared to be some kind of narrow-necked gourd, filled with fresh water to which she added a couple of drops from one of the containers. It tasted odd and peppery in the mouth, but the aftertaste was not unpleasant. Altogether he ate a very good meal, and the missing cup of coffee was the only thing he would have liked to round it off.

The afternoon had passed peacefully enough after that, whiled away with talk. They had tried to come to some grasp of each other's lifestyles, but it had been difficult. The conversation had been a little wary and hesitant, occasionally flowing more freely as they grasped at similarities – but these were few. Many of the differences were so great that there was no bridging the gap in their experience; and the attempt had left them foundering, staring at one another across a gulf of incomprehension. How did one explain the concept of television to someone whose only encounter with electricity was the sight of a bolt of lightning? And how did one convey the marvels and complexities of a life lived as part of the circle of life and death to one whose food came from a supermarket or a restaurant?

Even in matters of religion they found little common ground. It was natural that Lidan should be intensely curious about the beliefs of one from another world; but the tangle of Christian belief and praxis which emerged from her questioning did very little to enlighten her. The central tenet of Christian belief, the Incarnation of God, she found profoundly shocking. She listened carefully to a rather jumbled account of the life of Christ, and was prepared to concede that he must have been a holy and wise man, but to believe that he was the Uncreated made flesh was beyond her. Trying to establish some kind of parallel between their beliefs, she found that the nearest divine equivalent for the role occupied by her Goddess was something Christians called an "angel", though even that didn't sound very close. Some aspects of Christianity actually offended her, though she did not say so. It was not her place to criticise his faith, but she could not think highly of any religion that took such a dubious view of the processes of life. To a Skair, life was sacred, and the act that made life was therefore sacred too. To condemn and confine it as Christianity seemed to do was not only heretical – it was not even sensible! Marital fidelity by choice was one thing, and a very good thing too, but to make it a Law – by the One! As well make it a law to only eat one type of animal for the rest of one's life. A sure recipe for disaster.

In his turn, Brendan was taken aback by the primitive nature of Kerriel's religious beliefs and practices. He listened in doubtful silence to the story of the origin of Skaira, which sounded to him like a myth, though Lidan insisted that it was a literal truth. She then moved on to a more general outline of her world's religion, and he found some of it very hard to accept. Reared in a faith that traditionally took a dim view of sex even within the bonds of marriage, the discovery that not only was lovemaking regarded as a devout act, but that temples of the Goddess effectively acted as brothels, made him inwardly shudder with distaste. He tried to imagine being in a marriage where either partner had the right to invite anyone they chose home to make love with, and couldn't. For all that he had to admit to being a somewhat of a hypocrite in that he didn't practise what he preached in respect of chastity, Kerriel's completely amoral attitude to it revolted him. Further, the polarisation of worship between the sexes seemed primitive in the extreme. He couldn't come to terms with the fact that men were obliged to worship a ball of flaming gas while women revered a sky full of stars – he was still in too much of a state of shock to hear the nuances of expression that indicated otherwise.

The subject had provided matter for a fair amount of cautious but good-natured argument, both parties anxious not to offend. Although aware that he was fighting from a fatally flawed position, given the means Lidan had used to snare him, Brendan felt obliged to defend the Christian ideal. They came to an uneasy truce in the end, neither convinced the other was right, but realising that there could be no decisive victory.

The light presently began to wane, and he wondered how late it would be before his companion felt it safe to leave. She took a nap early in the evening, warning him not to leave the hut without waking her. He passed the time dozing and wondering what was happening back on Earth now. Until (or unless) his promised return was effected, he supposed that time was passing there as if he had simply disappeared off the planet – which indeed he literally had, though his colleagues had no way of knowing that. It was a fair bet that matters were getting a bit frantic by now. There was a plane to catch. The police would certainly be involved soon, if they weren't already. He wondered if his family had been informed yet, and his heart ached for them even while he clung to the belief that he could still rearrange reality and make all the suffering something that had never happened. In an hour or two the others would just have to leave without him, and carry on as best they could. Lucky that he had such a talented understudy in Kevin – the lad was well able to cope with the role, little as he could ever have imagined being thrust into it under such circumstances.

The matter of clothing had been a bit of a puzzle. He couldn't go out naked, and the Skair had no clothes. They had finally taken one of the blankets, folded it double, cut a hole in the fold and put it over his head, using a strip of leather to tie it around his waist. For extra protection she punched a couple more pairs of holes above and below the waist, and threaded through strips of hide to tie it closed before wrapping the belt around it. What he actually looked like in it he dared not imagine, but it was surprisingly warm. For footwear he had a piece of deer-hide wrapped sackwise around either foot and tied at the ankle. Gucci they were not, but at least they would protect his feet.

Lidan woke at last, and yawned widely, giving him a first real look at the entire set of miniature but ferociously pointed lion's teeth in her mouth. "So. I think it will be safe enough now. Stay here a moment, Kelti, while I scent." She stretched luxuriously and padded out of the hut. For a moment she stood perfectly still outside, listening. There was no sound. The wind had died down and there was no movement among the trees. After a while she walked down the hill as far as the edge of the woodland, where she again paused to listen. Her head was up, catching the breeze, while her tail dipped to allow its ultra-sensitive tip to touch the ground, searching for the faintest vibration. Still nothing. The green depths were silent. She was not altogether happy with the silence, but what was she to do? They could not stay here indefinitely. At least she could be reasonably confident that there was no threat to the Starborn in the immediate vicinity.

She went back up the hill, paused for one last uneasy look around, and beckoned him out. He came to her quite readily, but she noted his pallor, though she had no way of understanding the reason for it – it was harder than he had thought to leave the only place on this world which had some tenuous connection with his own. Neither of them spoke as they went swiftly down to the forest. Again she paused, scenting and tail-touching. Nothing. Her first intention was to seek out the nearest Manyé settlement. Although the shy, self-effacing Wood-People took no part in Venel quarrels, indeed rarely understood the nature of them, they were sometimes surprisingly well informed on the doings of the outside world. They said, "The forest knows", and could not elaborate on the theme. If they knew nothing, no harm had been done. If she could prevent it – which would be difficult, with a folk who were so much a part of the earth and the things that took life from it – there was no necessity for them to see the Starborn or know of his existence: what they did not know of they could not reveal to others. They were too honest to be suborned to treachery, but in the same way they were too simple to understand the necessity of secrecy.

The two moved through the woodland without speaking. They had already decided on this course, so there was no need to discuss it. Lidan paused occasionally to examine trees where any other passing Skaira would have scent-marked; there was no sign. She herself refrained from marking them, though in ordinary circumstances she would have done so: the fewer signs she could leave now, the better. She even refrained from emptying her bladder until she could straddle a small stream and urinate into the flow of water.

There was no way in which his companion could have realised how eerie the gathering dusk was to Brendan. Darkness was a familiar element to her, and the wood was her hunting ground; she was entirely at home here. To him everything was increasingly threatening. It would have been enough of a trial in good daylight. With darkness coming on it was really frightening. For one thing, Lidan walked so quietly that he could hardly hear her, and with his inadequate night-vision there were several times when he literally lost sight of her, even though she was never more than a couple of feet away from him. He derived some reassurance from the regular soft touch of her tail, which she instinctively used like a Skair mother keeping contact with a cub. Sweat crept down the back of his neck. In addition, he could not help envying the effortless stealth with which the Skair moved. Try as he might he could not walk anything like as quietly, and as the twilight deepened he became still clumsier. They were using what looked like a trail, but there were roots and stems of creeping plants sprawling across it, and he stumbled over them with embarrassing regularity. In decent footwear he would have had enough problems; in these makeshift moccasins he was at a far more serious disadvantage.

Eventually Lidan stopped and looked at him with concern. "Are you hurt, Kelti? Tired?"

"Tired of tripping over these blasted plants," he said in an undertone, freeing his foot from the latest ambush. "I'm sorry, Lidan, but I just can't see where I'm going too well."

"There is something wrong with your eyes?" she asked in quick anxiety.

"No. It's just that humans can't see in the dark."

"Can not see in the dark?" She was completely taken aback. "But what do you do at night?"

"Sleep," he said tersely.

The Skair added another astonishing facet to her knowledge of humankind. She should have remembered the brightly-lit surroundings on Earth, providing compensation for the humans' defective eyesight. But it was going to cause problems if they could only travel by daylight. She considered her options. They were few. She did not like to interfere with the Starborn's physiology, but the risks of not doing so were too great. With a sigh she reached out towards him.

He resisted the instinct to recoil after the last contact. Her fingers brushed his temples, and he felt something like a tingle of cold; he caught a murmur, again in a harsh-sounding language he could not interpret, and suddenly the near-darkness around him became lighter.

"What the…" He heaved a sigh of relief. It was completely astounding to see what a difference it made. Even his ridiculous shoes wouldn't slow him down unduly now.

"I do not like having to do that," she said quietly. "I should not interfere with the way your God made you."

"I think it's fantastic." He hesitated. "Can your – magic – can you do anything with it?"

"No. There are rules, many rules that we must not break. For most of us, we can only change the way things operate – the degree, if you will. We cannot make anything completely other than itself. Only one Skair can do that – the Princess. She has the Royal Words, the sorcery that can change matter. And she too must obey rules governing how it is used. Power is not a game. It is a responsibility, and a heavy one."

"So I should imagine." They set out again. Brendan found himself wondering what it would be like to able to do magic – real magic, not just sleight-of-hand or illusions. It was an enviable ability. What would the penalty be for breaking the rules? Probably nothing very pleasant. But to be able to literally change matter! No wonder the use of such a power was rigidly controlled. The potential for misuse was incredible. A Skair Princess must be a remarkable creature to be able to resist tinkering with the world around her. No human he could imagine would be able to do so. What was the saying? 'All power corrupts, and absolute power corrupts absolutely'. Oh, at first the tinkering would be humanitarian. Stop the wars, put an end to the starvation, make politicians tell the truth – one hell of a spell that would be! – but it wouldn't stop there. Perhaps God had been wise to refrain from giving such powers to humanity.

They walked on in silence for what he estimated to be about three miles. The night was now absolute, and but for his new night-vision he would have been practically blind, especially in such thick woodland. From time to time he caught a glimpse of sky between the branches, but there was thick cloud cover. According to the Skair, the season was late autumn and he would have expected most of the trees to be shedding their leaves, but on Kerriel far fewer species did so than on Earth. There were also more winter-flowering species, and the scent of these drifted on the air. He had also learned that even in the middle of winter, snow was a rarity. The continent on which the Forest of Three Stars lay was on slightly more southerly latitudes than the British Isles, and enjoyed less variation in seasonal temperatures.

Presently Lidan stopped. She listened, but could hear nothing. Nevertheless, she looked around for a safe nest to leave the Starborn in. A nearby stand of bushes offered a haven, and he did not argue when she told him to sit down in the middle of it and be very quiet for a while. He was aware of the indignity of being left in hiding like a fawn, but it was hardly clever to rebel, even though he was frightened by the prospect of being left alone. She must feel it less of a risk for him, however alarming it might be; it did not need words to convey her anxiety to him, and until he had a far greater acquaintance with the situation it would be wiser to do as he was told without comment.

Praying that he would be safe, but not daring to take him with her into a situation where her instincts were warning her of danger, Lidan prowled forward, using all her skill to move as silently as a shadow. She knew that the village was now close, and at this hour of night the inhabitants would be sleeping, but still the silence was too profound. Again and again she paused, scenting the air. The breeze was against her, it was blowing in the wrong direction; fortunately it was fitful and weak, and unlikely to advertise her own presence to any nose less sensitive than another Skair's.

Suddenly the forest opened out. There was the village, a cluster of simple huts each built about a living sapling. The Manyei would cut no wood, and made their dwellings around the trees they loved. This meant that such structures were fallible in the matter of waterproofing, but the Wood People saw nothing amiss with getting wet. Their bodies were made to cope with such conditions, and they accepted rain as naturally as did the trees themselves.

She stood scenting and listening for several minutes before breaking cover. Nothing but her moved. As silently as a cloud she stole forward. She crept between the huts, and stopped as if she had been struck. For a moment she could not believe the evidence of her senses. A small sound escaped her, a moan of mingled shock and disbelief. When she had recovered herself a little she went around the rest of the village, such as it was. The air was sharp with the smell that made the saliva run in her mouth. Everywhere the tale was the same. She pressed her hands to her face. "Why, Mother Shieih? Why?"

No-one answered. The night was quiet. There was no threat here now. She would have to fetch the Starborn; it was certainly not safe to leave him alone anywhere. Her brain reeled with the effort to understand as she hurried back to where she had left him. Not until she inhaled the scent of him did she realise how frightened for him she had become. He was there and he was safe. She wanted to hurry him away from the village, but there was probably nowhere safer they could be at that particular moment: she was too scared now to risk returning to the hill. As a proficient killer, she could look on violent death unmoved, but even she was aghast at the slaughter of the peaceful wood-folk. His reaction to what they would find in the village would undoubtedly be worse than hers; she had gathered that he did not have to kill to eat, and had probably never even seen a kill at first hand. Unfortunately there was no way he could be spared the sight of the village's occupants, or at least of what was left of them. To tidy them up would be to betray her presence if whoever had carried out the carnage should happen to return. Certainly the attack had been recent; the blood was still fresh. She pushed forward among the bushes and took Brendan in her arms, hugging him desperately. She could smell the fear-sweat on him, and for a moment searched wildly in her mind for an alternative that would spare her adding to his terrors. There was none. He had to be told – to allow him to walk innocently into such scenes would be unforgivable. She could hardly compose herself enough to get the words out. Who would do such a thing? Who would slaughter the Wood-People, who harmed nothing, who did nothing but care for the forest? Why? Why? Mother Shieih, why?

"They're *all dead*?" He sounded stunned. "But – you said they're harmless!"
"And so they are!" She fought to keep her voice down, to stifle the wail of horror and shock. –"No-one would harm Manyei, no-one! But someone has! And they can not be far away, so I must hide you in the village – they are not likely to go back there."

Fear clutched at his stomach, but he nodded. It was logical.

Some moments passed before Lidan could nerve herself to bring him out of hiding. She strained every sense, hating the silence that grated on her nerves. Nothing. The hackles all along her back were bristling with apprehension, her upper lip trembling away from her teeth. As they began the seemingly endless journey to the shattered village, the need for haste warred desperately with the need for stealth. Again and again Lidan pulled them to a halt, listening, scenting and looking, and each time Brendan froze. He had never experienced the presence of literally mortal danger, and more than half of him screamed to have the Skair take him back to his own world and safety – now! Somehow he kept silent. She couldn't just walk away, therefore neither could he.

They reached the village eventually without incident. More time passed in listening, but nothing had changed. As they moved cautiously forward, Brendan took a deep breath and steeled himself.

The first body somehow did not look real. So pathetically thin, a tumble of limbs sprawled aimlessly on the turf, its eyes staring sightlessly at the clouds above. He could not help hesitating to get a better look. The Manyé was more like what he would have expected an alien to look like, at first glance. Its body was almost skeletal compared to that of a human; the head looked slightly oversized. The hair was very fair, almost silvery in colour, swept back severely from the fine-boned face. The eyes were large and lustrous, or would have been before glazing over in death. Perhaps the strangest feature were the legs, like a deer's as Lidan had said, with tiny neat cloven hoofs. A faun lay dead in front of him, and for a second he had strayed into Greek legend; but this was no legend and the Manyé was no faun. It – he could not tell its sex – was disfigured with great stains of clotted blood. Someone, or something, had taken great pleasure in hacking the wretched creature to death.

The sense of unreality did not diminish with the discovery of more corpses; if any-thing it increased. The whole grisly scene was so ugly, so senseless, so pointless. The entire population of the village – about thirty souls in all – had been slaughtered like cattle. Mothers with tiny children had not been spared: all lay dead, hacked repeatedly and savagely about the head and body. Not one had escaped. Nothing moved around the place except for a small woolly animal – Brendan correctly guessed it to be this world's equivalent of a sheep, though the shape of its nose reminded him more of a tapir – that wandered disconsolately between the huts, uttering small piping sounds. Only the fact that the People of the Wood never tied or penned any beast, but allowed their flocks to come and go as they pleased, had saved it from sharing their fate. Lidan ducked into one of the huts, pulling him with her, and sank down on to the floor, holding her head. Nothing had prepared her for this. It was worse than anything she could have imagined. When conflicts broke out there could be violence, but there were rules as well. There was no *reason* for the village to have been attacked!

When her panic had abated a little she began to consider what her next move should be. There were few alternatives. If the situation had deteriorated in this terrifying way, she could no longer rely on her own ability to protect the Starborn. It followed that the most sensible alternative was to enlist the help of others, and there was no help for it: she would have to go to Vanreil and tell the Skaira who lived there what had happened. What they would make of the tale was in the hands of the Goddess, but it was absolutely imperative that no harm should befall Kelti, and who better could protect him than the mightiest in the service of Shieih? Whatever they felt with regard to what had happened between him and Lidan, they would be bound to honour the wishes of the Goddess by whose command he had been brought here.

It was a relief to have the decision made. Now there was nothing left to do but wait here for a few hours, and hope that those responsible for this sickening act made themselves scarce. The Holy Mountain was some distance away; for all that the range in which it rose was clearly visible from her hill. Ordinarily the miles would have been of little account, but now they stretched in her mind into an endless distance. All that way she would have to keep him secret, keep him safe, and keep him alive. The responsibility was crushing. He was kneeling beside her, looking out through the doorway at the bodies. His face was grim. It was well that he understood the danger, but Mother Shieih! Who could have anticipated that the danger would be so great? Who could have given the orders for such an act? And why? The questions returned over and over again to hammer at her disbelief.

Still, while they waited she might as well put the time to good use. There was cloth to be had in plenty, the village had had good weavers and there had been no pretence at plundering the huts. She found a bolt that would serve her purposes, and she had the knife at her belt to cut it. A brief search uncovered a hooked awl and a length of thin twine. Brendan stared when he realised what she was doing; in the midst of all this carnage it seemed ludicrous that she should be fitting him for clothes. Nevertheless, he would not be sorry to be rid of his makeshift tunic – the blanket was warm enough, but it was far from draught-proof. It was unfortunate that they couldn't improve on his footwear, but at least he could have trousers again.

For all that she was unused to such a task, Lidan worked swiftly while her companion snatched a couple of hours of uneasy sleep. By Earth standards, the garment that eventually emerged was almost laughable. It was rather like a baggy boiler suit, with the front slashed open and tied up with twine. She did not attempt such niceties as hemming, and the knife that was designed for killing was not good at cutting cloth without leaving ragged edges. Nevertheless, it was certainly an improvement on the blanket. When he woke up Brendan got into it gratefully, and pulled the lacing tight up the front. He could still keep the tunic for extra warmth if he needed it, but at least he no longer felt a complete idiot in what he was wearing. Considering the circumstances it was probably ridiculous of him to worry over his clothes, but he had an obscure feeling that as the sole representative of his world he ought to care what impression he made. Lidan had seen him at his best; he was not anxious for her fellows to mistake him for some kind of walking scarecrow.

By the time they were finished, the night was well advanced. There was even a hint of the far-off dawn in the air, some infinitesimal change in the smell of the breeze. Surely by now any evildoers would be gone, wearied by their night's achievements. Warily Lidan put her head out of the hut. There was still nothing to be heard or seen, but there was no longer the unnatural hush about the forest that there had been. As far as she could tell (and the Good Goddess guide her aright!), it was safe to venture out. It would be well to make a start. They had far to go.
"Come, Kelti. Let us leave this place. It is accursed," she said in a low voice. Brendan wasn't going to argue. The scene was bad enough in the darkness; he had no wish to see it in good daylight.

They started walking.

6

They did not stop until the morning light was well towards its full, for Lidan was anxious to make as much speed as possible towards Vanreil. In her mind it had assumed the nature of sanctuary, and they could not reach it fast enough. Eventually, however, they had to call a halt. They found a place where a shallow gorge cut the forest, no more than eighteen or twenty feet deep but offering several deep undercuts where they might safely wait out the hours of daylight. On her advice they had foraged for food as they travelled, plucking fruit from trees and bushes they passed and eating it on the march, and Brendan was glad of it now. Although he was not full, he was not hungry enough for it to interfere with getting to sleep; and despite the couple of hours' rest he had snatched in the Manyé village, he was tired – not so much physically, as he was superbly fit, but mentally. He needed to blot out for a time the strain of his worries, the sense of threat. The undercut – it was hardly large enough to be called a cave – which they finally selected, was floored with fine gravel, but it could have been a featherbed and quilt as far as he was concerned. He stretched out on it gratefully, pillowed his head on his folded tunic, and fell fast asleep.

Lidan too was tired, but she did not immediately follow his example. The exigencies of their situation did not excuse her from prayer, and she faced the East and the departed night, and quietly made her devotions. The period of prayer over, she looked around and considered. It was good that they had found such a hiding-place, but she disliked the fact that they could be crept up on and surrounded with ease. Still, short of going up to keep watch while Brendan slept, there was nothing much she could do about it. She actually considered doing so, but the risk was too great. She simply dared not leave him alone for any length of time. Without malicious intent of any kind there were animals who sometimes frequented such a place which he might not recognise as a threat, or might not wake in time to defend himself from. And she herself could not go on indefinitely without rest. Worried though she was, she could force herself into the half-waking doze her people called 'hunting-sleep', where all the parts of the brain not monitoring her surroundings were able to shut down. It was not as refreshing as real sleep, but it was a good deal better than nothing.

Common sense urged that she follow this course, and she did so. She lay down with both hands in contact with large pieces of stone that would transmit vibration from any approacher. The most sensitive of her monitoring systems, the tip of her tail, was placed carefully between two boulders; the tiniest tremor through these would set off the alarm hairs. It was virtually impossible even for another Skair to creep up on one in 'hunting sleep' – to some degree they were safer from being surprised in these circumstances than they were when she was awake. She cast one last uneasy look around then put her head down again. The ground was silent and still. Anxious or not, she had to get some rest... The predator's part-sleep swallowed her, helped by the faint sound of Brendan's steady breathing. The morning advanced, and noon came and went. Still the forest was as peaceful as ever, and the two lay concealed beneath the overhanging bank, while beside them the stream murmured placidly in its bed.

The sun around which Kerriel circled had passed its height in the sky when the sound first made itself heard. So faint at first that it was more a quivering in the ground than a movement in the air, it was nevertheless instantly detected by the nerves crammed into Lidan's tail. It sounded an immediate alarm, jerking her fully awake. Her predator's reactions were too finely honed to thrust her into any betraying movement, but adrenaline began pumping into her system. Too far yet for any sight or scent, even if she had not been hidden below the level of the forest floor. She turned her head to press one of her ears firmly to the ground. Hooves – many hooves, and they were coming this way. It might be one of the herds of deer that roamed the woodland. And it might not. Venelai rode deer as saddle-beasts. In smaller numbers she might have been able to pick out an individual set of hoof-falls and analyse its impacts – a ridden beast's feet naturally struck with greater force than a wild one's; but with this number of animals there was no way she could do it. The chances were that whatever they were, they were coming for water. Her first impulse was to wake her companion and flee. But to where? Would they be as safe out in the open where they could be seen at a distance and ridden down with ease?

Snarling soundlessly, she glanced around at the geography of their hiding place. It was fortunate that the place they had chosen was beneath a particularly steep part of the gully bank – no rider in his senses would attempt to take his mount down at this particular spot, especially not when there were easier places of access. Equally fortunately, the course of the stream meandered, so that there were bends at either side of them – one of the things that had recommended this particular hiding-place to her. The only danger would be if there were any approaches to the opposite bank. The undercut was not deep enough to allow them to get far enough back to be invisible to anyone looking from directly opposite. She could not tell as yet whether the oncoming animals were on this bank or the other one: and by the time she could be certain, it would be too late to look for another refuge. For a long moment she hesitated. From that one angle they were completely exposed. But up on top they were visible from almost any direction, and there was no thick vegetation in this area where they might hope to hide more effectively. They would have to stay where they were, and pray to the Good Goddess that they might be safe.

As the hoofbeats drew closer, she shook Brendan gently by the shoulder. His first muzzy awakening soon cleared into understanding. The sound was even audible to his hearing by now, and they lost no time in pressing themselves as closely as possible to the back of the undercut. He did not need telling what Lidan had already seen: that from most angles they were reasonably safe from detection. The opposite bank was the danger. Luckily it rose at a slight angle and was higher than their own, which would deter a casual approach. They could not depend on that, however. The vegetation which grew to the edge was not high enough to hide them from anyone on horseback, nor indeed from anyone of average height within a couple of feet of it – and Lidan had said that Venelai were bigger than humans. How much bigger it was a little late now to speculate. If their worst fears were fulfilled, he was about to find out for himself. He ignored the discomfort of small roots and embedded stones digging into his back. As the sounds grew closer he glanced at Lidan to see her reaction then almost wished he hadn't. Her ears lay flat against her head, and there was a red glow behind the amber eyes. A human face could never have got its lips that wide apart; and the set of teeth she was displaying were inhumanly white, with pointed incisors and long, curved canines...

The sound and vibration of the approaching animals grew louder and stronger. The gravel beneath them shivered to it. Then suddenly, when it seemed that it could get no closer without a tide of animals cascading into the gully, a voice shouted an order. There was a flurry of turning hooves, blurred with the protests of thirsty saddle-beasts that could smell the water. More tellingly, there were also a couple of nervous squeals from one or two who could also smell the Skair beside it; but the Venel riders evidently took these for fright at the drop in front of them. Brendan and Lidan relaxed with shudders of relief: the patrol was above them, not in front of them. Their relief was premature, however, for next moment a sudden flying bulk cut out the sun. One rider, bolder or more foolhardy than the rest, had spurred his mount straight at the gully. It was a dangerous move, for it was a very wide leap for the already tired animal to make. For an instant disaster seemed to have been averted, for the front hooves cleared the drop, while the hind ones scrabbled frantically at the brink. Then a large stone half-buried in the bank was dislodged by the weight. Part of the ground gave way under the struggling animal, and with a scream it fell backwards, bringing its rider with it.

Lidan had only a split second to make her decision and act on it. Even as the soldier and his mount plunged towards the ground in a shower of loose earth and stones, she was leaping forward. There was a chance he might survive the fall with no more than superficial injuries, and if that happened all their chances were gone. She was well aware of the size and weight of the saddle-beasts Venelai rode to war, with their racks of antlers sharpened to deadly weapons. A fractional error of timing on her part would bury her under soldier and mount, and probably kill her outright. Afterwards she could only attribute it to the intervention of the Good Goddess that she had survived the insane risk she took in that moment. Even before the combined weight hit the streambed she was on them, grabbing for the helmet. No claws, no knife, there must not be a mark left on the body. Her left hand closed on the thick curved beak, her right fist crashed into the hollow behind his neck. Even as her front paws plunged desperately to avoid the crash of the deer's weight landing, she exerted all her upper-body strength to wrench his head backwards over her fist. His spinal column snapped audibly, then she was hurling herself away from the thrashing antlers and flailing hooves as his unfortunate mount kicked away from the bank. A frantic glance told her that the dead soldier still had one boot thrust through the stirrup loop as the saddle-beast staggered upright, but the other had slid loose and his body lolled perilously. Worse still, the deer cried piteously as it tried to put its weight on a shattered hind leg and almost fell again. The situation allowed her no time to pity its plight. She lunged forward again and bit at its soft muzzle. Her teeth did not close to leave betraying marks, but the terrified animal reared away from this new nightmare. Somehow on three legs it got itself away along the stream, hobbling and crying out, drawing away the attention of those above who had witnessed the start of the incident, but hopefully not its unexpected ending.

The voice of authority screamed above the sudden hubbub. The words could not be understood, for it was not in the Common Speech, but there was no mistaking the tone. The patrol turned right and rode quickly along the bank of the gully, not stopping until they reached a spot perhaps a hundred yards further on where an area of slippage provided a safe way to reach the water. Then there was the sound of splashing as several made their way to retrieve their comrade. The cries of the suffering saddle-beast stopped abruptly, and presently a trail of blood floated down the stream. There followed an agonising wait for the two listening, while the officer examined his dead man. Lidan had scrambled back to protect Brendan, and prayed beneath her breath for the help of Shieih of fang and claw.

Whether by divine intervention or simply because the situation appeared to provide its own explanations, however, the officer evidently found no grounds for suspicion. Balked of the opportunity to punish the offender, deprived of a valuable fighting man, he marshalled his remaining troops into disciplined order with sharp commands that rang along the course of the stream like the cracks of a whip. Back beneath the undercut, Lidan allowed herself to breathe again. She listened intently for any word she might hear that might provide her with any clue as to the identity of this force. Soldiers were usually in the command of a lord answerable to the Emperor, and the Forest of Three Stars was unique on Kerriel in that it was not part of the territory of any king. These here could be part of an Imperial division. If that was so, in ordinary circumstances she could reasonably have requested an escort to wherever she wished to go. There was no way she could do it now however – even if she had not just killed one of them to keep her presence secret. The Starborn's safety must not be compromised; there was no telling how the Venelai would react to him. They might well want him taken to their overlord, whoever that might be. Whether they would be ready to defy a Skair to accomplish that end, she would not know unless she tried it. All her experience argued that no one would dare to defy a Daughter of the Stars about her Mother's business, here in the Holy Woods; but no one would slaughter a village of defenceless Manyei either.

Finding themselves at the brink of the stream, the patrol evidently decided that it was as good a place as any to allow their beasts to drink. It lengthened the suspense for the two waiting just downstream, but at least it was an indication that Lidan's gamble had paid off. At last all the beasts were watered. The officer barked a command, and the patrol set off with a jingling of harness. Praise the Goddess! They continued off to the right, until they eventually found a place where the leaning banks on either side constituted an easy leap across. The ground trembled to the impact of the landing animals, and then the soft thudding of the hoofbeats slowly died away into the blue-green depths of the forest. Lidan gave a soft growl of relief, and relaxed her hold on her companion. Her face loosened from its ferocious rictus, and her ears returned to their upright position.

"Well thank God for that." Brendan straightened with a shudder, and wiped his sweating palms down the sides of his thighs. The entire incident had happened so quickly that he had not had time to really take in the details of the doomed soldier and his mount; they were an unpleasant blur in his mind, and he preferred it that way. He avoided looking at Lidan. The practised, brutal efficiency with which she

had killed the soldier had turned his stomach, though he understood why she had had to take the risk. "I take it those were the Venelai."
"Yes. But I do not know in whose service. The holy woods do not belong to any lord, they are sacred ground. Whether the Emperor would claim some jurisdiction over them, I would not care to say. It would be hard to establish any grounds for such a claim. But there is no law to prevent any lord or any king sending troops here – though there is no stronghold to attract them, no town to attack or defend. I do not know of any reason for them to be here. It is very strange." She thought again of the slaughtered Manyei, and saw from her companion's pale grim face that he shared her suspicions. She saw too, with regret but without surprise, that his body language towards herself had changed: she had been right to fear his reaction to bloodshed. What could she say? It had been necessary, and he must know it. If necessity were not a good enough reason in his eyes, no other she could advance would do better. "Well, this has changed nothing. We still head for Vanreil. If you will stay here, I will go up and find food. There should be plenty to hand here, I will not be gone more than a few minutes."

With which she left the undercut, waded around the left-hand bend of the stream and was lost to view.

Left alone, Brendan tried to get comfortable again, though there was no way that he was going to sleep. He was still shaky with reaction, and had some mental adjustments to make before he could think of carrying on. He lay down, but unfortunately the exhaustion which had given the gravel such an illusory sense of softness had passed off now, and he was too aware of small stones digging into his ribs. He sat up again, and shook out his tunic. Something fell out of it on to his foot, making him jerk his leg back in alarm. For an instant he could not make out what it was, but as it hurried for the shelter of his other leg, which was equally promptly moved out of range, he got a better look. It reminded him of a crab, though there was no visible eye area and as well as having no claws it had a multiplicity of legs whose action was like that of a millipede. It was about four inches in diameter, and reddish in colour. He put the tunic down again and watched his odd visitor scurry into shelter within the folds. Carefully, for the sheer want of something to take his mind off what had just happened, he knelt down and peered inside at it. Since it had no discernible eyes he could not say for certain that it peered back at him, but he fancied that it was returning his scrutiny. Caution prevented him from trying to touch it: there were no visible claws, but there might be hidden teeth. Nevertheless, its crab-like appearance was illogically endearing, and he watched it with interest. It did not move, except for small incessant motions of the tiny feet, almost as though it was dancing on the spot. He wondered what was the purpose of this, but some five minutes' close observation did not bring him any closer to a guess.

Lidan returned just then, with an armful of the 'cognac pears' that he had enjoyed so much the day before. She looked surprised at finding him down on all fours with his nose almost touching the folded material, and put down the pears at once to come and see what was amiss. His find was soon explained, and the Skair unceremoniously upended the tunic to tip out its occupant for a second time. What happened next was too fast, and too unexpected, for Brendan to intervene. The crab-creature fell on to the gravel in front of Lidan, and in one lightning move she had swiped it up in one paw, tossed it into the air and bitten it in half. The part inside her mouth went down in a single swallow. The second half was tossed casually after it with the back of one hand. A trickle of what was undoubtedly blood ran down the side of her jaw, and was wiped away with the same blithe disregard. Some bony part of the creature required a little chewing, and she cracked the pieces between her strong jaws with noisy relish. She did not need live food again yet, even the fruit she had eaten was more for the pleasure of eating with a companion than the necessity of it, but no Skair except one with an incredibly full belly would turn aside from a gift snack like this.

Her action should not have come as such a shock to Brendan, but coming as it did on top of the killing of the Venel soldier, it was the last straw. Familiarity as a companion had begun to erode his awareness of the essentially alien nature of the Skair. The brief glimpse he had had of what her people called the *ngeih,* the battle-snarl, had not quite succeeded in reminding him of what she really was. Insensibly he had begun to regard her as a woman in a fur coat. He could have found excuses for the murder of the soldier, but the natural action of a natural predator in that moment appeared to him almost obscene. To make matters worse, he had quite liked the crab!

Lidan might have had difficulty in interpreting many of the finer nuances of human expression, but there was no mistaking the amazed disgust on Brendan's face at that moment. She was no less surprised by his reaction than he had been by her action. Did his people walk away from food when their supply was uncertain? Another succeeded the thought: was he simply upset because she had not offered him a share of the helti? Perhaps humans liked crunchy food. She hadn't thought of it, but then there hadn't been much worth sharing. She could certainly find him another, which he could have all to himself. If he liked them that much she would make a point of visiting watercourses where they were common.

Charitably deciding that the second theory was by far the likeliest, she turned aside and shifted a couple of the larger stones nearer the stream. As she had expected, she found quite a sizeable helti sheltering beneath one in the cool damp gravel. She picked it up and handed it politely to Brendan. "You can have this one," she said, pleased to have made amends for her discourtesy so quickly.

It was now her turn to be astounded when he almost slapped her hand away. He knew that he wasn't being either logical or fair. She had had to kill the soldier; she had probably saved both their lives by doing it. She wasn't a woman in a fur coat, and he'd seen humans eating oysters with just the same relish. Neither logic nor fairness had much to do with the revulsion he felt, however. The whole horror of his situation had suddenly rushed over him like a wave. *He*, not she, was the alien here. He wanted something, anything, to be familiar. He was miserably, desperately homesick, and the staring Skair was revolting and uncanny.
"Take me home."

She looked at him, and turned away slowly to replace the helti in its hiding place. She put the stones back gently, so that it should not be crushed.
"Did you hear me?" he almost shouted.
"Yes." The great amber eyes met his unflinchingly. "I am ready."

Wasn't she going to argue? Plead? Try to make him change his mind? His brain churning with rage and shame, he turned around and pressed his face into the wall of the undercut. He couldn't stay here. He just couldn't.

When he looked round again there was a gap in the wall a couple of feet away where none had been before. It was a black blank, but out of it came the smell of the shower gel he used. He did not need to be told that all he had to do was walk through it. He walked towards it and leaned forward into the blackness. Although he could see absolutely nothing, his other senses told him that he was in a shower cubicle. One step and he would be there. One step and he would be home, and safe. He could go down to breakfast and the chaffing of his friends, collect his luggage and be rounded up with the rest of the flock, catch the plane after phoning his parents from the airport. Home. Safety. Family. One step was all it would take.

He sat down on the gravel and wept.

7

It was in a chastened but resolute frame of mind that Brendan set out with his companion that evening. He had been stupid and unfair to act in the way he had, and he had awkwardly apologised to Lidan for his behaviour as soon has he had recovered some composure. He was unsure even now, however, that she really understood why he had acted in that way – come to think of it, he wasn't entirely sure he understood it himself. It felt, however, as though his outburst had been in some way a catharsis. He was calmer now, more sure of his own strength under pressure. He also felt that he had some legitimate reason for hope: if he had had the courage to turn down the escape which he had so desperately wanted, there was no good reason why he should not face the unknown test which awaited him with equal fortitude. There must have been some good reason why he should have been singled out to come here. It must surely mean that he had the capacity, in some way, to succeed. He couldn't expect not to be scared. All he had to do was to live with the fear, ultimately to conquer it. All his professional life he'd had to cope with pressure; it was an old and intimate friend. Admittedly this was pressure of a far different nature – he was facing not simply defeat but probably death if he failed in what he had been brought here to do. But he reflected with a wry inward grin that death would probably be rather less daunting than Adrian in one of his carping moods, and he'd coped with them often enough.

Part way through the night they came to a place where the forest opened out for a space. The first thing to strike him almost like a blow was the sight of the sky overhead. It was the first time he had seen Kerriel's night sky clear of cloud, and the host of stars gazing down was fairly staggering. He was accustomed to the relatively modest dusting of twinkling points that adorned the nights of Earth, and this sudden glory took him completely by surprise. He had enough of an acquaintance with astronomy to understand instantly what he was seeing: well over half of the sky was dominated by the incredible brilliance of a spiral galaxy. What it must be like to have an unimpeded view of it from high ground was beyond imagining. Part of him realised anew and with horror just how far from his home he must be, to see such a sight. Another part, the artist who took such delight in the complex forms of the dance, could not help but respond to the beauty of it. A vast motionless swirl of stars hung suspended in the blackness of space, spilling a faint shimmering radiance on the forest that turned a trail of vineflowers sprawled over a bush into an iridescent garland of magic. Like the displays of the Aurora Borealis which he had seen a couple of times on Earth, it seemed impossible that such a spectacle could be completely silent. Beside him, Lidan too looked upwards. She brought her arms forward, turning them so that the insides of the wrists were exposed, and said something beneath her breath. After a moment she relaxed again, and turned to her companion. The light was ample to show her the stupefied look on his face.
"Are there no stars on your world?" she asked softly. She hadn't noticed any during her visit – the glare of the street lighting had blotted them out.
"Yes – but nothing like these," he answered equally softly. "They're so beautiful. Do you have a moon?"

She had seen the silver shield in Earth's sky, and knew that several of Kerriel's sister-planets had satellites. "No. The stars rule the night. Shieih is the Lady of the Stars, Skaira are called the Daughters of the Stars. It is a title of great honour." Staring upwards at a sight he knew he would remember for the rest of his life, he had to agree with that.

They travelled for the rest of that night without incident. As dawn was breaking on the following day they found another Manyé village, again destroyed. The inhabitants of this one had disappeared completely. Emerging from a vain search of the semi-underground room where they would have planned to sleep away the cold months, Lidan stared around with sombre eyes. All the signs pointed to a departure in haste. The few possessions of the Manyei who had lived here were scattered where they had been dropped.

Brendan bent and picked up something from the ground. It was a musical instrument, extremely simple, just a thick woody reed with holes cut into it and a narrow mouthpiece at one end. Glancing at it, Lidan told him that it was called a 'nuluoi', and was used by all three races, though this was a difficult skill for those Venelai whose beaks were strongly curved. He enjoyed playing music as well as dancing to it, and the temptation to try the primitive thing was strong, but he refrained from doing so. He had no way of knowing how far the sound it would make would carry in the silence of the early morning, and no wish to alert any ears that might be listening for sounds that there should no longer be anyone here to make. Still, it would do no harm to take it with him. By all the evidence, the previous owner had no use for it any more. He managed to thread part of the thong fastening his boiler suit through it, so that it hung against his chest out of the way.

Lidan, meanwhile, was prowling around and examining the ground. From time to time she lay down and nosed over it, but her frown told her perplexity all too clearly. Presently she stood up and shook her head. "Mother of Stars, I do not understand it." She looked at the ground again and sighed deeply. "Where have they all gone? There have been soldiers here. Many soldiers, none on foot. But the scents are cold and fading. They have been gone for many hours. I do not understand any of it." She stared in frustration at the rustling layer of leaves beneath the trees, which hid tracks with such ease. Over clearer ground she might have had a good chance of following them – but that was a skill that called for much time and patience, and of time she had little or none to spare.

"Couldn't they have run away? Still be in hiding? Perhaps they heard about the other village."

"It is possible. Manyei know many things one would not expect. But somehow, it does not look like it. Do not ask me why – I just do not think so." The small sharp incisor teeth nibbled at her underlip. "They are not – how should I put it? – imaginative enough to stay away. They would flee, and then forget their fears and return. It would be hard to make them understand the necessity of abandoning the place where their fathers and forefathers have lived as long as the trees have grown there."

Brendan remarked that something must have done so, hard or not, for there was no sign that anyone had come back, or was about to do so; the forest all around them was silent and still.

"You would not hear them, Kelti. I do not think your ears are sharp enough. Sometimes even I could miss the sound of a Manyé who does not wish to be heard." She stared around at the trees, still frowning. "Still, I see no reason why we should not stay here for a little while. It is as good a place to stay until the evening as any." In addition to the fact that the huts would provide concealment, there was food in plenty. Another night's travel should bring them to the foothills that surrounded Vanreil. Perhaps then she could relax a little.

*　　　　*　　　　*

Warlord Stiv'aran, Emperor-Elect of Kerriel, stood very still in the shadows. The thing in his hands glimmered faintly in the low light. Even the jewels on it were quenched. So slight a thing, set against what he had done to get it there.

On a sudden impulse he lifted it to eye level. The blackness within looked back at him accusingly. The flat golden horns reared at either side. The last time he had seen this, it had been on the head of the man who was – had been – his dearest friend. Whom he had sworn to support and defend with his every word and action. Who could have foreseen then what was to happen?

He turned his head slightly. On the other side of the room a woman was seated quietly, watching him. The late evening light slanting through the window gleamed on the silvery feathers on her beautiful slender head, woke glimmers in the gold threads woven into the fabric of her long tunic. Although she said nothing, there was a hot intensity in her gaze that belied her composure. Her hands rested lightly, protectively, on the swollen mound of her belly, cradling the egg that it contained. An inconvenience, that, but not necessarily an insuperable one. According to the physicians, it would not be long now before she went into labour. She would have to be guarded – incessantly guarded – whilst she brooded the egg. When it hatched, he would be in attendance. If it proved to contain a female, he would marry the hatchling before the downy feathers on her head had time to dry. If it contained a boy-

She was not stupid. She knew, she must know, what had happened to the other offspring in the royal nurseries. The pregnant junior queens had mysteriously disappeared too. He was not taking any chances of posthumous hatchlings challenging his dynasty in future years.

There were moments even now when he was startled by how far and fast events had moved. It had all begun on the hunting trip earlier that year, when one night he had heard something crashing into the forest not far from where he and his companions had been encamped. The noise had woken them from a sound sleep, and they had been guided to the place by a smell of scorching. There they had found a piece of what looked like dark rock, lying in a saucer-like depression in the ground. At first it had been far too hot to touch, but they had fetched water from a nearby stream and poured it over the surface. The clouds of steam that this produced had had a most peculiar smell. And it was as they inadvertently inhaled it that their minds had begun to see things in quite a different light. It was as if someone had opened a window on new and astonishing possibilities, never before guessed at. For some reason it had never occurred to him before how easy it would be for him to acquire the Horned Crown. How desirable, even necessary, it was that he should do so. His blood claim was good – there were better, but they were not beyond his power to deal with. A little planning, a little ruthlessness, and the thing was done. The Emperor was trusting with his friends, did not come armed to Council meetings. There was no search by his guards at the door. The thing could not be accomplished at once, of course. Such a coup would have to be synchronised with the elimination of all those other rival claimants, or the effort would be wasted. Still, such matters would not be difficult to arrange.

And so it had proved. The friends who had accompanied him on that night had fallen in with his plans with enthusiasm. They had picked up the hunk of rock, and brought it back with them to Thervanil. It was now enshrined with all due reverence on the altar of Aiyeh in the Great Temple, and when he was crowned he intended to insist that the priests worship it. That this might be difficult to enforce, he was aware. The Great Lord was personified in the glory of the sun, and his temples had no images. Nevertheless, it was sometimes astonishing how persuasive suffering could be; and in the pursuit of his intentions, Emperor-Elect Stiv'aran was ready to use all the persuasion that was necessary.

He lowered the Horned Crown. In fact it did not look much like a crown; it was in the shape of a war-helmet, made of solid gold studded with gems. A great diamond glittered on the brow of it, directly above the heavy curving beak-guard. The horns symbolised his leadership, the helmet shape his ability to defend his empire on the field of battle. For uncounted ages it had been the imperial diadem, echoed by the golden horns that reared from the throne on which the Emperor sat in state: a symbol of the power that was now within his grasp. The only creature that could thwart him now lay hidden within the ex-Empress's belly, the only legitimate heir of the man he had murdered. His arms were already bloody to the elbows – he would not allow a male brat to stand in his way. He would delay assuming the Crown until the egg hatched; if he could marry the Heiress, his claim would be unassailable. If events fell out otherwise, he could and would hold the throne with brute force. On the whole, he would prefer to do the thing legally – chiefly because it weakened the case for any opposition – but legally or otherwise, he was going to keep what he had taken.

He had considered taking his predecessor's widow Mia'naan as his Empress, but had eventually rejected the idea. Her intelligence and hatred combined to constitute a threat, albeit a minor one. If it should be necessary to dispose of her son by Sevi'nke, she would have the motive as well as potentially the means and the opportunity to dispose of his own, no matter how carefully she should be guarded once she conceived to him. He had weighed up the risk of having a potential heir endangered, and decided against it. However, it would placate her powerful family if she were retained as a junior queen, and this he had decided to do. It would matter less then if she found some way to avenge a dead son by destroying her new lord's offspring. She was undoubtedly very lovely, and proven fertile – it was a pity that she should be tiresomely loyal to a dead man. Perhaps exposure to the scents still exuded by the rock in the Shrine might improve her grasp on the realities of her situation. It would be many years before a daughter would be of an age to be bedded; until that time he would use her as a breeding queen. Any ruler bred freely, using children to cement alliances and bolster his power. It would do no harm to have several high-ranking brood hinds in his stable, and he felt desire for her that was undimmed either by the ferocity of her gaze upon him now, or by the swollen outline of her body. If there was no daughter, she would still be safest kept under his control. She would undoubtedly resent becoming junior to whichever woman he eventually took as his Empress, but that was her problem.

Quietly, with movements that were as graceful as they were economical, the Venel lord moved forward and replaced the Horned Crown on the small, ornate table where it had rested. The slanting light now fell directly on him, gleaming on the light body-armour that he had not yet stripped from his lithe, muscular body and gilding the pale, almost blond feathers of his head. Born to power, he carried the unconscious arrogance of his House in every line of him. Even among a people who respected strength he was already on the way to becoming a legend. He had inherited the senior position in his family at quite an early age when his father was killed in one of the Imperial wars; had spent five years patiently analysing his situation, consolidating his power and learning his trade around the Imperial court. Then he had taken the field against a rebellious minor king whose forces outnumbered his by four to one, beaten him soundly and brought him back a prisoner to the Imperial court for a public and bloody execution. One man in four from the beaten army had been executed, and the remainder were set free and escorted back to their own lands, where they took the oath of allegiance to the Emperor and were immediately paid the balance of their wages by Stiv'aran's officers. As a first step on to the public stage it could hardly have been bettered, earning him the admiration of the people, the stunned quiescence of the conquered country and most importantly of all, the gratitude of the Emperor. He had been careful not to trade on it during the years that followed. For all that Venelai had the heads and many of the characteristics of birds, Stiv'aran had many of the instincts of a cat. He walked like a shadow and pounced like a bolt of lightning; he had the capacity to make men afraid, and used it. Nevertheless he was not capricious. When not occupied with war he often sat in court and gave judgement, earning himself a reputation for justice as well as ferocity. Slowly the Emperor's gratitude had matured into trust and then into friendship. Now all that was gone. The world had changed. No-one could have told from the steady gaze of the dark amber eyes above the cruel hooked beak whether he ever regretted it; or whether the years of faithful service had never been anything other than a preparation for his sudden and staggering seizure of the Horned Crown.

At that moment there was a movement in the doorway, and one of his most trusted lieutenants entered. Stiv'aran saw with chilly amusement that the man could not quite suppress the automatic gesture of reverence towards the silent, seated ex-Empress.

"Your commands are obeyed, Great Lord." His tongue stumbled a little over the still-unfamiliar salutation. It had gone out from the Palace like a shock wave that the Emperor was to be addressed from now on with the title hitherto reserved for a god. "The Palace at Weruavwe is in flames. All within are dead."

"All?" The word cut like a knife of ice.

His liegeman hastened to amend his error. "All but two, Great Lord. As you instructed."

"Ah." He inclined his head. "And those?"

"Also as you instructed. The one's under close guard, bound and gagged. The other – allowed to escape. But not so as to suspect. We pursued her for many hours."

"In which direction?"

"It was as you foretold, Great Lord. All as you foretold." He bowed himself out, and the Emperor-Elect was left to the satisfied contemplation of another completed step in his plans. It was incredible what ideas occurred to him when he was in the presence of that piece of rock. Sometimes, if he had not been too intelligent to dismiss the idea, he could even imagine that it was talking to him.

He was slightly taken aback when the voice broke the silence.

"Have you no fear of the Goddess, that you do what you have done?"

A lesser mortal would have raged, cursed, heaped invective on his head. The ex-Empress Mia'naan reduced him to something unworthy of that much notice. He looked at her with admiration, and wondered whether she would maintain such frigidity when she was beneath him in bed during her next period of oestrus.

"I'm not afraid of anything that can be out-manoeuvred, Mia'naan," he replied amiably. "And if the Goddess had the power and the will to avenge Her own, I doubt if I'd be standing here now." "What the Goddess wills done may be done by Her Daughters. You have struck a blow that will not be forgiven."

"I've destroyed the hive, but the queen is in my power. Who'll dare move against me now? Even the Skaira are realists, for all they spend their lives staring at stars. If they want their Princess alive, they'll accept me. If they want her to remain alive, they'll crown my Empress. Whomever that may be," he added lightly. "Unfortunately, madam, it won't be you."

"At least you have said one thing worth the hearing," she said coldly.

He leaned towards her. "Don't worry, Mia'naan; you haven't been forgotten. There's a special place for you in my plans." He took her by the shoulders and lifted her; like all male Venelai he was immensely strong. A couple of paces had her pinned to the wall, and he held her there with one hand against her throat while the other slowly explored her body. Presently the pupil of the one eye visible to him contracted suddenly.

"I do not consent," she said clearly.

"Don't you, Mia'naan? Remind me to ask you another time whether I care." He pulled her away from the wall and forced her on to her knees. There should be no accusation that he had endangered the egg. During the brutal act that followed she remained totally silent, but even so the awareness of her pain and rage acted on him like a stimulant. He had never taken an unwilling woman before; the heretical thought flashed through his brain that perhaps rape was forbidden in order to keep men in subjection to a woman's whims. Well, those days were over. When he had finished, he rose from her with a laugh. "I've spoiled my surprise, I'm afraid. But at least you won't have to worry about what place you'll occupy in my life from now on."

He left the room. Mia'naan remained kneeling in silence for some time, containing the mental and physical suffering until it could be channelled into prayer. Her own powerlessness rose up to choke her. She herself might well never have the chance to take revenge for what had been done to her, but surely the Good Goddess did not need telling what had taken place, the supreme salute to Her befouled and demeaned into filth. Just as surely She of fang and claw did not need urging to avenge Her slain Daughters and the dead queens, and especially the murdered children, more piteous victims of the madman who now plotted to have himself crowned Emperor.

"Mother Shieih, avenge us!" whispered the ex-Empress, beating the sides of her face against the cool marble floor. "Avenge us all!"

8

The heights of Hergath were before them, the first mountain in the range that contained Vanreil the Mountain of Storms. This formidable great range was the spine of the continent, extending for many miles to the north where some of its higher peaks were crowned with snow already, a covering that in some years would never completely yield to summer. To reach the foothills here it was necessary to cross a bridge, a narrow span over a gorge that plunged to blackness among the thinning trees. The crevasse was not particularly wide, perhaps twenty feet across at its widest point, but legend said it was bottomless. At any rate, it was dark. It might have been that it was only the lingering night that made its depths so impenetrably black. No plants grew near its edge or clung in its crannies; and there was no sound at all from the darkness below. The two companions emerged from the woods and after cautiously checking that the coast was clear, crossed a meadow to where the bridge sprang from the earth. Lidan had restrained Brendan from his first impulse to circle the bridge head and take a closer look at the gorge from beside it; now she hesitated before setting a paw on the stone, and looked searchingly at her companion. "Kelti, be careful crossing this bridge. It is – not ordinary."

He stared at her, and at the bridge. It looked ordinary enough to him. Old, incredibly old; and perhaps not the safest structure he could have wanted to have for the only way of crossing the terrifying depths below. But there was nothing visibly strange about it. "In what way – not ordinary?" he asked warily.

She looked at the top of the arch. "I can not explain it. It is not unsafe. That is not what I meant. But there are spells on it, and for good reason. The gorge is a place of strong, ancient sorcery. Its name is Geirion, 'The Sorrowing'. Do not stop once you have set foot on the bridge. If you hear anything, do not listen. And above all, do not look down over the side."

"You're not exactly filling me with confidence." He eyed the structure. "Isn't there another way across? Can't we go round it?"

"Geirion extends for a great distance, and nowhere is it truly safe to cross. The bridge is as safe a way as any. If you do as I have said, all should be well."

"Now that really has made me feel better." It was a very narrow bridge, not wide enough for two to go abreast across it, and its age and apparent fragility made it appear wisest that they go separately. Brendan watched narrowly as Lidan padded on to the structure. Her ears were half-flattened, her tail held low and taut. He noted that she did not vary her paces in the slightest, and stayed in the exact centre of the gap. The balustrade on either side was about the right height for her to grip, but although she held her hands close to them she did not touch. Whether this was for any particular reason she did not say – if it had been dangerous she would surely have said so; but he felt it would be safest to copy her as exactly as possible.

She was across. He walked the few steps to the near end of the bridge. It began at a surprising distance from the edge of the gorge, as if even the builders had avoided coming too close to the place. Her warnings had put him on edge; there was a light sheen of sweat on his palms. He resisted the urge to take hold of the balustrades. The stone was a very light grey, and seemed to glitter faintly in the thin light of dawn, as if there were chips of mica in it. A couple of inches down from the top there were two chiselled lines, with carved symbols between them. It did not look like writing, though it might possibly have been some kind of hieroglyphic text. Looking closely, he saw that the work was extremely old, perhaps as old as the bridge itself. Weathering had blurred and softened the edges.

It was no good; he had to cross. He took a deep breath. Instinct shrilled at him to rush at it, but he thrust it down. One step, another, another. Steadily, lightly, not pausing, not hurrying. He could hear his own breathing, and concentrated on controlling it. The stones were quite even, so there was no danger of tripping. No need to hold on. Just keep going. Lidan was watching him, and he tried not to see the tension in her face. Here was the top of the arch. Half way home. He squashed the panicky urge to break into a run. Nothing had happened to him. Nothing was going to happen -

It came down on him like a vast black blanket, a miasma of despair deeper than any he could have dreamed of in his worst nightmare. He stopped, forgetting everything except the horror from which he would never escape. He could no longer see or hear; every thought was paralysed. His knees buckled. There was a vague, unimportant sensation of scraping as his arm and side slid across rough stone. If it had mattered, he might have been aware that he was toppling sideways over the balustrade. He would not have felt the long fall, and the impact would have been utterly merciful. As it was, he felt nothing and remembered nothing. Suddenly in the blackness there was a point of light. In the same instant there was something else – he could only interpret it as a phrase of music, though it might have had perfume in it. He tore air into his lungs with a gasp. The music, or the perfume, strengthened. The light brightened. The darkness hesitated and drew back a little. His left hand clenched on the top rim of the balustrade, the heel of his right scraped for purchase to push him back and up. If he had been even a little less fit he might well have failed; as it was he needed every bit of his strength to claw his way back across the stone, while the light and the music sang to him and the perfume filled his nostrils. He fell to his knees on the bridge, shaking, and felt the darkness slip away from him. The brightness surrounded him, strengthening, comforting and healing. He recognised the perfume now: it was one his mother always wore. There might have been a voice, but there were no words. He knew Her now. "Shieih..." No reply, but the brightness shimmered. He put his sweaty forehead down on the cool stone. When he raised it again the world was ordinary once more.

It took him a couple of moments to gather the courage to stand up. When he finally did so his knees wobbled, and he clutched the stone sides of the bridge. Nothing else happened, however. Lidan was watching him, her face the colour of chalk, her tail rigid with apprehension. Not a word was spoken until he stepped off the end of the bridge and on to the blessed earth again. Then she pounced on him, uttering his name in ecstatic little growls, hugging and patting him as if to reassure herself that he really was still in one piece. He half expected a scolding for fooling about when he had been so stringently warned, but she knew full well that he had not been fooling about at all. She as a Daughter of the Stars was immune to the cold spells of Geirion; that did not mean that other races would be as fortunate, and as an Otherworlder he must be particularly vulnerable.

The moment was so charged with relief that he so far forgot his ambivalent reaction to her alien nature as to return her hug. It was not so different really, once you got used to a hug from something so strong and leonine; he was growing fond of her quaint face with its lion features, and had almost ceased to notice the fact that like all her kind except heavily-pregnant mothers she customarily went about bare-breasted. This fact had disconcerted him at first, but the total lack of sexual connotation had robbed the continual sight first of its novelty, then of its effect on him. He only noticed occasionally now, and though he could not help but remember how well her breasts had looked (and felt) on a human body, the Skair body which they now adorned had no sexual appeal for him whatsoever. He could hug her without any inappropriate reaction, and it felt natural now to do so. Close up, he would have expected her to smell like an animal, and even now he was slightly surprised that she did not: her naked upper half didn't have any odour that he could detect, but her hair and fur had a faint resiny perfume from the oil she used for washing.

"By the One!" Her voice was shaking. "I thought you were gone!"

He glanced over his shoulder. The bridge was still there, solid and innocent. Below it, the gorge was deep, dark and silent.

"What was it?" His own voice wasn't exactly steady.

She shook her head. "I will tell you – but not here. We must go further on before we rest – and I would have you as far from here as possible."

"Now that I can live with." He was extremely glad to turn his back on the spot. He wasn't surprised that even the trees and plants seemed reluctant to grow too close to the edge. What sort of dreadful place was it that even nature avoided?

They did not have far to go to reach the bolt-hole that she had had in mind for their halt that day. The rock of which the mountain range was largely composed was fissured in many places, and at the foot of Hergath there were several caves. One of these in particular ran far back into the mountain. Lidan was glad to find that no animal had taken it over as a lair, as it would be a good place to hide while the sun was high.

"We should be safe here," she said, prowling into the dim recesses of the cave. "And I am glad to be among the mountains. Another day should see us at Vanreil."

"And then the fun really starts." He sat down and began to massage his legs. It felt natural to continue on to his usual exercise routine, loosening the various groups of muscle around his arms and shoulders: just because he was away from his world didn't mean he should allow himself to get out of condition. The familiar movements were oddly reassuring, a link with home. The Skair watched him with great interest.

"Just how much *are* you going to tell them?" he asked finally, lying back to bring his knees up towards his stomach. "Everything? The whole works?"

"It would not avail me to do otherwise. The greatest minds on Kerriel are here, those high in the service of the Goddess. There are those who could read from my mind everything I had tried to conceal, and it would be thought insulting that I had tried to hide the truth."

"You have telepaths?" He sat up. "Your people can read minds?"

"Some, not many. It is a gift, and must be trained. And it is not done lightly, under any circumstances. Do you remember that I touched your mind with mine? That is as much as I can do. I have not the gift. Those with Thought Power carry a great responsibility. They are in demand, especially when there are legal disputes. Of what use is it to lie to one who can read thoughts?"

He nodded. Now that was something that would come in handy on Earth. Nevertheless, he was not entirely comfortable with the idea of encountering somebody who really could read his mind. There was much about his own world that he was uneasy about revealing to anyone who didn't live there; it would probably be an unedifying picture to anyone looking from outside. Admittedly there were times when it wasn't too pretty from the inside, but he was curiously defensive about it. Flawed it might be, but it was still his home, and he didn't want any outsider passing judgement on it. It was a good thing that there were the restrictions on the ability to look inside somebody's head: it must be a hugely personal thing to do. He still disliked the memory of Lidan's mind touching his own. It had been horribly invasive, for all it had been so gentle. Not that he blamed her for doing it. He had been in such a state of shock that he could probably have gone on denying reality indefinitely. She'd had to snap him out of it somehow.

His thoughts returned to the narrow escape he had had so recently, and he turned to the Skair again. "The bridge. You said you'd explain."

She sat down opposite him, and heaved a sigh. "So I did. By the One! I do not know where to start."

"At the beginning?"

"Very amusing! But I am not sure you will believe it. It is an ancient tale – so ancient that the bridge yonder has been built and rebuilt over the gorge of Geirion more often than the storytellers can remember. I cannot say how much of it is truth. We were told that it was true, and certainly there is deep sorcery at work in Geirion. But what is its nature, even we, as Daughters of the Stars, cannot say."

She sat up a little straighter, and stretched her forelegs out so strongly that the great grey claws slid out of their soft housings. For a moment or two she was silent, and Brendan watching her had the feeling that she was arranging her thoughts carefully. Which indeed she was; on Kerriel, Skaira were the guardians of the truth, and such stories as these were passed on word-perfect from generation to generation. To tell them was a responsibility, and one that every Skair was taught to respect. Finally, she half-closed her eyes and began.

"The story goes that in the dawn of the world, there were the two Powers who had been put into the world, to guard and guide it. And they were a part of the Great Dance, the act of continuous creation. By their will, life came into being on what had been a barren planet. The grasses and the trees grew, but no beasts walked among them. For long it remained so, until the next part of the Dance, when it was time for life to take on new forms. The two Powers – we call them Aiyeh and Shieih – became lovers. From their joining sprang three animals, the forerunners of all the beasts that were to walk on the face of Kerriel. They roamed the world in peace and plenty, giving birth to their offspring, and every year another type of animal emerged. Even the four 'speaking' races – there were four of us then, for Skaira came later – were born of the Three.

"Thus was our world made, and it was wonderful. I do not say that there was no pain, nor that there was no death, for this is a world for mortals and all mortals must die. Nevertheless it was wonderful. The gods walked among us, and the very plants rejoiced in their presence.

"It happened one day that the firstborn of the Three was walking beside a great lake, and a voice spoke to him out of the air. It was certainly a god, and it warned him that Aiyeh and Shieih were displeased with the creation they had made, and planned that it should be destroyed. And the Animal believed it, for never in that world before had a lie been uttered. He went to the other two and told them, and in fear they tore open a great rent in the ground and concealed themselves in it.

"When Aiyeh and Shieih looked for their children, then, they were nowhere to be found. In great perplexity the Powers questioned the sea, and the clouds, and the deep forests, and nowhere was there any sight of the Three. And then Shieih looked down at the earth, and asked were the Three within it, and the earth did not answer.

"Then the Powers saw the great rent in the earth, and came to it, and looked down and saw the Three hiding in terror; and Shieih asked in great hurt and amazement what was their purpose. And in that moment the Three knew that they had been deceived, and their shame was terrible. They told their Mother and Father what had been said, and swore that they should stay hidden in the earth for ever, for they had believed evil of their parents, and did not deserve ever to see the light of sun or star again. And though Aiyeh was silent for rage at the thing that had been done to His children, Shieih was more thoughtful. 'You shall stay as you have said,' she told Her children, 'but out of evil shall come good. In a time to come there shall be the chance to make amends for all. Until that time, the one who deceived you shall be banned utterly from this world. Be of good heart. Even your fall must have its place in the plans of the Uncreated.'

"And there they have lain until this day, and the very earth sorrows with them. It is perilous to approach the gorge, for many who have done so have stayed to grieve until the heart could bear no more. Thus does the bridge spring wide and high, to keep unwary travellers as far as possible from the sorrowing of Geirion."

Her eyes opened fully again; she shook her head and flicked her tail to and fro. "Well, that is the story. You can believe it or not, as you choose."

"Hell's bells!" He considered, frowning. It was almost impossible to believe that the story was literally true. It would have been comforting to have been able to dismiss it as the fairy tale it sounded like – Lidan had told it in a deeply stylised way, obviously hallowed by many centuries of repetition. How could it be true? Nothing could live that long. And the creation story was a variant of the one found on his own world, and every world with rational beings on it must have something similar to explain the origin of existence. And yet – he himself had experienced something completely beyond his power to explain away. If he had known the story before crossing the bridge he might have been able to claim that he had been mentally influenced by it; he had not. The sensation, the paralysing sense of despair, had caught him completely unawares. He wished he had enough science to know if there could be some rational explanation. It was entirely possible that some completely natural physical phenomenon was at work – perhaps some gas or combination of gases was leaking up from below ground, which acted as a particularly nasty hallucinogen when inhaled. That sounded reasonable. More reasonable than some crazy story about incredibly ancient animal ancestors shutting themselves up for millions of years because they'd fallen for the wiles of Kerriel's equivalent of Lucifer. Funny how there was that parallel in the Creation stories, though. There always had to be a killjoy coming along to spoil the party.

And yet – given that his theory about a hallucinogen gas was somewhere near the truth – what was he to make of his rescue? Another part of the hallucination? Perhaps. It was possible. But the very fact of his being here spoke for the existence of something, or some One, of powers beyond his comprehension. That Someone had certainly influenced his existence in bringing him here. It would not be unrealistic to expect Him – or Her – to continue to ensure his survival. "I did not think you would believe it," said Lidan matter-of-factly. She had been watching him.

He shook his head slowly. "I don't know whether or not I do. There's something there. But what it is – who knows?"

"It is nothing to concern us now, anyway. We should sleep now, for tonight's travel will be harder among the mountains." She lay down, and lifted a forepaw invitingly. He moved over, spread his by now rather ragged blanket tunic beside her – he still carried it with him, it helped to make sleeping on the ground slightly less unpleasant – and lay down against her ribs, appreciating the warmth of her fur. It was odd, but by no means unpleasant: like snuggling up to a gigantic teddy bear. He smiled at the thought, put his head down on her forequarter, and relaxed. He began drifting towards sleep, but a faint movement of the body against his alerted him to the fact that she was looking at him.

"What's up?" he asked drowsily.

"Nothing of moment. I was only thinking that my cub will lie thus when she is born. By the One! I hope she is prettier than you!"

Seeing the betraying tongue-tip quiver, he grinned in response. "You didn't seem to think I was that bad-looking when you were on Earth, as I recall!"

"*That* was different." She put a paw across his face, and pushed gently. "You are impertinent, Kelti. Your mother did not beat you nearly often enough."

"Did yours beat you?"

"She did not need to. I was a model cub."

He made a vulgar sound that expressed derision in any language, and she grinned too. "Well perhaps not all the time. But I think she thought me well enough – until I left her." The smile left her face; the focus of her gaze lengthened past him. "You left home – did you quarrel?" He straightened a little.

"I do not say you could call it a quarrel. We lived at Weruavwe, at the Palace. My mother is high in the Princess's service. I too could have been – but I did not want it. I saw the place to which I brought you, many years ago while I was wandering the forests. It drew me back ever afterwards, and I could not banish it from my mind. And I decided that I wanted to live there, as what my people call an 'out-lairer'. My mother was grievously disappointed. She did not understand."

"But you still left."

"It would have been a death to have stayed. She did not try to prevent me; I was old enough to choose my own path. But she was hurt and angry. I do not visit her

– I think it would only reopen the sore of my folly in her eyes." She was silent for a while. "Perhaps when we are both older there will be a time to be reconciled. I hope so. It is a grievous thing to have one's mother alienated. I still believe that I was right to leave, but I wish that it had not cost her so dearly."

"Every chick has to leave the nest sometime. My mother cried her eyes out."

"Neither of us cried. Perhaps it would have been better if we had. Though Skaira do not weep easily." She sighed. "Well, I hope that her life has brought her compensations. She always loved the halls of power, and she was a friend to Princess Thaskan from when the First was weaned. It is well to think that she is where she belongs – and to hope that she too has come to the same understanding of me."

He touched her gently. "I'm sorry."

"For what fault of yours? It is all history now. Old history. I had what I chose – and by the word of Shieih, my choice was blessed. I do not regret it. Now, little Kelti, we should sleep. Talk is well enough, but we have hard travel before us. Sleep well." And she lay down and closed her eyes; and in a few moments her breathing lengthened. Brendan watched her for a minute or two longer. So even on other planets they had the same problems with their kids. He supposed it was pretty inevitable that mothers never did think their offspring were ready to fly the nest; was thankful that the occasion of his own leaving had been emotional but without rancour. Drowsiness crept over him once more. He put his head down again, listening to the reassuring double thump of the heart sited just under her withers. Soon they were both asleep.

9

It was with slow steps that he turned towards the door. For ten years – all his adult life – he had been a soldier. Orders had to be obeyed. And yet – and yet –.

The comparative darkness of the stable was comforting. The great animal beside him moved with accustomed grace towards the waiting manger, and began to eat. Teho'evan envied such a quiet conscience, as his war-stag must have. His meal too was waiting, but he had small appetite for it now.

Ignoring the puzzlement of the groom whose usual tasks he was performing, he slipped off the stag's bridle and saddle, putting them neatly in their places. He picked up a brush from the shelf, and began to groom the animal's coat. There was no escape from his thoughts there, however. The actions were far too automatic. Again and again, superimposed on the glossy dark hide, he saw scenes that would haunt him for the rest of his life. He had had orders. Did that justify him?

True, he had not believed at first. He had even protested. By the One, who could have dreamed that such an order would ever be given? What could be the reasoning behind it? But it had been quite unequivocal. He had not been the only warlord to walk out of the Council chamber with a stunned expression. The Shining One knew that others had had more formidable tasks than that allotted to him; but surely none could have had one more distasteful.

Why? Why? The question beat at his brain. Never in all the years had such a ceremony been called for. Why now? Why this appalling act, performed in the honour of something the participants were not allowed even a glimpse of? (A new manifestation of the Shining One, said the priests. Had he imagined the glazed glare in their eyes?) There must be a suitable sacrifice.

A suitable sacrifice? To the Lord of the Fields, the god of green growing things and the harvest? His brain reeled at the thought. It was Shieih of the dark hours who took pleasure in ritual bloodshed. Could there have been some terrible mistake? And if there had been, what of his own part in it?

And what of Shieih? What of Her likely response to the commands given to the luckless Takh'rai, to burn the Skair Palace at Weruavwe and slaughter almost all within? It was obvious enough why it had been the Chief Archer who had been selected to carry out the attack: a bow and arrow was the only weapon against which a Skair was completely defenceless. He was glad that it had not been his duty to motivate his men for such a task: it made the mind crumple to imagine what revenge the Goddess might take against those responsible. It had been difficult enough to keep control of his own squadron as they carried out their allotted orders. Fortunately neither he nor they had known the ending; he did not know if he could have enforced his authority if his subordinates had understood to what fate they were escorting their wretched prisoners.

"Father Aiyeh!" He buried his face in the stag's hide. I had orders, he pleaded. I didn't know what was going to happen. And when I found out – what could I have done? The priests said it was demanded. The Shining One is to be worshipped in a new way from now on.

Wasn't the old way good enough? Wasn't it right and proper, part of the eternal balance, light and dark, God and Goddess, life and death? Why should Aiyeh suddenly thirst for blood, whose holy drink was the blessed rain from the clouds that made the fields green? Why a new manifestation, when the God was still visible in his might, blazing from the sky? But surely the priests should know such things? Who better placed than they to understand the ways of the God?

The grooming was finished: the stag's coat shone, from the heavy shoulders to the dappled rump. He took a cloth and began to polish the great antlers, while Freharehen angled his head in hopes of having his master rub the bases of the large ears. Without even thinking of it Teho'evan obliged. The animal sighed with pleasure, and closed his eyes.

It was growing dark. Turning from the stag, he began aimlessly checking the blades of the spears stacked in the rack ready for fitting behind the saddle when he rode to war. Henanei his wife would be waiting within, and wondering why he lingered so. Had she heard the news? The city must be buzzing with it. It had already been rocked to its foundations by the murder of the Emperor; but such things as a change of the ruling dynasty were not totally unheard-of. The Venelai were a warlike people, and the Horned Crown had tempted men before to do murder. The new occupant of the Horned Throne would be accepted eventually, as long as he proved capable of the task. He had already proved himself clever and ruthless, two very necessary requirements for holding on to what he had taken. What his motive was for ordering an unprovoked attack on the Skair Palace was anybody's guess. No doubt he had his reasons. It would be extremely unusual for any Skair to intervene in Venel politics, but it was not hard to imagine that the murder of children and the 'disappearance' of the dead Emperor's junior queens would provoke some kind of sharp response from Weruavwe. Perhaps Stiv'aran's attack had been designed to pre-empt this, as it would undoubtedly have acted as a focus for whatever discontent his coup had stirred up. Whether it would have been dangerous enough to justify killing so many Skaira was hard to say. It was unlikely that the Palace hierarchy would have felt the matter grave enough for actual physical retribution. They would certainly have viewed the new Emperor as guilty of grave offences against the Goddess, and probably never have enjoyed the cordial relations with him that they had with Sevi'nke, but in the end it would probably have boiled down to being considered as an internal imperial matter. The mere fact of ordering the deaths of so many of the Daughters of the Stars was too much for most men to comprehend. Stiv'aran evidently did not share the widespread reverence for Skaira, and could not have any fear of the Divine retribution which most would expect to follow such a staggering act. Teho'evan uttered a low groan. Nothing was making sense any more, and now he himself was soiled with the blood of innocent victims.

He turned and looked out of the window. The sky was clear. The city was quiet. Most folk had returned to their homes for the evening meal. He should be at table by now, but how could he sit down to eat, with the pictures he could not erase so vividly before his eyes? How could he face his wife, knowing what he had participated in? 'Bring them', had been the order. And he had brought them, a whole village of frightened and bewildered Manyei who asked what was happening and could not be answered, because there were no answers. He could still see in his mind's eye the headman standing at Freharehen's shoulder, looking up at him and asking humbly how long it would be before they were allowed to return to their village, as their flocks would need tending? His voice had dried in his throat, but somehow he had managed to croak out, "Soon," hoping against hope that he spoke the truth. Then he had given the orders. His men had harried the villagers to the city at the best speed that could be managed, hating the task: what honour was there in bullying the People of the Wood? And why bring them to the city in the first place?

The questions had been answered with a vengeance when the villagers had finally been herded into the courtyard of the Temple of Aiyeh. The priests waiting there had been armed with axes. The great golden doors had been barred, preventing escape; and then the killing had begun. Mercifully only a few of the soldiers had escorted the prisoners within, or there might well have been a rebellion on the spot. They, like he, had stood rooted with horror and shock as the priests began hacking at the screaming Manyei. Prayers had mingled with the shrieks of the wounded and the groans of the dying, and the golden paving of the courtyard had run with blood. Not one was allowed to escape, from the headman to the youngest child in its mother's arms.

He should have acted. He should have responded to the appalled faces of his men, looking to him to give them a lead. Somehow he should have done something to prevent, even if it had cost him his own life in the doing of it. Now he had to live with his shame, and only the feeble justification that he had been following orders.

Wearily he walked towards the house. His young wife was waiting in the doorway, her eyes anxious. She looked as if she would have liked to put her arms around him for comfort, and he deliberately side-stepped to prevent her doing so. He felt dirty, soiled, and did not want her tainted with his corruption.

She had been on the verge of asking him what had happened, but was wise enough to remain silent. Such discourtesy was most unlike him, and was a sure sign of how deeply troubled he was. To force him to talk was not the best way to go about mending matters: he would open up in his own good time. Until then, it would be safest to maintain some semblance of normality. Trying to break the tension she sensed but did not understand, she offered him a plate of bread. He took it as though he did not know what he was doing, sat down at the table and stared blindly at the plate. Next moment his fists rose and crashed down on the wood, crashed and crashed again, heedless of the jumping tableware and the spilled food. "Forgive me! Forgive me! Shining Father, forgive me!" His talons clenched and writhed in his blue-black feathers as he lowered his head and sobbed. Henanei stood aghast, her hands clasped on her belly. She had news for him that would gladden the heart of any husband, but this was certainly not the time to reveal her secret. What could possibly have happened to him, out there in the city where nothing was familiar any more? Tentatively she moved towards him, but he was instantly aware of it. His hand shot out and thrust her away. "No! I'm dirty – dirty! You'll soil your hands!"

She stood still, hurt and utterly bewildered, her honey-coloured crest shifting in alarm. He did not look dirty to her. Then she realised that he was not referring to anything that water would wash off. Her heart contracted with dread.

But whatever he had done, he was still her husband, and the father of the child to come. He had a right to her loyalty. And she did not believe that he could have done anything dishonourable: it was not in him. She walked forward, ignoring his hand, and knelt down beside him. Quietly she leaned forward and rested her head on his lap. It was a gesture of the deepest trust, and for a moment she feared he was not going to react. But presently she felt his hand come to rest on the back of her neck. His body still shuddered with grief, but there was less tension in it.

"You should leave me, wife. I'm not worthy of you now."

"I don't know what you've done. I don't care what you've done," she said steadily. "I'm your wife in the sight of the Goddess, and I know that you'd do nothing wrong in the sight of the God."

He laughed at that, a sound of unimaginable bitterness. What, after today, could possibly be wrong in the sight of the God? The world had run mad. Only here was there some semblance of sanity. Thank the Shining One for Henanei. He could not tell her yet, though sooner or later she would have to know and it was best that he should tell her rather than another. He did not know if the truth would be too much for her, despite her brave words. How many women would remain loyal to a husband who stood by and did nothing while innocent civilians were slaughtered? For now, he would not put it to the test. He wanted her suddenly, for comfort in a desperate world. Gently he lifted her and walked to the bedroom. It might be for the last time, but they would honour the Goddess together. And if ever the chance came for him to make amends, might the Shining One give him the courage to seize it with both hands.

* * *

The ex-Empress Mia'naan stood up and moved to the window. Never in her life before had she known this feeling of helplessness. Never before had she been penned up, guarded, spied on. And certainly never before had she felt such hatred as she did now.

She looked out across the city, resolutely giving no sign that she was aware of the instant attention of the guard beneath her window. What was happening out there? Had they all accepted what had happened? If there was resistance (Mother Shieih! Let someone, somewhere, have the courage to strike back!), it had not yet made itself felt. Perhaps in the circumstances no one felt it appropriate. After all, done was done, and Venelai were realists. Rebellion would not bring back the dead, and probably not do the living much good either. Was there anyone who would raise the Red Standard over the fate of a child not yet even hatched from the egg?

Restlessly she turned away. As she walked, her hands caressed the swollen mound of her belly. Who could ever have guessed that the day would come when she cursed her own fertility? For what was in store for the infant within? If it were a girl-child it would be allowed to live, she could guess that much, and she knew for what purpose. Stiv'aran would be an utter fool not to seize the opportunity of cementing his hold on the Horned Crown by marrying the

Heiress; and be he whatever else he was, fool he most certainly was not. If it were a boy-child the same merciless reasoning would be applied. The Emperor-Elect would definitely not permit a male Heir to live. There would be a regretful announcement from the Palace to the effect that the child had died in the egg – most probably due to the criminal carelessness of his mother in brooding it. Any counter-tale she might put forward (assuming she ever got the chance to do so) would be dismissed as the self-justifying squealing of a careless and hysterical female. The Goddess defend her if ever she fell pregnant to Stiv'aran. She would not put it past him to have her bound for the term of her pregnancy, and forbidden to brood her own egg when she was delivered of it. He was utterly without scruple, seemingly without fear, certainly without compassion. She had never encountered anyone like him.

And yet – how, how could her husband have been so mistaken in him? For Emperor Sevi'nke had trusted him utterly, and Mia'naan had had the greatest faith in her lord husband as a judge of men. In the most ironic of circumstances, he had planned to make Stiv'aran the Great Guardian of his heir when he or she should be born: a position he certainly would not have awarded to anyone of whom he had had the faintest shadow of doubt. Sevi'nke had not been the blindly trusting sort: he would not have held his throne for so many years if he had been naïve. He had been a stern but just ruler, in private capable of much tenderness, and she had held him in considerable affection. His death had been not only a shock, but also a grief to her. Shock had probably been uppermost. It had been so totally unexpected. She had not even been allowed to see his body before it was hurriedly given funeral rites – she was growing so cynical now that she could wonder whether he actually *had* been given a funeral. In ordinary circumstances any Venel male of rank was sent to meet the Sunrise in a burning ship commissioned especially for the purpose, but it would have been so much more practical for Stiv'aran to have simply had him shovelled him into a hole in the ground and left him to rot in dishonour. If ever the Good Goddess allowed, a full search should be made, and the most intense enquiries. He might have paid for his misjudgement with his life, but he should not be deprived of the Emperor's funeral that was his due.

That was hardly the most pressing issue at this moment, however. Her primary aim must be escape. She had no fears for her own survival: Stiv'aran would not make the mistake of harming the woman who might be carrying his future Empress, and once she was delivered of her child he would use her for breeding, thus ensuring the acquiescence, if not the co-operation, of her House. Her brothers might not approve of him, but with the prospect of imperial blood relations being bred from their sister they would not intervene. To be sure, if she did not happen to produce a female posthumous child to Sevi'nke the position would be slightly different; it would not be as advantageous as being related to the Heiress in whose right Stiv'aran would claim the throne, but even imperial bastards were of high station at court and could wield considerable power. Like most Venelai, her family were realists. They had liked Sevi'nke, insofar as liking him was relevant – the fact that he was Emperor had been more important than any other consideration that could possibly have been advanced. This would be exactly the case with Stiv'aran. What he was, what he did, would be completely eclipsed by the fact of what he wore – the Horned Crown.

So, she could not expect help from her family. Any members of the imperial entourage who might have been likely to resist Stiv'aran's coup had been dealt with in the hour of Sevi'nke's assassination. Several had been killed in the same Council meeting. She had heard, but could not believe at first, that a Skair who had been bringing a message from the Palace had also been killed. There was no point in disbelieving it now, however. She had heard every word of the report of the attack on Weruavwe. How she had not fainted on the spot only the Goddess knew. *Skaira* slaughtered! And so many! For what reason? Mother Shieih, why, why, why had he ordered such a thing? Why take such an appalling risk? Did he think that the other Skaira would tamely accept it? Had he no fear of the Goddess? Yes, from what he had said it was clear that he had ordered that the Princess be taken unharmed, and kept captive as his hostage against her subjects. It was hard to understand how he could believe that that would suffice to protect him against the wrath of Shieih. At some point – and it was only incredible that thus far the hour delayed – the Goddess would avenge Her own. In the meantime, Mia'naan could only watch, and wait, and pray for a chance to escape the net. She knew that her pregnancy was near its end. Once the egg was laid she would be watched even more closely. So if her escape was to be made at all, it must be soon. Perhaps all was not as hopeless as she feared. Perhaps (the Goddess make it so!) there were still those who only waited their moment to strike against Stiv'aran. Surely there must be someone out there!

She knelt down before the small altar she had made of a stool draped with a blue cloth. Her own had been smashed, and this wretched substitute would be taken from her as soon as any of her captors came in and saw it; nevertheless it was her own little gesture of defiance to a hopeless situation and a dark future. She had spent many of her waking hours there ever since the moment when her world had started its falling apart, when the screams had begun shattering the peace of the Women's Quarters and armed soldiers at her door had forcibly prevented her from leaving. Powerless for the first time in her life, she had had to watch as a fleeing child had been pursued down the corridor outside and hacked down within six feet of her. The little one's mother had been shrieking in the grip of two other guards. She should have been safe, everyone knew she was in oestrus and could not possibly be pregnant… but, there had been no exceptions. They had dragged her away with the others. Mia'naan had flailed with her fists at the unresponsive guards, demanding explanations. They had not answered. Perhaps they had had no explanations either. Not until many hours later, when the Palace had finally fallen into a dreadful numb silence, had Stiv'aran darkened the doorway. After that, she knew everything there was to know. Except why…

She emerged from her dark reverie to find that her talons were gripping desperately at the blue cloth, as if to a lifeline. Carefully, with an effort, she made them unclench. She had no offering to place but her own worship, but even Stiv'aran could not take that from her. On that cloth she must place all her troubles, handing them into the care of the Goddess. Whatever her fate, Shieih would watch over her. At least she had that consolation. The One of fang and claw would not desert Her own.

*　　　*　　　*

In the Temple of Aiyeh all was quiet. There were no priests in attendance at this hour. Normally the doors and windows would have been flung wide to admit the glory of the daylight, but the orders had changed. Now the windows where closed and shuttered, and dark cloth hung across the doorway, so that anyone entering must brush through it. Not so much as a chink of light entered to be reflected in the walls of beaten gold. There was only one worshipper, the Emperor-elect. Stiv'aran knelt before the altar, his wrists exposed in the traditional posture of supplication. His eyes stared sightlessly, and mist seemed to wreath around him.

The stone on the altar shuddered slightly. Had anyone touched it, they would probably have been burned by the intense cold of it. Stiv'aran did not try. He was incapable of making any independent decision by this time.

The presence within the stone regarded him with satisfied malice and amused contempt. It was sweet indeed to have corrupted such a man. At some point it might even be worth while to allow him to understand what he had done; the realisation might well overturn his sanity. Not for a while yet, however. There was still far too much to be done with such a useful instrument.

So far, things were proceeding according to plan. The Venelai were too accustomed to obeying orders, too rigidly hierarchical, to put up much organised resistance to a man who had usurped the position of supreme power in their world. It was possible nevertheless that given the circumstances there might be a rebellion, but this was by no means certain. Several of the minor kings might well choose the time of unrest to launch attacks against their neighbours, but the additional suffering that this would cause was no more than a garnish on the chief dish. The attack against Weruavwe had been accomplished successfully: it had been vital to secure the Princess, muzzling the chief danger from that direction. It would not pay to underestimate the power residual in the First Among Skaira, for all the restraints placed upon it. Now that power had been disarmed. The one other whom he had allowed to escape had acted as expected and was even now on her way to the other power-arm of Skairesse. So far, so good. That too might pay dividends – and if not, she could always be gathered in at some other time. Soon he would order more Manyei to be brought. The least significant of the three dominant races of Kerriel, theirs was a simple society that belonged intimately to their surroundings. They believed that the trees were their brothers, and nothing would induce them to shed the blood of any living creature; if there was power in them it was deep and diffuse, the power of the abiding earth. There was no harm in such pitiful beings, and no threat either, but their suffering was entertaining, and there was always black joy in wanton destruction, no matter how insignificant the victims. Besides, the shock of having to bring them to their deaths was a useful way of weeding out the loyal among the Imperial troops from those less – trustworthy. The tally of deaths thus far was nothing, *nothing* to what was to come. The whole world would soon be a reeking bloodbath.

Aeons ago, a wandering asteroid had struck the barren planet where he had been cast into exile. From the resulting explosion, one significant solid piece had escaped the pull of gravity and hurtled into space. For millions of years he had waited, watching while this fragment of his dark world had wandered the airless reaches of the star-system. The Law was the Law: he could not be forbidden to reside on the rock of his own world. No matter how small a piece; no matter where it might happen to land…

An immortal's perception of time is different from those whose span is determined by their mortal form. He could not have expressed in comprehensible terms the length of time he had wandered from galaxy to galaxy, sowing ruin in his wake. Encountering the impotently fuming Guardian of one world to which he had just introduced the concept of biological warfare that would ultimately destroy every living thing on it, he had received the strange, bitter warning that he should beware the Two and the stranger from the West beyond the East. He had disregarded, almost forgotten it, until he meddled with Kerriel, a world that had two Guardians, and for the first time he encountered a force of resistance that had been sufficiently powerful to confine him to the black hell of the outermost planet of this system. Imprisoned there, he had for the first time experienced some terrible conception of the passage of time – the slow, futile grind of hour after hour watching the bright star around which his prison circled.

Esdiol of Tharnil had long dreamed of revenge. He had found means to evade the Two. And as for any 'stranger' he might encounter…

The chance was here. He was not about to waste it now.

10

"At last!" Lidan heaved a sigh of relief. "That yonder is Vanreil, the Mountain of Storms. The Holy Place of Shieih."

Brendan too heaved a sigh of relief, but not because he was pleased to see the goal of their journey; he was more pleased that they had finished the scramble up the mountainside in such poor light. With his improved night-vision, starlight would have served well enough to illuminate his footing, but the clouds had come up and with them the first rain he had felt on Kerriel. It was unfortunate, though probably inevitable, that this should happen when they were completely without shelter of any kind. He had draped his blanket-tunic over his back, but the rain had fallen steadily and soon everything he was wearing was wet through. Luckily the night was not cold. He minded the rain more for the effect it had on his footing than for the discomfort of it. There was nothing as definite as a path across Hergath, and after leaving the cave they had been obliged to climb as best they could across the steep slopes. Now he really did miss proper shoes, preferably ones with a good grip on the soles. But for the fact that his feet would probably have been cut to ribbons in the first five minutes, he would have been tempted to remove his hide moccasins altogether. They certainly did not have the grip he would have preferred, nor did they offer much protection to his ankles. Still, in the circumstances they were still better than nothing. He had made no complaint, but climbed on as best he could in the wake of the more agile Skair, envying her four paws with their long claws for grip. They paused to rest occasionally, but the comfortless surroundings discouraged lingering; and besides, it would not be wise to be caught out in the open in full daylight if they could help it.

They crested Hergath in the dawn, and saw the valley that contained the Temple Complex spread out before them, hemmed in and protected on every side by the huge range of mountains. It was far larger and more lush than Brendan had expected, a hidden jewel in such an unpromising setting. He saw the glint of water on one of the heights alongside this one, and on another the long silver ribbon of a waterfall that must be many hundreds of feet high. But ahead of them and slightly to their right frowned the mountain to which Lidan had pointed, Vanreil the Mountain of Storms.

It did not look welcoming. Much of it was completely bare rock, dark blue in the pale light. There were thin scarves of rain blowing across it. The very crest was hidden in low cloud.

"We will not go first to Vanreil," said Lidan, looking happier than she had done since they left her hut. "We will go to the Temple Complex. There you can rest and eat a proper meal, whilst I discuss our situation with the others."

This prospect did even more than the easier downward going to brighten Brendan's outlook. He hadn't gone hungry on the march; Lidan had made a kind of sling from grass stems, which she'd slung around her withers and filled with whatever food offered. Constant snacking was not as satisfying as a solid meal, however, and he would be glad of the chance to sit down, relax, and eat a balanced dinner, or whatever the next meal might be after their arrival. He was finding it hard to adapt to the lack of a schedule for eating: it was something that had never occurred to him before that on Earth human beings were the only animal who actually knew when and from where the next meal would arrive. The removal of this certainty was far more disconcerting than he would have expected. He'd never thought much about food before, mainly because he'd been certain of his supply of it. Now that the supply line was considerably less certain, he was shocked and illogically embarrassed to find how much the subject occupied his thoughts. It seemed that the instincts for survival were still alive and kicking beneath the veneer of civilisation. The worry over what the inhabitants of the Complex might think of him had receded somewhat in his mind. Whatever they made of him, he could not imagine that they would refuse him food and shelter, especially since he had been brought by the command of their Goddess.

With this in mind it did not seem so important to stop and seek shelter during the daylight hours, even though they were both weary and had originally planned to seek shelter among the corries on the mountain's inner face. Here in the holy valley they were in far less danger; and they paused only to eat a handful of sweet pink berries from the sling before pressing on down the far side of Hergath. Resting on a ledge with the valley spread out in front of him, Brendan found himself thinking with a faint sense of surprise that he'd miss the odd intimacy of travelling alone with Lidan. Walking such distances wasn't much fun, especially in such poor footwear, and sleeping on the ground at night was less, even with his tunic for a blanket to spread over a heap of ferny stuff to make a bed of sorts – fortunately the nights were warm, so he needed no covering, and they'd been lucky with the weather, which had been almost entirely dry. Nevertheless, despite the ever-present sense of danger he realised now that he'd actually rather enjoyed the experience. They'd had quiet conversations while they walked and before they fell asleep, and he felt that despite the gulf between them they were on the way to becoming friends. The presence of other Skaira would probably change all that. Still, it would be a burden eased for her, having the sole responsibility for protecting him; and being an optimistic, easy-going sort he hoped that the others wouldn't have too much of a problem accepting him.

They set off again. The morning advanced. Towards noon they reached the edge of the woodland, and Brendan felt that they were indeed almost at the end of their journey. Even the rain had slackened and now only fell in sparkling showers. Every now and then the sun gleamed through the cloud cover to light up the forest canopy above them. Their spirits lifted, and for all that they were very tired indeed by now, they kept up a good pace.

Perhaps their renewed optimism made Lidan less cautious than was wise. At any rate she did not notice the solitary rider and his beast off among the trees on their left, and the breeze blowing from the wrong direction did not give her warning. Not until the sudden beat of hooves sounded did she spin around, and so fast did the attack come that even she might have been too late but for Brendan's acute reflexes. He hardly had time to take in the oncoming stag and rider, but he saw the naked sword. He hurled himself away from the sweep of it, feeling the blade slice through the tunic still slung across his back. The sudden fiery pain across one shoulder told him he hadn't escaped completely, but as he fell among the undergrowth he was able to keep rolling, getting himself away from the hooves. In the next instant Lidan acted. With a completely inhuman scream of rage she sprang at the Venel, every claw agleam. Her hind paws hit the stag's body and gouged deep, sending the animal into a frantic rearing turn. Her forepaws, knife, free hand and teeth took the rider as her weight hurled him from the saddle. Never in his nightmares had Brendan imagined the scene that followed. The Venel seemed to put up some kind of a struggle, but it was brief and bloody. The Skair did not waste energy in making any other sound, and her victim's throat was very soon too mangled for so much as a death rattle to emerge from it. Even when he was dead – very visibly dead – she did not stop. Her hackles were a hedge of fury all along her back as she gouged at the body with her forepaws, spitting and snarling down at it.

The impact with the ground had torn the sword from the rider's hand, and it had fallen at a little distance away. Quite automatically Brendan went to pick it up. It was made of what looked like steel, but it was surprisingly light. The long blade curved slightly and was sharp along both sides. He felt better with a weapon of some kind in his hand. Common sense told him that he had no training in swordplay and would stand no chance at all against anyone more skilled, but the psychological boost of being armed was immense – especially after what had just happened. He had taken care not to move his left arm as he bent to retrieve the sword, but the experimental swing even with his right still tugged the flesh of his back, and a fresh stab of pain punished his lack of caution. Wincing, he put the sword down again for a moment and carefully felt the back of his left shoulder. His hand came away smeared with red, and he could feel wetness seeping down his ribs, but as far as he could tell it was no more than a long thin cut. He had been lucky – very lucky.

He turned back to where Lidan had just abandoned the body with a parting curse. She was bloody all down her front, and her eyes were still smouldering as she spat out a few small feathers. A short way away among the trees the stag had come to a halt. It too was bloody from the encounter, and stood trembling, its reins trailing. He felt sorry for it. Lidan saw him looking, and glared at the stag, pulling her lips back to expose her teeth.

"Oh, come on, it wasn't his fault," said Brendan, trying not to feel sick. "Can you have a look at my back?"

"Son of the Dark One!" growled the Skair, with another furious glance at the corpse. "Turn around, Kelti. I will not hurt you more than I can help."

He did as he was told, and tried not to flinch as she gently pulled away the edges of fabric from the wound. More muttered curses followed. After a moment she turned aside and padded into the undergrowth, where she bent over and picked something. She returned with a handful of what looked like dried pea-pods. When split these proved to contain a substance like fine cotton wool. She opened several, and carefully wiped the wound with the contents. That done, she pulled wisps from another and gently dabbed them on so that they stuck to the cut, helping the blood still seeping from it to congeal. A last trickle escaped from the deepest part and ran down his back, and she quickly dabbed it with her tongue – curiosity had got the better of her.

"No great harm done. When we reach the Complex I will ask a Healer to examine it, but I think it only a scratch. But I am indeed sorry that I did not guard you better. I was careless, and you have paid the penalty for it."

"Could have been worse." He resisted accompanying the words with a shrug. "But wouldn't it have been better to try and take him alive? Find out what he knows?"

"Alive? And risk having him rescued, so that he lived to boast of his deed afterwards? No, it would not! To draw a weapon in this valley, and attack one under the protection of a Skair! By the One! I am only sorry that he did not have two throats, so that I could tear them both out!" She glared at the body again. "Besides, he was not of any rank. It is doubtful that he would know much of value, even if he had lived. And our situation is complex enough without having a prisoner on our hands."

That was logical enough, he had to admit. He wasn't keen on going much closer to what was left of the Venel even to satisfy his curiosity; he could see even from here that it was not a pretty sight. But there was no doubt that the soldier had been perhaps eight or nine inches taller than he, and far more powerfully built around the now shattered torso. It would have been difficult to keep him under control with only the two of them to guard him and for only one of whom he would probably have felt any fear. He would always have been a threat to their secrecy and their security, and the chances were that once brought to the Complex for the judgement of the inhabitants; he would probably have received short shrift from them anyway. Still, that wasn't quite the same as being summarily slaughtered like a bullock. Once again Brendan felt the gulf between their cultures yawning between them.

"Can you ride?" Lidan asked suddenly. He looked at her in surprise, then saw her considering the stag. The obvious drift of her thoughts made him grin. He had used to ride quite regularly at home in Galway, but it was some while now since his hectic lifestyle had allowed him the time. For a moment he was tempted to make a vulgar play on the term "getting in the saddle", but suspected that Lidan's sadly literal mind would probably not understand it if he did, and having to explain the joke would rob it entirely of humour. She wondered why his grin widened momentarily.

"Well I've ridden a horse on Earth, I suppose it can't be that much different." Not much, if you were prepared to overlook the spread of antlers and trust that the 'aids' were similar. It wouldn't take too long to find out if they weren't. "But do you think he's going to let you come near him?"

"When you are astride him he will have to do what he is told," she answered crossly. "He is only a stupid animal, after all."

"Hmm." It didn't seem to him that any animal would have to qualify for Mensa to want to avoid proximity to someone who had just torn holes in its hide. And if it came to a power struggle between a large, strong, frightened animal and a comparatively puny and inexperienced rider, it didn't take much imagination to work out who was going to come out the winner. However, it was worth a cautious try: if it didn't succeed he was no worse off.

Leaving Lidan where she was – the stag certainly wasn't going to stand still while she stalked it – he walked slowly towards the nervous animal. He would have picked a handful of foliage if he'd known what it ate; it was a pity he had no equivalent of a lump of sugar to hand. The stag watched his approach with increasing anxiety. When he was within about eight feet of it, it threw up its head, brandishing the antlers and showing the whites of its eyes. He interpreted this correctly as a display more of fear than aggression, and went on walking, though he moved even more slowly. The trailing rein had snagged on a branch of a fallen tree: a tug of any determination would have freed it, but the impression of being tethered evidently conquered the temptation to bolt. A couple of minutes later Brendan was able to catch the rein and put out a gentle hand towards the stag's nose. It was a handsome animal, though bigger and stronger than the red deer he'd seen on Earth; its coat was the colour of ripe corn, with a streak of white fur down its breast and belly. The large velvety nostrils fluttered inquisitively against his skin as the animal inhaled deeply of his scent. The spread of the antlers was formidable, and he noted that each tine was sharpened, but it made no aggressive movement towards him.

"Poor old thing." He ran his hand up the underside of the jaw and around to rub the base of the ears. The stag relaxed and rumbled with pleasure. Stags evidently had much the same taste in tactile treats as horses did. After a minute or two Brendan gently pulled on the rein. The animal moved forward willingly enough, and stood still again when the pull ended. He moved round to the nearside of it and leaned his weight across the saddle. The stag did not seem to object, though it looked around curiously at him. The saddle was more built up than the type he was used to, almost like those seen in Western films, and instead of an iron stirrup it had only a loop of leather. Still, neither of those should pose much difficulty. Now for the real test. He glanced around for something to use as a mounting block: ordinarily he would have hoisted himself aboard with no difficulty whatsoever, but the exertion would drag on the new wound in his shoulder and probably rip it open again. The fallen tree would serve nicely. He guided the stag into position, climbed on to the trunk and again leaned his weight across the saddle. No hostile response. Ignoring the pain in his shoulder as he leaned down, he opened the stirrup loop and fitted his foot into it. For a moment he hesitated. Then he mounted. The stag sidled restlessly, blowing, and tugged once or twice at the rein; but it answered readily enough to gentle pressure from his heels. He'd been relieved to note that the harness included a type of martingale preventing the head from being thrown far enough back to give the rider a jab in the face with one of the antlers' tines, but his mount showed no inclination to try it. His face wearing a look of considerable delight, he rode the stag towards Lidan. The Skair did not look exactly friendly, but she refrained from any movement or expression that might be interpreted as an intention of renewing hostilities; the stag must have been used to the proximity of Skaira at some time, for after a few anxious snorts and a bit of side-stepping it seemed to accept her. Lidan glanced at the claw-marks on its hide and opted to leave well enough alone: they were flesh wounds only, and attempts at first aid would probably not go down too well. Brendan looked confident enough on its back, but she had no wish to put his riding capabilities to the test of trying to stay on a bolting animal in thick woodland.

"So. That is well," she remarked. "It will be easier for you to ride than walk, and we have travelled far already today." At his request she picked the sword up from the grass. There were still traces of his blood on part of the blade; she scowled, cleaned it on a patch of grass and handed it to him. It rested in a sheath fitted to the saddle, and he tested how easy it was to draw it if needed.

He couldn't help glancing back at the body. "Are we just going to leave him there?"
"What would you suggest? Honourable burial for such scum? By the One!"
"He was probably just following orders," he answered mildly.
Lidan showed her opinion of that by raising her tail and spraying in the direction of the corpse. "That for following orders! He has come by his deserts, and I have no pity for him! I hope his body is eaten by scavengers and his soul wanders for eternity!"

There was no reply to be made to such unforgiving hatred: it was hardly possible to preach Christian forgiveness to one who'd never heard of the Gospels. Nevertheless, her unsparing lack of charity saddened him a little. It seemed so pointless to bear a grudge against the dead.

They started out again, and although from that point onwards they were both much more vigilant, there were no more alarms. At an hour or so after noon they made a brief halt beside a small lake, where Lidan found some freshwater shellfish – she offered Brendan a share, but he declined it. He took the opportunity instead to wash the stag's wounds, which it seemed to appreciate; he was growing fond of the animal, and had named it Adrian. ("After all the times he's been on my back, I'm going to be on his." Lidan had not seemed to get the joke, even when he'd explained it.)

Half of the afternoon passed. It had not appeared as long a way as this when they had looked down from Hergath, and Brendan was so weary he was almost asleep in the saddle; he envied the tireless stride of the Skair who seemed immune to exhaustion. He almost did not notice when she suddenly stopped and brightened. "Praise the Goddess! We are safe!" She pointed ahead. The trees thinned out, and there among them he could clearly see buildings.

At last they had reached the Temple Complex.

11

For all that had gone before, for all the fact that he had thought himself now beyond shock, Teho'evan still looked down and wondered how under the face of the sun things had come to this.

The Skair lay completely motionless, eyes closed, hardly even seeming to breathe. The whiteness of her fur was soiled and bloody, the gold ruff at her withers sticky with sweat. Her golden hair had been cut – hacked almost up to the nape of her neck with something as clumsy as a knife. So needless, so pointless. So infantile. Her paws were bound, her wrists tied at her withers. The cords were brutally tight, as was the leather gag in her mouth. She had been wounded at some point, and the gashes had not even been washed. Fortunately the cuts showed no sign of infection yet. The soft pink flesh at the tip of her nose was dry and wrinkled, a sign of dehydration; the fur between her hind legs was stained and smelly – she had not even been allowed to stand in order to evacuate with dignity. He had not seen her before, but only one Skair line of descent had that brilliant, beautiful colouring. If he hadn't already known, it would have told him who she was: Thaskan, Princess of the Skaira.

"Aiyeh!" he muttered under his breath. He had been given the task of escorting the prisoner into the city – Stiv'aran was not taking any chances of her being rescued by sympathisers. He had expected a captive, treated with respect. Another few days of such treatment and he could well have been taking over responsibility for a corpse. He glared at the oafs who had brought her from Weruavwe. Was not captivity enough, was not the murder of her people enough, that so respected and revered a person was reduced to such indignity?

At a gesture his own men moved forward and took the bridles of the geldings that drew the cart on which she lay. The jolt as it moved forward again did not even make her open her eyes. Perhaps she was unconscious. He hoped so, for her sake.

The word had got round (somehow it always did), and there were many in the streets to watch the sad procession. Few people made any comment – it was no longer safe to say what one thought in public – but even fewer could completely hide their shock and dismay. He rode at the head of it and was ashamed to be seen there, for horror that anyone should think such a spectacle was anything to do with him.

Once again the orders had been specific. Thaskan was to be taken the Temple of Aiyeh and imprisoned there, in a room especially prepared for her. He had seen the bolts and bars. A criminal would have been less securely held, and a criminal would have been allowed freedom behind them. There was to be no freedom for Thaskan. Bound she arrived and bound she must stay, and woe betide anyone who dared to meddle.

Orders were orders, and what could he do? He had not enough men to prevail against those who had brought her thus far, even if he gave in to the crazy impulse to free her. He outranked their commander, but was far from sure that he could convince him that there had been a change in plans; and having a running battle break out in the street would be disastrous, here where the imperial troops could be so quickly and easily reinforced. It was not as if Thaskan was in any state to help herself even if he cut her loose. There were no Skaira in the city to whom he could appeal for help either – Stiv'aran had seen to that. The Princess was isolated and powerless, and her Goddess appeared to have deserted her.

After what seemed like the longest and most nightmarish ride of his life, they finally reached the Temple. The cart was unfastened in the courtyard, and a makeshift stretcher of planks brought. There was not even a blanket on it. Raging inwardly, Teho'evan helped his men transfer Thaskan on to it; warily noting the slightly erected crest that betrayed his mood, they were as careful as possible, but the semiconscious Princess moaned softly, though her eyes still did not open.

"Carry her inside. Gently!" Not caring for the moment what anyone thought, he took one corner of it himself. It did not weigh as much as he would have expected: Thaskan had not only been kept short of water, he realised savagely, she had not been fed either.

They got her somehow into the cramped, bare little room with its newly barred window. It had originally been a storeroom, and laying planks across two empty chests had made a bed of sorts. To save disturbing her any further, he thought it best to rest the stretcher on top of this – it would be larger, and there was no bedding laid there that would make it more comfortable if they transferred her to it. The official who had been Stiv'aran's observer at the event departed to inform his master that the prisoner was safely delivered, and Teho'evan sent a scorching glare after him and ordered water to be brought.

After a slight pause (there had been some confusion over what the water should be brought in), his lieutenant came in with a shallow bowl and clean cloths.

"You're a mind-reader, Keri." He dipped one of the cloths in the water and began trying to trickle some of it into the Skair's mouth, cursing beneath his breath as it ran down the leather gag and pooled on the wood beneath her.

"Don't even think of it, *Lathaichan*," Keri'khai said softly, not needing to be a telepath to know the thought that had entered his senior officer's head. "We're still being watched."

"I know. The Dark One take it!" He took her head in his hands and tried to manoeuvre it side- ways, tilting her jaw upwards. Another try with the dripping cloth seemed slightly more successful: he thought that at least some trickled past the gag, for she swallowed once or twice. He dared not try to give her too much at once, for fear of choking her. Instead he began gently cleaning the two visible wounds, ensuring that they were indeed as free from infection as they appeared. There was no other treatment available, but at least they seemed in no danger of festering. Then he cleaned her face, keeping the rest of the leather dry as far as possible. He knew that drying leather contracts, and had no wish to add to the Princess's torment.

'If I could only get her to a bath,' he thought – but didn't say aloud, knowing it to be not only ludicrous but also literally dangerous. Still trussed with such brutality, even if she regained consciousness Thaskan would almost certainly drown in a bath, and there was no possibility that he would be allowed to untie her. Even betraying that much concern for her welfare would put him at risk: the Emperor's warlords were not supposed to sympathise with his prisoners, no matter how exalted these might be or to what depths of misery they were now fallen. He could justify cleaning her wounds and giving her water by saying that he feared for her life, seeing that she was injured and dehydrated when she arrived. If Stiv'aran wanted her alive, as he presumably did, he would not be best pleased to be presented with a stiffening corpse.

He resumed trying to drip water into her mouth, persevered for some while in his self-appointed task, and succeeded in getting what he felt to be a reasonable amount of water into the Skair. Keri'khai knelt silently beside him, and one or two of the soldiers watched from the doorway. The four guards Stiv'aran had appointed arrived, checked on their prisoner, and took up station outside the door. A fifth was positioned outside the window.

"Well, I don't think there's anything more I can do here." Teho'evan sat back on his heels. And at that moment the one thing he had been dreading happened. Thaskan opened her eyes.

Suffering had made them sink back into her head, but they were still alert, intelligent, alive. There was no way she could talk to him, but the tawny triangles fastened on his face and softened slightly. The inclination of her head was so infinitesimal that even Keri'khai might have missed it if he had been less observant. Nevertheless Thaskan conveyed her gratitude for the first kindness she had encountered in her captivity. Not quite all the world, it seemed, had fallen into the realm of nightmare.

He wanted to say so much at that moment, but almost anything carrying any overtones of regret or sympathy could be interpreted as treason. Alive, he might – might – have some chance, somehow, of helping her. Dead, as he very shortly would be should Stiv'aran have any doubt whatsoever of his loyalty, he would be of no use to anybody. He offered her more water, but she closed her eyes again and seemed to sleep. Perhaps she felt it wiser to do so, and who was to say she was wrong?

With no further excuse to linger, he rose and strode from the room, Keri'khai at his heels. The scene within stayed with him, however. For all that it was no work of his, he was ashamed. He had felt shamed too often of late, and hated the feeling almost as much as he hated his own confusion.

Outside the Temple, he gestured to his lieutenant to accompany him to the adjoining gardens. These were part of the Temple and cared for by its priests, as part of the worship of the Good God who made all green things grow. As they entered by the gate in the wall, he was almost surprised to find that here nothing had changed. There were few flowers, this was not the season for them, but the autumn foliage was at its best and there were even some winter-flowering trees coming into bloom. There were benches set here and there for the benefit of those who came to pray in such serene and beautiful surroundings, and he chose one close to a pool whose motionless surface mirrored a particularly lovely lalaio tree. Not only was it well worth admiring the lalaio as it trailed streams of bronze leaves towards its reflection, the bench was sited so as to be well out of range of any inquisitive ears.

Aware that he was about to take a grave risk – with the world turned upside-down as it was, there was no guarantee that even Keri'khai was trustworthy – Teho'evan sat down and signed to his subordinate to do the same. They were both silent for a while, but it was a relatively comfortable silence; they had fought together in the Imperial army for some years, and felt no need to fill every pause with conversation. Released from formality by the permission to share a seat with his commander, the lieutenant sat to all intents and purposes enjoying the view; but though his bronze head turned only imperceptibly, the wide-set eyes ceaselessly scanned the empty garden.

"Have you heard the latest?" Nothing there had changed; even on campaign Keri'khai had had an uncanny knack of garnering gossip. "Shas'kare has had to send part of his division into Three Stars. Special orders, he said."

"What, have they managed to find another village of Manyei to slaughter?" asked Teho'evan bitterly. Guilt was still gnawing at him. His sleep was nightmare-ridden; he was still haunted by the memory of one that had jerked him awake in a cold sweat several nights running, in which he'd been stumbling through a dark and trackless forest, crying out in terror for someone to come to his aid. "I thought they'd cleaned them all out by now."

"I don't think it was for that. He didn't say so. Something about 'a stranger'. It seemed odd at the time."

"A stranger!" Teho'evan gave a bark of utterly mirthless laughter. "He could try the Imperial Palace. By the One, there's a stranger there, and but for a babe in the egg he'll be sitting on the Horned Throne very shortly!"

"Not so loud," cautioned the older man. "You don't know who may be listening."

"I know *you're* listening." He turned to his lieutenant. "Tell me if I'm wrong. You've worked with Stiv'aran, you've fought for him – I haven't. Is this like him? Sevi'nke trusted him completely, and he was no fool. Oh, I know –" the strong slender hands with their curved talons moved in a quick gesture – "we both know the temptations of power. I suppose there's no man breathing who could say he'd never be tempted if he had the chance to snatch at the Horned Crown. But to serve loyally for so many years, to pass up many a better chance, then to do the things he's done – you can say better than I – *is* it like him?"

Keri'khai was never to be rushed into comment. He considered the matter in silence for a time. Finally, "No, I wouldn't have said so. He's clever, and he can be ruthless when he has to be. He was never afraid of bloodshed. But he was – seemed to be – honest and honourable. Sevi'nke wasn't alone in trusting him. I suppose we were all wrong."

"Were you?" he demanded passionately. "I don't think so. I don't believe so much can have happened under ordinary circumstances. A coup, yes, maybe even Stiv'aran could fall into the temptation. He might have his reasons. But by the One! What reason could there be for attacking the Skaira? Did you know that Takh'rai never left the Palace at Weruavwe? When all the Skaira were dead he went into the chapel there and took poison, and they found a letter on his body saying it was the only way he could make amends for what he'd done! And his victims were less defenceless than mine! When I heard it I wished to the One that I had the courage to do the same!"

"Courage? Or cowardice?" said Keri'khai tersely. "His life might have served to avenge them. Yours still might. There's no field of action in a funeral boat."

"And precious little here, that I can see."

"Little's better than none. A day's patience may bring your chance. Our chance," he amended, turning to look in Teho'evan's eyes with an unusual frankness. There was a tacit understanding that his superior's trust had placed them, for this while at least, on an equal footing. Teho'evan was glad of it. Keri'khai was a reserved man, his friendship not easily won but well worth having. He had a feeling that in the days to come he would have need of a friend at his shoulder.

* * *

Stiv'aran rose from his knees and turned to the doorway, strangely troubled. Today there had not been the same reassuring sense of certainty in the Stone. It had seemed withdrawn from him. Initially there had been urgency in the demand to know that the order to send troops to Three Stars had been carried out. Reassured on that point, it had retreated into brooding.

He was still no nearer knowing why the order should have been given – and hardly noticed the fact that he was actually questioning it. If there was a stranger in Three Stars, it hardly seemed worth sending half a division of men to hunt for him. If the stranger had appeared in Thervanil it would have been rather more of a threat. One individual at such a remove surely could not be all that important; and to order him slain on sight was appallingly sweeping. It gave every man in the detachment *carte blanche* to kill everyone he came across who was not personally known to him.

Still, there could not be too many individuals roaming Three Stars anyway, and those who were would just have to take their chances. What were a few more deaths to the tally?

He must visit the Empress later today. Ex-Empress, he corrected himself – the old title had slipped out automatically. Mia'naan had accepted her new status with seeming calm. Perhaps this was on account of the lethargy common to heavily pregnant females. She was carefully guarded but had not betrayed any awareness of the fact, although it must irk her. He intended to question her physician closely before the visit: her pregnancy must be very near its end by now. This did not mean that she was less attractive, only that he must refrain from any unnecessary violence if she resisted him. His superior strength meant that her resistance was futile anyway, but so far she had not come sufficiently to terms with reality as to submit with any pretence at cordiality. He was strongly tempted to bring her from the Palace to the Temple, but that would involve the presence of a strong armed guard to get her there; in her condition, she would be far too tempting a target for would-be rebels. All in all, it would be wisest to keep her safe and secure exactly where she was. In any case, it was basically safer tactics not to have all one's prisoners in the same location.

He was pleased with the progress of his other important prisoner, however. He had already visited Thaskan, and her condition was entirely satisfactory. She was weakening hourly. It would not take more than a couple of carefully chosen volunteers to bring her through the Temple when the time came, and the next stage of the plan could be put into operation. She would be so weak by then that the power in her would not be able to resist the influence of the Stone. The keystone of Skairesse would be corrupted. Through her, every one of her subjects could be made accomplices in the subjection of their world.

Stiv'aran thrust away his doubts. The plan was too good to fail. It *would* not fail. The Princess was under his control. If all went according to plan, the

Temple at Vanreil would be neutralised until too late. He had the army under his thumb. The ex-Empress was his prisoner, and with her the unborn child who could be the only threat to his accession. Who could possibly be a threat opposing all that?

12

At first glance, the Complex appeared to be deserted. Lidan had not said how many Skaira lived there, but there were more than a dozen buildings. These were all of stone, and looked old. They were all quite alike in construction, two-storey, with stone staircases going up the outside of each. It was probably logical that these should have broad, shallow steps going up at a relatively gentle slope; it would be difficult for a front-heavy Skair to descend a steep incline. All had climbing plants trained over them, though it seemed that for most the flowering season was over. A stream of some size had been diverted to branch among the houses, and more flowers grew along the banks. Skaira, it seemed, were fond of flowers: a trait he would somehow not have expected in a race of predators with a talent for sorcery. There was a large pond in the middle, with a particularly fine lalaio tree weeping over it. Altogether the whole scene was one of rural idyll. Brendan didn't know whether or not the silence was to be expected – he somehow didn't see Skaira as being a rowdy lot. These houses could be filled with them and he wouldn't know it.

Lidan came to a halt beside the pond, frowning. She was not entirely surprised by the quiet, the Complex did sometimes appear quite deserted even in normal circumstances, but even so she would have thought someone would have noticed their arrival by now. A casual glance out of a window would have been enough to bring the inhabitants of any house out like bees from an overturned hive.

Still, it might be that a meeting had been called for some reason. For certain there would be someone in the Hall who could tell her where the First Priestess would be found at this time. It would be best to lay the whole affair before Varei at once, and then she could take counsel with her senior priestesses as to what should be done. Lidan almost ached with the need to lay down at least a part of her burden, if only temporarily. To have someone else know – to be able to sleep in peace, knowing that she was not the only defender the Starborn had in this hostile world – Mother Shieih! Let me find Varei soon!

She led Brendan confidently towards the largest building in the Complex. The doors were closed, but that in itself was not significant. If a meeting were in progress it would be usual to shut the doors.

"Stay outside for a moment," she said as they reached it. She had grown so used to him that she hardly noticed now how peculiar he looked, but he was going to come as a terrible shock to her fellow Skaira. It might be best if they were prepared in advance. Besides, it would be to her advantage if she could come upon her sisters in council: it would mean that she only had to tell her story once. She glanced about, but there was still no movement; natural caution, however, made her look around for somewhere he might be a little less noticeable. Close beside the door was a large clump of ferns. It would do no harm for him to sit among them for a few minutes until she could call him within. He looked surprised, then resigned. Very likely he would not be sorry to sit and rest for a while. (Across the clearing the stag had wandered over to sample the lalaio leaves, which probably wouldn't make it all that popular with whoever was in charge of the gardening.) There was a convenient space between the fern and the wall of the building, and his utter weariness evidently made it comfortable enough. He sat down with his back against the wall, closed his eyes, and appeared to fall almost at once into a light doze.

Reassured that he was now fairly unnoticeable from most angles, Lidan turned back towards the door. She was surprised to find how nervous she was, now that the moment was upon her. It was not that she expected to be disbelieved – Skaira did not lie – but there was no saying how her audience were going to react to her tale. And there was certainly no saying how they were going to react to Brendan when he was before them. The Temple of Vanreil housed the greatest priestesses on Kerriel. Varei was equal in rank to Princess Thaskan herself, though her realm was the sacred and not the secular. It mattered beyond belief what they thought and did in the next few minutes: without their help, she did not see how her quest could possibly be accomplished.

Taking a deep breath, she pushed the doors open. She was taken aback by the crowd within. It seemed to her in the first moment that every Skair on the Peninsula was assembled there, and save for one, they were all perfectly still and silent.

That one was on the dais at the front of the Hall, and for a couple of seconds Lidan did not know her. Then recognition came. Copper-haired and wiry, with a narrow, humourless face, she was from Weruavwe and had been among Thaskan's retinue. Riyeth was her name. She had been high among those who practised Thought Power, a naturally gifted telepath. Their paths had crossed occasionally, but nothing had given Lidan the impression that here was a possible friend. From what she had seen, Riyeth was far too unlike her for any sympathy of minds; she was impulsive, outspoken and aggressive. But for her telepathic abilities she would probably have fitted well into the Warrior class. There was no aggression in her at this moment, however. Her voice dominated the Hall, and in it there was more than a trace of hysteria.

"We must do nothing, nothing to endanger her!" she was almost screeching. "They took her alive, we must not threaten them!"

Lidan blinked. She glanced around at the crowd as Riyeth continued to rave. First Priestess Varei, middle-aged, kindly and indecisive, was standing to one side of the dais, and looked as if she were about to faint. Many of her fellows appeared in like case. Here and there one was frowning. Near the door was one of these, a sturdy individual she recognised for a friend, Kanehar the Healer. Closing the doors quietly behind her, Lidan moved unobtrusively towards her. A touch on the elbow brought the Healer's gaze around to her; the frown on the broad, normally placid face gave way to a look of surprise. This was immediately followed by one of compassion, to Lidan's surprise and alarm. What could have happened? What was Riyeth caterwauling about?

"Ill met, Lidan, but I am glad beyond words to see you safe," said the Healer, leading her to one of the corners at the back of the Hall. Automatically they rubbed ears together, the Skair equivalent of the kiss of kinship. "Have you heard anything of what has happened?"

"Nothing. I have news of my own. But – what is wrong?"

"Weruavwe has been attacked." Kanehar hesitated; she looked as if she had aged twenty years since Lidan had last seen her in the early summer. "There is no easy way to say it. All the Skaira in the Palace were killed save Thaskan, who was taken prisoner, and Riyeth who managed to escape and bring us word. When it was all over, the building was set on fire – she saw the burning from high among the hills. Your mother was almost certainly among the dead."

"My mother?" Lidan almost staggered. "Shieih! There has been some mistake. It is not possible! The Palace! Nobody would dare!"

"Someone has dared," said the Healer soberly. "It is the truth. Riyeth barely escaped with her life. You can see she was wounded."

Lidan's head whipped round. Clear to see were the dark marks on Riyeth's forequarter, and even as she stood she was favouring her left foreleg.

"It is not possible," she repeated faintly, though she could not deny the grief that now welled up inside her. Whatever her faults, Riyeth was no liar. "Kanehar, who? And why? Why?"

"By the One! Would that we knew why!" She passed a square, capable hand wearily across her forehead. –"Riyeth says that the soldiers were from an Imperial division. They were archers, and skilled – our people had little chance against arrow fire. There was no warning, just an attack. Many gave their lives trying to save Thaskan from capture, but they did not succeed. Riyeth felt their deaths. The Princess is a prisoner, and we do not know what they intend for her."

"An Imperial division?" whispered Lidan. "Has the Emperor run mad?"

"There is no longer an Emperor," replied the Healer heavily. "That, too, we have just heard. Sevi'nke was assassinated some days ago. His slayer waits for his unborn heir to hatch from the shell, but all the other royal children have been murdered."

"By the Goddess!" She felt as if she screamed with shock, but the sounds were strangled in her throat. "Even the children too!"

"It is logical. If he is to mount the Horned Throne, he will want no challenge from the shoots of the dynasty that he has deposed. If the egg produces a female, he will probably marry her to legitimise his claim. A male will go the way of all the others."

"And this is the rotting offal that Riyeth wants left in peace?" Her voice rose in anger, but it was hardly noticeable in the uproar which had broken out in the Hall.

"That too is logical. He has Thaskan as his hostage. Her life may well depend upon our quiescence." "By the One!" Now she really did scream. "He murders children, he kills almost a hundred Skaira and kidnaps our Princess, he assassinates the Emperor and slaughters villages of Manyei, and we are to leave him alone?"

"What is this of Manyei?" demanded Kanehar sharply. "This we had not heard."

In as few sentences as possible Lidan told her about the two villages she had encountered on the way to Vanreil. It hardly seemed credible in the circumstances that the occupants of the second had escaped the fate of the first, though it had not overtaken them in the village itself for whatever reason.

"Varei should hear of this at once. Was this your news?"

"No-." Lidan hesitated. "Yes. Part of it." Instinct was warning her now that introducing the Starborn into this super-heated atmosphere would be incredibly dangerous. "I would prefer to talk that over with you before I discuss it with Varei or the others. And not here."

"It is something more important than the Manyei?"
"Yes. No. Yes." She frowned. "It is extremely important. And for now I think it is going to have to be kept secret."
"Then you have my ear." Without further ado the two Skaira left the Hall. Lidan closed the door carefully after them, and looked around intently. Then, without another word, she took Kanehar by the arm, drew her to the clump of fern, and parted the fronds. Brendan looked up sleepily, saw a second Skair looking down incredulously at him, and stiffened.
"By the One!" Kanehar had forgotten to breathe for a good twenty seconds. "What is it?"
"He, not it," said Lidan sharply. "He is Starborn, brought by me from another world at the bidding of Shieih. His name is Kelti – at least, it is not, but that is what I call him. It is he who can save us, but we do not know how. I have brought him here for safety, but after what I saw within I do not know how safe he is here."
"And you do not want *Varei* told of his existence?"
"By the One! Did you not hear them in there? They are beside themselves! Show them some- thing out of the ordinary, something that may be held responsible for the things that have happened, and what will they do?"

Kanehar opened her mouth to argue, and shut it again. As a Healer she was aware of the manifestations of hysteria, and there was no denying that it had been present, and spreading, in the Hall behind them. Slowly she extended a hand, palm upward, towards Brendan.
"I am honoured beyond the telling to meet with you, Starborn Kelti," she said steadily. "My name is Kanehar eré Seleti, and my life is at your service."
"Pleased to meet you," responded Brendan, getting to his feet. He put his hand cautiously forward to touch the Skair's, unsure whether Skaira shook hands as humans did. It seemed that they did not, for as soon as their fingers met she withdrew her hand. She cast a single intensely curious glance over him, then became practical.
"You are right, Lidan. We have to hide him, at least until they have settled down a little. When – no, the questions can wait. Come, we will go to my house. We are fortunate that I have it to myself at the moment, there are no patients there."
"But where is – no, I had forgotten. She must have gone to the Training School this summer. Has there been word from there? Do you think the cubs will be safe?"
"Who can tell?" the Healer stared briefly into the distance, her face drawn as she thought of her cub Falair, many miles away with the other youngsters. "As safe as anywhere here. We have received no word, so I must hope they are well, at least for the present. Varei sent a Speaking Stone ordering the teachers to take them to the best hiding places they can find. In such times, what else could she do?" She sighed. "Now, we had best hurry. They will not stay in there forever, and Kelti must be hidden before even one emerges. Carry him there if you can – the less scent we leave around here, the better." And as soon as Lidan had taken Brendan on to her back, where he sat uncomfortably aware of the ridges of her spine, and trying to prevent his weary legs from touching the ground on either side of her, Kanehar moved forward to where he had been sitting and sprayed urine there.

Luckily Kanehar's house was quite close – it was quite a large one, as it acted as the infirmary when there were sick or injured Skaira to care for. No one had come out of the Hall before they reached it. Kanehar went in first to check that the coast was still clear; signalled that it was safe; Lidan carried Brendan within, whirled and shut the door. Then she sighed with relief and signed to him to get off.

"I don't believe this." Brendan dismounted thankfully and sank to the floor with a groan. –"What's gone wrong? Why am I not safe now?"

"Our world is in turmoil, Starborn. Indeed and indeed, I am sorry that you have had so poor a welcome." The Healer was going around the room releasing the ties that held the single simple blue drapes aside from the windows. The light dimmed, but they were now safe from being seen by anyone passing outside. "We have just received news which has set everyone by the tail, and it will take a while for many to come to their senses. When they have calmed down it will be much safer to reveal you to them." "But what have I done?" he asked in bewilderment. "Why would they take it out on me?"

"You have not *done* anything. At this moment, what you *are* is all they will see. A stranger. A threat. Something on which to vent their fear and anger. Alas, even Skaira are fallible." She bowed her head. "There have been terrible events in the last few days. Our Princess has been kidnapped, her retinue murdered. The Venel Emperor has been assassinated and his children slain. Lidan has spoken of even Manyei slaughtered, but doubtless you know more of that than I. Events so terrible have not happened since Skaira came into being. It has thrown us all into confusion. Forgive us. Until they have had time to come to terms with it, they will be dangerous to themselves and to others. I would not have you endangered needlessly by those who would be your defenders if they were in their right senses."

"Kanehar is right," said Lidan wearily. "You did not see them, Kelti, and I am glad. It was not a creditable sight. But at least I can redeem one promise that I made. Here you can sleep in safety, and Kanehar will provide us with a meal." She turned to the Healer. "We have eaten sparely and on the march since setting out, and Kelti is hungry and tired. I promised him that here we could sleep and eat. Can you find good food, such perhaps as you think suitable for him? He will sleep sounder with a full belly."

"Is there anything that is forbidden?" asked Kanehar, not wishing to innocently break some religious taboo.

"No. Except that I don't eat raw meat." Conflicting emotions were warring within him: relief at being temporarily safe, and a shattering dismay that the refuge had turned out to be as dangerous as what they were fleeing from. But over anything else, he was tired, bone tired. He shuffled over to lean against the wall, too exhausted even to stand up and move to the broad couch beside the table which stood at the centre of the room. He looked around wearily, taking in the simplicity of the furniture – the couch, the table, a wooden structure that he took to be some kind of bookcase – the bare stone floor and unadorned walls. The room's only ornament was a stone vase in a corner with a branch of copper foliage in it. Directly opposite him was a door that he would later learn led to her surgery. Lidan lay down beside him, and after a moment he rolled over to drape his torso over her forequarters, laying his head on her withers. Even the smell of her fur was now reassuringly familiar.

"I am sorry, so sorry," she said softly as Kanehar left the room. "By the Great Goddess, you have not deserved this of us."

"It's not your fault," he yawned. "Perhaps by tomorrow they'll have calmed down."

Privately she felt that he was being optimistic. There were individuals within the Hall quite capable of feeding almost indefinitely upon their own frenzy. Still, he did not know that, and it would be cruel and possibly unnecessary to crush his hopes. A night could indeed change many things.

Kanehar was both observant and quick thinking. She had noticed the stag beside the tree, and her first action was to catch him. His presence would alert others, and the Starborn's scent was very plain on the saddle. There was a stable attached to the infirmary, and he could be hidden there. Quickly she led him within, put an armful of fodder into the manger, and left him there with a quick glance to see his wounds were in no danger of festering. The saddle with its betraying odours she thrust into a dark corner where it would be least noticeable; the ragged piece of blanket draped across it she dropped across her own withers to take inside. No one was likely to look into the stable, and if they did she could always say she had found him straying riderless; this was technically true enough. Safety taken care of, her guests needed food. She foraged quickly. Within ten minutes she was back in her house, laden with plates and bowls. A sack strapped to her back proved to contain several loaves of a substance very like bread; a jar under one elbow contained what was unmistakably wine, what would have been a rosé on Earth, scented faintly with honey. One of the bowls contained a couple of steaks – cold, but cooked (there had been Venel visitors expected that day, but it was perhaps not surprising that they had never materialised), and another was full of some kind of chopped vegetable mixture. Another bowl was full of raw meat, and this she handed to Lidan, who began eating it rather more daintily than she ordinarily would have done. Brendan took one of the steaks, tore a couple of wedges out of the bread, and began munching his way into the most inelegant sandwich he had ever made in his life. It tasted like manna from heaven.

Perhaps half an hour later, the two Skaira stood looking down at the soundly slumbering form of their visitor. He looked absurdly small in the fur-strewn expanse of Kanehar's bed.

"I am so full of curiosity I could burst," the Healer admitted with a faint smile, "but I think you are almost wearier than he. Sleep soundly, Lidan. I shall be downstairs, and nothing will move in the night but I shall hear it."

"Tomorrow morning I shall tell you all," said her friend, yawning cavernously. "But it is so good to know I can sleep properly at last. I have had nothing but hunting-sleep since he came."

"Then sleep now, before I have you for a patient." She watched the younger Skair climb into the bed, careful as a mother not to disturb the Starborn. Lidan sank down into the furs with a lack of grace which betrayed her extreme exhaustion, gave a prodigious stretch which extended every claw to its roots, and relaxed with a groan. In a breath or two sleep swallowed her. Kanehar paused for a moment, comparing the different sounds of their breathing. Then she shook her head and padded downstairs, leaving them to their desperately needed rest.

13

"It is almost beyond belief. Still – he is here. That is the final proof." Kanehar looked at Brendan with great respect. "Do you feel better for your rest?" "Much, thanks." He was sitting up in bed eating breakfast. She had brought food up to them about half way through the morning, and her Healer's experience had prompted her to provide a jug for him to empty his bladder into before he ate. He had become attuned to the Skair matter-of-factness about these things, and felt no shyness about doing so; the Healer took it downstairs at once and tipped the contents carefully into a part of the stream where the current ran swiftly – to her sensitive predator's nose the urine had a most distinctive smell and any Skair detecting it would be curious. (Fortunately a short shower the previous evening had disposed of any lingering traces of his presence outside.) That done, she had returned to her guests attacking their meal. Skaira did not wholly share the human attitude that it was impolite to talk and eat at the same time. It fell largely to Lidan to tell Kanehar the tale of Brendan's arrival. She did so honestly, leaving nothing out. He listened quietly, adding a comment when it seemed necessary; it was interesting to hear it told from another viewpoint. He also took the opportunity to compare the ways in which the two Skaira differed from one another. At a guess, there was perhaps ten years' difference between their ages. In size, Lidan was considerably the slighter of the two. Kanehar was very solidly built, broad-shouldered and sturdy. She made Lidan appear almost willowy. Her fur was many shades darker – Lidan's fur and head hair was honey blonde, Kanehar's a deep russet. She emanated calm reliability, sitting there on the floor with her front paws folded and her arms crossed. The tale Lidan told was listened to with deep attention; her eyes widened when she heard of her friend's honouring the Goddess with Brendan on his world, but although there were plainly a thousand questions she would have liked to ask, she did not interrupt.

When the tale was done, she asked permission to examine him. That did make him feel a little shy, but he understood that her curiosity was professional. He had stripped off to get into bed, and now simply pushed down the furs to let her see and do what she would. To take his mind off what she was doing, he lay back and went on eating. Breakfast consisted of more bread, split and spread with honey, and some of the cereal cakes he had had in Lidan's house. This was washed down with large quantities of fruit juice, served with bits of fruit floating in it. Finding early on that Brendan preferred juice chilled, Lidan had touched the bowl and murmured something. His next mouthful had almost frozen the back of his throat. The Skair smiled at his face of astonishment.

Kanehar's examination did not in fact take very long. She touched him occasionally, but this seemed to be only from an interest in the various textures of his body. She questioned him as to the location of his vital organs, and was deeply interested in what he could tell her of their functions. (Medicine on Kerriel was nowhere near as advanced as on Earth, and some of the ideas he put forward were intriguingly novel to her.)

At last: "Well, I have done. I have seen all there is to see without using a knife. And that I think your faithful guardian here would not permit." She patted

his leg, pulled the furs up over him again and leaned back. "Now, Lidan, we must consider what our plans should be. Do you wish to go to Varei now?"
"I do not know." Lidan frowned. "It depends on how much calmer she is. And that depends on what voices have been bawling in her ear since yesterday."
"I think that she should be told about the Manyei, and also that you were attacked close to here yesterday. That is important – where there was one soldier there may be others, and our people should be warned."
"And what of Kelti? Varei has no Thought Power, but there are many around her who have. I do not want his existence revealed prematurely when we are still not sure how they will react to him."
"There is no problem there. I will go to Varei, and tell her that you arrived late last night, exhausted after being attacked. You have told me about the Manyei, but it is my judgement that it would be unwise to question you further at this time. They will not search me for more information. What would I be likely to know?"
Lidan looked at her admiringly. "Very clever. Not an untruth in the whole!"
"Who needs untruths? The truth is the best camouflage one can have, if used properly. Now, I suggest that you finish your meal and get some more rest. I will go to Varei and tell her what she needs to know." And being a creature habitually sparing with her words, she left the room without further speech and went downstairs to beard the First Priestess in her den. Her intentions were twofold in doing so: not only would she be passing on information that it really was important that Varei should have, but she could use the occasion to find out the current state of the atmosphere around the Complex. For all that she entirely agreed with Lidan's wish to keep the Starborn out of danger, it was not going to be well received if it was discovered that he had been brought in and deliberately hidden from the Temple hierarchy. The sooner his existence was disclosed the better in that respect. Nobody likes to feel that they have been kept in the dark unnecessarily, and when they had calmed down the senior Skaira would be sensitive to even an unspoken suggestion that they might not have been completely responsible for their actions had they seen him when he first arrived.

There was a silence when she had gone. Mostly this was because both of her guests were still finishing their breakfast, but both of them had much to think about as well. Last night Lidan had been too stunned with tiredness to feel the real impact of the loss of her mother; it came home to her now with full force. She grieved for Gisar, and for the dreadful manner of her death. True, they had never shared much of a viewpoint, but all creatures have only one mother to lose. And to lose her in such a way! If the defence of Thaskan had been a success, at least Gisar would have died accomplishing something worthwhile. But her death, and all those others, had been for nothing. For *nothing.* And why, why, why? What had any would-be Emperor have to gain from alienating the most feared and respected wielders of sorcery on his world, and earning himself the incalculable wrath of Shieih? Such pain, such misery, and for what? *For what?*

Brendan, meanwhile, had no idea that the killing at Weruavwe had had any such deep personal significance for Lidan. He was suffering something of a nervous reaction that was affecting his ability to think clearly about anything. The emotional seesaw of the previous day had affected him badly, and he was conscious of a rising anger. Not towards Lidan, nor Kanehar, nor even the other

Skaira who were now, it seemed, a new and unexpected threat to him. He was angry with Shieih who had had him brought here, brought and dumped with a guardian but no instructions. If he was supposed to be saving the world, wasn't it about bloody time somebody told him how he was supposed to do it? All they seemed to be doing at the moment was blundering out of one death trap into another, and the strain on both Lidan and himself was appalling.

Presently, unable to keep silence any longer, he turned to face her. Trying to keep his voice completely neutral, but not succeeding quite as well as he would have liked, he asked, "Have you any idea at all where we go from here?"

Obliged to answer him before she had had time to order her thoughts a little better, she too was unable to control her face and voice completely. He was aghast at the naked grief in her reply. "Shieih have mercy on me, Kelti, I do not know. The world has run mad, and I do not know where to turn. You should have a better guardian than I. I have failed you."

"Good God, no!" He got up quickly on to his knees, and grabbed her by the shoulders. "Don't say that. You've kept me alive. You weren't to know what would happen."

She looked at him, and the amber eyes were pools of tears. "I am sorry, Kelti. I did not mean to burden you with my sorrow. I told you that my mother was at the Palace, in the service of Princess Thaskan. We believe that she was among those slain in the attack."

"Oh, Christ." He dropped his hands momentarily. He hadn't remembered, hadn't made the connection when Kanehar told him the previous day that the Palace had been attacked. He couldn't bring himself to trot out the conventional phrases of sympathy. Of what use was it to say how sorry he was? It wouldn't bring her mother back to life, nor lessen the grief of her loss. "Are you sure?"

"As sure as I need to be. She would not let Thaskan be taken while there was breath in her body." The tears spilled over, and trickled down the blunt nose. "She would not have grudged dying as long as she could have succeeded. But she failed. She died for nothing. And I pray to the Goddess that she never knew."

He couldn't take this, looking at her grief and doing nothing. He leaned forward and put his arms around her. She resisted for a moment, then collapsed against him; she made very little sound in her crying, but the wetness trickled down his neck. He still couldn't make himself trot out any of the trite efforts at consolation that are helplessly resorted to on such occasions; there was nothing to say, and he said nothing. Her arms were around him, and the strength in them was frightening, but he bore the discomfort in silence, smoothing the long blonde hair and trying not to notice how the fur on her ear was tickling his nose.

After perhaps five minutes she pulled away. Her eyes were still wet, the lids reddened, but she was making a visible bid for composure. "So. Weeping for the dead is one thing – but my mother would have wanted vengeance, not tears. I had hoped for reconciliation between us, but it is not to be. As the Goddess wills, we must be reconciled beyond the Endless Ocean. It seems that she and all the others were denied the honourable end that should have been their due – therefore I am more bound than ever to do all I can to bring down the son of Tharnil who was her slayer. And though the One send me better wisdom if my wishes guide my judgement astray, that task I am certain is yours also."

"You know who he was?"
"I know what he is, not yet who he is, but be sure I shall find that out. I called him a son of Tharnil – Tharnil is a place, not a person. It is the Dark World, where the Power I told you of was exiled after he was flung forth from our world. He was chained there so that he might work no more evil, and ever since that day anyone who does his work is called a son of his world. It is a saying, no more."
"Just a saying?" he asked slowly.
"That is all. Why do you ask?"
"I don't know." He stared unseeingly at the wall. "It's just that – I got a cold feeling when you said it."
"You are not ill?" she asked anxiously, touching his forehead with the back of her hand. "You have no fever?"
"It wasn't that sort of cold." That was a stupid thing to say. How many sorts of cold were there? Apart from degrees, cold was cold was cold. Or was it? There wasn't any better way to describe the chill that had come over him when she used the casual phrase; and it hadn't gone away when she explained the term. If anything it had deepened. He crossed himself, much to Lidan's puzzlement. His slightly shamefaced explanation of the act did little to enlighten her, but although she did not say so his feeling the need to make a protective gesture alarmed her. Shieih had not spoken to her, but that did not mean She would not find means to convey information. And why should the Starborn be disturbed by what was in effect only a legend? Were his people perhaps very superstitious about such things?

But – by the One! Tharnil! It was not possible! No, there must be some other explanation. Esdiol of Tharnil had been banished, bound forever to the stuff of his world. He could not have broken the ban, it was not possible.

But suppose – just suppose – that somehow, by some incredible turn of fate, he had managed it? What would he desire for the inhabitants of Kerriel and the Daughters of the Goddess who had exiled him? She shuddered. Shieih would be beyond his reach, but what better vengeance could he have than to destroy the world She cherished?

Impossible! She thought vehemently. He would not dare. Aiyeh and Shieih would destroy him. What they could do once they would do again. Unless, unless – for some reason – they could not. Unless they had to find some other way, to bring in a subject of a world over which neither he nor they had sovereignty. Unless they had to use a Starborn.

Her tears drying unheeded on her ashen face, she stared at Brendan. Did she dare give him any hint of her suspicions? Mother Shieih! He was human, he was mortal and fallible, and she did not want to be right. Had he been brought here to combat a *god?*

She could not tell him. He had a right to know. She still could not tell him. She might be wrong. The whole thing was too incredible for words. It could not possibly be the truth. And yet, and yet –

It fitted.

<u>14</u>

"By the One, I am glad you are here. I was about to send for you." Hargen drew Kanehar quickly inside the First Priestess's house. "I think your skills are needed."

"Varei is ill?" asked the Healer in quick anxiety; that was a complication they did not need. She cast a quick look around, but only the Senior Priestess was within earshot. Praise the Goddess that it was Hargen who had had the initiative to come in search of competent help: if the need was there, she was one of the few whom Kanehar could trust with the truth.

"Not yet," said the other grimly, "but if we can not silence Riyeth for an hour or two it may come to that."

"Oh, by the One!" muttered Kanehar crossly, relaxing. "Could you not have made Riyeth sleep? She must need it."

"By the Stars! Do you think we did not try? Garlah suggested that when she had told her story to everyone she might perhaps be able to find rest – thus, the meeting in Hall. It was a good idea, but it did not work. She is as bad as ever. I have tried to reason with her for three hours. She will not rest, nor allow Varei to rest. And while the First can not sleep her retinue will not either."

That did not sound too promising. Kanehar had hoped that there might have been at least a few strong spirits present who would able to take control of the gathering, and even go some way towards damping down the initial hysteria that Riyeth's news had produced. It seemed that her hopes were unfounded. One of the drawbacks in dealing with telepaths was that when they were upset they tended to broadcast extremely strong emotional thought patterns, often quite without intending to do so. It was doubly unfortunate that the telepath with whom they had to deal in this instance was likely to be totally indifferent to the distress her irresponsible behaviour was causing to those around her. Riyeth was no crueller than the average Skair in ordinary circumstances, but she was volatile at the best of times, and the dreadful experience that she had undergone had sent her completely out of control. It would be difficult, if not impossible, to make her understand that for her own sake as well as everyone else's around her it would be wise to try to calm down.

Her voice was audible even from here, with two closed doors in between. The words were indistinguishable, but Kanehar recognised with some apprehension that the note had not changed, except perhaps for the worse. Called in the previous afternoon to examine and treat Riyeth's wounds, she had felt it wise to leave a strong dose of sedative. It would not have been possible to deceive the patient as to what this was, even if the Healer had wanted to do so, and she had flatly refused to drink any of it. Hargen now confirmed that she still wouldn't take so much as a sip.

"Then I will have to order her to drink it, if all else fails," said Kanehar briskly. "Matters are ill enough without her making them worse."

"You can order her to do anything," Hargen replied with a shrug. "Making her obey you will be the difficult part."

This in itself was an indicator of just how bad the other believed Riyeth's state to be. From very early on, it had been written into Skair law that the orders of a Healer were paramount. Even the First Priestess would have to produce extremely strong reasons for disobeying the professional judgement of a senior Healer such as Kanehar; that Riyeth, who was of comparatively low rank, would be crazed enough to do it was probably the strongest evidence possible of the seriousness of the situation.

"By the One, Hargen, is she sane?"

Another shrug, and an expressive wave of the tail. "She thinks she is."

Listening as the voice from within rose to ever more frenzied heights, Kanehar was increasingly inclined to doubt it. Most certainly it was time and past time that she intervened. There didn't seem to be anyone here capable of imposing order on the chaos, and it was desperately necessary that a full Council be called, calm and orderly enough to consider dispassionately all the events of the past few days and decide what their response should be. The rest of the world needed a lead, and it was surely the responsibility of the First Priestess and her advisers to provide one. Allowing one hysterical voice to override all the others would hardly help matters; but Riyeth's telepathic powers were so strong that unless she could be reasoned with, or silenced in some other way, she was fully capable of paralysing the ability of all of her seniors to make any decision whatsoever.

"You still have the sedative, I take it?"

"Unless she has thrown it away since I came out. I sympathised at first, but after listening to her screeching all night, my sympathy has worn thin. If I had stayed within I might have ended by boxing her ears."

"That might have been the best thing. The Goddess knows if she will not drink the juice I may end up boxing them myself."

Hargen grinned in spite of herself. She had been as shocked as anyone had by the news Riyeth had brought, but she had run out of pity fairly quickly when the overwrought Skair had gone on and on caterwauling about her experience instead of turning to what should be done to amend or avenge matters. It was not hard to imagine what a terrible shock it must have been for a hunter to become the hunted, but at least Riyeth had survived. She, more than anyone else, should be taking the lead in striking back against those who had murdered her fellows and kidnapped her Princess. Instead of which, she was just sitting in there squawking away like a witless fowl, and preventing wiser heads from taking order without her help. Hargen had not been the only one of the Senior Priestesses who had begun to run out of patience, but she doubted that Varei would approve of the ear-boxing programme, and had thought it best to make an exit. She had indeed been on the point of sending for Kanehar, feeling that it was a Healer's province to take control where others were out of their depth; but she would not be displeased if the treatment Kanehar ended up dispensing did include a timely box on the ear. Varei would not be able to object to what a Healer thought necessary, and it would relieve the feelings of many of her retinue who had been obliged to spend a wearisome night enduring Riyeth's raving.

Kanehar pushed through the double doors into the Audience Chamber, and went through it without stopping to exchange more than a nod with the several Skaira there who had not had the resolve to follow Hargen in escaping but had been unable to steel themselves to stay in close proximity to Riyeth. She winced at the sudden increase in volume, and had to pause and take a deep breath before laying her hands on the second set of doors to the First Priestess's personal apartment, and pushing them open.

Her first thought was that it was lunacy that no one had sent for her before matters reached this pass. She had never seen anything like the dreadful creature who reeled around the Chamber, shouting incoherently into the ear of whomever she was closest to at the time. Foam dripped from Riyeth's jaws. Her eyes were rolling in her head. For one terrible instant Kanehar thought that she had literally gone mad, but when she could make the intense effort to block out the frenzied waves of emotion that battered at her, a moment's calmer observation brought her nearer the truth. Riyeth was not insane, but so exhausted that she was no longer capable of feeling exhaustion; her brain could not switch off, but was endlessly reliving the horror at Weruavwe. If she went on like this much longer it was entirely possible that she would simply drop dead. Whatever she was, whatever she had done to others, she did not deserve that. A glance showed the bottle of sedative, disregarded on a table. Kanehar strode to it, picked it up and gestured to Hargen. The two Skaira closed on Riyeth from either side. Without saying anything Hargen took hold of her arms and pinned them to her sides. As she wrenched around, jaws parting for a scream of furious protest, Kanehar thrust the mouth of the bottle between the foam-speckled teeth. Sheer surprise took most of the contents down her throat, more than enough to do what was required. A far stronger concentrate of the *vhi'the* that Lidan had used to calm Brendan, it was very quick acting. The sweetish fumes drifted up her twitching nostrils as she automatically swallowed, and almost at once, even before she had got through her initial burst of abuse of her assailants, her voice started to slur. Her legs wobbled. Several of her more quick-witted fellows sprang forward to help catch her as she began to totter. With an immense effort she got out a few more garbled curses, then pitched forward and was unconscious even before she was carefully lowered to the floor.

The effect was instantaneous. Had tension been registered as heat, the room would have lost fifty degrees in as many seconds. Most of the twenty or so exhausted individuals who had been sitting or miserably prowling around seemed on the verge of collapse themselves. Varei was on her couch, her face grey with strain, and almost fell backwards into the furs and rich cushions there as the tension disintegrated.

Cheering would have been undignified in the circumstances, but there was a muted ripple of sound that carried definite overtones of relief.

"Praise the One!" said Hargen, who was never deterred from saying what she thought by mere considerations of politeness. "Carry her to one of the couches outside, and Kanehar can have her disposed of as she will in due course."

Kanehar opened her mouth to say automatically that Riyeth should be taken to the infirmary to sleep it off, but remembered in time and shut it hastily. The very last thing she wanted was Riyeth waking to find herself sharing quarters with an alien.

"She will be well enough in the room outside," she said. "Someone should keep a watch on her from time to time, but sleep is what she needs most. If she shows signs of stirring before dawn, call me again. She should sleep until full daylight at least, and preferably until tomorrow's dusk. With the Goddess's blessing, she should be more herself when she wakes."

An anonymous voice growled that it would be even better if she was more someone else altogether, and there were several snorts of stifled, weary laughter.
"Peace!" Varei sat up again and made an attempt to re-impose dignity on the gathering. "The Goddess knows Riyeth is not to blame. None of us knows how we would have come through such an ordeal as she has endured."

Several of her juniors looked as if they tactfully refrained from comment. Kanehar followed their example and said nothing, although Hargen grunted. Seizing her opportunity, the Healer stepped up to the First Priestess and made the customary gesture of respect. "I have news, First Priestess," she said formally. "We have had one other come from the outside world, out-lairer Lidan eré Gisar. She has told me two things of significance, which I have to draw to your attention. The first is that at least two villages of Manyei have been attacked in Three Stars; the inhabitants of the first were killed there, those of the second driven away to some fate unknown. The second is that she herself was attacked, by an armed Venel soldier, within the borders of the holy valley. It would surely be wisdom to command that our people do not go out singly, and are careful when they go – and still better, that they should not venture out at all if it may be avoided. We are not so many that we can afford to lose even one of us."

Around her there were gasps of dismay and disbelief.
"Was Lidan badly hurt?" demanded Hargen.
"By the grace of the Goddess, no," replied Kanehar. "But she was exhausted and in shock when she arrived, and I have ordered her to rest. For the time being she needs solitude and quiet, and time to recover from the shock of her mother's death."
"By all means," nodded Varei, who was now recovering herself a little now that Riyeth's overpowering mental presence had been removed. "She may have all the time she needs. Doubtless when she is ready she will come to us."
"Doubtless," agreed Kanehar. "And in the meantime, First Priestess, as the Senior Healer present, I would make a suggestion. Everyone here is tired. It would do no harm for all of you to sleep. If anyone thinks it beyond them, I have sedatives that will help. Tonight or tomorrow it will be possible to call a full Council and consider what we should do, but to do our best in the crisis which has befallen us we should have our minds at their keenest, not half-stunned with tiredness."

A 'suggestion' of this nature did not quite have the force of an order, but Varei was thankful enough to fall in with it. "You speak wisely, Kanehar. We should all return to our houses and rest. I am sure you can provide for those too troubled to sleep."
Looking around at the gathering, every face registering the blankness of exhaustion, the Healer thought that she was extremely unlikely to be besieged by prospective patients; and so it proved. Almost twelve hours of bearing with Riyeth had worn everybody out, and the gathering dissolved with relief. Varei was the most fortunate, being already on her couch. Everyone else made their reverences and stumbled out to the blessed peace of their own houses.
"Praise the One!" said Hargen again as they joined the exodus. "I began to fear that nobody would ever restore sense in there. Do you follow your own advice?"
"It would be sensible. And when am I not sensible?"

“Whenever you have other things to do,” replied the other, looking at her penetratingly. –“Well, I am sensible and I am going to my couch. If you have a need, do not call me. All you will get is abuse.”
“But of course,” said Kanehar, smiling. “You would be the last person I would be likely to call upon.”
“Good.” And understanding one another perfectly well, they parted.

15

Brendan's sleep was uneasy. He was still tired from the previous day, and welcomed the chance to go back to sleep after breakfast; but his dreams were strange and vivid. Some of them were of a vaguely erotic nature, though he never saw a face; some reflected with uncomfortable clarity his sense of being lost. At one point he heard a voice that seemed familiar – perhaps he'd dreamed it before? – but he could not understand the language, though it cried out to him in desperate urgency. And the last, the most horribly real, had a knife in it. This knife was hidden in the darkness and he had to draw it, though the agonising pain as his hand closed around it was almost enough to stop his breathing; but it was necessary, necessary, necessary, and he had to draw it if it killed him in the doing of it…

He woke, and sat up with a jerk. His left hand was icy cold and almost lifeless; he had to literally use his other hand to help bend the fingers of it. He couldn't quite brave himself to put it under his right armpit to warm it up. A suitable alternative was immediately available. Lidan was also asleep, right beside him. She had rolled up among the furs and was as warm as toast. There was no way she would notice his hand if he rested it gently against the thick ruff of fur at her withers, and it would thaw out pleasantly from the heat of her body. Why it should be so cold when the rest of him was quite warm was beyond him; perhaps he'd been sleeping on it and crushed the blood supply out of it for a time. The idea was followed within seconds by the act. There was no difficulty in finding a space between the furs for his hand to slip through, and though she had told him that Skaira in general were fairly resistant to cold, he was still most careful not to touch her flesh. Almost immediately he felt the fur he was seeking. Still careful not to press too hard, he lowered his hand into the ruff to reach the warmth that would be trapped within it.

It would be hard to say which of them exploded with greater violence, or which of them had the greater fright. Lidan catapulted away from him as if she had been shot, uttering almost a scream of terror. Taken completely aback by the magnitude of her reaction, he threw himself backwards and fell off the bed. The scene would have been rich in comedy if there had been anyone present and inclined to laugh at it.

"By the One, what has happened?" Kanehar burst in at the door, expecting to find the occupants under attack from at least half a division of infantry. She found them instead wallowing in furs at either side of the bed, and Lidan looked as though she was in the grip of some nightmare. She was crouched down and glaring madly about for the threat she had sensed so clearly, too overwrought to realise that she was hissing like steam venting from a partly covered pot. Her hackles were erect, her ears flat, her claws bared; her tail lashed with fury. Brendan's attention was now divided between his hand and his head, which had had a bang on the floor and now had an ache in it. His language was intemperate. Happily most of the phrases he used lost much in the translation.

For a moment Kanehar was unsure which of them was more in need of her help. She opted to go to Brendan, and helped him up to a sitting position. It was self-evident where he was hurt, and with gentle fingers she explored the bones of his skull. No breaks, though he might well end up with a bump for a while. She also checked the cut across the back of his shoulder, which the fall had opened up again. "You will live. Now I had best find out what is amiss with the boiling pot over there."

Lidan stared at her with sleep-blurred eyes, a little calmer by now but still hissing intermittently. Kanehar initially ignored her confusion, making a brief but thorough examination to check that no bones had been broken. Lidan watched her as though unsure who she was or what she was doing, but did not protest, though the Healer's warily observant eye noted the claws glinting from her patient's paws again once or twice.

"No, no harm done. Can either of you tell me what happened?"

They both replied at once, and she threw up her hands against the storm of words. "No, not both of you! Kelti, what of you?"

"It was nothing!" he answered in angry bewilderment, climbing back on to the bed. "I woke up with a cold hand – I must've gone to sleep on it. All I did was to put it on her fur to warm it up – I swear I never touched her skin, I knew it might disturb her if I did. And she went completely mad!"

"Sorcery!" Lidan almost screamed. "I felt *sorcery!*"

Kanehar's head whipped round. It was far too serious an allegation to be dismissed out of hand, no matter how far-fetched it might be. "Have a care, Lidan! You were asleep, and maybe dreaming. Kelti touched you – it might be that for all his care you felt the cold. Is there any possibility that that was what happened, that in the confusion of waking you mistook the chill of his hand for that of sorcery?"

"By the One!" She gestured frantically. "You are awake enough – *you* feel him!"

The Healer frowned. It seemed nonsensical. But there was no doubt that Lidan needed to be convinced that there was nothing sinister involved, and there did not seem any simpler way of doing it than by proving her wrong in the way she suggested.

With a sigh, she turned to Brendan. "You will permit it?"

He shrugged. What harm could it do? He held out his hand. It really must have been badly compressed whilst he slept: it was still tingling. He watched Kanehar extend her fingers to touch it; from the casual movement it was obvious that she knew how silly the whole thing was. Next moment she whipped her hand back as if she had touched something red hot, and spat. Lidan also spat. Both Skaira hissed at him, and he recoiled. Their amber eyes were wide with fear and shock.

"Mother of Stars!" gasped Kanehar, controlling herself. "She said you had no magic!"

"God Almighty, I haven't!" he shouted in panic. How did one escape from one's own hand? - "I swear, I haven't! It's nothing to do with me!"

"Then how has it happened? What have you done?"

"I wish to Christ I knew! I was having a dream, and I woke up, and my hand was cold!" He was now holding it at arm's length, being unable to get any further away from it. "It was a dream – just a bloody dream!"

"A *dream!*" Thrusting down her terror, Lidan lunged towards him. Dreams were sacred, a means by which the soul could leave the body and wander where it would. "Kelti, do you remember it – *do you remember it?"*

"Some of it," he replied, backing away from her. "It was all dark, and there was a knife. I had to take it out of the sheath but it hurt my hand, so much I think that was what woke me up. I couldn't stand the pain in my hand any more. That was all. It didn't make any sense. It must have been just that I was lying on it."

"A knife?" said Kanehar sharply. "Did you see it at all?"

"No. I told you it was dark." He looked down at his hand. There was still a blue shade to it, and the memory of the agony of it in the dream was scaldingly vivid. Kanehar exhaled, and the two Skaira looked at one another.

"Is it possible?" whispered Lidan.

"The Goddess knows." She sat down as if exhausted. "But – he has touched something in his dream. Something of dreadful power."

"I never left this room," he said steadily, sure of at least that much. "If I was sleepwalking or something, if I touched anything, it must have been in here."

"You did not sleepwalk, Kelti. I was wakeful downstairs, and rest assured I would have heard you moving. You dreamwalked. Your soul, your spirit, walked. It went ahead of you as your guide, as doubtless the Goddess called it to do." The Healer looked full into his eyes. "I do not know why this should be, but I think that Lidan shares my thought. There is on this world a weapon, a knife, not made by any craftsman who ever breathed its air. A Skair who lived many, many years ago brought it here, though she would not tell from whence it came. She named it Irvathil, the Avenger, and left it in our care, in the safest of safe places, warning that it should never be taken forth or handled for any reason until the Goddess ordained that it be done. And there it has lain ever since."

"Shirah," said Lidan quietly. Reverently she touched the bracelet on her wrist. "Her name was Shirah. She was my *eréai*."

"You are descended from her? Lidan, I never knew that." Kanehar looked at her with wonder. – "So it is appropriate. What Shirah began her *eréan* will finish."

"Perhaps." She was very pale. "We must go to Irvathil, then. Or bring it to him."

"I think – I think," Kanehar spoke very slowly as if she were working the thing out as she went along, or perhaps listening for a silent voice of contradiction, "I *think* that it would be best if he were to take it from its hiding place in person. That seems to be what he did in his dream, and we should not scorn the only guidance we have had."

"Let me get this straight." He had been listening intently, trying to glean what information he could from a conversation that somehow had no longer included him. "You want to take me to where this thing is kept, and make me take it out. I'm sorry. I don't know if I can do it. You don't know what it felt like – it was burning my hand off. And you want me to walk around holding it?"

"You certainly must not walk around with it in plain view – it would be the greatest folly imaginable. And to draw it would place you in the gravest danger. We would not ask – or allow – you to do so." Even the sturdy Kanehar could not repress a shudder at the thought. Although a Healer, she too took her turn in caring for the Shrine on Vanreil. Most of the adult Skaira in the Complex did so, and had to handle the case in which Irvathil the Avenger was stored as part of their duties. It had to be kept reverently clean. Nevertheless, although neither a Priestess nor a telepath even she had been able to sense something of the dark force within, and if she had ever been even slightly tempted to disobey the stern injunction never to open the case, that faint emanation of malevolence would have cured her curiosity completely. The thought of the innocent Starborn being exposed to whatever would be released with the drawn weapon itself was enough to make her blood run cold.

"Then if I can't use it, what's the point in me having it at all?" he demanded. The fact that he wouldn't be expected to handle the thing was a relief, but at the same time he felt illogically insulted, as though they were treating him like a child forbidden to touch an adult weapon. He couldn't help flinching slightly when Lidan leaned forward and touched his hand: it had been nearly forgotten in the heat of the discussion, but although it had regained its normal colour she could still feel the faint cold tingle of sorcery clinging to it.

"I think, I believe, the pain was a warning," she said softly. "In truth, I do not know what would happen if Irvathil was drawn. I do not want to find out, and indeed I would rather leave that dreadful thing where it has lain these many years, and keep you far from it in safety. But if it is meant for you there will be a safe path through the danger. There is a reason, and we will find it. Shieih will guide us. I swear it."

He made a wry face, but said nothing, massaging his hand and flexing his fingers. It felt normal again, but the memory was still horribly real; and he couldn't quite dismiss the evident fear the Skaira felt for the weapon with which his fate now seemed somehow to have become entangled.

"Now we must certainly tell Varei," remarked Kanehar. "If he is to be taken to the Shrine, she will have to know. And then the uproar will really begin."

It was natural that Brendan did not understand what she meant by this phrase, but Lidan grimaced. It would have been bad enough revealing the presence of an alien in their midst. To have to compound the shock by saying that he had to enter the Holy of Holies, which no male had seen and lived to tell of since it was revealed to the very first First Priestess of the Skaira, would well and truly set the gathering by the tail. Without receiving a direct command from the Goddess, it was quite possible that Starborn or no, well over half of the assembly would flatly forbid him to set foot in the place; and if the essentially peace-loving Varei found from somewhere sufficient courage to overrule them it was hard to imagine what would follow. Strictly speaking, the rule of obedience to the First Priestess should silence the opposition: but what the situation might become if many felt – as they undoubtedly would – that the act Varei was sanctioning was the blackest sacrilege imaginable, was fraught with dreadful possibilities. Any Skair would defend the Shrine with her life against defilement. Could it, would it come to the point where a sizeable body of honest dissenters felt the need to hold it with bloodshed against their own sisters? The nature and location of the Shrine made it eminently defensible. It could be held long against attack by only a handful of defenders; this was something that had seemed vital all those years ago, when the newly-created Skaira had still reeled from the destruction of the Temple of Shieih in Thervanil, the holiest place of worship in the world at that time. And each costly minute wasted, each costlier life needlessly lost, was another gain for whoever or whatever was the true enemy, who could ask for nothing better than that his foes should kill each other.

At last: "*Must* Varei know?" asked Lidan quietly.

Kanehar shot her a considering glance. "You know what you are suggesting, and what we would risk. You also know the difficulties involved. It is one thing for us, but quite another for Kelti. Found in our company, in an unsanctioned visit to the Shrine – he would not live to tell of it. There would be no chance to tell our story, no time to offer reasons or excuses. We would all die."

"We will all die, soon or late. Our need is urgent. To place the matter before Varei is to place it before the Council. To leave it to their judgement is to put our errand at risk. There are many – too many – who would want him kept from the Shrine. I can name you a dozen in a breath who would forbid him to touch Irvathil. Dare we put our duty, our destiny, in hazard because we were afraid to risk our lives?"

"I am not afraid," said the Healer drily, "but trying to choose the surest way to achieve what we desire. I do not see that the most dangerous way is necessarily the best – perhaps I have had more experience than you of sewing back together the results of taking risks. And besides, this does involve one other. I think that Kelti has a right to voice an opinion: it is his life, also, that you would risk."

Aware that Brendan would not understand the situation to which they were referring, she explained it to him in as few sentences as clarity permitted. He listened closely, asking whatever questions seemed pertinent. When the explanation was done, he sat quietly for a few minutes, thinking it over. The alternatives were finely balanced.

He found it easy to believe that a religious hierarchy charged with the sole care of a deeply valued centre of worship would contain individuals to whom the idea of any possible departure from the 'status quo' would be unthinkable. It was less easy to imagine that someone with supposedly supreme authority would not have the power to overrule resistance – it was like envisioning the Vatican College of Cardinals successfully rebelling against the Pope. However, given that the circumstances were exceptional, the bone of contention a serious one and the opposition passionately sincere, it wasn't too hard to understand Lidan's suggestion that it would be the wiser course to avoid the risk of asking permission and not receiving it. For there was no saying that Varei would be on their side anyway; and if she was not, there would be no chance whatsoever of getting into the Shrine and taking the relic stored there. And on that rock – unless there was some miraculous intervention, for which so far there seemed little reason to hope – their enterprise would founder completely.

After a while he looked up at the silently waiting Skaira. "Assuming I have the vote – and assuming I said go for Lidan's idea – just how difficult would it be to get us up to the Shrine and down again without being found out?"

"Very difficult," Lidan admitted heavily. "It is not that so many go, but there are always one or two in attendance. We would need the connivance of at least one Senior Priestess, and how to go about obtaining that, I have not the faintest idea."

Kanehar started to smile. "Do not be uneasy on that score. If that is the wish of both of you, I may be able to help you there."

* * *

Late on in the day Kanehar had brought their prospective co-conspirator to the house and introduced her. In some ways, although he would have been hard pressed to say exactly how, Brendan had found Hargen very much the most intimidating of the three. She was not as solid as Kanehar, though taller than either her or Lidan, but she had a reserve, almost a stateliness, that the others lacked. As a Senior Priestess she carried an unconscious air of authority, but beyond that was a sense of what he could only describe to himself as 'otherness'. All Skaira, by Lidan's account, had some command of sorcery. With Hargen he could almost have felt it without needing to be told. Her colouring was striking: hair and fur were a bright auburn, almost the shade of a tiger's, while the fur of her ruff and underbelly was creamy. She had heard most of the tale from the Healer before she arrived, so he did not see her in the first moments of surprise, but when finally introduced to him she had looked far less at his body than at his eyes, and he found her intense gaze more than a little alarming. The temptation to break eye contact was very strong, but he resisted it, though with her more than with either of the others he was immediately aware that he was dealing with a dangerous predator. She too had some degree of telepathic power, and he sensed that should she choose to use it he would have no defence against her whatsoever. And yet, she had not been unfriendly. Once released from her summing stare he was accepted as part of the group, and from then on she treated him as an equal, listening gravely whenever he had anything to say.

As the day waned, Kanehar brought wine and bread for them all, while Lidan explained quietly to their Starborn guest that this was an ancient custom that had sacred meaning. It was the first meal that Brendan had eaten seated at a table since leaving Earth, and he was self-conscious about it, especially once aware that the occasion had some religious significance; he had no knowledge of this world's polite table manners. There was a dreamlike quality about it all, with the late afternoon light filtering through the drawn curtains and the three part-leonine alien creatures calmly occupying the other three sides of the table. Hargen had brought in an armful of blossoms from one of the flowering trees outside and dropped clusters of them all around, so that the air was full of the scent of them. The bread was sweet and crumbly, almost like cake, with thin slices of fruit served alongside it. The plates were of wood, as were the goblets into which Kanehar poured the wine, a bluish liquid that was faintly fragrant and startlingly sparkly on the tongue. Lulled by the sense of relaxation and security, Brendan studied his three companions. The temptation was there to imagine them in a human environment; it was not hard to envisage them as cats. He smiled at the thought. Lidan, slender and intense… she would be the sort of cat who sat upright on the hearthrug of an evening, watching pictures in the flames in the hearth. Kanehar – well, even as a Skair she exuded a certain cosiness. Given an accommodating lap, the Kanehar-cat would be purring in it. Hargen, though – Hargen would be a creature of the night, a ferocity in the shadows, a sorcerer's familiar.

Unaware of his wandering imagination, towards the end of the meal Hargen produced what was unmistakably a musical instrument, something that resembled a harp but was made in two separate sections, designed to be played with both hands and one paw. Brendan watched in real fascination as she quickly checked the tuning of it and played a couple of gentle arpeggios. The great claws of her right forepaw moved with astonishing delicacy on the thin silver strings of the bottom section while her left curled around the base to hold it steady. She did not sing, but as the tune rippled out into the room all three Skaira joined in; the sound they made was not quite a hum and not quite a purr. He could neither follow the tune nor remember it clearly afterwards, though for many hours he could hear odd phrases from it wandering through his thoughts.

Afterwards it was the time for prayer, and though in ordinary circumstances no man would have been allowed to witness this ritual in its full form, by tacit consent they allowed Brendan the great privilege of doing so. They washed their hands and faces beforehand in herb-scented water, and tied an identical broad band of blue velvet embroidered with silver across their foreheads, leaving the loose ends fluttering across their unbound hair. Then they lined up side by side, facing the Holy Mountain, and began the ritual.

As a dancer himself, Brendan watched what followed with the deepest interest. He had found it hard to imagine Skaira dancing, but when they began the stylised movements that to them were an integral part of prayer, he could not help but be stirred by the incredible grace of them in motion. It was not quite a dance as he understood dancing, but there was something of heavy rhythm about the complex and flowing motions that accompanied the low chant that he could not describe in any other way. He did not know what they meant, but he had no doubt that each was deeply meaningful. The dancers' faces were inhuman and fierce, but their eyes shone with such joy that he felt almost an intruder for witnessing it. On the first day of his enforced visit, Lidan had related the strange, perhaps mythical story of how Skaira had lost the male half of their sexuality, and had said that they had been compensated for the loss; at the time he had wondered inwardly what could possibly compensate for such a deprivation. Now, seeing that inexpressible rapture in the luminous amber eyes, he was answered.

16

'To be used for no evil, and to harm no creature, and to uphold the Law: the sword of peace, the rod of pity, and the judgement of a gentle understanding.'

The phrases drifted through Princess Thaskan's mind like silver fish in a vast dark ocean, hardly seen and no longer comprehended. Vaguely she was aware that they mattered, that they mattered dreadfully. How, or why, was beyond her. Even her own identity was hard to remember. Occasionally she could still catch hold of reality, but the effort required now was appalling, and the reward hardly worth the expenditure. Even the pain had retreated into dull familiarity, almost to the point where she would miss it if it were no longer there. Only movement brought on a renewal of the excruciating agony in her stiffened joints, and she had learned not to move. In the past day or two her strength had begun leaking away in what in her lucid moments she had known for the initial stages of blood-deprivation. If it went on for another three or four days she would die of it. Perhaps whoever was responsible for her plight was unaware of this: she could only hope so. Death had no fears for her. Only a continuation of her inexplicable imprisonment and torture had the power to frighten her now.

Even time had begun to lose its reality. At first, tormented as much by her own powerlessness and rage as by her physical suffering, she had lived through a year in every hour. Pain had prevented sleep for a long time, but eventually she had lapsed into some kind of insensibility more resembling coma than sleep. Now this was overtaking her more and more often and for longer and longer periods. There had been a time when she had fought it, had known that it was a forerunner of the endless sleep, and it was too early for that: her people needed her, and she must not abandon them. Now, severely weakened and close to despair, she welcomed it, hoped on each occasion when the darkness began to gather that this was the time when it would not draw back on this side of the Endless Ocean. Shieih had deserted her. She was abandoned in the midst of her enemies, and it seemed that only in death was she to find out why.

Sometimes she still dreamed, though not often: and they were dreadful dreams, when she relived the attack on Weruavwe. It had come out of nowhere. The first thing she had known was the shriek of the wounded guard at the outer doors. After that it had been utter horror and confusion, the Palace erupting into a battlefield shot through with the *whitt-whitt-whitt* of arrows. There were many bowmen, far too many and far too skilled. Her people were not ready, not massed, and in too many cases not armed. Though she knew that the first instinct of every one of her subjects had been to come to her, risking their lives without a thought of flight, the attack had been planned with deadly precision. Barely half a score had made it into her chamber and turned to defend her, roaring curses and defiance. One by one they had fallen, pierced by a rain of arrows. Sureh had had a cub at foot, had defended the baby with her body; the cub's screams had cut through the uproar, shrill and terrified, until an arrow had taken her in the throat. At that the already mortally wounded Sureh had gone completely mad. With Gisar and a couple of others she had hurled herself forward, uselessly trying to reach their attackers: only valiant Lehar had done so, and she was so wounded that she died as she struck at the first enemy. Nanla had actually slipped on the pools of blood on the floor and broken her back: the crack had been audible even through all the chaos. They had shot her as she died. With all her people dead or dying about her, Thaskan had stood up as straight as possible for the wounds she herself had sustained. A couple of stray shots had taken her, one high in the shoulder and one in the side. Both were only flesh wounds, she had taken worse in making kills; and they should not prevent her from meeting her death with dignity. There had been a long, terrible pause. Why did they not shoot and make an end of her?

She had been utterly incredulous when they had advanced on her with ropes. It would have been very easy to kill at least four of them, and she was tempted to do so: it would have been some inadequate vengeance for her slaughtered subjects. *It is not justice to punish tools when the hand that moves them goes unscathed.* She had not wanted to heed the thought. The corpses piled around and in front of her cried out for her to avenge them; the incandescent red rage in her breast craved for the sight of her claws rending Venel flesh, for the taste of their blood running in her mouth. But would even her dead subjects want injustice heaped upon injustice? A Princess could not lay aside one of the most important lessons she had been taught, just for the sake of relieving her feelings by killing something.

It had been the hardest thing she had ever done, standing quietly while they took her prisoner. Her muscles had shuddered and jerked with the control she had had to exert over them. One of the men who had tied her had passed some comment in his own language that betrayed the depth of his misunderstanding of that involuntary shivering. The officer to whom he made it had obviously been wiser than he; the jest had been rewarded with a backhanded blow across the face that had felled him to the floor. Now, she did not know whether she could have submitted so tamely if she had understood with what barbarity she would be treated once a captive. It was obvious why they had gagged her: they feared her sorcery. It had not occurred to her that they would not untie her, not feed her, not allow her to stand and stretch the stiffness out of her cramped limbs occasionally, not even allow her the dignity of voiding her body wastes without soiling herself. Nor that she would be left to run half crazed with wondering why the attack had been carried out in the first place, and what was happening elsewhere. Nobody told her anything. Nobody even spoke to her. The officer who had evidently been in command of the attack had not been with the detachment when it left Weruavwe. If she had been able to ask questions, it was unlikely that they would have been answered. Her years of rule had given her some ability to interpret the body language of all the races of Kerriel, and close observation of the soldiers who held her prisoner and now escorted her south to Thervanil convinced her that that they were deeply uncomfortable in her presence, for all that they carried out their orders meticulously. They had had to do what they had done, but they did not like it. They certainly did not ever meet the eyes of the prisoner they had taken.

Then, at the end of that nightmare journey, they had brought her into the city, and into the Temple of Aiyeh. This in itself was blasphemy. Skaira were not permitted to enter it, even if they had wished to do so. In ordinary circumstances it would have been an act of incredible disrespect for any Skair even to enter the courtyard. For the Princess to be taken into the very heart of the building – she had half expected the stones to crumble around her. It had been there, however, that she had encountered the one tiny act of kindness that had given her something to cling to in the miasma of horror that her world had become. He had been a total stranger, and young, despite the leather wristbands that had proclaimed his position of authority. And yet he had had the compassion to give her water and clean her face, and she had sensed his revulsion at her plight. It was not clear how, or even if, his sympathy might be turned to account. It might well be that he would not want to help her even if the opportunity offered, and the Goddess knew that there seemed little enough chance of that. But Thaskan did not think so. As a *Lathaichan,* a warlord, he had to have courage, and he had already shown that he had compassion. It was not much of a hope, but it was better than none at all.

But the hours and the days had passed, and nothing happened except for the stealthy worsening of Thaskan's condition. It seemed a long time ago now that she had had the energy to care. Now care and hope alike had slid into the abyss of despair, and she waited only to die. Once or twice a day they brought her water, though never enough. No food was offered. She had gone past the cruelty of hunger, and was now light-headed in her periods of wakefulness. Her guards had reported to someone out of her view that she had begun to laugh occasionally: that of course was a lie, for what under the stars had she to laugh about?

* * *

Teho'evan turned from the door with a beating heart. He had dreaded this order, and hoped against hope that it might come. Why it had come his way, he had no way of knowing; what he intended to do now that it had, he had even less idea. His hands shook as he buckled his scabbard into place at his belt. He had spent half the morning sharpening his sword: it had an edge on it now that could cut the north wind. The desperation in his breast warned his head that his heart was being tempted to involve him in something extremely dangerous, if not outright suicidal. Henanei said nothing, but watched him with wide anxious eyes. She had been quiet ever since she had learned about the Manyei, but it had not been a quiet of withdrawal so much as one of bewilderment. She had not turned from him in their bed, but once or twice he had caught her crying. There was something on her mind, but she was not yet ready to reveal it, and he had not pressed her. If she were considering divorce (and he would not blame her if this were the case), he was in no hurry to be told of it. Perhaps this was one of the factors behind the recklessness he contemplated. It might well be better to die attempting to redeem his shame than to live with only his guilt for company in a world he no longer recognised.

He was relieved beyond words to find Keri'khai in charge of the squadron. It should not have been a surprise. His lieutenant had always found ways and means of being where he was most wanted, even when least expected. And yet, for a moment he hesitated over whether to order him back to the barracks – a pretext would not have been hard to find. His own ruin was one thing, but why should he expect Keri to share it? The man had a wife and child. There was enough on his conscience already without burdening it with the grief of a widow and an orphan.

He must certainly be a weakling, for he said nothing as he swung up into Freharehen's saddle. The news had gone through the city an hour ago that ex-Empress Mia'naan had begun labour. It had been no surprise that Emperor-Elect Stiv'aran should send out for reinforcements. The delivery of the egg could well act as a trigger to any discontent thus far dormant, and it would certainly be wise to have the brooding mother heavily guarded. The egg contained the legitimate heir (or heiress) of the Horned Throne, and it would be the target for every power-seeker in the Empire. From the moment of her delivery Mia'naan would never be alone for a moment, and certainly never allowed to touch her egg without being under the closest observation. In the circumstances, it was even a little surprising that she was to be allowed to brood it at all: true, after birth it was natural for the mother's body temperature to rise slightly to facilitate brooding at the correct temperature, but it was probably as well that there were no brooding queens in the Women's Quarters any longer. Stiv'aran would have had no compunction in secretly removing a less important egg and substituting the one containing the future heir, leaving it to be innocently brooded by a woman who would have no incentive to destroy it.

The squadron clattered through the streets in an orderly fashion, wasting no time in getting to the Palace. There were already extra soldiers on guard there: Stiv'aran was taking no chances. Many nobles had been summoned to witness the delivery of the egg. It was traditional that they each make a mark on the shell when it dried, so that at the Hatching they could be assured that no substitution had taken place. In actual fact there would have been no difficulty in forging such marks but it was still part of the imperial tradition, and the Emperor-Elect would not neglect anything that would establish his claim more firmly. Teho'evan glanced about him as they dismounted in the courtyard. Hard to imagine how he could possibly stage an escape with Mia'naan in the face of such overwhelming odds; she would be weakened from the birth, and they would have the egg itself to look after. However Stiv'aran might have reacted to an abduction attempt on the ex-Empress, there was no way on the green earth that he would allow that egg to be snatched from under his beak. And yet, even as he was forced to acknowledge the near-impossibility of what he contemplated, Teho'evan still could not bring himself to abandon his hopes. Even as he gave orders for the disposition of his squadron – and they had to be tactically justifiable, even though he worsened his own chances thereby – he still hoped against hope for a miracle. It was quite possible that he would be called to attend on the Emperor-Elect as he too witnessed the delivery. In such proximity, perhaps somehow, by some divine gift, some opportunity would present itself.

As they turned to go inside, he found Keri'khai at his shoulder. This in itself was no surprise, but what his lieutenant was unobtrusively holding out to him was. A small image, no larger than the palm of a hand, woven out of the stalks of seeding grasses. Great skill had been used to mould the body, even to suggest the ripple of hair down the back. The lower belly bulged. Around the brow was a tiny wreath of white flowers. "It may be appreciated," Keri'khai said in a completely expressionless voice.

"You are a genius, Keri." He tucked the thing carefully out of sight in a fold of his tunic. It was traditional for small gifts to be given to an expectant mother, and no one would question his wish to join those who would bring the usual good-luck offerings. (The One knew where his lieutenant had obtained the thing, with fear stalking the city as it was, but he always had known which doors to knock on.) He was confident of being able to keep the exact nature of his gift safely secret; he would be expected to disarm himself before entering the delivery room, but apart from that he would not be searched. Who would suspect him of carrying such a thing to the ex-Empress? But he thought she would appreciate it, nevertheless, even if she could not display it openly. In happier times, no delivery room would be found without at least one votive image.

* * *

In the Empress's Quarters, Mia'naan rose from the couch and began walking around the room, watched attentively by the two physicians in attendance. Her labour was at a comparatively early stage, and she was permitted to remain secluded until the delivery was considerably closer. She could hear the low murmur of conversation in the room outside, where the nobles awaited her entrance. Nobody had told her whether Stiv'aran had arrived as yet. She did not want to know, did not want to set eyes on him, certainly did not want to have to go through the ordeal of laying her precious egg under his predatory gaze; but what she wanted and did not want was of no relevance whatsoever, and she knew it. A spasm of pain rippled through her, and she arched her spine and rubbed it. In ordinary circumstances a Skair Healer would have been present, partly to add her supervisory skills to those of the Venel physicians and partly to bring the blessing of the Goddess of blood and birthing on the happy event taking place. The two Healers present had some experience in midwifery, but it was still faintly and absurdly worrying that the tradition of the Skair being present could not be observed. As if there were not greater things for Skaira to worry about at this moment! And as if the child within the egg were not accursed already, doomed either to die in the shards when his sex was discovered, or to be united in her first breath to the murderer of her father.

Outside the sun was setting, and rain clouds were coming up with the dusk. It would have been good to be allowed to walk in the gardens; Sevi'nke would have allowed it, as would any prospective father, agreeing to anything that might even temporarily ease the anxiety and discomfort of labour. She would not even bother requesting it of Stiv'aran. She would not give him the satisfaction of refusing her. For a moment she paused by the window, breathing in the cool air. There was a breeze blowing from the East, from the sunset and the holy woods. For a moment she even thought that she could smell the trees, the cold heights of Vanreil and her sister peaks Hergath and Sikkthi, Frinéini, Olcalgar and Hernarué. Some years ago she had visited the Complex, and had been granted the rare privilege of doing worship at the Shrine itself. The memory had stayed with her, and came vividly now. The great cave with its divine Image, the secrecy and the terror and the holiness. Another memory surfaced. To one side of the cave was a wall, behind which the blind Seer was confined. She rarely spoke, living in communion with the Goddess she adored. But as the Empress had passed, there had been a cry from behind the wall. Phrased in the Old Speech, it had naturally been quite unintelligible to the Venel, but the Skair Priestess accompanying her had looked startled. "The Seer blesses you, Empress," she had said. "She calls down strength upon you." No one had been able to offer any reason why she should have done such a thing; one did not ask the Seer for explanations. Nevertheless she had known that the Skaira had been surprised and awed by the incident. Perhaps only now was that strength needed? 'Mother Shieih, protect me,' she thought as a fresh contraction began. 'Protect this child, who has done nothing but be conceived. Whatever we have done, however You have been offended, forgive us all. Defend us. Be again our Mother.'

At that moment there was a knock on the door. She turned her head: any distraction was welcome at that moment. It was no one of importance, however. Just another of Stiv'aran's minions, doubtless sent to check on her progress. She turned away again as another contraction gathered force: they were coming more swiftly now. Soon she would be moved to the other room and the ordeal would really begin. She did not listen to the brief murmur of voices, and was surprised and annoyed to find the young warlord at her side. He handed her something with remarkable clumsiness, and they both dropped it. Her size made it hard for her to bend, but she automatically tried to do so when she saw what it was. He bent in the same moment, far more gracefully, and retrieved the gift. A *sh'uerin*, a birthing charm, made in an especially lucky shape. She would have her Skair in the birthing room after all, even if it must be kept safely hidden in her robe. Her anger evaporating, she inclined her head in thanks, and he walked out of the room without a second glance. For that moment as they both bent, their heads had been close together. *"You are not friendless, Gracious One."* She had not imagined the almost inaudible whisper; she was not imaginative, and had certainly not expected any message. 'Gracious One'! How long it seemed since anyone had saluted her by that title!

Unobtrusively, feigning a movement of acute discomfort over the next contraction, she looked at the physicians. They were inept spies, and would have betrayed any suspicion they had felt. No sign of it. Their role as Healers was far more real to them than that of Stiv'aran's eyes and ears, and they were far more intent on monitoring her progress than on keeping the watch they should have done on a seemingly harmless visitor on a commonplace errand of kindness.

Feeling something perilously like hope stir in the dull grey torpor of despair that had been growing on her, she glanced again at the window. The sun was setting in wreaths of fiery cloud, and one of these was standing high in the wind-torn sky. It was not hard, in her suddenly winged mood, to make a figure out of the cloud, a figure that raised mighty arms in protection. The next contraction was growing, the pain worsening with each one, but now the pain was almost an irrelevance. *'You are not friendless'*. It might well come to nothing, but merely to know that someone cared was like cool water after almost unendurable thirst. She lowered her head. Nobody in the room could have heard her whisper, but She of Fang and Claw would hear. The physicians were close beside her now. It was kind of them to make it sound as if she had a choice, when in fact she had none. A few moments ago it would have galled her; now she responded almost gaily. Her prayers had been answered. Shieih had not forgotten her. Compared to that, what did anything else matter? She was about to give birth, and deliver the egg that contained the trueborn heir of the Emperor. It was an honour, and she would not allow a triviality such as the presence of one scoundrel to spoil an hour that might well be the greatest of her life. The future was between the paws of the Good Goddess, however black the present might seem.

They were opening the doors. Beyond them was the sudden stir and rustle as the assembly realised that she was about to make an appearance. Mastering the latest surge of pain, she walked forward with a dignity that befitted an Empress.

'You are not friendless'.

17

'At some point,' thought Brendan morosely, staring into the near-darkness, 'I actually *agreed* to this idea.'

It had seemed fairly sensible at the time. Once presented with both sides of the discussion, Hargen had agreed at once with Lidan that it was best not to consult the Council on the question of whether or not he should be taken to the Shrine. (Kanehar looked as if she was still not wholly convinced, but made no further objections.) From the way in which she immediately began discussing ways and means of ensuring that he reach it and leave it again in safety, undetected, it would have been quite easy to imagine that Hargen spent her life plotting. This was not in fact the case, she was a stranger to deception, but hidden beneath the rather forbidding surface was a strong sense of humour. Given that she could accept that it was the wish of the Goddess that the Starborn be taken to the Shrine, she found nothing wrong with making sure he got there as swiftly and safely as possible; and the prospect of spiriting him away under the unsuspecting noses of her sisters appealed to that sense of mischief.

It was her suggestion that the safest way to get Kelti up to the Shrine undetected was to conceal him in a rolled-up hanging. Part of the Shrine was partitioned off with an embroidered tapestry. From time to time this had to be exchanged for another one and taken down to the Complex to be washed and treated with herbs which inhibited the mould that could take hold in the damp atmosphere of the cave. It was time for such an exchange to be made, and there would be no difficulty in getting hold of the replacement one. Hidden in it, the Starborn could be carried up to the Shrine without any danger. The scent of the herb mixture would go far towards masking his scent, unless anyone was interested enough to come up to the tapestry and sniff it; and in view of the fact that most Skaira found the smell rather too strong for their comfort when it had first been treated, this was unlikely. They could even sling it across his stag, taking the animal along for his use afterwards – if anyone questioned where the beast came from, they could simply say he had been found straying and they were putting him to good use. A docile and valuable animal could sometimes be viewed in other lights than simply a tame lunch; and in ordinary circumstances Skaira did not kill domesticated beasts. For one thing, their predatory instincts were honed to respond to things that ran away, and most would have had difficulty in attacking something that simply stood there and looked at them.

Everyone had approved of the idea. Brendan could see flaws, but since these were mostly to do with his comfort during the process, they seemed relatively minor. He considered raising them, then decided not to. After all, the idea was to keep him safe, not necessarily in cushioned bliss. He could put up with the limited discomforts for the brief time it would be necessary to keep him wrapped up and hidden.

Which was how he came to find himself staring at the few visible details of the inside of the tapestry, and wondering how he had ever been crazy enough to agree to this insane idea and condemn himself to the most excruciatingly uncomfortable journey he had ever endured in his life. Never having travelled in the position before, he had never realised how inefficient the body's shock absorbing system is when slung sideways across a moving animal. He had been sparing with the wine that afternoon, and soon found reason to be glad of it. To keep his width as narrow and inconspicuous as possible they had wrapped him with his arms above his head, not down at his sides. Although this was an improvement in that he felt very slightly less pinioned, the unnatural position soon made his shoulders begin to ache, and the blood supply to his arms was a little inadequate. They had been careful to lay him face down across the saddle and had tied the ropes as loosely as possible in the circumstances, but it was still hot, horribly confining and dreadfully uncomfortable. It was fortunate that he had not the acute sense of smell of a Skair, or the strong scent of the tapestry might have brought him close to fainting. He had not expected to feel something close to real panic at his total inability to move, and the proximity of the heavy cloth to his face seemed to obstruct his breathing. The position of his arms helped to provide a little natural space, but it seemed very small, and he gulped at the occasional eddies of air that drifted in. For some moments after they had secured him inside the hanging he had been afraid that he was going to lose control completely and start shouting. Then from somewhere had come the realisation that the fear, if not the physical sensation, was very like stage fright. That he had felt, and conquered, many times. There was a knack to it, a discipline he had had to learn. He shut his eyes, breathing slowly and deeply. Mentally he leaned against the wall of the wings, lifting each foot in turn and pulling it up towards his buttocks, loosening the muscles in his legs. His mind emptied, the sounds from the auditorium diminished. The steps were clear in his memory, imprinted on his brain by hour after hour of pitiless rehearsal. The dance was the thing: the audience was for the time being an irrelevance he must forget. Slowly he grew calmer, his breathing shallower. The music pulsed through his body, the music he loved. So real was it momentarily that he almost opened his eyes to look around for Adrian, poised in his shimmer of white to make his grand entrance to start the show.

The voices broke his illusion – others were speaking, greeting Lidan and asking her questions. Kanehar dismissed them fairly gently, saying that her patient wished to make her evening prayers at the Shrine in gratitude for her safety, and would answer questions when she returned. This was evidently accepted, for the voices retreated. The stag plodded along in silence for some time, while Brendan tried with varying degrees of success to recapture the illusion which had given him a fleeting sense of home, and might help him to ignore the discomforts of this unorthodox method of travel.

"Did Shieih say nothing at all of why he must be brought?" asked Hargen presently, as they began the ascent of the long ravine cut into the side of Vanreil so many years ago.

"No, only that 'only one not of this world can save it'." The Skair exact memory had no difficulty in recalling the phrase precisely. "He had a dreamwalking that took him to the Shrine, as best we can understand it. He himself could only tell that he had drawn a knife from darkness, which caused him great pain in the drawing. But his hand when he awoke was in deep cold from dark sorcery – Kanehar and I both witnessed it. Therefore it seemed to us that what he must do, whatever it may be, must involve Irvathil somehow."

"It is hard to know what one man, even a Starborn, can hope to achieve against what has been let loose on this world." The Priestess stared upwards to where the first hesitant stars were visible. "If we had some knowledge – some *reason* for what has happened! But it is all so senseless. The harder one stares at it, the darker it becomes. There is no fathoming it."

Kanehar said nothing. Lidan padded on for a while in similar silence, wondering how wise it would be for her to share the terrible idea she had had that morning. Was it fair of her to keep her suspicions to herself? Would it not be much better to advance the solution that would fit the situation, even if by so doing she risked it being laughed to scorn? By the One! If only the idea *could* be laughed to scorn. If only it had not begun to seem so dreadfully, horribly likely. If only someone could convince her it was not true.

Hesitantly she began to speak; and to avoid alarming Kelti with what might only be an absurd theory, she did so in the Old Speech which she knew he did not understand. First of all, she admitted that the idea that had come to her was preposterous in itself, but that once conceived she could not dismiss it from her mind. There were objections, seemingly insuperable objections, which she herself had raised. These excepting, the idea made sense. Tharnil had come to Kerriel. In human terminology, Hell had come to Earth.

There was a long silence when she had finished. She was aware that the instinct of both her companions was to reject the idea. Even as she herself had done, they were trying to find an insurmountable flaw in the theory. But also as she herself had been, they were brought up against the unthinkable. It could be true. For what other reason could the bringing of the Starborn have been necessary, and why else could it be needful to arm him with a weapon of indescribable power with a nature as marvellous and mysterious as his own? If he were to combat mortals, he would have needed nothing more than mortal weapons. He had been led in a dreamwalking to Irvathil, the legend in the darkness, even before he knew that such a thing existed. Here, surely, was the clearest indication of the magnitude of the enemy. Handed down from mother to daughter through all the generations of Skaira since its arrival in their world, was the knowledge that Irvathil the Avenger had some part to play in Kerriel's destiny. Could it be that here, now, was the place and the time for that prophecy to be fulfilled? Exactly what part the dark blade had to play, and when, even Shirah had had no way of knowing.

"Mother Shieih! Is it possible?" asked Kanehar at last. "The tales tell clearly that the Dark One was banished, bound to the earth of Tharnil. How could he possibly have broken the ban and returned? Aiyeh and Shieih would never permit it. It could not happen."

"*Something* has happened," said Hargen bleakly. "Someone is at Tharnil's work, and Kelti is to be armed against whoever – whatever – it must be. Irvathil is a mighty argument. Without that, I would have been tempted to dismiss Lidan's idea. But such a weight shifts the entire balance of the evidence. It was brought here for a purpose, and so was he. It may well be that no lesser combination will suffice to save us."

"No, but Hargen! Esdiol! The Dark One himself! Do you honestly believe it possible?"

"Until today I would not have believed *he* was possible," replied the Priestess, nodding towards the stag's precious cargo. "But there he is. Explain it away as you will, there must be a mighty reason behind his coming. And the evidence for what that reason may be is convincing enough for me to say that whoever the evildoer is, he breathes Tharnil's air, even if he does not go by the name of Esdiol."

"By the One!" Kanehar exhaled deeply, shook her head and went to the end of the tapestry nearest to its occupant's head. Switching to the Common Speech, she said softly, "Are you well, Kelti?"

The reply from within was enough to reassure her that he was not in danger of death, though it could hardly have convinced her that he was enjoying life; he was vilely cramped, sweating, felt as if he was half-suffocated and by this time was feeling extremely seasick. So far they had not encountered anyone else in the ravine, but it wound around the side of the mountain in such a way as to make it possible to see only a short way ahead, and the sandy floor meant that a Skair could move on it almost soundlessly. Sympathetic though she was to his plight, they dared not release him yet.

Perhaps ten minutes later they arrived at the second site of worship on the mountain, where a natural outcrop had been extended to form a great platform poised over space, floored and pillared with marble and roofed with sky. Mara-Ilessi, the Place of Seeing, opened on the panorama of Three Stars drenched in the last light of a windy sunset. Across at the far side lay one of its attendant priestesses, sleeping. Hargen frowned. At this time the three priestesses should have been offering the Twilight Salute. Leaving the others to wait at the gateway, she strode across to the errant one, and bent over her to shake her into wakefulness. The others saw her stop suddenly, and stoop to look closer. Then with horrible suddenness, she swerved around and came racing back. Her ears were flat against her head, her hackles bristling; her tail was rigid behind her. Automatically her hand was clawing for the knife that she kept at her belt when hunting, but knives were not worn for worship and she was unarmed. The other two Skaira were hissing in alarm even before she reached them. "Out! Get him out!" she snarled, gesturing at the rolled-up hanging. "The Shrine is under attack!"

"The -?" Kanehar's mouth opened but no sound came out. Not waiting for a response, Hargen began tearing at the knots binding the tapestry. Lidan leaped to her side to steady it as Brendan began to struggle for freedom, too cramped and claustrophobic to bear the confinement a second more than necessary. Between them they got him down safely, but for a few minutes he was totally unable to stand up; his sense of balance was in chaos. He had to kneel, gasping the fresh air into his lungs, and bringing his arms down by degrees as feeling and control returned to them. His internal organs felt as if they had been shaken about so much they would never get back to their proper places, and to begin with he was completely unable to make sense of what was going on. While they waited for him to recover a little, Kanehar went over to the body at the other side of the paving, examined it briefly and stood back with a grim expression. She also looked at certain marks on the edge of the rim, where there was scoring and blood. Not much doubt where the other two priestesses had ended up. The drop beyond was many hundreds of feet high, and the forest below would have hidden their broken bodies without difficulty.

When she returned, Brendan was enough in control of himself to stand, even if it meant leaning against the stag's shoulder. Lidan and Hargen were looking up the continuation of the path that led to the Shrine itself. On their faces were identical expressions of savage intent. Bared teeth glinted.

"We are unarmed," said the Healer quietly. "And we do not know how many there are."

"Not quite," Brendan answered the first objection. He pointed a little groggily to the sword still strapped against the saddle.

Kanehar glanced at it and shook her head. "I am no warrior. I know that Lidan and Hargen are not. And pardon me if I am wrong, but I think that you know little of swordplay. Those things are well in hands that know how to use them, but of little use to the unskilled."

"We are not unarmed." For all that Lidan's voice was low, the ferocity in it was terrible. She lifted a forepaw whose naked claws gleamed in the tawny light of the setting sun. "And there are not many, or the smell would linger more. I have been scenting the floor, and I count six at most."

"Six only, to kill three Skaira?"

"Six archers would be more than enough," interposed Hargen. "I thought that Tarseh yonder had been knifed, but the wounds are too jagged. They shot her, then cut out the arrows when she was dead, saving them for re-use."

"Then all the more reason why we should go back and alert the Complex," said Kanehar shortly. – "Three of us and an indifferent swordsman, against archers? It would be madness."

"We should have one weapon on our side that they have not," answered the Priestess harshly. Her tail was lashing.

"You do not suggest -?"

"No, of course not Irvathil. In any case, they are between it and us. I mean surprise. We are on our home territory, and we know of their existence. They are on foreign ground, and do not know yet that they are discovered." She glared upwards, to where the end of the Way was hidden among the heights. "Besides, I do not want to risk their being allowed to escape whilst our tails are turned. I want them dead."

"I too. I vote that we take them now," spat Lidan.

"And what of Kelti? Will you endanger him too, for the sake of killing?"

"I think Hargen's right," said Brendan unexpectedly. The three Skaira looked at him in surprise; he coloured a little, but went on doggedly. "If they get away they may kill other people. If we can take them by surprise, we've got the best chance of taking them out. Killing them, I mean." He was startled to hear himself saying it. Back on Earth it would have been unthinkable; what he was counselling was murder in all but name. But was it? This was a war, and he was caught up in it. The circumstances didn't exactly allow for niceties of behaviour.

Kanehar sighed. "Then I withdraw my objections. Let us go, but Kelti must go last. I do not doubt his courage, but he should not be in the forefront of a battle."

This was agreed to as no more than wisdom, and with great care the three Skaira led the way up the continuation of the ravine. Brendan had considered whether he would be better riding the stag or on foot, and had decided on the latter. Still aching and nauseous, he was also extremely nervous, and his anxiety was far too likely to communicate itself to the animal and make him hard to control. For the sheer comfort of having a weapon in his hand, he was holding the sword, but the grip was not designed for human fingers and was less comfortable than he would have wished. Now that the die was cast, he wondered if he had gone completely mad to vote for this. What experience had he ever had of killing anything? In his teens he'd gone through a phase of rifle shooting, but he'd never wanted to actually kill anything with it. Once or twice he'd trained the sights on rabbits, but the knowledge that he could have hit them if he'd wanted to had been enough. He'd never pulled the trigger. Now his hands were sweating, his pulse thumping. He could almost feel the hatred emanating from the three Skaira, and was thankful it was not directed at him. 'Adrian' followed him docilely, seeming unaware that anything was wrong.

In almost complete silence, save for the stag's soft hoofbeats, the four completed the journey up the remainder of the ravine. At the very top the path swerved suddenly and the walls gave back to an open space perhaps twenty paces wide. At the far side of this was the open mouth of the entrance to the Shrine, a narrow and unadorned cavemouth that yawned black in the rock face.

Rather than risk discovery, the Skaira had tacitly decided to rush around the corner. If the soldiers were still occupied in the Shrine, no harm would be done: if they were outside it, this would be the best way to take them by surprise. Silently gesturing to Brendan to stay back, they crept up to the last bend. Obeying a mad impulse, he swung stiffly up into the saddle and sat there, the reins wound in his left hand, the sword in his right. Sweat ran down his back. He felt hot and cold and sick. The stag sidled gently, blowing; some sense of tension must now have communicated itself to the animal somehow, for the hairs on its shoulders lifted slightly and its neck arched, bringing the wicked tines of its antlers to the fore. In front of him the Skaira went down on to what he supposed crazily would be termed 'all sixes', their fingertips gently brushing the floor. He heard one of them draw in breath, and then it was expelled in a war cry that echoed around the heights of Vanreil like the avenging scream of Nemesis.

They charged.

18

The six Venelai had indeed come out of the Shrine, and were preparing to mount their stags and make their escape. Their profane business had gone without a hitch, and now their only thought was to get away to safety before dividing the spoils.

Suddenly attacked by three screaming Skaira, the stags had contributed hugely to their riders' downfall by going completely mad with fear. One had gored its rider as he attempted to bring it down from its terrified rearing; another soldier had had one foot in the stirrup and was unable to free it as his mount exploded sideways. He was dragged past Hargen, and made the second casualty as the Skair landed a full-power swipe on the side of his head. The snap of his neck was clearly audible. Kanehar, evidently forgetting her reservations and abandoning her commitment to healing, launched herself full at the foremost of the remaining four, who had somehow got astride his stag and was attempting to control it. Her weight took over both the stag and the rider, and in her rage at the desecration of Vanreil she spared neither of them in the use of her claws and teeth.

Hargen and Lidan were slightly slower in coming to grips with two of the others, and those few seconds allowed the one at the very back to gather his wits. He waited, controlling his plunging beast, until the furious Skaira had attacked his fellows; then he saw an opening and spurred forward frantically, ignoring the bloody chaos around him. The chance of attacking the Shrine and plundering whatever fabulous treasures it contained had been too good to miss, but he had not counted on being discovered, and felt no loyalty to his doomed fellow thieves. He was too intent on escaping to see that the seventh stag in the affray had a rider unknown to him. It was a complete shock when the animal suddenly leaped across his path, and the two stags collided with a clash of antlers. He would have drawn his sword, but he still had hold of the plunder from the Shrine. The flash of steel told him he must drop something or lose all, and with a cry of mingled rage and fear he allowed one cloth-wrapped bundle to fall and groped for his sword. Next instant there was a Skair clawing at his stag's rump and with a shriek the terrified animal plunged forward, ignoring everything but the necessity of escaping the death that sank bloody talons and teeth into its flesh. Had his attacker been experienced enough to take the chance offered, the matter could have been settled there and then; but Brendan had never tried to fight on horseback, was completely unable to aim a single blow without risking injuring his own mount, and did not know that he should have let his stag's rein loose to allow it to drop its head and use the sharpened tines on the other beast's suddenly exposed throat. The robber could hardly believe his good fortune, but was not about to waste it. He dropped into the shelter of the antlers, where nothing but an extremely skilled thrust could reach him, and somehow held on while the two stags shouldered past each other. He had only an instant to get one incredulous glance at the other rider before he was through and free, and able to set spurs into his beast's flanks and make good his escape. Lidan's grip was not sufficient for her to hold on, and she had had to beware of the frantic kicking of the stag's hind hooves as it fought for freedom. She had not been close enough to wrap her forepaws around the legs and bring the animal down, and she wailed in savage frustration and disappointment as she saw her intended victim career around the bend and vanish at a speed that would take him into Three Stars and safety within minutes. Skaira could achieve a very respectable speed at a sprint, but they had nothing like the ability to keep up with a fleeing stag. She could do nothing but watch him go. The remaining riderless animals raced after him.

It was over, and the reaction hit Brendan hard. He leaned forward over the pommel of the saddle, shaking. The sword slipped from his hand and clanged on the paving. He wanted very much to be sick, but swallowed the nausea, unwilling to disgrace himself in front of the Skaira who seemed indifferent to the slaughter they had inflicted. This time he had had a really good view of the Venelai, and they had filled him with horror. For all the leonine strangeness of the Skair face, at least there was some similarity to a human one; and the Manyei were not so dissimilar except for the overlarge eyes and narrower jaw. To see a 'human' intelligence and purpose in what was effectively the face of a bird of prey was inexplicably dreadful to him. He had wanted to turn and run, not draw those great hostile golden eyes on himself; and from where he had found the courage to intercept the one who had managed to break away from the rest, he had no idea. If the soldier had managed to make any sort of attack he could not have hoped to parry the first thrust. That this had not happened was solely due to Lidan, who had killed her victim in time to see the danger and had acted to avert it.

None of the Skaira had taken more than flesh wounds in the fight, but five out of six of the enemy lay sprawled in death. The one who had been gored by his own stag might have had a chance of surviving, but Hargen had knifed him with his own dagger.

"One lost. Tharnil take him!" said the Priestess, scowling. "Bravely tried, Kelti. I am glad you were not hurt."

"No thanks to me." He straightened up and dashed the sweat from his face. "I'm sorry I couldn't stop him."

"I am glad he did not stop you. Imperial troopers, these. Scum!" She spat down at the nearest. – "Well, I suppose we must go into the Shrine and see what has happened there. Not that I need to see, nor even desire to, but it must be done."

Kanehar sighed. "I do not imagine that they will be in need of my services. Yet it would indeed be best to make sure."

"We must go," said Lidan tautly. "We must find out what that offal has taken. And pray that in their haste they did not find what was hidden."

Without further words, the three Skaira headed for the cavemouth. Assuming correctly that they expected him to follow, Brendan dismounted and bent to tie his stag's rein to the nearest solid object, which was unfortunately one of the bodies. It was the closest he had come yet to one of the Venelai, and he was able to take in the details of the dark bronze-coloured armour, the heavy body. The feet were encased in boots, but the lax hands were visible, with their long scaly fingers and claw-like nails. He did not look more closely than he could help at the feathered face whose glazed yellow eyes glared sightlessly at the gathering night. As he stepped back away from it in distaste, he almost tripped over the object which his erstwhile opponent had been forced to let fall. He picked it up, unwrapping some of the bindings in curiosity. It was a small slender case of what looked like black wood, about the length of his forearm and about five inches in width. It was quite light, and a gentle experimental shake produced no sound, so he thought in some disappointment that the contents couldn't be all that valuable. Still, it was something saved out of the losses. He tucked it under his arm and went after the Skaira.

He never had liked confined spaces all that much, and his recent ordeal wrapped in the tapestry had done nothing to improve his feelings for them. It was therefore not easy for him to step after Kanehar's tail as it disappeared into the dimness of the cave. Even his intensified capacity to see in the dark was hard put to make anything out in the narrow passage, which almost immediately began to slope down. Fortunately the flooring was completely even, so that even when the light failed he was able to walk with reasonable confidence, his hands extended to brush the wall on either side of him. Every so often the soft tip of a tail would touch him reassuringly, as the Skaira measured their pace to his.

Perhaps half way down the passage, the darkness ahead began to be relieved by a faint light. Lidan had explained the nature of the Shrine and how it had been revealed to the first First Priestess, who had been led to the Holy Valley shortly after the Skaira had come into being. He was therefore not surprised to hear now the unmistakable pattering of falling water. The passage led through a cavern where an underground stream fell down beside the path. The water was held to be holy, and the rare visitors of any race other than Skaira were expected to bathe in it to purify themselves. Candles were kept burning in the cavern, as they were in the Shrine itself further on. The sound grew louder, and the light stronger, until suddenly the last turn revealed the cave. It was not large, perhaps fifteen feet high and twenty in length. In the wavering candlelight he could see that the path swerved to the right and ran along the edge of a drop into which the waterfall plunged from the crevice high in the left-hand wall. The amount of noise was explained by the fact that a single slab jutted out from the path directly into the waterfall, very evidently put there on purpose to provide a site for the ritual cleansing to take place. The candles were placed on rough ledges on either side of the fall, and in their light the ceaseless cascade of water glittered like a rain of diamonds.

"Wait a minute," said Brendan quietly. The Skaira turned to him in concern, and looked startled to see that he was unfastening the front of his clothing.

"Kelti -," Kanehar began, but Hargen gently motioned her to silence. Watched by the three of them, Brendan stepped out of his boiler suit, leaving the case carefully underneath it, took off his moccasins and walked naked to the edge of the slab. Common sense shouted at him that this was stupid, that there was no time now to observe the proprieties; ignoring it, he looked carefully at the surface of the stone in front of him. The incessant play of the water on it made it hard to guess whether it was slippery or not. There was no moss to make it treacherous, and the dry part underfoot was rough and grainy. He glanced down at the drop on either side of the slab. It was not that deep, five or six feet, but footed with jumbled rocks into which the stream drained away. A slip wouldn't kill him, but it would probably mean a broken ankle. He put a foot forward cautiously, letting his toes get a good grip before he put any weight on it. The cold of the water was so intense that he was hurried into moving forward faster than he'd intended because if he hesitated he probably couldn't have gone through with it. As it hit his body he drew a great involuntary gasp of air, and then his head was in it too and the chill made his senses swim. Steeling himself, he raised his arms to break the flow above him; to the watching Skaira he was a figure of moving stone, haloed in millions upon millions of drops of glittering light. Once the initial shock of cold was mastered, it was intensely exhilarating. Swivelling to let the water run over his flexing muscles in icy ribbons, he even noticed to his surprise that it was having quite a different effect to that usually produced by cold water. This was not surprising to the Skaira. Long ago First Priestess Shirah had referred to the spring as 'the Giver of Gifts', and although she had never explained why this should be so, ever since then it had been understood that its nature was magical. Skaira coming to the Shrine washed their hands in it as a matter of course. They now accepted this manifestation of its power without comment, but it was a measure of how greatly Brendan's outlook had changed that he did not immediately curl up with embarrassment. Instead he stepped calmly out of the water, shook off the excess water from his body and smoothed it from his hair, and got back into his clothes, shrugging off the puzzlement that they did not feel damp and clammy as he would have expected.

Evidently accepting what he had done – was he imagining it, or were their glances approving? – the Skaira led the way into the second half of the passage. The friendly candlelight faded behind them again. A very ancient tradition laid down a precise series of steps, almost like a dance, which should be used down this passage; in their anxiety and haste the three Skaira obviously trusted that the Goddess would understand and forgive them for not using these. After several turns and twists they saw ahead the light from the Shrine, but it was not the usual comfortable glow of votive candles. This flickered and flared, and with it was the smell of burning, overlaying another and more sinister stench.

Not hesitating, for their noses as well as their logic assured them that there were no enemies lying in wait, the three Skaira stepped into the Shrine. After a moment, Brendan followed them. Kanehar went to the body of the Duty Priestess, but as she had expected, there was no help she could give. To their horror, the wall on the left had been broken down; sprawled across the gap was the thin, lifeless form of the Seer, whose bloody claws testified that she had exacted a price for her life. But worst of all, the sight that drew muffled shrieks of disbelief and dismay, was the raised empty hand of the great Image before them. Genshenna the Star of Heaven, the Crown of Shieih, was gone. Incredibly old, older than Skairesse itself, it was the most revered relic in their world; and it had been stolen.

Weeping without even knowing that she was doing so, Lidan darted forward. Her hands scrabbled frantically in the darkness at the foot of the Image, where the cloak fell in folds and the shadows clustered thickly. Again and again she thrust to and fro, but emerged empty-handed and ashen-faced.

"Gone! Mother Shieih, it is gone! The sons of offal have taken Irvathil!"

"Oh, by the One!" Hargen refrained with difficulty from some extremely imaginative cursing. – "There is no help for it. We go in pursuit. And pray to the Goddess that his stag falls lame."

Brendan stood looking about him without saying anything. The light came from the flames where the hanging they had intended to replace lay slashed and burning. There was not much in the Shrine, apart from the huge stone Image at the far side of it, which stood upright in untouchable majesty. If he had thought about it at all he would have expected this to look like a Skair, but it was a strange conglomerate figure, two-legged, composed of features he could recognise as belonging to the three different races of Kerriel. The face was indeed rather more leonine than that of a Skair, its parted jaws glittering with rock crystal teeth. The firelight glinted in the great amber eyes, making them look strangely alive. One taloned hand rested lightly, almost protectively, on her belly, swollen in pregnancy. The other was raised, and cupped as though designed to hold something. It did not take much intelligence to deduce from the anguished stares of the distraught Skaira that whatever this had been it was now missing. Hargen rose on her hind legs to peer vainly and hopelessly into the empty place, and fell back shaking her head. Her face was contorted with misery and rage.

He took out the case from under his arm. It was unlikely that he was going to be that lucky. It didn't look anything like the right size or shape to be held in such a place. For a moment he almost tossed it aside as so much rubbish; then he shrugged, and stepped forward. The soldiers had thought it worth stealing, so maybe it might contain something that someone would be glad to know was not lost after all: some small personal possession of one of the dead Skaira perhaps. He hesitated briefly, not wanting to break in on the mourning of his companions, but even a little bit of good retrieved from catastrophe was better than nothing.

"Lidan – that soldier. You mustn't have noticed, but he dropped this." He held out the case. She turned listlessly, saw it, and stared in disbelief for a second. Then she yelled, a roar of delight that echoed around and around the cave, making the flames waver as they devoured the last threads of the tapestry behind her.

"Irvathil! Oh, by the Good Goddess! Irvathil is safe!"

"*What?*" The other two spun around, and came hurrying to touch the thing as if only thus could they believe in their good fortune. Brendan was suddenly extremely sorry to be holding it: his casual grasp suddenly became fingertip contact, and he was relieved beyond words when Lidan removed it from his hands. She handled it with great reverence but no fear, turning it over and over to make sure it had sustained no damage. He noted that she made no effort to open the small silver catch that secured the case. "Aren't you going to open it?" he asked.

From somewhere out of her emotional turmoil the Skair found a smile. The Starborn's innocence was sometimes astonishing. "There is no need, Kelti. If any of those sons of Tharnil had opened it, they would have learned their error. It is still within." She pressed the case to her forehead with indescribable thankfulness. "Now we must go, and go quickly. Hargen was to have been Duty Priestess for this night, but others may well follow for private prayer as I was supposed to have done. Even if Kelti were not discovered to have been down here – the smell of burning should mask his scent – it would not do for any of us to be caught amongst all this. There would be no explaining it to everyone's satisfaction."

"I think that I should stay," said Kanehar quietly. "The bodies should be taken care of, and the Shrine put to rights. It is not right to leave it thus, as though we knew no more and cared less than those offal above us."
"We may need you, Kanehar." Lidan's voice was almost pleading. This was a development for which she had not been prepared. "I am sure that the Goddess would understand."
"She might. I would not. It is my duty, Lidan." The Healer's reply was gentle but immovable. – "And those who come are entitled to an explanation, once you and the Starborn are safely away."
"She is right, Lidan," said Hargen evenly. "You and I will protect Kelti. If we are not to have the entire Complex on our tails, it will be well to have a voice raised in our defence. And Kanehar can speak for us as well as any."
"Well, if it is thus." She gave in with a sigh. "Now, Kelti, we must go. We have been fortunate this day, and I would not press our fortune too far. Come, we have to go now, and swiftly."
"Had you thought of where?" asked Hargen.
"Wait!" Kanehar lifted a hand. "Do not speak of your plans in my hearing. What I have not heard, I can not be made to reveal."
Lidan nodded. "Yes. That is wise. I will speak with Hargen when we leave."
"If you would heed my counsel, do not stop to talk until you are back in the forest. There is no saying that that vermin who escaped has not been seen, and others may come to investigate. You do not need my counsel to have a care with our Kelti here." She smiled at Brendan. "You will be in my prayers every hour – and I am glad that you understand why I can not go with you, much as it would please me. I should have liked to be in at the kill."
"Who knows who will be where when the hunt is over? I shall look after him for you." She hugged the Healer briefly. Brendan came over for what he knew would probably be his final farewell to the sturdy Skair to whom he owed so much. For all that their acquaintance had been so short, he felt that they had become friends; he would miss her. A hug seemed too familiar, a handshake too formal. He hugged her. She grinned, hugged him back and licked his ear with a rasping tongue. "Live long, little Kelti. Behave yourself."
He grinned back. "Life's too boring when you behave yourself. Ask Lidan."
"You are impertinent, Kelti," said Lidan, colouring vividly but smiling in spite of it. "And Kanehar does not know what you mean."
"Oh, I think I can guess," replied the Healer drily. "Thank the Goddess I am very nearly unshockable. Go now, you three, and have a care that you meet no one on your way back down. Hargen, you should go in front, and if you do encounter anyone tell them that the Shrine has been attacked and they must come with you to fetch help. Then you must use your own ingenuity to rejoin Lidan and Kelti when opportunity offers. Time is not on our side, and I shall not rest easy until I know that you are far from here and safe."

She stood and watched them leave, then turned and went down into the attitude of the deepest reverence before the Image. Her forehead rested on the floor, and for a long time she listened, hearing nothing but her own pulse and the soft sound of her breathing. Her mind went blank, though her soul wept for her poor murdered sisters. They were between the paws of the Good Goddess, safe on the far side of the Endless Ocean. It was those still here, still caught in the toils of mortality, who needed her prayers: most of all Lidan and Hargen and their terrible responsibility, Kelti the Starborn, on a world far from his home and launched on a quest that would test him to limits far beyond anything he could have ever have imagined.

"Have them in your care, Divine One," she whispered. "For my heart misgives me that there will be sorrow enough in this land before the end."

19

It was time.

Stiv'aran looked down at the motionless body of the Skair Princess, and knew that he had very little time left before the decay of her body processes became irreversible. He turned back one of her eyelids, and the eye within had rolled back and did not move. Her breathing was so shallow it hardly moved her ribs. The physician at his elbow radiated anxiety in case even now it was too late to save her: few Healers save Skaira themselves could claim much expertise with Skair physiology.

"Lift her," said the Emperor-Elect shortly. The six soldiers deputed to the task moved forward smartly, took hold of the four corners and the sides of the stretcher, and raised it. They had not realised how thin and light Thaskan had become: it took far less effort than they had expected to move her. The jerk made the Princess's head loll backwards. Dried blood and foam encrusted the leather gag. Her lips had shrunk back as her dehydration worsened, exposing the large canine teeth embedded in the rope. She made a faint sound, but did not move.

The Temple was silent as they carried her through the echoing passageways. It was very early, perhaps an hour before dawn. This was the time when the power of the Night was waning, and the sorcery in the Skair would be at its lowest ebb. Now was the ideal opening for attack, when she was weakest and most vulnerable. Looking down at her as she was carried in front of him, Stiv'aran thought that it would surely take very little to destroy what was left of her true identity. A few breaths only would serve. And then – what a weapon he would have in his hands!

Ever wary for unexpected developments, he had had fully armed and trusted men posted at various points of the way. There was no way to be sure that even now there was no danger of a rescue attempt. The passages were peaceful, however. No stranger materialised. Waiting beside the Inner Shrine, as he had been ordered to do, was the warlord Teho'evan. It had been in Stiv'aran's mind for some days that it would be appropriate to admit this promising young officer into the secret of the Shrine. Today seemed to be a propitious day for doing so. He could assist in this momentous step towards the subjection of the world. It would be merely the start of the rise to power he could expect as a loyal lieutenant of the next Emperor. He was the scion of a great and powerful House, one that carried much weight among the nobility of Kerriel. His family was related to almost every other of note through marriages down succeeding generations. Securing his support, and thereby that of a good proportion of his friends, family, allies and dependants, was a logical precaution for any prospective Emperor. The rewards for such loyalty were there for the taking. Stiv'aran was prepared to be generous: nothing suggested the possibility that Teho'evan was the sort of fool who might bite the hand that fed him.

Unaware of these plans being made for him, Teho'evan watched from behind a mask of impassivity as Thaskan was carried past him. Seeing her now, he was truly astonished she was still alive. Had Stiv'aran had her brought here to inflict the final terrible offence, to have her die in the holy of holies devoted to the

Lord of the Day? By the One, what could Thaskan have done, what could anyone have done to earn such hatred? More mysterious still, what could he hope to accomplish by it? What possible difference could it make where the Princess's spirit took its merciful leave of its suffering shell, when she would fly straight and sure to her Mother's arms no matter what Stiv'aran did to what remained? And what then of her subject Skaira whom her captivity had kept quiescent? They would boil over, and surely there would be no hope of holding them.

He was so busy with these thoughts that at first he did not realise that the Emperor- Elect had signalled to him. He blinked in surprise as he caught the second, slightly more emphatic signal. Stiv'aran wanted him to follow them inside? For what reason could he possibly want him there? He was surrounded by picked men; he could have no need of another, and one whom he hardly knew at that. Still, an order was an order – and who was to say that this was not an answer to prayer? His heart beating suddenly faster, Teho'evan stepped forward and walked smartly after the little group who passed in through the great double doors to the inmost heart of the Temple.

Only the most privileged of those who were not priests were ever allowed within the Inner Shrine, and Teho'evan was conscious that it was an enormous honour to set foot here. His first look around was a shock, however. Though few were admitted, the nature of the shrine was not secret. The prayer room elsewhere in the building was built along the same lines though on a larger scale, made to accommodate hundreds of worshippers. Its walls were of yellow marble, unlike those of the Shrine itself, which were plated in solid gold, eternally reflecting the light of the flame kept burning on the altar in miniature mimicry of the glory of the sun. In all other respects, however, it was a reasonably faithful copy. Having visited it often, Teho'evan naturally expected that the Shrine would be warm and bright, though the windows would of course be shuttered out of reverence for the Night. But there was no flame on the altar here. There was a brazier of sorts on the floor in front of it, its sullen red glow casting a faint light around itself but doing little to pierce the gloom. The walls were all but invisible: it would have been easy to believe that there was a scum on them, if such a thing were not utterly unthinkable. Shadows clung in every corner, and darkness hung like a palpable presence where the radiance of flame should have been, on the altar in the very centre of the room. It was late autumn, so it was not to be expected that the room should be warm; but there was no explanation whatsoever that could account for the dreadful chill in the air. Teho'evan shuddered with the cold, and with more than the cold. There was suddenly a faint sound from on the stretcher in front of him. She could not be aware of where she was: it was not possible. But it came again. Somehow, from some unimagined nadir of existence, Thaskan was dragging the strength to utter the only defiance she had left. She had not the strength to raise her ribs for greater volume. It emerged as hardly more than a breath. But it came again, and went on coming. The Princess was hissing.

Halting directly in front of the altar, Stiv'aran bowed to whatever the darkness on it contained. Then he turned and looked down at her with a faint, indulgent smile. There was awareness, but not enough to save her. He could feel the Presence in the Stone behind him, rising in readiness. In a very few moments those last embers of selfhood would be extinguished, and she would embark on a new life as his tool. One of his subordinates was standing ready with a goblet of fresh warm blood, the drink that would be the first step in bringing back Thaskan to her new existence. He gestured, and the men lifted the stretcher that they had momentarily set down, and carried it forward. They put it down again directly in front of the altar, and retreated. Then he gestured to Teho'evan also to come closer. It would be most appropriate that he and the Skair should share a conversion to the True Faith.

Teho'evan moved forward on legs which he was surprised still obeyed him. Six steps carried him to the side of the brazier, so close to Thaskan that he could have leaned forward and touched her. Inside his head he was praying frantically for protection, but he managed to keep up an unmoved front. He did not know what was happening, but every instinct was screaming of danger. The small soft feathers down the top half of his spine were rigid against the back plate of his armour. Could Stiv'aran have learned of his treasonous leanings? Was this some bizarre punishment?

"Have no fear," the Emperor-Elect's voice came smoothly. "This is an honour, warleader. A token of my appreciation of your loyal service."

He stepped to one side, leaving Teho'evan and Thaskan alone in front of the altar. For some moments nothing happened. The warleader looked down at the Skair, still emitting tiny, feeble hissing sounds. The gold and white hackles were lifting. He could see her bound hands weakly trying to clench, the points of the claws showing. Her eyes were half-open, but the pupils that should have been wide and alert were thin in the cloudy amber. He would never have dreamed that there was this much life still left in her. What was going on? His breath came fast and shallow: he had never been so terrified in his life.

The darkness was growing, moving forward. It was surrounding them, cutting off even the faint light from the shrouded windows. The air had gone stale and flat, and smelled metallic. In front of him, however – surely he was imagining it? There was a strange pale glow beginning. He was not imagining it. It was coming from Thaskan. It swelled and brightened, outlining her body with shimmering purity. He had always known that Skaira were called the Daughters of the Stars; now he saw that core of sorcerous radiance exposed. It was the most welcome thing he had ever seen. If such a thing had been possible, he wanted to lean forward and dive into it, as into cool water in blistering heat. But there was soon a change. The darkness gathered slowly closer. The light wavered, began dimming. Thaskan struggled feebly. Through the gag she cried out, a minute and suffocated sound. Teho'evan glanced around wildly. He was ringed by Stiv'aran's henchmen. Even emaciated as she was, Thaskan was too heavy for him to lift unaided. She cried out again as the darkness ate towards the heart of her brightness.

The despair in the sound was terrible; it cut through the creeping tendrils beginning to coil softly around his brain, and he knew that he had to save her in the only way he could. Before anyone could stop him he took the one step forward that was necessary, drew his sword and bent over the Princess. The blade took her in the throat, a skilful stroke that was deep and smooth so that there should be no need for a second. Her eyes flashed open and met his for a split second, tawny triangles of gratitude; then they rolled and went sightless. The light of her power blazed into unbearable brilliance for an instant and then disappeared as though it had never been. Around him the darkness splintered and recoiled, and the temple vibrated with a soundless scream of rage. Stiv'aran lunged forward, but he was too late: Thaskan was beyond his reach.

With a vicious, unnatural speed and strength he smashed his fist into the side of Teho'evan's head. The warleader was hurled sideways by the blow, his senses spiralling briefly into nowhere; but with him he took the triumph and the horror of what he had done. He hit the floor hard and awkwardly, one arm taking the impact, and the agony of snapping bone jerked him back into consciousness. Before he had fully regained his feet, the Emperor-Elect's men closed in. They tore off his body armour. Boots and fists crashed into his unresisting body, but before he could be beaten to death Stiv'aran intervened. The thugs drew back, allowing their leader to look down on what was left of the felon who had ruined his plans. Teho'evan was not yet quite unconscious. He sprawled on the floor, breathing with difficulty, watching his blood pool in front of his face as it leaked copiously from the cut above one eye. He was going to die in the next few minutes, but he regretted nothing: except perhaps that Henanei would never know what had happened to him. For what seemed a very long time he waited for the beating to start again. Above him and around him there was silence. Stiv'aran's gaze was one of unspeakable, freezing malevolence.

"No," said the Emperor-Elect at last. "Nothing so quick and easy for you, traitor. I'll make you wait until something suitable is devised, something that will make all men understand the price of treason. I'll make you pray for death, but it won't come for you until the agony has made you less than an animal. And your wife will watch every second of it. After which, she too will die, and there'll be an end of your House for ever."

Teho'evan's head moved slightly. He should have foreseen this. He should have arranged for Henanei. 'Mother Shieih, protect her,' he prayed desperately as his senses started to whirl from loss of blood. 'I've done all I could for Your Daughter. Protect my wife…'

Stiv'aran watched the consciousness fade from the golden eyes, the nictitating membrane come up. His fury had congealed into ice. There were still many possibilities to explore, even though this one had been so unexpectedly closed against him. The warlord could wait, chained in the foetid cell Thaskan had occupied, until the appropriate punishment had been decided upon. There was no hurry. The anticipation of what was to come would be one more refinement upon his suffering, and Stiv'aran was in no hurry to put an end to it.

At his gesture, his henchmen tipped Thaskan's stiffening body off the stretcher without ceremony, and bundled Teho'evan on to it in her stead. The orders were brief. They marched off to obey, and the Emperor-Elect watched them go. He spared one bitter glance for Thaskan, whose face now bore the serenity of her invulnerability, despite the disfigurement of the gag that was still in place. It would not do to leave that offal here to stink. He would have to make arrangements to get rid of it – but secretly. As long as the other Skaira thought she was still alive, they would not move against him. And who was to tell them?

He had to have leisure to think. He needed to rearrange his plans, and he would take the uttermost pleasure in devising for Teho'evan a punishment that would live in men's minds as long as tales of suffering were told. When he was calmer, and had had all the blood cleaned up off the floor, he would come back to the Temple. It would not be reverent to commune with the Other with his mind in such turmoil. He bowed shortly to the Stone and strode out of the room.

His mind a black maelstrom of rage and disappointment, Esdiol watched him go.

20

"Wake up, Lady! Quickly!"

The fog of heavy sleep was slow to clear from Henanei's brain at first. When the hissing whisper came again, however, she realised with a shock of horror that there was a total stranger in her bedroom. With a muffled shriek she jerked backwards, scattering the cushions among which she had been sleeping. Her husband was absent, on some business for the Emperor-Elect at the Temple. And here was some intruder in their house, in her very room, and what could he possibly want with her?

She was not long in finding out, for the half-seen figure thrust a bundle at her that proved to be her clothes. "Dress! As fast as you can!"

Whatever she had feared, putting on her clothes did not equate to even part of a threat. Her terror receded a little, but did not disappear: there was far too much strangeness in this situation for danger not to be involved in it somewhere. The voice was authoritative, and she thought that she had heard it before. Not often – but somewhere –. She climbed out of the bed and with shaking hands began pulling on her clothing. Her unknown companion waited, not turning his back but averting his head to give her all the privacy that was possible. The half-light from the window gleamed on naked steel: he held a drawn sword in his hand. Something about his attitude told her that he was listening intently, and she tried to keep her own movements as quiet as she could.

"We must leave, get out of the city," he hissed as she finished and turned towards him. –"You're in danger. Do as I say, and make no noise." A thousand questions crowded on to her tongue, but the sudden terrible belief in what he said silenced them all. If they escaped from whatever threatened, there would be time enough for explanations. The silence and the darkness breathed threat over them.

A few moments later they were at the back door of the house. There was a garden, and at the foot of it ran a small alleyway. They picked their way cautiously through the half-seen trees and plants, stopping every so often to listen. He opened the gate slowly and with great care, and breathed what sounded like a prayer of thankfulness. There were three saddlebeasts there. A fine rain had been falling; the dark coats were beaded with moisture, the large ears swivelling curiously. The stag tossed his great antlers nervously in the greyness, his nostrils dilating to scent his master. The other two animals were hinds, and one of them already had a rider. In the darkness this was no more than a shapeless figure, surprisingly bulky, but being astride a hind it was probably a woman: hinds were far more docile and easier to control. Henanei had no hind of her own, as she was an indifferent rider at best. Ordinarily she would not have needed her rescuer's cupped hands to hoist her into the saddle even so, but suddenly remembering her condition she accepted his help gratefully. He mounted his own animal with the ease of years of practice, and though she still could not see his face clearly she suddenly knew who he was: her husband's lieutenant Keri'khai. With the recognition came the lessening of one fear and the increase of another. Where was Teho'evan? What had happened to him? The third rider must be Keri'khai's wife, Faesanei, and the reason she looked odd was because wrapped in her riding-cloak she was carrying their child, still sound asleep despite the night alarm. Henanei realised with a stab of fresh fear that the danger must be very real and very close – even his wife and child must be endangered by what he was doing.

Without further words, the three of them rode out of the alley and into the silent streets. It was very early, the sky tinged with the first suggestion of the dawn light. The misty rain was still falling, and the sleeping city looked unfamiliar and threatening. Doorways and alleys watched them ride past. From a tree somewhere a bird's call pried at the silence. At the sound Keri'khai pressed his heels lightly into his stag's sides and increased the pace a little. It was never wise to underestimate Stiv'aran; they might have been followed, for all his caution. Teho'evan's house was close to one of the city's gates, but that would have been too obvious. They made for one of the others, fortunately not at too great a distance from it. It had not been difficult to arrange for picked men of their own squadron to be on guard duty there at this time – he had had the queerest feeling that the orders for his lord to be at the Temple at such a strange hour might well have unforeseen consequences, and it was always wise to ensure an avenue for escape, even though it might not be needed. He had been among the detachment Teho'evan took to the Temple, and though he had not been admitted to the Shrine he had seen all too clearly what had been carried out of it. Taking care not to make any move that might draw attention to himself, he had taken the rest of the detachment back to the barracks and supposedly returned to his own quarters. There he had waited half an hour to give any watcher the impression that he had settled down, then left by the window and gone by a roundabout route to his own house. His small sturdy wife Faesanei was waiting for him with the baby, who had gone to sleep. He had taken her some way into his confidence, and fortunately she was not in the habit of asking inconvenient questions. In a couple of moments they were astride their mounts, which he had saddled and left waiting in readiness, and he thanked the Shining One that he had had the foresight to buy an unremarkable animal for a spare. Even if it had been safe to risk a detour to Teho'evan's stables, he doubted whether Henanei would have either the strength or the skill to control Freharehen; and a woman mounted on a war-stag would be far too noticeable even if she had.

They were passed out of the gate without difficulty, and breathed a little easier as they headed for the uplands. The saddlebeasts were fresh, and extended their pace willingly on the soft turf. Ahead of them the hills in the East began to grow faintly visible, outlined against the still-dark sky. Keri'khai had not been able to come up with any viable safe haven within the confines of the city, and had no choice but to take his charges out of it. In view of recent events, he did not know how safe they would be with the Skaira at Vanreil, but he could not think of anywhere safer. He was well aware that taking them to the infuriated Skaira was a dizzyingly risky thing to attempt, but surely, he reasoned, in return for news of their Princess, the Daughters of the Night would not refuse sanctuary to innocent womenfolk. He himself intended only to see them as far as Vanreil before returning to Thervanil. Apart from the fact that it was extremely unlikely that he would be allowed to stay there (and it was quite possible he would not be allowed to leave it alive, if he reached it at all), he knew that Teho'evan was still alive, if barely. There might be some chance of rescuing him, and if there was he intended to be ready to seize it.

It was obvious that if his own responsibility for Henanei's escape should become known, he himself would be in danger the moment he set foot in the city again. This was why he had taken the precaution of also removing Faesanei and their baby daughter Narenei. As far as he could tell, their escape had gone unnoticed. He could rely on the gate guards to be blind and deaf on the subject of who had passed through; and they would be relatively safe to be so, since the city had five gates and the escape might have been made through any one of them. A blank having been drawn at the nearest and most obvious escape route, it might even be assumed that the fugitives had made the mistake of seeking safety elsewhere in the city, which would mean that men and time would be wasted in a fruitless search. He was strangely certain that Stiv'aran was quite capable of extending his malice to his victim's wife, and knew that he was keeping faith with Teho'evan by ensuring her safety.

He was so wrapped up in his thoughts that he did not see Henanei's pleading glances. She had obeyed him without question, and would continue to do so, but his silence on the subject of what had happened to her husband was more frightening to her than their flight from the city. Finally she could bear the suspense no longer. "Sir, for the love of the One tell me what's happened!"

"Would to the God I knew, Lady," he answered grimly. "Your husband's under arrest. I don't know why, but I do know he'll rest easier if you're not within Stiv'aran's grasp. And as my own family might suffer if it were found I'd helped you escape, I'm taking you all to the Skaira at Vanreil."

"Arrested-?" Her voice emerged as a thread of sound. "It's not possible! He was loyal!"

"Loyalty to Stiv'aran isn't necessarily loyalty to the good of the Empire," he replied. "You must know how troubled he's been. He did something – I wasn't with him at the time, but even Stiv'aran doesn't have a valuable man beaten half to death for no reason."

"Beaten?" She swayed in the saddle. "But he'll live? You're certain?"

"Lady, in this world I'm certain of nothing. I think the Gods have deserted us. And when that happens, a man must do his best on his own. Your pardon, but I think we should make more speed now the light's better. The sooner we're into the forest and out of sight from the City, the easier I'll be." And without further words, he leaned over to touch his wife with a gentle hand, and spurred his beast forward. Even burdened with her daughter, Faesanei could ride almost as well as her husband. Henanei was not as fortunate, and her fear and grief for Teho'evan almost overcame her. But whether her husband was alive or dead, she had his child to care for. It might well be that the jolting of the ride was the last thing she should have had to endure in the circumstances, but it was certainly better than falling into the clutches of the evil man planning to mount the Horned Throne. Her saddlebeast leaped forward after the other two and she hung on with grim determination. If they were to be caught after all, it should not be because she had slowed them down with her poor riding.

21

"We are in great danger here." Hargen made the point matter-of-factly; she did not think Lidan needed telling. "I understand your reasoning, but we must take precautions. It will not do for all of us to go to the Pool. If you wish to take Kelti, well and good, but I should remain outside to keep watch. There is still a possibility that someone may have picked up our trail, for all the care we have taken."

"I do not like splitting up," said Lidan with a frown. "You are right I know, but I wish there was some other way."

"What other way is there? We cannot both go and leave Kelti alone; if we have been followed, he will be safer inside with you than out here with me. And it would not be right for me to take charge of him and part him from you unless circumstances dictate it. He was entrusted to you, and I have no wish to run counter to what the Goddess has ordained."

"Oh, very well. But be careful. They will have discovered the Shrine by now, and the uproar will be worse than ever."

"That, to put it mildly." Hargen sat down at a point on the mountainside which afforded her an excellent view of the valley below, but which could not reveal her against the skyline. Her two companions began the climb to the crest, likewise being careful not to betray themselves more than their colouring made inevitable. They had waited for the approach of dusk before moving on to the windswept slopes of Sikkthi, to become less visible to keen eyes at a distance. It was fortunate that the season was late and the grasses and low scrubby vegetation were fading into duns, yellows and browns, with here and there a patch of stunted wind-torn bushes whose leaves were a vivid shade of orange. Lidan's blonde fur blended in well with the sere grass that covered most of the slope. Kelti's strange garment had originally been creamy in colour, but was showing the wear and tear of his adventures. This in itself was no bad thing as it helped to camouflage him, while the brown tunic-blanket he was carrying around his shoulders would help to disguise his distinctive shape at a distance. Their main danger lay in being skylined as they went over the crest, and Lidan was well aware of it. Before they would have become visible, both she and Brendan went down on to their stomachs and began crawling.

It had rained again the previous day, while they were busy making a cautious and circuitous journey around the edge of the valley to reach the foot of Sikkthi. They had rested through the middle hours in a thicket, and Brendan had managed to get some sleep, but didn't feel much better for it. He had pretty well had to give up worrying about what he looked like, but as he wormed his way forward now through wet vegetation and across patches of damp bare earth, he still winced at what this was going to do to his already filthy clothes. Kanehar had not been able to risk washing his makeshift boiler suit, though she had beaten out as much mud as possible and mended a few tears. He had been able to bathe (which he had desperately needed), and to wash and comb his hair, and he had even been able to borrow some kind of scalpel from the Healer to use as a razor. She had also shown him a kind of twig which when bitten broke down readily into a fan of soft fibres that he could use for cleaning his teeth. Personal hygiene thus attended to, he felt considerably better – at least his mother would recognise him now, even if the process of shaving had provided the watching Skaira with a mixture of surprise, amusement and anxiety. No one on Kerriel grew beards.

Lidan had explained to him why they had to make what could well prove to be an extremely risky journey to the mountain called Sikkthi. Hidden inside the crest of this was a sacred pool, which was the reason for their visit. The Skaira claimed that it would reveal answers to questions, which was a pretty mind-boggling concept, but they were evidently deadly serious about it. They intended to ask for guidance as to where they should go next – all alternatives seeming equally dangerous. He could have stayed near the path with Hargen, but the chance to see a 'magic' pool was far too intriguing to pass up.

Once well over the crest they were able to straighten up again and get back on their feet. Brendan recognised instantly that the broken-edged hollow was the cone of an extinct volcano, filled now by a huge still lake. It was not far down to the edge of this, a scramble of perhaps three hundred yards over a mixture of scree and boulders. Both of them had to be very careful with their footing; the going was treacherous in the extreme. It was a little surprising that such a place did not have a path worn to it by inquirers over the years, but he had gathered that the site was far too holy for casual use. The asking was done in a ritual hallowed by the centuries, with words that only Skaira would know. In that way the sanctity of the place had been preserved; and indeed it was impossible not to be impressed by the sheer majesty of the scene. The sky was cloudless now, already dusted with stars bright enough to defy the late light of the sun. Another hour would show them in all their glory, and Brendan had still not got used to the sight: he could have sat looking up at them for hours. The great lake of Sikkthi – it was strange that the Skaira called it a pool, he'd been expecting something a couple of yards across – lay in its hard stone bed, unsoftened by a single leaf of vegetation or a blade of grass. There did not seem to be any wind, for the surface of the dark water reflected the sky with the unbroken purity of a mirror. It was indeed an awe-inspiring place. He could understand that any race who believed in magic would regard it as inherently magical; now seeing it for himself, he had less difficulty in imagining that the lake was indeed actually capable of what the Skaira claimed. Still, it was one thing to get within hailing distance of belief, quite another to actually witness something as an indisputable fact.

They reached the foot of the slope without incident, and at Lidan's gesture Brendan sat down on a large boulder. His heart was beating rather fast. Apart from the first day, their circumstances had not called for the use of sorcery, though the mere fact of his being here constituted ample evidence that Lidan had powers unexplainable in human terms. Now – if what the Skaira claimed was true – he was going to get a grandstand view of something that could only be regarded as supernatural. Half ashamed of his own nervousness, he crossed himself and waited.

Composing herself to the proper state of mind, Lidan stepped to the water's edge. She waited for a moment or two, concentrating on reaching the part of her mind that her people called the Old Knowledge. This was where the Old Speech, the spell-speech, was stored: Skaira did not have to be taught this language, but were shown at a certain age how to recall it from their subconscious. It was much the same with sorcery. Their capacity for it was inborn. As soon as their elders were certain that they were responsible enough to be entrusted with the power involved, they were taught the rules that governed its use and then shown – almost reminded, so instinctive was the knowledge – how to use it.

Now. She began the ritual movements, slow and graceful, again almost a silent dance though she did not move from the spot where she stood with the water lapping gently at her forepaws. For the use of sorcery, as with prayer, it was considered reverent to unbind the hair, and she had shaken it loose so that it fell cascading to her withers. For travel she invariably kept the sides of it caught into braids that she tied at the back, keeping the rest of it tidy and out of her view. The plaiting had made a rippling effect that was most attractive, and for no particular reason the suddenly sinuous movements of her body brought back to Brendan unexpectedly and very vividly the events in his hotel room – how many days ago? He had lost count. The memory unfortunately gave him an erection, and with the indirect object of his lust absorbed in prayer, it felt completely inappropriate. He was forced to alter the way he was sitting for embarrassment in case she turned around and saw it. For all that he tried very hard to think of something else, he still wanted to watch what Lidan was doing, and he could not dissociate the almost erotic swaying of her body from the feline grace of the woman with whom he had shared a bed. The pressure became increasingly uncomfortable.

Fortunately, the Skair suddenly went still. She called out, in the language he had heard her using with the other Skaira on Vanreil: it sounded to him like nothing so much as ice breaking in so many various keys, a language of brittle consonants and swallowed vowels. After a brief pause, when she seemed to listen for something he could not hear, she called out again. Then after another, shorter pause, she said something very quickly and looked down. He was several paces behind her, but he could still see that the water had begun to ripple in front of her, not at all the way it would respond to wind on the surface or a current beneath it. After a moment or two he could see what looked like submarine light beginning to glow. The illuminated area was not large, perhaps ten feet or so across, and cast a wavering radiance upward into her face. There were colours in it, muted pastels for the most part, but from where he sat he could not make out any picture. Drawn by intense curiosity, held back by fear, he got to his feet but did not move closer. Fascination had disposed of his inconvenient physical reaction to her: all his thoughts were now concentrated on what was happening in the water, but he did not know if this was for him to witness or not. Lidan stared down into it as if turned to stone.

It would have been hard to say accurately afterwards how much time passed while the Skair stood watching whatever the Star Pool had to tell her. He thought it had been about five minutes, but it might have been three times that by the time she made a gesture almost of dismissal and turned away. The light died away slowly. Too curious to be properly wary any longer, Brendan stepped forward and looked into the water. He saw something, very faint and very far down, that looked like a tower. Around it were other buildings, but the vision was fading too fast now for him to get any impression of what they might be. Very soon it was gone completely. The water was still again, dark and cold, plunging sharply to depths at which he could only guess.

And yet – and yet –

"It's so beautiful," he said aloud, looking around slowly at the vast broken bowl of the cone, at the still water reflecting the sky and its now even greater scattering of stars. The gigantic glowing heart of the spiral galaxy had begun to appear, a vast jewelled frieze on the apricot sky with its double shimmering on the mirror-smooth surface of the lake; every moment another hundred stars slipped silently into view to peer down at their reflections. The place had an inexplicable serenity all its own; the crazy thought came to him that dying here would be very peaceful. "Even if it wasn't magic, it would still be amazing. I wish I could stay here. I think it's the most wonderful place I've ever seen in all my life."

"Beautiful?" Lidan was looking up at the sky, and she shuddered. "Is your world so dreadful, then, that you think Sikkthi beautiful?"

He frowned in perplexity. It would have been impossible to explain where the attraction of the place lay; he had been fortunate enough to have visited some of the most beautiful places on Earth, and there was no way in which the two experiences could be compared. Nevertheless, he let the description stand. After a moment or two longer he turned his back on the lake and went to her; and thus neither he nor she saw the water ripple again, sharply, though there was neither light nor sound. If Lidan had been less troubled, she might have heard the tiny click of pebbles shifting. Brendan did not.

"Did you see what you wanted?" he asked.

She was still looking up at the stars. He was horrified to discover that she was crying, the tears sliding down her cheeks silvered by starlight.

"What I wanted? By the Goddess! I did not *want* to see it. Anything else – anywhere else! I am not strong enough!"

He felt as though his heart had suddenly jumped into his throat. Whatever he had expected, this was not it. He tried to say something, and no words came out.

She looked around at him, and saw his sudden pallor. It was wrong that she should be frightening him like this, but she herself was too frightened to dissemble. She had told herself and the others that she had come to Sikkthi to ask for guidance, but it was only now that she was brought face to face with the knowledge that she had actually been praying for a way to evade the truth. And the truth had stared up at her from the shifting, shimmering water: the tall golden tower of the Temple of Aiyeh in Thervanil, with the buildings at its foot wreathed in impenetrable darkness.

Now she had to tell him. And when she told him he would have to go back to his own world, because he did not want to die, and who could blame him for that?

"Forgive me, Kelti," she said in a choked voice. "I have suspected this, but dared not tell you for hope that I might be wrong. I have discovered what has happened to this world. Esdiol has returned to it."

"Esdiol-?" The name meant nothing to him, and painfully she reminded him of the story she had told, the ancient tale of the making of Geirion and the breaking of paradise. That led to the explanation of what she had seen in the Star Pool – he had seen the tower for himself, but had not had any idea where it was. As he listened to her the chill of the mountain tops gathered closer. The silence breathed coldly on the back of his neck. It had been one thing to wonder about the truth or falsity of the Geirion story when it could be dismissed as a purely academic issue. Now it really did matter whether the story was true. Was there, could there be, some kind of Devil-figure loose in the world?

"You say this – Esdiol – is in the city over there? Thervanil?" He stared into the West. "And we have to go there?"

"I asked to be shown where we should go. That was the reply. And if he is there, we can not hope to prevail against him." She scrubbed her face with the back of one hand. "I have told you that magic has rules: and one of them is that there is one place where my powers are out of reach. And that is the place where the Lord Aiyeh is worshipped, in the Great Temple of Thervanil.

"Do you understand?" She looked pleadingly at him. "If we go there, I will not be able to save you. I will not be able to make a door between the worlds so that you can escape. And I can not risk that."

He sat down, and was silent for a while. "I suppose there's no chance you could have got it wrong?" Bloody stupid question, he thought, even as he said it. She shook her head. There was another silence.

"Look. Let's take the worst case scenario. If this Esdiol got hold of me, what would he do? Kill me, I suppose?" He couldn't make it sound quite as dispassionate as he would have liked. Try as he might, he couldn't disguise his fear.

"No. That he could not do." Her voice was muffled. "The ancient texts say that there are rules that even gods must obey. He must have some foothold here, and it gives him power over the inhabitants of this world. But on your world he has no hold. He has no authority over your people. To destroy you would destroy him, and he knows it."

"So why would I be in danger from him?"

"He can not work against you directly, but he can use others as tools to destroy you. He will have no shortage of followers – he was even able to order an attack on Weruavwe and the murder of almost a hundred of my people. Ordinarily no one would dare to raise a hand against any Skair. Now he has so worked upon them that they dare to go even into the heart of Vanreil itself in search of plunder. It seems that all this stems from the man who intends to become the next Emperor, and it is he whom we must fear. He has nothing to fear from killing you, and if he believes you to be a threat he will do it."

"I see." And he didn't like the look of the situation at all. He would have been other than human if he hadn't been dismayed by the prospect of going to a place where the safeguard upon which he had come to rely was suddenly removed. A place moreover which was the home of an ambitious bastard with a nasty taste for bloodshed, who would have no hesitation about disposing of any threat to himself he could get his hands on. 'I've done everything I can,' he thought desperately. 'They can't expect me to walk in there and be killed. I'm not a hero, for Christ's sake. I'm just a bloody dancer, and I've got a family to go back to.'

But that was the problem. It was evident that Lidan wasn't expecting him to go anywhere and be killed. She wanted to send him home where he would be safe, even though by doing so she sacrificed whatever faint hope there might have been of him pulling off the impossible and saving her world. And he had a family to go back to, and wanted them now more desperately than ever, but if he went what had she to go back to? Her mother had been murdered. Her world would be smashed into smithereens. And she would have the deaths of thousands on her conscience because she did not want to risk his life. He looked at her with a new and grave insight. Skaira might not have menfolk, but he suspected that whether she understood it or not, at least one had learned how to love. He felt humbled by the discovery, and a little frightened by it too. It was no small thing to be so precious to another living being.

Still – wasn't it too much to ask of him? To walk into such danger, into the clutches of what by any human definition was a supernatural power equivalent to the Devil? Too much to ask of anyone. He didn't want to die.

But he didn't want to just give up either. He'd worked his way to his World Champion title by not giving up, not wanting to fail. He'd never been a quitter, and he must have been brought here because there was a way for him to succeed. Nothing that Lidan had seen or said indicated that anything in that respect had changed. Could he live with himself if he crept home to safety and left Kerriel to its fate? Wasn't it better to keep faith with something about himself he'd taken pride in, and aim for the stars? So it might cost him his life. It wasn't a pleasant prospect, he was no keener on dying than anyone else, but it wasn't as if death wasn't going to get him sooner or later no matter what world he was on at the time. It would surely be better to die trying than to live the rest of his life with the ineradicable shame of having been too scared even to give it a shot. He sighed. Sometimes, back on Earth, especially when exhaustion was black iron in his muscles and his knees and ankles ached from practising, he'd wished he could cultivate a more realistic approach to accepting defeat. He'd never got around to doing it. It looked as though it could well be the costliest omission of his life. He stood up and stared upwards at the glory of the sky. Too much to ask, that the world should be left with no one to wonder at the beauty above them. There was no help for it. He had to try.

With a new respect, a new gentleness, he put his arm around Lidan's shoulders. She looked at him with the dumb resignation of an animal waiting to die.

"Come on," he said softly. "Hargen'll think we've fallen in and drowned. We'd better get on our way before all the rest of them come after us, don't you think?"

She stared at him, her eyes widening with shock. Her face worked convulsively. She did not want him to die: she did not want him to leave. And she could not guarantee his survival. How could he possibly prevail against the powers that were ranged against him? But what of her trust in Shieih who had told her to bring him here? Would the Good Goddess have had her bring him only to see him die in vain? How could anyone find their way in such darkness?

'As with all journeys. One step at a time,' the voice of Rerafa the Dance tutor at the Training School echoed in her head from long ago, quelling a complaint that one dance was harder than all the others to learn. It was true enough. She had asked for guidance, and had been given it. It was not right that she refuse what she had asked for. She leaned her head briefly against Brendan's, thanking the

Goddess that She had sent one who had the courage to see the horror ahead and still keep walking.

"Come. Let us go," she said.

22

"I repent nothing. If I had the time again, I would change nothing. I am sorry if this displeases anyone, but it is the truth." Kanehar sat in front of the assembly with folded arms and a totally unmoved face, although she did not need to be a telepath to pick up the waves of horror, shock and rage beating out of her audience. "He was too valuable to be exposed to any unnecessary risks. The Good Goddess had shown us what was to be done, and we took what seemed to us the best way of doing it."

It was not to be expected that many of her hearers would relish being referred to, however obliquely, as 'unnecessary risks'. Her ears flattened slightly to protect the delicate insides from the volume that assaulted them.

"You thought that we – we, your sisters – would harm him?" asked Varei in horror, when she could make herself heard. A slender creature compared to most of her subordinates, she was extremely intelligent, but often reluctant to think the worst of anyone. The power of her office was so great that she had never had to exercise the power of personality, and as a result sometimes found herself being carried along by events instead of directing them. She stared at Kanehar now with genuine amazement, her reddish-bronze fur fluffing up slightly with the shock of such an accusation, and her tail upright like an exclamation mark.

"Yes. I thought it was possible. And I still think it." The Healer spoke bluntly. "The events of the past few days have struck us all to our very hearts. I would lay upon no-one the burden of doing in the heat of the moment something that they and many others would live to repent of in days to come."

"And yet you felt yourself immune to the possibility of wrong?" said Argan sharply. The torchlight glinted on her gold armbands as she leaned forward to rest the heels of her hands on her folded forelegs.

"None of us are that. But the rightness of my actions is for the judgement of Shieih, and I am satisfied with the result thus far. The Starborn is on his way to wherever he must go, and he has Irvathil, as he should. He is well guarded and guided. For the rest, I trust the Goddess."

"You had no right!" shouted Resat, one of the Masters of the Warrior Arts, and one of those of whom, rightly or wrongly, Kanehar had had the darkest suspicions. "You have set yourself up as a judge of us all!" Such was her rage at the insult that she actually had one forepaw raised and held; much more provocation and she could well bring it down in a slap, and the fight would have been on there and then. Healer or not, even the placid Kanehar was not of a temperament to refuse a challenge in open Council.

"I had the right, and the duty, to judge in what direction lay the surest safety for Kelti." She raised her voice to make herself heard over the angry responses. "And if anyone doubts me, let her recall it to memory the last time that the judgement of a Healer was so called into question that she was arraigned as if in court before her fellows and treated with less courtesy than a convicted felon. For I am certain that such behaviour has never been seen in my lifetime, nor in that of my *eréaihin*."

It was close enough to an accusation to give many of her hearers pause, and too fair for most of them to deny the impropriety of their treatment of her.

Even Resat seemed to become aware of the fact that that raised paw was quite shocking in the circumstances – Skaira could and did fight if disagreements could not be settled by more amicable means, but it was quite out of order to issue such a challenge in Council, in front of the First Priestess. She lowered it reluctantly.

Kanehar had been discovered keeping vigil over the ruin of the Shrine on Vanreil, and the Priestess who came upon her had wasted no time in trying to get to the bottom of the matter herself, but had brought her straight down to Varei. It had been unfortunate that one of the Skaira attending the First Priestess at the time had been a telepath. Seconds later, every Skair in the Complex had come racing to the Hall, and what had started off as a confidential meeting had become something alarmingly close to a trial.

The Healer was telling the truth when she said that she repented nothing that she had done. Faced with her current audience, she repented it even less. The news of what had happened in the Shrine had redoubled the hysteria in the Complex. Many seemed inclined to view Kelti's presence there as one of the worst parts of the entire affair, and for some it was, incredibly, *the* worst: to these, it was one thing for unsanctioned visitors to defile the place, but quite another for Skaira themselves to actually take in a pollutant. All three were guilty of the vilest sacrilege, and no excuse was sufficient to justify them.

In the front row, and thus far silent, sat Riyeth. A lean creature, whom one of her detractors had once uncharitably summed up as "All bones and bad temper", she shook now with the violence of her outrage. The hackles of her copper fur were erect all along her lower spine, and her ears were completely flat against her head. From time to time her lips writhed back away from her clenched teeth. For all that she said nothing, her eyes spoke for her. Luminous with rage, they burned on Kanehar's face with an intensity that the Healer could not help but notice. A lesser soul might have been intimidated. Kanehar was not impressed. It merely reinforced her belief that she had acted with nothing but wisdom in keeping Kelti and Riyeth apart.

"Where have they gone?" asked Argan more moderately, realising the justice of the Healer's indirect complaint. "Surely you have no objection to telling us that?"

"And if you have, we have means of discovering it anyway!" growled Mesca, one of the senior telepaths.

Kanehar flicked a glance at her. "You are welcome to try. I do not know where they have gone. I made certain that I would know nothing of their plans, so it could not be bullied out of me."

Varei flung out a hand as Mesca surged upright. Hissing but obedient, tail rigid with suppressed rage at the implied insult, she sat down again.

"Why do you take this attitude, Kanehar?" the First Priestess asked almost pleadingly. "You know that none of us would force you to reveal what you wished to keep hidden. Mesca spoke in anger, she would never act upon her words. One would think that you wished to enrage and alienate your sisters, and I know that is not true."

"I wish for no such thing. I wish for one thing only, and that is for Kelti to be safe, so that he may accomplish what he was brought here for. And if that enrages or alienates any or all of you, so be it. Shieih is my judge, and it matters nothing if every voice here is against me, if She holds me justified."

"You are arrogant!" roared Resat. "You have no right to exclude us from such decisions! We are every bit as able as you to judge the situation and care for him! With a greater number to guard him, his safety would have been better guaranteed than it is now!"

Kanehar finally lost her temper. She hurled herself up to her paws, snarling, and such was the fury on her face that half of her audience shrank back.

"You understand nothing, Resat! Do you think it was pleasant, to have to look upon my own people and say that a defenceless being from another world, one brought here by the act of the Goddess, was not safe in their hands? Do you think that I enjoyed the necessity for secrecy, that it gave me pleasure to have to own up to Kelti that I could not trust my sisters with his safety because they were so distraught that their judgement might be impaired? By Shieih! I was ashamed – ashamed – ashamed! He is Dancer-born, the Favoured of the Goddess, risking his life for ours of his own free will! You should have been his foremost defenders, and yet I see those here who would tear him asunder for no greater crime than having looked on the Shrine and lived to tell of it. I did what I thought best at the time, and hearing and seeing now what I see and hear, I repeat that I repent of nothing. If this is a court, I plead guilty. Sentence me if you wish. I have done!"

"Of course it is not a court!" said Varei hastily. "You mistake us, Kanehar. Certainly it was a shock to hear what you had done, but I believe you acted only with the best of intentions."

"If you believe it, you are in the minority here," replied Kanehar grimly. "And if you do believe it, then I ask you to believe also that it is in Kelti's best interests if he is not followed. The more are with him, the more noticeable he will be. And his best guarantee of safety is secrecy, not numbers. Numbers did not prevail at Weruavwe."

"They were unprepared at Weruavwe," snarled Resat. "Unprepared, unarmed! We should be neither, and he would be safe!"

"Safe from Venelai, perhaps!" retorted Kanehar. "Safe from fanatics, perhaps not!"

This was too much. The room exploded. Half were roaring for the Healer's blood, half were agreeing with every word she said. A dozen arguments broke out. Several looked likely to end in blows or worse. Only the presence of the First Priestess prevented serious violence, and even that was perilously thin restraint. Tempers were lost, insults traded. Varei was left almost unheeded at the edge of the storm, gesturing miserably for everyone to be calm. No First Priestess since the Creation had been so comprehensively ignored by those under her authority. It was not Varei's fault, but her misfortune, that she was basically a gentle creature, totally out of her depth in such a crisis.

When something vaguely resembling a suitably respectful silence had eventually been restored – it had taken several of her most senior Priestesses with extremely loud voices to do it, and not even they had managed to achieve a completely submissive hush – Varei made a final attempt to pour oil on troubled waters.

"Well, done is done, and whether it was ill or well is in the lap of the Goddess. What we must do now is to decide our future course."
"Follow Lidan," said Resat promptly.
"Leave her alone," said Kanehar, equally promptly.
Uproar broke out again.

Varei succumbed to despair.

*   *   *

Three days later, Emperor-Elect Stiv'aran looked down with hooded eyes at the soldier sprawled in front of him.

Warleader Shas'kare stood to one side, his attitude one of contempt. He was a warrior of the old school, hardened to bloodshed and committed to obeying orders to the letter: it was not what his troopers had done which had infuriated him, but the fact that they had disobeyed orders for the sake of going looting, and thereby cost five lives from his Division. The watery sun from outside glinted on the dark armour encasing his powerful body – he was very rarely seen without it – and the darker feathers on his square blunt head. His deep-set orange eyes glittered.

It had not been possible to cover up what had happened at Vanreil. The five dead soldiers had had to be accounted for. Their surviving accomplice had tried to spin a tale about what had happened, but Shas'kare could smell a lie a mile off. He had had the miscreant's belongings thoroughly searched, and the results spoke for themselves. No man living had ever seen what had been in one of the bundles, but when its wrappings were removed and the unearthly radiance filled the warleader's tent, no man there doubted what they were seeing. The possible ramifications of what the wretch and his fellows had done were far too grave for Shas'kare to dismiss. He had been sent to Three Stars to search for a stranger, not to incite the Skaira there to raving pitch. If the odd Skair happened to be killed, well and good, he was not afraid of that, and he was not particularly troubled by the sacrilege to Vanreil either. But the effect on the inhabitants of the Temple Complex of having their shrine desecrated and looted, its guardians killed – well, that was something else altogether. And to add to all, the soldier had babbled out some crazy tale of something half-glimpsed during the escape from the vengeful Skaira who had discovered them. It might have been an attempt to divert attention from his own activities by focussing it on something his seniors might find more interesting, but a beating had not made him change his story. It might be strange, but it sounded like the truth, and the orders had been about a stranger.

All in all, Shas'kare had decided that Stiv'aran ought to be told at once. Leaving his half-Division in the capable hands of one of his senior officers, he had brought the offender to Thervanil at the best speed that their over-ridden beasts could produce. The Emperor-Elect had granted him an audience immediately, and listened in silence to what he had to say. He had examined for himself the loot from Vanreil, which the warleader had brought for evidence in case it was needed, and was glad enough to surrender into other hands – superstitious or not, the possession of Genshenna made him uncomfortable. Then together they had questioned the thief.

The Emperor-Elect had been prepared to use every means at his disposal to get at the truth, but the wretch before them was pitifully ready to tell everything he knew, in the hope that it might save his skin. He disowned all responsibility for the attack on Vanreil – his companions had forced him into it, he said – but after relating the events in the Shrine, during which he had behaved with truly remarkable restraint if his account was to be believed, he passed on to the part in which Stiv'aran was really interested. It was unfortunate that he had had no more than one brief wild glance at the other stag's rider, and that had been partly obscured by the tossing antlers. Nevertheless, he was quite certain that he had seen something unlike anything he had ever come across before. His description was reasonably accurate in the circumstances, though had Brendan been privileged to hear it he would probably not have recognised himself, and if he had guessed would undoubtedly have been most insulted.

Even discounting a third of the account as imagination, however, and another third as embroidery, what remained was enough to trouble Stiv'aran deeply. Ignoring the soldier still grovelling on the floor, he met Shas'kare's hard glance for a moment and turned away to pace to the other side of the dais. (The carved figures on the wall stared back at him indifferently, and a corner of his mind made a note that this particular frieze would certainly have to be replaced: it depicted Aiyeh and Shieih confirming the Emperor and Empress in their authority.) Unseeingly he looked down at the table where the stolen things were laid out: most were ordinary enough, offertory bowls and candlesticks, valuable more for their workmanship than for the silver they were made of or the gems set into them. One piece alone had been re-wound in its wrappings, so that the light from it no longer danced on the walls like sunshine reflecting on unquiet water.

It was an old habit of his to turn the heavy bracelets on his wrists while he was thinking; the rough-cut gems in the massy gold were cold against his talons. So, something unaccountable had come to Vanreil, and the Skaira were in possession of it. The attack on the Shrine could well be enough to tip the indecision he think he had Thaskan as hostage, and keeping her in the Shrine at Thervanil had prevented any of her people from touching her telepathically, so that they still would not have any way to discover the truth. Whether her supposed survival would be enough to suppress their instinct to avenge their murdered Priestesses and defiled Shrine, there was no saying. It should be enough – they held their Princess in the greatest reverence, and she had not yet borne her daughter. Logic dictated that with Thaskan in his grasp he could offer almost any provocation and get away with it. But he had not counted on this. Short of actually killing Varei as well, there was not much worse he could do to them. Would they keep their claws sheathed? Could they? And who, and what, was the stranger? What part had he to play in the game?

He had not paid much attention to the existence of 'the stranger' in Three Stars, apart from obeying the command to have Shas'kare's men deployed there to kill him if found. It had not been clear to him that the stranger might not be merely from another land, but from another world. This altered the entire picture. He must be found, and destroyed, with all speed. And the Skaira would surely not be slow to perceive and make use of any weapon sent to their hands. All in all, it would be wise to take precautions, and at once.

Stooping, he buried a knife up to its hilt between the soldier's shoulder blades. A faint gasp was the only response; the body slumped. Not even bothering to withdraw the weapon, he stepped over the corpse and gestured to Shas'kare. They had much to do. The warleader must advise him what troops were where, and how quickly they could be mustered.

They left the room.

23

“One comes.” Hargen raised her head. Instantly everyone stopped, and the two Skaira lowered their tails and stood perfectly still, analysing the vibrations in the ground.

“Three,” corrected Lidan presently, and Hargen nodded. Automatically they looked around, growling, for the best place to seek cover. It was unfortunate that this part of the forest was quite open; it would have been hard to find adequate hiding places for themselves, let alone the stag. The two Skaira shared a glance that went not so much over Brendan’s head as under his mount’s nose. They had been lucky so far, meeting no one in two days’ travel. It seemed that their good fortune had come to an end. If they could not hide they would have to fight, and kill, for they could not take the risk of allowing anyone to escape with the news of Brendan’s whereabouts. His existence was probably known already, thanks to the escapee from the fight on Vanreil. By bringing him away with all possible stealth, they had hoped to foster the belief that he was still at the Temple Complex, under the protection of the Skaira there. It should have been the safest and most logical place to house him – who would have believed that events would prove otherwise? As hiding places were in short supply, so were suitable sites for an ambush. They had followed the usual route towards Thervanil, though taking care not to follow too closely the broad unpaved way worn through the forest by generations passing there. Now they had to act quickly, and Hargen led the stag aside, gesturing to Brendan to dismount. He was the easiest of them all to hide, the growth around the bole of one of the larger trees would conceal him, and a riderless stag would not attract that much attention. Left with his reins trailing, ‘Adrian’ looked puzzled for a moment and then began grazing. Even without being tethered, he would not stray far from his new owner, who treated him far more kindly than the previous one ever had.

Understanding enough to keep him silent in hiding, ignoring the voice that called him a coward for allowing the Skaira to face the danger without him, Brendan crouched behind the tree, raising himself just enough to peer through the screen of withering leaves and twigs. Hargen had had charge of Irvathil, but she had silently handed it to him, and that too he understood. If the worst came to the worst, they would spend their lives to ensure that he made his escape with it. What he should do in those circumstances was beyond his imagination. It would have helped if he had had any real idea of what he should do when he reached Thervanil. Getting back to Earth was something he could worry about if he survived. At present, just surviving was enough of a worry.

The hoof beats were close enough now for them to be audible. They were not those of animals ridden fast, but to the experienced ears of the Skaira they conveyed weariness. It was nearly evening, and the saddlebeasts had been on the move almost since dawn. From time to time they had been rested insofar as their riders had dismounted and led them for a while, but even at midday there had only been a few moments’ pause. Growling softly in unison, Lidan and Hargen exchanged glances that confirmed their plan of attack, and stood waiting in open view on the path for the Venelai to appear.

Keri'khai was moderately pleased with their progress thus far. He was proud of the way both the women had endured a difficult journey without complaint, though he knew his wife was concerned for their daughter. They could not afford to go more slowly, however: if the pursuit was up, they had to keep going to have any chance of outrunning it at all. He had allowed as little time as possible for resting the weary saddle-beasts; the animals were strong and healthy, but even they could not be ridden day and night without foundering. From time to time he had had all three riders dismount and walk for a while to ease the burden a little, himself carrying Narenei in a cradle made by knotting his cloak into his belt. The sooner they reached Vanreil and a hope of safety, the sooner he could turn back and ride for Thervanil and Teho'evan – if he was still alive by now. If he was – and his lieutenant prayed to the Good God that it might be so – there might yet be ways and means of averting disaster.

He was taken completely aback by the sight of two Skaira waiting for him. His initial, automatic reaction, a surge of joy, was instantly quelled by more sinister considerations. No Venel was going to be taken for a friend by any Skair on this world any more. He would be lucky to get the chance to open his beak before they charged. His soldier's instinct told him that he was in deadly danger, and his hand twitched towards his sword. He stopped the movement, with difficulty. Hardened campaigner though he was, sweat broke out on his back. There was no possibility of missing the hostility in the amber stares. The claws were bared, the ears flat. Both the Skaira were armed with belt knives, which he recognised as being of Venel military origin. The fact that so far they had not drawn them was small comfort: he knew the legendary speed of a Skair's reactions. Faesanei uttered a small sound of fear and reined in, clutching the baby to her more closely. Henanei also stopped, turning her hind across the other woman's in a probably futile gesture of protection. If he tried to talk to the Skaira and they attacked, it would only require one of them to deal with him, and the two women would be helpless without a male escort, even if they were permitted to escape by the other. Fleeing instead of trying to communicate might or might not save them: there could well be other Skaira nearby. Whether in the circumstances even the baby would be spared, there was no saying. Cubs had not been spared at Weruavwe. And what chance would there be for her if she did survive? There were predators aplenty in Three Stars that would make short work of an abandoned infant.

Dry-throated with fear, not so much for himself as for his family, Keri'khai did what was probably the hardest thing he had ever had to do in his life. He dropped the reins loose on his mount's neck, freed his feet from the stirrup loops and rode slowly forward, his hands raised level with his shoulders. If they attacked him now he would have no chance; it would be doubtful if he could even stay on his stag if it reared in terror from their charge. When he was several yards away from them the younger of the two Skaira put a hand on the hilt of her knife, but somehow he kept his hands high and his legs relaxed. Responding to the faint pressure of his thighs, his mount went on walking slowly towards her, but though she still held the knife she did not draw it from the sheath.

He was perhaps six feet from them when the older put out a hand. The nervous stag stopped immediately, its great soft ears flicking. Four amber eyes were fastened on his face as though they would rip his soul out from behind it.

"In the Goddess's name, I'm asking for your help," he said at last. "These women are in danger from the man who's trying to make himself Emperor. Your enemy's enemy should be your friend, and these badly need your protection."

"Is not yours sufficient?" asked the younger one. Her lips shuddered back from her teeth as she spoke, so that the light gleamed on the curving fangs. "Are Venelai such benefactors of ours, that you expect us to care who of you is in danger from another?"

"They haven't committed any crime, haven't done anything against anybody." He spoke a little desperately. "This woman's husband was kind to Princess Thaskan in Thervanil, and he's in prison back there. I don't want anything for myself; I only want to see them safe and get back to the city, to help him if I can. I don't think your Goddess would want you to take revenge on women and children, no matter what their menfolk have done."

"Do not teach us of the Goddess!" spat Lidan. Her hackles lifted in outrage. "There was small reverence for the Goddess when Weruavwe was attacked, Vanreil despoiled! Do not dare to invoke Her for your own ends!"

"*Vanreil* attacked?" He hadn't known. It had been hopeless enough before. Now he knew there was no chance at all. They were all four going to die.

Hargen put out a restraining hand. She had no difficulty in reading the genuine shock and dismay on his face, and her own hostility receded a little; but she knew that Lidan would still find it hard to resist avenging her mother on any available Venel target.

"You spoke of Thaskan," she said evenly. "Is she well treated?"

Lying was extremely dangerous: it was too well known how many Skaira were telepathic. On the other hand, telling the truth was probably suicidal. He took a deep, shuddering breath. "No," he said flatly. "She was alive when I last saw her, but barely. Stiv'aran's had her starved, the God knows why. He must have some reason, but what it might be is beyond me."

For one instant he knew that death was so close to him that he heard the lapping of the waves of the Endless Ocean. Then the Skaira seemed to step back and become normal again, though in actual fact they had not moved at all.

"That took courage," said Lidan grudgingly in the Old Speech. "Do you believe him?"

"I would not have believed him if he had told us what we wanted to hear. I think he is honest, and I know he is brave. And he is right when he says that Shieih would not wish us to avenge our dead on women and children."

"He is impudent, to try to teach Skaira the will of Shieih!"

"He is desperate. After what has happened, we should be his enemies, and the enemies of all his kind. When you beg help from an enemy, you do not always consider the propriety of the arguments you use, only their likely efficacy."

"Hargen, we can not afford to burden ourselves with them! What of Kelti, and our mission?"

"Yes. I know." The Priestess stared thoughtfully at the waiting soldier, who watched their indecipherable communication as though trying to understand it by

the concentration of his gaze. – "He wishes to go back to Thervanil. And Kelti must go to Thervanil. It seems to me that this may be an opportunity we can not afford to miss."
"You want *him* to take Kelti?" Lidan almost shrieked.
"It would be easier for him to gain access to the city than for you. I do not suggest that they go alone together, that would be folly at best. But he could perhaps find means to get you through the gates that would not be possible otherwise. If we protect the women and the child, he is under an obligation. This would be a means to repay it."
"By the One! Seven of us, going to Thervanil?"
"No. Three." Hargen looked at her intently. "I will take the women to Vanreil as he asks, in return for help for you and Kelti. That is, if you agree. If you do not, we will let them pass and go on as we had originally intended. I will force nothing on you."
"By the One!" said Lidan again. She paused, thinking the idea over. The risks were manifest. They knew nothing of this soldier, not even his name. She had much faith in Hargen's judgement – but to entrust Kelti's safety to one whom they had only just met, who might be wholly unworthy of trust, who could so easily betray them… But with the women as hostage for his good behaviour? Always supposing they were of some significance to him in the first place – that this was not some fiendish trap laid for them by the Dark One…

And yet, and yet, it was a good idea. The main problem facing them had been how they were to get Kelti into the city when they got there. With the help of one of the Venelai themselves, that could well be overcome very much more easily than it could possibly have been if they were on their own.

The main drawback, assuming (a large assumption!) that the Venel was trustworthy, was the fact that it would mean that Hargen was lost to her. She had relied upon having the Priestess as a back up for Kelti's safety. If the worst came to the worst, surely Shieih would show Hargen how to send him home. If they adopted this plan, it would mean that she and she alone was again responsible for his safe return to his own world. But Shieih had entrusted him to her in the first place. He *was* her responsibility – the man who had been, for that brief time in that other world, her lover…

Had Shieih sent this soldier, this Venel, to her to show her the way forward? And if so, dared she reject the gift?

But suppose he was a tool of the Enemy? How could she tell? And dared she take the risk that it might be so?

She gnawed at her lower lip, not knowing she was biting so hard that blood sprang. Finally, "Tell him to dismount. Tell him that they must all dismount and come to us."
Hargen glanced at her. Lidan was still watching the soldier, watching him with the terrible concentration of the predator. Without comment, and without any explanation, she relayed the command.

Keri'khai hesitated for a long moment. He had not understood a word of the Skaira's low-voiced conference, and the nature of the Old Speech prevented him from gleaning much information from the tone of their voices. It did not need a mind reader to detect the hostility of the younger one, however. Insofar as he was able to read Skair facial and body language, the older was nearer neutrality. Would she stand by and allow her junior to attack them? If he shouted out to the women to flee, he might be able to keep the Skaira busy for long enough for them to get away. But if they escaped, where had they to run? And what then of Teho'evan?

He glanced around at his companions. "Dismount."

There was no point in watching to see that they obeyed him: women did obey their menfolk. He leaned his weight forward and slipped his left leg easily across the saddle, springing lightly to the ground. His sword was now on the other side of the saddle, and out of his reach. The knife at his belt was sharpened to an edge that could cut the wind into slices, but it would not save him if even one of the Skaira came for him. He did not reach for it. In a moment or two he heard the soft sounds of the two women drawing level with him. Wrapped in Faesanei's thick, wine-coloured cloak, Narenei whimpered softly, catching her mother's tension.

"What relation are they to you?" asked Lidan, returning to the Common Speech but keeping her voice toneless.

"This is Henanei, whose husband is my commander. This is Faesanei, my wife, and Narenei, our daughter."

The Skair gazed at him with suddenly slitted eyes, her upper lip wrinkling malignantly. "And if I were to say, I will slay one of them to avenge our dead, and let the rest of you go free, whom would you offer me?"

"I'd hope you'd be merciful enough to kill me instead. At least you'd take your victim without a fight."

"And if I refused?"

"Then you'd have to choose your own victim. And you'd have to kill me before you touched any of them." He said it quietly but firmly. His hand rested on his belt, close to the hilt of the knife there.

Her eyes and mouth returned to their normal shape. She did not precisely smile, but the tension went out of her face. Whether or not they were who he had said they were, he valued the women and the child. It was something.

"I agree," she said to Hargen, again in the Old Speech. "But the women must not know of Kelti's existence. The fewer let into that secret, the fewer can tell of it."

"Then how will you persuade him to co-operate?"

"If he wishes his womenfolk taken to Vanreil he will do as he is bidden."

"Lidan," said the older Skair gently, "he is not an animal. I understand how you must feel, but do not blame the entire world for the actions of a few. He will respond better to trust than to coercion, even as you yourself would do."

"Trust him? I do not know him."

"And if you treat him unjustly you never will know him, and thereby deprive yourself of the possibility of trusting him. Do not alienate a possible ally. You will need all the help you can find to keep Kelti safe: it would be folly to deprive yourself of it by venting your pain on an innocent man."

Lidan grimaced, but the truth of the Priestess's words was self-evident. "I still can not trust him."

"I do not advise you to trust him, but to treat him as though you do. You are wise enough to deal so that you learn in due course whether or not you are justified. If

he betrays you, his women will die by my hand – but do not tell him that unless he earns their deaths."
"Why not?" demanded Lidan, mystified.
"Because if he is the man I believe him to be, he will not need to be told. He will protect you from gratitude for their safety better than he would for fear of it."
"Now that I do not understand. But you have mingled with these folk more than I; if you say it is so, I will believe you. Now, we have talked enough. Take the women and go. I still do not want them to see Kelti."

Hargen inclined her head. Briefly she told the Venel that she was willing to take his companions to the Temple Complex, which had not so far come under attack and would be the safest place for them, in return for his escorting her companion to Thervanil. "And one other, of whom she will tell you presently," she added. "If you agree to this, I shall be answerable for the safety of your womenfolk, and I ask that you be answerable for her and the other while they remain with you."

Keri'khai did not answer immediately: he did not believe in hasty decisions. Nevertheless, it did not take much thought to see the advantage for the women in being taken to Vanreil by a Skair. Assuming the Priestess was making a genuine offer – and if she were bent on killing, there was nothing he could do to stop her, but Skaira were known to disdain falsehood – they were considerably likelier to be admitted there under the protection of one of the Daughters themselves, and his protection along the route would probably be rather less effective than that of the formidable Priestess. He was deeply perplexed as to why any Skair should want to go near Thervanil: it would appear suicidal in the circumstances. Still, that was their affair. If that was the price of seeing his women safe, he was quite prepared to pay it. "I agree," he said. Turning, he embraced his wife and bent to rub a gentle beak along the soft down of his daughter's cheek. "It's the safest way for you. I'll come for you when it's over."
"Keep safe. We'll be waiting." A soldier's wife, who had long ago learned how to cope with the fact that her husband lived in constant danger, Faesanei was not in the habit of displaying her feelings, but that did not mean she had none. She held Narenei tightly because she could not hold her husband to her and protect him. She mistrusted the Skair who was to accompany him to Thervanil. And who was this 'other'? Would she ever see either of them again?

Henanei too was obliged to choke back protest. She shared Faesanei's distrust of Lidan, whose hostility was thinly veiled. Keri'khai was the best hope her husband had of escaping Stiv'aran's malice: was his safety to be put in hazard for some nameless plan of the Skair's? But womenfolk did not argue with a man's decisions. They could only pray to the Goddess that he had made the right one. They went back to their saddlebeasts and remounted, saying nothing.

Hargen turned and gestured to them to follow her, shooting one glance at the tree where Brendan had remained hidden throughout. "I had not thought that I would not have the chance to take leave of Kelti," she said a little sadly to Lidan, using the Old Speech for the last time. "I must hope that the Goddess brings us together again. As soon as I have them safe in the Complex I will come after you again with all the speed I can."

“Go with Her blessing.” Lidan hugged her. “If needs be I will make your farewells for you.”

“So that you both succeed and live, farewells can be dispensed with. Will we not all meet again beyond the Endless Ocean?”

“I know it. But sometimes in these troubles, it is hard to keep it in mind.” She bent her head and wiped wetness from her eyes. “Go quickly. The night draws on, and I would have us well apart before we rest again.”

“Go with the Goddess.”

And so they parted.

24

Brendan, meanwhile, had been having a small adventure of his own.

Left behind the tree, he had very properly remained completely silent. He had watched the first part of the encounter, wondering what was going to happen. The distance between himself and the others had prevented him from hearing much, though the tension was clearly visible. He had been puzzled at first by the physical differences between the foremost Venel and the two who remained behind him: unlike human women, female Venelai do not have prominent breasts. Their heads were smaller and more slender, their shoulders more narrow: he had begun to guess at the truth even before one looked down to speak to the bundle she held in her lap. He gazed at them with interest. Two women and a baby. Illogical as it might be, somehow it seemed to improve his perception of the Venelai in general to find that they had families like humans. It was easy enough to see that the armed male was putting himself between his females and the threat presented by the Skaira, and from the menacing aspect of Hargen and Lidan, he was a brave man to do it. Brendan found himself hoping that there might be some happy ending possible to the encounter. He had no illusions as to the willingness of the two Skaira to slaughter anyone they felt to be a danger to their mission, and prayed that he would not have to witness the killing of what were obviously innocent civilians. At that moment, his safety did not seem worth the price of such brutality. He saw the two Skaira begin to confer between themselves, which was reasonably encouraging – from what he knew of them, it was unlikely that having made up their minds to attack they would have needed to discuss it. The longer it went on the more hopeful he became. He was not destined to watch the whole of it, however. Something touched him on the leg.

Thinking initially that it was his stag nuzzling him for caresses – he had discovered early on that the saddlebeasts were very tactile creatures – he put back a hand to rub the broad muzzle he expected to find. His fingers encountered something quite different, and the reflex of shock brought his hand back like lightning, his head jerking round.

It was not the stag. It was a smallish animal, perhaps a foot and a half in length excluding the tail, and a foot or so high at the shoulder. Its fur was silvery in colour, dappled with rather beautiful rosettes of darker grey. The lushness of this was rather like a cat's, especially where long silky tufts of it fell from the bases of the ears, but the shape of the head was more like that of a dog: the muzzle was long, the ears soft and floppy. Its legs and plumed tail were long and slender. And to complete the illusion, it was wearing a collar.

Brendan loved dogs. He was only momentarily disconcerted by the fact that the animal's eyes were not at all like a dog's, but silvery like the rest of it. Moving gently so as not to startle the visitor, he extended his hand again, holding it with palm down and fingers closed as was wise when dealing with an unknown dog. The animal smelled his skin carefully, looking up intently into his face as it did so. Then it jumped into his arms.

The suddenness of the movement almost knocked him backwards. As hopeful as he had been of a friendly response to his overtures, he hadn't expected anything quite this friendly. The last dog to do this had been the Labrador-cross pup he'd adopted in his early teens. The name was painfully ready in his memory: Topaz. As the soft fur was crushed against his nose he breathed in a scent that was uncannily familiar: Topaz after a run through the warm bracken on Slieve Elva, with the sun on his back and the heather in flower…

There was suddenly a lump in his throat. A dog. A lost dog, looking for security. Smelling like Topaz. He always had been a sucker for dogs. He couldn't turn this one away. No matter what Lidan thought.

To give himself something else to think about while the pain of the long-buried memories subsided, he looked at the collar. Perhaps there was some kind of identification on it that Lidan or Hargen might be able to decipher: it might even be possible to trace an owner. Perhaps someone, somewhere, was searching for a lost pet; the way he had searched, though without hope of finding, across the rain-swept slopes of the Burren, the day Topaz had died.

Oh, this was *futile.* The people on this world had more to worry about than one lost dog. Lidan was more likely to eat it than sympathise with it. That didn't mean he didn't have to care, he decided obstinately. He was going to keep it. But not call it Topaz. No. He put the animal down, though it continued to snuggle against him, making little treble cooing noises in its throat. He examined the collar again. It was made in one piece, not buckled. Most peculiar stuff: he couldn't decide what it was made of. It had the texture of metal and the resilience of rubber, and it was not wholly pleasant to the touch. Not unpleasant, just …a little cold, and very slightly tingly. It too was silver in colour, with a surface that was beautiful to look at, reflecting the late evening light in shimmers. He could not find any markings on it at all.

What should the dog's name be? Come to think of it, before he decided, shouldn't he find out what sex it was? He lifted one of the hind legs, that being the easiest check from his angle. Unless this sort of animal had its genitals elsewhere, which seemed rather unlikely, it was a bitch. So, a suitable name for a bitch. Something appropriate. *Uisge* came into his mind from nowhere. Whiskey? No, wrong colour. But it wasn't the wrong colour. *Uisge beatha,* the colourless illegal 'poteen' that burned its way down the throat and lay simmering in the stomach. And the literal translation, 'water' was very apt. The silvery fur with its darker markings could be thought to look like the surface of a pool dimpled with raindrop circles. So, Uisge it should be. He murmured the name into its ears and it pushed its nose into his face and blew lovingly at him.

"By the One!" Lidan was staring down at him in amazement. "Where did that come from?"

"I don't know. But you mustn't eat it," he said quickly, remembering the unfortunate incident with the helti all too clearly. "I want to keep it."

"Why?" asked the Skair. "What use is it to you?"

Use? Were all Skaira so unsparingly practical? He couldn't think of where to start to explain, and he didn't want to talk about Topaz. "I just want to keep it."

"Well, I suppose it will do no harm. But if danger threatens, it looks to itself. I am not endangering you for the sake of looking after a strayed rodent-chaser."

"Is that what it is?"

“The Venelai keep them for company, and to keep their houses free from vermin. There is a proper name for them, but it is in their language and I can never pronounce it properly. We just call them ‘rodent-chasers’. It is all they are.”

The Venelai rose another few points in his estimation. They kept pets. Clearly Skaira did not understand the concept, that much was clear from that dismissive description.

“Keep it if you wish,” she went on with a sigh. “Now, there are more important things I must speak to you about. Our plans have changed. We have spoken with the Venelai back there, and come to an arrangement.”

“We’re not going to Thervanil after all?” Hope rose in him so giddily that for a moment he was almost sick with it.

“Unfortunately, that has not changed. We have decided that Hargen must return to Vanreil, taking with her the Venel females and the child. In return for their safety, the man will escort you and me to Thervanil, and do his best to get us into the city undetected.”

“And you think that’s a good idea?” He tried not to let his own doubt of it show in his voice.

She brushed a hand wearily across her eyes. “It is our best chance of getting into the city without being discovered. He seems a good enough man, and he is grateful for Hargen taking his females under her protection. Now I must introduce you to him. He has been told that you are not of this world, but he will probably still be surprised when he sees you.”

Brendan was getting a bit tired of being astonishing. If ever he made it back to Earth, one of the first things he intended to do was to go out on a busy street and walk down it without one single person looking at him twice. It would be so *restful.*

He patted Uisge reassuringly and stood up. Across the clearing only the Venel soldier was visible, staring. He looked around for Hargen. There was no sign of her.

“We felt it best if the women did not see you. Hargen was sorry to have to leave you without farewells, but it was best for your safety. She will come after us again when she has left them at Vanreil with Varei and the others. Now come and meet Keri’khai.”

“Keri- what?”

“Keri’khai.” She pronounced it slowly so that he could hear the small aspiration that divided the two syllables. “All Venelai males, and females of high rank, have names that derive from both of their parents. It is a very ancient custom. Come and be introduced.”

With some trepidation, he stepped out of hiding. Lidan’s more experienced eye noted the feathers shifting slightly on Keri’khai’s head: he certainly was shocked by Kelti’s strange appearance.

“What do I say?” asked Brendan in an undertone. ‘How do you do’ somehow seemed a bit inappropriate in the circumstances.

“Just say what you said to Kanehar. He will not expect you to speak to him in his own language.”

It was harder than he would have expected to walk up and look the soldier in the face. The Venel was considerably taller than he – about four or five inches, and frighteningly muscular around the chest. He was also fully armed, and the light glinted off the bronze breastplate: his clothing was like something from ancient Greece or Rome, with a short grey tunic beneath the armour and a deep blue cloak buckled at the shoulder. Brendan had become fairly used to the inhumanity of Skair eyes, but the round golden glare of the Venel's falcon gaze was deeply disturbing. For a brief moment he felt a sick resurgence of the shattering loneliness he had felt on first finding himself on Kerriel. He craved for the sight of a human face. Illogically, it troubled him somehow that creatures so unlike his own kind should have something that would probably be defined as immortal souls. He was glad that the claw-like hand was not extended for a handshake; he would not have wanted to accept it. For reasons he would have been hard put to define, beyond the fact that he was made to feel very small and puny in comparison, he disliked proximity to the soldier. This was nothing personal – he would have felt the same for any of them. The total absence of humanity in the face robbed him of any ability to read it; he couldn't even have placed any reliance on body language. Keri'khai didn't say anything, so he felt obliged to offer some kind of civility, but for the life of him, he couldn't remember what he'd said to Kanehar. In the event, he said "Pleased to meet you", which was more polite than true. He wasn't sure how truthful the soldier was either, when he replied courteously that it was an honour, but probably wasn't exactly thrilled either.

Keri'khai was indeed extremely perturbed by the revelation of the nature of the 'one other' whom he had to escort to Thervanil. He could now understand perfectly well why the Skaira had not wanted the women to see this strange Starborn creature, and was grateful that their desire for secrecy had spared his charges a nasty shock. Lidan had explained to him no more than was necessary about Brendan's presence on Kerriel, but it was not hard to guess that she intended him as a weapon against Stiv'aran. Given that assumption, the lieutenant was perfectly ready to help her in any way possible – even more so than he had been originally. To press her for more information yet was probably a waste of time. He was realistic enough to understand that she must be extremely protective of the odd, skinny creature, and would not welcome curiosity from one whom she had no reason, as yet, to trust. Perhaps in due course she would find it within herself to open up a little: there must be a story well worth hearing behind this. Despite his awareness of the forces arrayed against them, the odds against success, Keri'khai found that his heart had unexpectedly lightened. It seemed that the Gods had not deserted them after all. What use this man would be, what powers were at his command, was only known to the Skair and to her Goddess. Until he had earned the right to be told, he was content to wait and trust them, doing his best in the meanwhile to safeguard his charges and smooth their way forward in any way possible.

He had been slightly surprised that the Starborn had acquired a pet (Uisge was stuck to Brendan's heels as if glued there), but the appearance of the stag, which came trotting after its new master, was less remarkable. He had already noted that the Skaira had Venel weapons at their belts, and he knew that Shas'kare's troops had gone into Three Stars with hostile intentions. It was not hard to infer that the Daughters had already had at least one encounter with soldiers, out of which they had come victorious. He thanked the God that they had been willing to talk to him instead of attacking him on sight, as would have been reasonable enough in the circumstances.

The two riders remounted. Practice had given Brendan some confidence in the saddle, and if the experienced eye of a real expert saw flaws in his technique, at least there should be no grave danger of his falling off if they were forced to make a run for it. Privately Keri'khai resolved that if the worst came to the worst, he would take Kelti into his charge and leave Lidan to deal as best she could. It was a horrifying prospect, but she could not match the speed of a stag, and it would be no use having all of them captured. What he should do with the Starborn then was anyone's guess. He would just have to hope that the situation never arose. In the meantime they were heading back towards the city. There was still some ground they could cover before the light failed entirely; and both he and the Skair were equally anxious to reach Thervanil with all speed. He had a friend and she a Princess to save. For one if not both of these, time must be very quickly running out.

25

"I knew that one of you would come back."

It did not come as quite the surprise that the speaker might have wished: it was, after all, another Skair whom she had been stalking, not some witless animal. Escorting the Venel women through the forest towards the Temple Complex, Hargen had been aware for some time that she had company, and of the identity of it. She had not believed it to be a threat, though she was not pleased by the development. Their journey to Vanreil had been uneventful, but she was glad to be back in the Holy Valley again, especially now she was free from the complication of having to conceal Kelti beneath her wing there. She was ready to face the expected recriminations; the prospect left her unmoved. She was also confident of being able to exert sufficient authority to ensure that the women under her care were allowed to stay with her there. It was wholly likely that their arrival across Sikkthi had been noted, since they had made no attempt to conceal it and it would have been no more than logic for lookouts to have been posted. In fact, had they not been intercepted at some point along the route, she herself would have had many unflattering things to say when she arrived at the Temple Complex. No, Resat had her failings, but she was quite able to organise the defences that no one would ever have imagined the Complex would need.

"So you are a clairvoyant as well as a telepath," she said shortly. "Come out, Riyeth. I can not imagine why you have felt it necessary to shadow me all this distance, it is not in the least entertaining." The berry-spangled bushes rustled, and Riyeth stepped out. She cast a single glance of withering contempt at the two women, and thereafter ignored them as though they did not exist. This was very like her, as Hargen remembered: she never had had room for more than one issue in her head at a time.

"What have you done with him?" she demanded without preamble. Her claws dug at the ground as the big soft paws shifted restlessly among the fallen yellow leaves.

"Keri'khai has gone back to Thervanil," replied Hargen blandly. "I escort his womenfolk to safety here, as you can see."

Riyeth's face worked. The tip of her stiff tail lashed. "Do not insult me. You know whom I mean. The Otherworlder, the vermin who has defiled our Shrine with his presence."

"Still as intelligent as ever, I see," remarked the Priestess.

"You are ignorant and arrogant!" snarled Riyeth. "You have polluted the Shrine with your filthy starborn whelp, and plot to put Thaskan's life in danger by your imbecilic folly! Now you will pay the price for it!"

"And is Varei well?" inquired Hargen.

For all her flippancy, the Priestess had been watching the other like a hawk. She was ready for the lunge, and evaded it with ease, delivering a stinging slap to Riyeth's flattened ear as she plunged past.

"I am not answerable to you, Riyeth eré Saleh! Do not assume a cloak that does not belong to you! If the First Priestess requires answers of me I shall give them, but to you I owe nothing, and seeing your attitude I would tell you nothing even if I owed all! And that is final!"

Her face a mask of rage and humiliation, Riyeth spun around. She did not make the mistake of trying to attack Hargen again, for the Priestess was considerably larger and heavier and swift for all her size. All Riyeth's strength was concentrated in her will, and her slight body shook with the violence of her frustration. For a heartbeat she hung as if poised between choices; then she seemed to shrink into herself, like a snake coiling to strike. For reasons that were not immediately clear, she stepped backwards a little.

"You will tell me nothing? I think otherwise, Priestess Hargen," she said softly. "I think you will tell me whatever I wish to know."

For one instant the older Skair genuinely did not know what she meant. Then she stiffened in incredulity. It was not possible.

"You would not *dare*," she breathed. The oldest taboo of all, older than Skairesse itself, the ultimate misuse of Power. They had all been taught from earliest cubhood the ruling words of their sorcery, the Words that governed every use. 'To be used for no evil, and to harm no creature, and to uphold the Law'… that was the first half of the very first sentence. And what Riyeth intended would violate all three parts of it. It was unimaginable sacrilege.

Riyeth merely smiled. There was no humour in it, simply a baring of fangs. Her eyes were colder than winter ice. "You think not?"

"You would not dare!" shouted Hargen, suddenly herself in a towering rage. "You have been a fool, but not until now a dastard! You do not know what you would risk!"

"I will not stand idle and watch while you and that other Tharnil-spawned misbegotten she-cat endanger Thaskan!" screamed Riyeth. Her mouth was suddenly contorted with vicious fury. "You will tell me everything!"

"Do you think Thaskan herself would countenance this?" roared Hargen. "Do you for one moment imagine she would think it worth the evil you would do to yourself?"

"It is of no matter, so that she is safe," hissed Riyeth. "You can not hide from me, Hargen!"

The Priestess saw the beginning of the movement, and knew that there was no reasoning with her, no stopping the cataclysm that threatened. Riyeth had taken care to place herself out of range of an immediate killing strike. A struggle would probably be unavailing; now that she had consented to the evil, it was already launched. For their own sake Hargen wanted no witnesses to what was coming: there was no saying now what Riyeth was or was not capable of. With reflexes that were surely honed by the act of the Goddess, she whirled around and slapped the spotted rumps of the waiting hinds, so that both sprang forward with squeals of shock. "The river ahead!" she shouted to the women. "Follow it downstream! Tell them what you saw!"

There was no time for more. The Power hit her like a battering ram.

Kanehar was sitting beside the pool enjoying the early morning sun. The furore over her activities with Kelti still had not completely died down, but after much heated argument she had finally prevailed on Varei to agree that as the one to whom Shieih had entrusted the Starborn's safety in the first place, Lidan should be allowed to judge for herself what was best for him. To placate those more urgent for action, they had also agreed to have a constant watch of telepaths on the borders of the Holy Mountains, so that any call for help could be answered swiftly. Resat had all her juniors standing by, armed and ready for action, and most of these were so infected by their leader's nervous tension that they had become too keyed up to sleep. The Healer had had to be stern with several about taking calming medication, and had resisted the urge to seek out Resat and hit her over the head with something solid.

She had wanted some time for solitude and prayer this morning, and had been brusque about achieving it. It was usual to go to the Shrine at such times, but despite the fact that the holy place had been thoroughly cleaned and put back to such rights as the circumstances allowed, she did not want to go there. There was still a gap where the wall was broken down and no Seer lived beyond it; there was still an aching emptiness in the Image's raised hand. Worst of all, for her, there was a tapestry hanging up that held too many memories for her to look upon it with comfort, at least until she could be assured that the one whom it had concealed was safely back in his own world.

A fine Healer she was, treating others for a malady she herself was sick with. At this hour she should be composing herself for rest. She herself should go to the cupboard where the jars of remedies were stored, and take a spoonful of the milky stuff that brought dreamless sleep. She could not bring herself to do it, however. The tiredness that was nibbling at the edges of her brain was less real than the restless sense of threat that had begun to pervade the rest of it.

As convinced as she had been, and still was, of the rightness of Lidan's belief that the best hope of safety lay in secrecy, she was still deeply worried. She had liked the Starborn for himself, and hated the knowledge that he was frightened and in danger. Subconsciously she had transferred to him the fears she had had to stifle as best she could for her cub, half a continent away and out of her power to protect. If she had known where he and Lidan had gone, she might well have followed them. It had been best that she did not know, even though Mesca would never have been allowed to take the information from her by force even if she had wanted to, but it was a pity that she could not find out now. She knew that several of her sisters had gone to the Silent Pool on Sikkthi in the attempt to find out, probably not with Varei's blessing; but she had put her trust in the Goddess, and had not been disappointed. There had been no answer. The pool had remained blank, much to the surprise and dismay of the questioners. Such a thing had never happened before. It had been far too strong an indication for anyone to ignore. If the Pool itself was keeping the secret, it was certainly not meant to get out. Once word had got around, no one else had dared to go up to ask.

She stared into the water, flexing her claws restlessly. The words of the litany she had begun to recite ran through her mind almost without thought. 'Lady of life making, bless us. Shieih of the Endless Ocean, receive us. Goddess of the dark hours, guide us. Mother of All Life, guard us. Firstborn of-"

Hoofbeats. Coming at speed. Almost in the same instant there was a cry of warning from one of the lookouts posted around the Complex. How had they got this close? What had happened to the sentinel at the west, the most sensitive approach, and the one that covered Sikkthi and the route to Thervanil? Who had been posted there?

The answer sprang into Kanehar's mind, and the formless sense of threat crystallised into one of impending disaster. She was already standing, ears swivelling to pin down the exact direction of the approach. The stream. They were following the stream. They were indeed coming from Sikkthi. Mother Shieih protect us. Riyeth, *what have you done?*

There were many waiting to respond to just such an alarm. Skaira boiled out of the houses, catching at knives, howling defiance. A dozen of the most senior of the Warrior Arts priestesses surged towards Varei's house, their body armour clattering together as they shoved to get in through the door to surround her. It was probably a mercy that sorcery could not be used in such circumstances: it was not meant for use in self-defence, or the Palace at Weruavwe could have been held against any attack. If the combined fear and hatred of the inhabitants of the Complex at that moment could have been channelled into sorcery, it would have been sufficient to annihilate an entire army, let alone the two desperate fugitives riding towards it.

Kanehar had no Thought Power. It would have taken the united voices of a dozen Skaira to make themselves heard in the uproar. Nevertheless, she filled her lungs and bawled out a single word: "WAIT!"

Everyone stopped. Dead silence fell. Heads turned timidly. The Healer realised with a mixture of shock and gratification that she had not shouted only with her voice. Well, well! Talents did sometimes make themselves known later in life, but this was something she had not expected.

"Listen!" she said crossly. "There are two of them. Only two! Do you think they would send two soldiers to attack us?"

Ears swivelled. Faces assumed sheepish expressions. Knives went back into sheaths. Nobody went back into her house, however – it was not to be thought that whoever was riding like that was coming on a commonplace errand, and any arrival might be bringing news. Even Varei was allowed to come out to the door, though her bodyguard neither relaxed nor disarmed.

Moments later, the two hard-ridden hinds galloped into the clearing. They were pulled up with difficulty; the panic of their riders had communicated itself to them, and several Skaira had to jump out of the way with more haste than dignity. Faesanei had the baby to look after, but Henanei almost fell out of the saddle, looking for the nearest authority. She knew that senior Skaira wore armbands, and she ran towards the nearest that she could see, a sturdy individual who hastened forward. "She needs help!" she gasped, in far too much haste and urgency to bother with the formal salutations. "Hargen – the other one's attacking her!"

"Hargen!" Kanehar's face went perfectly white. What in the name of the Goddess was Hargen doing back at Vanreil? She could understand all too well why Riyeth was attacking her, now that she had found her. But where was Lidan, and most urgently of all, where was Kelti? If Riyeth got her claws into him, his life would not be worth a snapped twig.

"Look after them!" she shouted, gesturing to one of her juniors she spotted nearby. "Resat – Kareh – Tolveren – follow me!"

Nobody argued, nobody looked at Varei for confirmation. Resat and her two fellow warriors sprang forward, needing no second invitation to get into action. Skaira were not built for more than a short sprint, but dread lent Kanehar wings as she hurtled up the path beside the stream. Even if they had had breath to spare for it, none of her companions asked questions. Others were on their trail; there would be no shortage of help if it were needed. What the Healer was praying for now was a miracle, and the horror that had closed around her heart forewarned her that none would be forthcoming.

They came upon her suddenly, sprawled to one side of a clearing. Kanehar almost missed her, but caught a glimpse of bright fur among the greenery. She swerved so sharply that Resat almost cannoned into her. "Hargen! Mother Shieih, Hargen!"

There was nothing to be done. If the Priestess had given in, Riyeth would have taken the information she wanted without doing damage – or perhaps she would not, there was no telling. Hargen had resisted with all the colossal strength that was in her. The struggle had been titanic, but Riyeth had finally won it. What remained was not enough to keep her defeated foe alive.

Kanehar fell down beside her friend and gently lifted the battered head. There were very few signs on the body: Riyeth had not needed to attack with her claws. In desperation Hargen had tried to dash her own skull against a rock or a tree-trunk to kill herself before the information could be stripped from her. With her enemy already tearing her asunder from inside, she had not been able to exert enough control and force to do it – the injuries were no more than superficial. If this had been all the damage, Kanehar would have been inexpressibly grateful; but even as she registered that there was still warmth in the skin she touched, the Healer saw the expression in the fading amber eyes, and knew that what had been done to Hargen was beyond repairing. Astonishingly, the Priestess had held on this long; but her grip was failing fast.

"The women – look after them," she whispered, discharging her last obligation. "I promised... Kelti has gone to Thervanil. Riyeth knows... could not stop her. Forgive..." The last word was no more than a sigh, and her life went with it. Blood trickled out of her nose and ears. Her body sagged into stillness. The silence was complete, as the three Warriors looked on, stunned and helpless.

"Mother Shieih!" Kanehar wrenched her head from side to side in anguish, then slowly lowered it and rubbed ears with her dead friend, leaving tears smeared across the cheekbone as she cradled the rapidly cooling torso. "You were the best, the dearest... I will kill her myself for this!"

Forgive, repeated the silence. But had it been a plea – or a last command?

26

Stiv'aran had a reputation for expecting his orders to be obeyed fast and thoroughly, and in Shas'kare he had one of the best officers in the army. The orders to deploy troops throughout Three Stars had depleted the forces immediately available to the warleader, but he made the best use of what he had. Within a couple of hours a considerable proportion of the remainder of his Division marched out of the city. He was far too experienced to send them out of reach of quick recall, should trouble rear its head inside the walls, but he also kept a strong defensive force of his best men immediately to hand. A steel net spread out around Thervanil. Should any foolish Otherworlder attempt to break through it, its meshes would simply close around him. And that would be the end of the affair.

It was sheer coincidence that a junior officer whose foremost passion was hunting commanded one of the patrols. In his free hours, this young man – his name was Lan'avir – devoted his energies to breeding and training a pack of hunting animals of a type unlike anything found on earth in the twentieth century. They were reptiles, about the height of an average dog, and like a dog they had an acute sense of smell. Essentially wild animals, few attempts had ever been made to domesticate them and their intelligence had been badly under-estimated. In his youth Lan'avir had been one of a couple of hunters attacked by a mother defending a nest, and having been lucky enough to kill her (though not before his companion had been quite badly savaged), he had found the eggs just on the point of hatching. Even then interested in all hunters like himself, he had taken several of the hatchlings home and reared them. The results had fired an enthusiasm that still dominated him to the extent that he was rarely seen without at least one of the beasts somewhere within call. He regretted the fact that army discipline did not allow pets on parade, but his best male, Calgax, was trained to wait, curled into a leathery ball, in the warmest available spot until called. This had been the case when the troop was called into action and despatched from the city. There had been so much going on that it had seemed safe enough to softly chirrup Calgax into position under his stirrup loop as the cavalcade passed out through the barrack arch. Fortunately at that moment Shas'kare's attention had been elsewhere. Calgax had trotted out in his usual place, moving lightly and easily on hind legs, his long tail extended behind him for balance.

The orders had been specific enough, if puzzling – they were to watch for, and if found, kill, any 'unusual' life form they might find in the forest. As the troop rode out across the grassy levels that separated the city from the edge of the woodlands, speculation broke out. What sort of 'life form' might they be searching for? A strange beetle? A bird? "Lieutenant Tah'sen – he's unusual enough!" – guffaws greeted this witticism.

"The One knows!" snapped Lan'avir, who had no expectation of finding anything, and suffered an uneasy suspicion that he ought to squash disrespect to his fellow officer. He was newly promoted, however, and not quite sure enough of his authority. "Just – keep your eyes open!" Still, he reflected, it was a fine morning, his war-stag was fresh and eager to run, and with any luck Calgax would pick up the scent of something worth chasing….

Lidan was bending to drink from a stream when she first caught the far-off sound of hooves. She froze, ears swivelling. An out-thrust arm caught Keri'khai and Brendan into stillness. Her hackles lifted as she identified the source. More of the accursed saddlebeasts, and they were coming from Thervanil. Soldiers – it was almost certain they were soldiers. She flung an anxious, suspicious glance at Keri'khai. If he were feigning alarm, he was a good actor. Brendan instinctively crouched into the greenery, but there was nothing like enough to hide them. The stag threw up its muzzle and whickered softly, its great ears twitching with interest; the lieutenant quickly covered its nose to hush it.

"Nowhere to hide," growled the Skair. "We have to go back. There is better cover at the far side of the hill."

Keri'khai stared around, evidently trying to work out some way of evading the patrol without retracing so much ground, but the trees in this part of the forest were well spaced and the undergrowth sparse and scrubby. Heartbreaking as it might be when they were so close to their goal, there was no alternative. They had to retreat, and quickly.

At first, though they set off immediately and kept up a good pace, there was more annoyance than fear. There was indeed plenty of cover on the opposite side of the low hill they had just crossed, and with any luck the patrol would take the track that wound around it and follow that for the ease of their mounts' legs. The fugitives had avoided using the track at all, for fear of leaving prints on it. They could take cover in the thickets that crowded in the lee of the hill and wait there for the patrol to pass, a comfortable distance away and blissfully unaware of them.

Brendan's heart was beating rather fast, but he was reassured by the evident belief of his companions that this was more of an inconvenience than a threat. He held his stag's bridle, trying to help it pick its way up the rocky slope down which they had scrambled so short a time before. Uisge leaped lightly up alongside.

They had just crested the hill, and were within perhaps a bowshot of the rhododendron-like shrubs that held out the promise of sanctuary, when they heard the sound.

It meant nothing to Brendan, but instinctively he stopped in his tracks. Such a thin, ululating wail, it sounded more like a wheezy far-off air raid siren than anything that could possibly have been made by an animal. The air went out of Lidan's lungs as if somebody had punched her in the stomach. She gripped the nearest tree, clutching it so hard that her claws ground into the bark and ripped it. Her eyes met Keri'khai's in a glance that shared a sudden appalled realisation.

"Lan'avir! Tharnil's blackness take the fool!" groaned the lieutenant.

"A garynon? Someone has trained a *garynon?*" whispered Lidan. "A soldier….?"

"Yes!" Keri'khai half turned, hand on his sword hilt. Alternatives crashed through his brain. He did not know Lan'avir at all well, but the reptiles he trained were widely discussed. It was dreadfully probable that the creature had picked up

Brendan's scent, or Lidan's. They were known to be relentless pursuers in the wild, trailing herds for many miles until an unwary individual strayed within range of attack by the pack. If its handler were intent on the chase, it would be difficult to persuade him to abandon it without very good reason. Lan'avir co-ranked him, and could not be simply ordered away.
"It will follow us," the Skair said flatly. "We can not hide from a garynon. We must fight."
"Against a patrol? We wouldn't have a chance." He glanced desperately at Brendan, who had gone pale. – "I know the man who trains it. He'll be in command of the patrol. I have an idea – but we have to get into heavy cover!"

Lan'avir sat bolt upright in the saddle when the shrill cry of excitement burst from his garynon's throat. He had stopped the patrol by the stream to allow the saddlebeasts to drink, and had had no suspicion at all that life was about to become so extremely enjoyable. Whatever the reptile had discovered, its scent led straight away into the forest, and by the way Calgax leaped forward, the nostrils flaring on the long narrow muzzle, it had been here only a very short time ago. Perhaps it was the life form they had been sent out to search for – but whatever it was, its pursuit and death would be a pleasant diversion!

Rallying the troop, he spurred his beast forward after the eagerly hurrying hunter. The prey had obviously been panicked; the trail led straight ahead. He hoped it would be something well worth the killing.

They followed the scent straight up the hill, and over the top. The garynon did not pause, but ran straight towards the belt of thick greenery that crowded among the trees on the other side. Lan'avir drew his sword and set spurs lightly into his saddlebeast's side; the reptile's sudden bursts of speed could be quite astonishing. They crashed into the bushes, and had to begin concentrating hard on staying in the saddle as branches caught and whipped at them. Calgax gave tongue again, an unearthly screech somewhere ahead of them; and next instant it rose into the sustained howling that signalled that the prey had been run to earth. Almost crying with frustration and excitement, Lan'avir spurred his saddlebeast across the final glade to where Calgax was crouching in front of a great stand of ferny greenery, head weaving as it went on emitting that crazed howl beseeching the command to attack. Pulling his mount up so hard it went up on its haunches, his men thundering to a halt all around him to share the excitement, Lan'avir hurled himself from the saddle, sword drawn, and advanced on the hidden quarry….
"*Stand for an officer!*" The bellow almost flung him back on his heels, and even silenced the garynon's wailing. A fully armed Venel lieutenant erupted from the ferns, a picture of wrath, adjusting his clothing. As he moved, the disturbed greenery parted to reveal an outflung hand on the ground, and a tangle of glimmering fair hair.
"What…." Lan'avir stammered. "You…." He stared at the hair. "I….."
"What in the name of Tharnil are you playing at?" the unknown lieutenant thundered. "Well?"

"I….." The luckless hunter prayed vainly for the greensward to swallow him. "I thought…."
"You *thought!"* roared the other. "Well try thinking something *else,* another time! Something *useful!"* He seemed to become aware of the eyes riveted on the thing on the ground. A hand, the wrong shape for a Venel's – the tumbled tresses of hair, almost silvery fair against the dark leaves…. He wiped a hand brusquely across a trickle of blood that had run down his thigh. The patrol was now staring him with mingled horror and admiration. Few of them would have thought of taking their body pleasures with one of the People of the Wood – evidently she had not been willing…
"Need a hand, sir?" offered one of them.
The officer's eyes narrowed. "Do you need your head?"
"Sir, I'm sorry…. I didn't realise…." Lan'avir was almost babbling with embarrassment. Even his promotion had been forgotten. "We'll leave you in peace now….."
"Good!" The orange glare transfixed him. "You say nothing about this, and I'll say nothing about you! Is that understood?"
"Perfectly, sir… perfectly…." He spun on his heel, dragging the bewildered Calgax with him by the collar. – "You men, mount up!"

Keri'khai watched as they got themselves back astride their mounts, some averting their eyes, others trying surreptitiously to get a better look at whatever he was straddling. "Get out of here," he said curtly.
A few ragged salutes acknowledged the order. Lan'avir cast a single nauseated look back as he rode away. His men followed him. None of them lingered. Within moments the hoofbeats had gathered speed, and they quickly died away into the green forest; but not until the very last echo had faded did Keri'khai dare to let his shoulders sag. His knees were trembling, and the feathers down his spine were saturated with sweat. He used the hem of his leather tunic to press the cut across the top of his thigh, carefully inflicted with his own dagger to provide the strategic trickle of blood. At his feet, Lidan and Brendan disentangled themselves from each other. Brendan was shaking, and Lidan not far from it.
"Christ!" said Brendan weakly. "You did it! It worked!"
"Yes," replied Keri'khai shortly. "It did."
"We have to thank you." Lidan sat up, and looked at him closely. "Is the pain very bad?"
The lieutenant straightened and stared at her. "My leg, I can bear. Do you know what I did?"
"Of course." She frowned, and said slowly, "This is a war. In war, there are always casualties. You are a soldier. You should understand that."
"I always knew it. Perhaps I didn't understand it till now."
Brendan looked from one to the other, understanding only a little of the tension that trembled between them. They should have been elated at their escape. Why weren't they?

27

"So now we are here. What we have to discover next is – how we get in." Lidan looked out across the distance that now separated them from Thervanil. It was not great, but as flat and bare as it was, it seemed a veritable expanse, and every step of the way of it they would be exposed to any eye that cared to look out and see them.

Brendan stood a little fearfully beside her. To one accustomed to the concept of 'city' as understood on twentieth-century Earth, Thervanil was a severe disappointment. On Earth, the collection of dwellings in front of him would hardly qualify as a modest town. He could see that it must be old: it contained three sets of walls, which it had evidently outgrown, and the fourth that now contained it was formidable. It looked like something medieval, and he supposed that in view of the fact that Kerriel appeared to have missed out on any equivalent of the Industrial Revolution, there was no reason for its architecture to be advanced. Nevertheless, he had read widely, and he knew the power that had been concentrated in many medieval fortress-cities. If this were indeed the power-base of the Emperor who commanded the allegiance of every ruler on the entire planet, as Lidan had told him, it wouldn't do to dismiss it just because it wasn't the size of Dublin.

Thervanil was built on the edge of the sea, like most Venel cities and towns: not for nothing were the Birdpeople known as the People of the Seaways. Its walls and buildings were mostly of an almost beige stone. The outermost, crenellated wall looked extremely strong; its builders had known all the tricks of defending its gates with huge bastions riddled with strategically placed loopholes. There were murder-holes above the great gateway, and though at this time the gates themselves stood open, the thickness of them was visible and it was not hard to guess that they would be reinforced with iron. The expanse of open ground that separated the wall from any of the surrounding woodland was not accidental either – it was meticulously maintained, so that there could be no possibility of the city's being approached under cover. It looked virtually impregnable, especially with the sea at its back as a supply route during siege. Most of the city's wealth and influence depended on maritime trade. The Imperial fleet controlled an ocean larger than the Pacific, and was feared and respected wherever ships plied the sea. The bare masts of many ships, both trading and navy, were visible at the quays partially obscured by the bulk of the frowning city wall.

The oldest part of the city had originally been built on high ground. The seat of power, the Imperial Palace, was an enormous building in the centre. It too had expanded far beyond its original limits as one Emperor after another added and improved according to his own ideas. Now it was a vast warren of a place, with halls and colonnades, gardens and apartments of great beauty. Architecture was greatly prized among the Venelai, and an Emperor could afford, and demand, the best. What had originally been the entirety of the Palace was now just the Women's Quarters, a delicate and beautiful confection of a place with walls and screens of pierced marble and floors of inlaid and polished wood.

There were many other tall buildings elsewhere in the city of course; lesser nobility built beautiful houses of their own. And the great Temple of the

Sun, Vanil with its great tower from which the priest of the day saluted the first rays of Aiyeh-Rising-from-the-Western-Sea, was sited at the far side of the city. Natural reverence dictated that no building must rise higher than the Temple from which the city took its name. Even from the hills the topmost courses of the honey-coloured Tower were visible beyond the Palace, bathed in the late afternoon sunshine; and even without being told, Brendan could have identified it from Lidan's fixed and horrified gaze. Their destination; his destiny.

"Was there anywhere specific you wanted to go?" asked Keri'khai, his voice neutral. He had been extremely careful to maintain the most formal of relationships with Lidan, but he was beginning to relax with Brendan. The two were too completely dissimilar to ever have become friends, but a process of tentative contact had begun. Despite their initially unfavourable impressions of one another, both felt a reluctant fascination. Without the inhibiting presence of the Skair, they might have thawed into communication more rapidly, but the Venel knew that she was extremely wary of his motives for engaging the Starborn in conversation. He was more than a little puzzled by the complexity of the relationship he could observe between the two of them: sometimes they seemed far more easy and affectionate with one another than he would have expected. They had a way, occasionally, of making oblique references that made them both smile, but which outsiders were clearly not meant to understand.

As he had expected, Lidan looked hard at him before she answered, and took time for thought. There seemed no alternative to the truth. So far he had acted fairly towards them, and she had been thankful for his help. There were far more soldiers abroad than she had expected, and they would certainly have been captured by that wretch with the tame garynon but for his intervention. She was forced to acknowledge reluctantly that Hargen's judgement had been more accurate than her own, and whilst relieving her of one worry it had made her uncertain of making decisions. Anxiety and mistrust still coloured her thoughts towards him, however. He was a male and a soldier, and he owed loyalty to his God, to his Temple and to his superiors; and everyone's gratitude had a limit somewhere…

Nevertheless, if they were to reach the Temple and confront whatever awaited them there, it was hard to see how they were to accomplish it without him. It would be hard enough to do it even with his help.

She sighed, and gave in. "We are going to the Great Temple. I know that you may be unwilling to take me there, it must go as ill with you as taking you to Vanreil would with me. But that is where we have to go, willing or otherwise."

"It doesn't surprise me," he answered. "That's where Thaskan's being held. I don't know what's happened, but it seems to me there's something dreadful, something evil there. You must know what you're risking going there."

"I know that better than you," she replied, shuddering. Even he could not mistake the fear on her face. "But there is no help for it: we must get there. Can you think of any way to do it?"

He had thought about it a great deal since they had set out; and various schemes had presented themselves, each less likely to succeed than the last. He had finally hit upon one which seemed marginally less suicidal than the rest, but had no illusions about what the Skair's reactions were likely to be. To put it mildly, she wasn't going to like it at all.

And she did not like it. She listened incredulously to the terse outline of the idea, and with difficulty restrained herself from exploding. It renewed all and more than all of her suspicions of the lieutenant. To allow him to take her into the city as his captive, bound and supposedly ill or injured, with Kelti concealed beneath her in the straw of a cart – by the One! What was to prevent him turning fiction into fact, once they were within? How could she defend either Kelti or herself if he turned traitor? How well it would suit his purposes! He could trade them for the life of his commander, if indeed such a person existed; he could name his price! And how would Hargen ever discover what had happened? There would be no way of telling her – this close to Thervanil, the use of Speaking Stones would betray the presence of a Skair as surely as shouting it aloud from the battlements. Keri'khai would earn Stiv'aran's undying gratitude, and Kerriel would lose its only chance of defeating the Dark One! And Kelti, what of Kelti? What would happen to him? If he were killed outright it would be the most merciful outcome. As a result of much painful thought, she had resolved that if she could not ensure his return to his own world she would give him the only other gift possible, that of a swift and painless passage to the next. Her own experience in a human body had given her more than enough information about its weak points: she could kill him so quickly that he would not even feel the snap. She cared about him enough to do it, though it would leave her nothing but the desire to join him beyond the Endless Ocean. But this plan did not even leave her the certainty of that!

Their journey had afforded her much time to wrestle with her own ambivalent reactions to the Starborn. Skaira had forfeited the privilege of having partners, but she alone of them all had experienced the wonder of shared sexuality. When the dreams came that heralded her pregnancy, as they came to all of her kind, her lover would have a face… By definition, Skaira were solitary. They sometimes made close friendships among themselves, but – was this friendship that she felt? For an Otherworlder, who at times amused and at times exasperated her, whose presence had come to have such meaning for her, but whose thought processes were as elusive to her as a butterfly?

"It sounds better than anything I could come up with," Brendan said with a sigh.

Lidan looked at him in amazement, more than half expecting to see humour on his face. Surely he did not think they should fall in with this preposterous idea? Could he not see the dangers?

He could see them perfectly well: he was not naïve, and he had a healthy desire to avoid taking risks. But he knew as well as she did that Keri'khai had already saved them at least once, and if he intended to betray them anyway it did not make sense that he should wait until they reached the city before doing so. He could have earned Stiv'aran's gratitude quite as well by bringing them to Thervanil as captives in fact as well as in name. It wasn't the world's most original idea, but it was workable. And if all three of them were unable to come up with a better one, they were going to have to try it whether they liked it or not. Otherwise they could just slink home to Vanreil and wait for the end, or sit about looking at the city's outer wall until they were captured. And by the numbers of soldiers on the move, that was going to happen sooner rather than later.

"Kelti…" The Skair spoke almost pleadingly. "This is folly. It is madness. I can not defend you in the Temple, and from the moment this soldier binds me I can not defend you outside it. Do not ask it of me."

He looked at her, and then at the city. Something twisted deep inside him, but he couldn't allow himself to feel it.

"That's my way home, Lidan," he said gently but implacably. "And I want to go home."

"I can send you home," she cried desperately. "Alive, and safe! I can not protect you, this way! You do not know what might happen!"

"I know what can't happen if I run home with my tail between my legs!" he shouted, not even realising that his fists were clenched as though he confronted an enemy. "I can't beat the bastard. And I've come all this way to do it and I'll be damned if he'll send me running before I even clap eyes on the son of a bitch!"

Keri'khai held his breath. Uisge peeped out from behind Brendan's legs and ventured a very small growl. Starborn and Skair held one another's eyes for perhaps thirty seconds, while many messages passed between them, none of which could ever have been put into words. It was Lidan who first broke the desperate staring.

"Very well," she said dully, at last. "We will adopt your plan, Keri'khai. Find us a cart, and whatever ropes you need."

As honesty demanded, the Lieutenant had already admitted to the Skair that he himself might well be in some danger when he returned to the city. He had absented himself without leave, though with the city in such an uproar this might have gone unnoticed, even considering the time that had elapsed. It was not very likely, however. And he was glad in a way to have something that would act as a diversion from his own activities: nobody was going to ask questions about where he had been if he arrived with a Skair as his prisoner.

He rode in through the great gates without any notice being taken of him – the guards knew him fairly well, although they belonged to a different Division, and he was cautiously heartened by their amiable acceptance of his arrival. Evidently no orders had yet been issued for his arrest, or he would have been detained there and then. His unauthorised departure would have been noted in his own squadron, but it had probably been put down to a flight in terror for his own skin when Teho'evan was arrested. The fact of his taking his family with him would have confirmed this theory. In the circumstances, nobody would suspect him of asking his worst enemies to give them refuge while he returned into danger. If he had been suspected of harbouring any intention hostile to the would-be Emperor, the order for his capture on sight would have been widespread and immediate; sometimes, he reflected, there were distinct advantages in being considered insignificant. Instead of going straight on to the barracks, he turned right and headed for the stable blocks. He was well known there, and nobody made any difficulty about lending him a cart to bring in some casualties from a fictitious accident. The stable staff were at that moment in a frenzy of panic over one of the Emperor-Elect's favourite breeding hinds which had gone into premature labour and was showing every sign of having a breech-presented fawn. As the hind's high-pitched cries of distress rose desperately, an almost palpable shiver of dread ran through even those who had no responsibility in the matter, and not a soul spared him a second glance as he led the placid gelding and its cart from the courtyard. So far, so good. He was not questioned at the gate; the guards there had orders to pay great attention to what came into the city, rather less to what went out of it, and were at present engaged in a particularly enthralling (if surreptitious) game with dice. They were likely to pay an enormous amount of attention when he came back, but that was a different story.

Still careful to appear casual, he rode back the way he had come, the cartwheels rumbling on the broad track where the years of traffic had worn the earth away down to the bedrock beneath. At the appropriate point, he left the road where it bent right and went south with the great woods keeping pace beside it, and turned on to the grassy rising ground. There was no difficulty in identifying where his co-conspirators were waiting for him, close to a stand of winter-flowering trees that stood out against the late evening shades of the forest like a shimmering cloud.

He did not know, and did not like to guess, what they had found to say to one another in his absence. The Skair was pale and quiet, the Starborn possibly even paler and quieter. If it had not been completely unthinkable, he would have drawn some very definite conclusions about what they felt for each other: but there must be some other reason for the tension that linked them the way the string linked the arms of a drawn bow.

Neither of them spoke as Brendan climbed into the cart and burrowed into the deep straw within. Uisge jumped in with him and was dragged into hiding too. Her face now schooled into something approaching calm, Lidan climbed aboard. She spread her weight carefully, making sure her heavy lower parts were not across Kelti at any point. Some of her upper half would have to lie across him, there was not room to avoid him completely, and besides it would help to keep attention from any part of him that might be visible through the straw by the time they reached their destination. Finally she was settled and ready. She looked up. Keri'khai was standing with ropes in his hands, and a length of rough cloth that would have to go into her mouth for a gag: nobody would attempt to take a Skair prisoner without silencing her. For a long moment Skair and Venel stared at each other. For a fraction of an instant he saw something incalculable looking out at him, something that raised the feathers on the back of his neck. Then she put her hands behind her withers without a word, and looked up into the star-sprinkled sky as he tied first her wrists, then her hind and forepaws together. The gag came last. She glanced down at the Starborn, a glance that was terrible in its fear and despair, and then opened her mouth. He had ripped off a piece of his tunic to make the best possible compromise between realism and compassion, and folded it ready. It was the work of a moment to insert it between her jaws and secure it with another length of rope. He did not like looking at his handiwork. There was something completely indecent about it. He had seen Thaskan like this, which should have been even worse, but somehow that had been different: he had not known Thaskan. And despite Lidan's obvious distrust, which he could understand, he liked her. He wished that there were some way he could reassure her that he was to be trusted, but he knew that words would be wasted. Only deeds would prove him in her eyes.

Heavy-hearted, he tied the Starborn's stag to the back of the cart. That could always be accounted for as a stray – if anyone should possibly have attention to spare for it, which was unlikely. They had agreed that Lidan should have been discovered sick in the forest – she was perfectly well able to feign illness, and it would be simpler than trying to fake an injury. As soon as they came close to the city walls she would 'fall sick', and it would be reasonable enough that he should take an ailing individual to the Temple instead of to the Palace. In ordinary times he would have taken her to her own kind, but neither of the Skaira in Thervanil had been seen since the day of Sevi'nke's assassination. Some of the priests of the God were competent healers, if not on the level of Skaira, and nobody would question his actions in taking Lidan to them. He could say, truthfully enough, that it would have been senseless to take a prisoner to the Palace who was likely to die on the way, when a detour to the Temple for treatment might ensure that she lived to give useful information later. No doubt there would be plenty of willing informants to take the news to Stiv'aran, and if the Emperor-elect wanted to see the prisoner for himself, which he might well do, the distance between the Palace and the Temple was not great. If by any ill chance he decided that the matter merited immediate attention, that would mean that their time for action in the Temple would be limited, but there was nothing that could be done about that. Given the fact that Lidan had not revealed what she intended to do there anyway, he could formulate no plans to deal with the situation. He would simply have to get her there and see what happened. Barring accidents, the plans seemed watertight enough. He bowed his head to make a brief, silent prayer to both Aiyeh and Shieih that the venture would have their blessings. It would need all the good fortune there was to have a hope of succeeding.

When he raised his head again, although he had not heard a sound, the situation had changed. There was another Skair in the clearing. About Lidan's age, but thinner, bearing the marks of exhaustion. Her coppery hair and fur were matted and stained. The great claws of her forepaws glinted in and out of their housings with nervous tension. It was her eyes that drew him, however: they were like amber lamps, lit with a fanatic triumph.

"My prisoners, I think," said Riyeth.

28

Keri'khai had not survived upward of a dozen battles by mistrusting his instinct. It told him now, even without a glance to see the reaction of his appalled prisoner in the cart, that this arrival was catastrophic. He would not have time to get to his own mount; he had just tied the reins of Kelti's, and would not have time to free it. There was no option. He was unarmed, save for a dagger. He had to surrender.

He could not surrender. Drawing the dagger, he flung himself at the astounded Skair. So confident had Riyeth been that there would be no resistance that for one moment she simply could not understand what he was doing. In that moment he was on her, and though in the very last instant she reared and swerved aside, she squealed with pain and fury as the gleaming blade bit obliquely into her upper arm. He would have struck again, but she was too fast: he never saw the blow that felled him. When his senses cleared he was on his back on the grass, and she was bending over him.

"I can put an end to your heroics, fool!" she hissed. Disregarding the blood dripping down her arm, she took hold of both his wrists. One paw was planted in the centre of his chest. Then, with a cruel smile that told him she was taking the greatest pleasure in the act, she jerked her heights backwards. Strong as his torso was, he was in the grip of a creature twice his weight. There was a double crack as both of his shoulder joints were dislocated. He thought he would go mad with the pain. Both of his arms fell back like things that did not belong to him as she released them, and out of the black agony he heard her laugh. "Alas! The bird is wingless! Sing, little bird! Sing us goodbye!"

Dismissing him from her mind as if she had wiped him out of existence, she turned away and strode to the cart. Lidan had been making strenuous efforts to sit up, but there was no way she could have done it: and she had realised that her struggles were threatening to injure Kelti beneath her. Riyeth looked down at her, still smiling without a trace of humour, and then gently parted the straw to look down at Brendan. He had not been able to see what had happened to Keri'khai, but he had heard a voice he did not recognise, and he could see Lidan's reaction to it and knew that something had gone dreadfully wrong. And when he saw the unknown Skair surveying him it did not need the frantic half-stifled hissing from his companion to tell him that he was in deadly danger. Various options flashed through his mind: none of them would be of any use. Even if he'd been able to extricate himself from beneath Lidan, he wouldn't have stood a chance against any Skair, whoever this awful gaunt newcomer might be. She was stronger than he, and faster, and something about her face told him that if he gave her any trouble, killing him would be less significant to her than swatting a fly. He knew of course that all Skaira were killers; but even the formidable Hargen had accepted him as one of their own. To Riyeth he was no more than a talking lunch.

"So you are responsible for it all," she said softly. "Not much of you, to cause so much trouble! But whatever you are, wherever you come from, I am sure you will be welcome as a trade!"

"You can't," he said desperately. "You mustn't! You'll spoil everything!"

"Spoil everything? I will achieve the only thing that matters! I will rescue my Princess! And if this traitress loses her life for conspiring with you against the lawful authority of the Empire, then so be it!" She spat at Lidan, then swung around and seized the rein of the gelding harnessed to the cart. It shied away from the blood on her arm, but she jerked at the leather straps savagely, and the animal followed perforce. Keri'khai's stag snorted uneasily, started to follow, then stopped and walked uncertainly over to where its owner lay in agony on the grass. It nuzzled at him, but he could not even say a word of reassurance: if he opened his beak he would never be able to control the screams. He listened to the sound of the cart's wheels dying away in the distance, and wondered how long it would be before a predator discovered him. The night had closed in. There was no one to help him; the slightest movement made his senses spin. He shut his eyes and prayed, but he knew that there was nobody listening.

* * *

Emperor-Elect Stiv'aran listened incredulously to the message that a Skair wanted to speak with him. He could not imagine what any Skair would want to talk to him about. As far as they were concerned, he had Thaskan, and that was it. Any request to see her would be refused. They had no means of forcing his hand, and that was all that mattered.

But as he read the message that the gate guard had taken down to Riyeth's dictation, he changed his mind very quickly. By the One! Could anything be more providential? He had wanted the stranger dealt with, and here was a Skair offering to hand him over! Certainly this was not an opportunity to be missed. He sent the guard hastening back to the city gate with the assurances of safe-conduct that Riyeth had demanded, and sat for a moment with his head in his hands, trying to decide what was the best way to make the most of what offered. He had originally ordered the stranger to be slain on sight, but it would be intriguing to have speech with him first if the chance was there. Then, whenever he should be of no further use or interest, he would be a truly unique sacrifice afterwards – there must be some special rite devised for the occasion, for surely no god on Kerriel had ever received such an offering!

And the letter had said something about a second prisoner too – another Skair, whom the first accused of conspiracy against the State. That too was most interesting! With whom had she conspired? The Otherworlder? To achieve what? And how? He would take pleasure in extracting every detail, now that it was academic. But the Otherworlder first. Yes.

He summoned an underling, and gave orders. It was late, but he had not yet eaten. It would be courteous to offer his guest a meal.

The cart rumbled to a halt in the courtyard, and was immediately surrounded by soldiers. Riyeth stood to one side, looking on with satisfaction as her fellow Skair was unceremoniously hauled out of the straw and let fall heavily to the paving. Abandoning any pretence at dignity, crazed with fear and rage, Lidan cursed through the gag, fighting the ropes that had been re-tied and added to until she was a mass of cords. Even her tail had been tied to one of her hind legs in an act of puerile spite. She had no chance; though she managed to sink the bared claws of one paw into the leg of one unwary soldier and rip it open to the bone. His fellows immediately closed in on her and exacted revenge, but she endured the vicious kicking in silence, the amber eyes blazing defiance.

Then it was Brendan's turn. When the layer of straw had been pulled away to reveal him there had been a silence, in which he lay tense and hating like a cornered animal, the cynosure of dozens of astonished inhuman stares. As long as they did no more than stare he could bear it, but as soon as the first hand tentatively touched him he exploded. All the fury and terror he'd had to endure and contain since coming to Kerriel found a vent at last, and for all that his rational sense told him that resistance was utterly futile, there was a huge sick sense of joy in the thud as his fist hit the nearest ugly head. Despite his disadvantage in being so much weaker than they, his smallness and strangeness startled and disconcerted them. He was as supple as a whip and fast on his feet, and they grabbed at him in vain as he hurled himself out of the cart, not even knowing that he was swearing in Gaelic at the top of his voice as he did so. There was no plan in his action, nor any real hope of escape whatever he did; it was simply impossible to him to just accept it any more, and he found a glorious if temporary relief in hitting out left and right as he dived among the packed bodies.

But though he might have the advantage among the bigger, slightly slower Venelai there was one other to whom his desperate attempt at flight was merely amusing. She watched him, purring softly deep in her thin body, and let her claws ooze from their housings. To kill – to strike that miserable skinny frame and feel the snap of bone; to close her jaws across his face and hold him down, feeling his warm blood running across her tongue and the ribs heaving under her as he slowly suffocated, and watch his eyes as he died… She grinned, and yawned so that every one of her teeth showed. A pity that the Emperor-to-be wanted him alive; by the One, she would have enjoyed it…

She pounced.

Perhaps half an hour later Stiv'aran was seated in the Throne Room, looking down at the new arrivals. The Otherworlder was standing beside the imprisoned Skair – Lidan was her name. Apparently his was Kelti, although so far he had refused to answer any question put to him. His fists and jaws were clenched; one did not have to be expert in the body language of his kind to interpret the rigidity of his body as mingled fear and defiance. The Emperor-elect surveyed him with a mixture of contempt and curiosity. So small and thin, dressed in some strange ragged, filthy garment, his skin scratched and dirty like that of any street urchin. Hardly a threat! What could he have hoped to achieve? What danger could he possibly present to anyone?

"I do not know what they planned, Gracious One," said Riyeth, concluding her explanation of her activities. "But they have defiled Vanreil and plotted against you. And I have come to offer them in exchange for our Princess whom you presently hold prisoner."

Stiv'aran looked at her, his eyes veiled. "You're offering a trade?"
"Yes." She met his gaze fearlessly. "We are not concerned with the rights and wrongs of who sits on the Horned Throne. I am certain that in exchange for her freedom, Princess Thaskan would be willing to forswear all hostile action against you."
"Indeed," he mused. "I think Thaskan's already ceased to regard me as her enemy. Well, I agree to the exchange." He gestured to the guards who surrounded them. "Six of you, take her to the Princess. See she's adequately taken care of."

Riyeth cast a look of unconcealed triumph at Lidan as she turned. She did not bother to speak; what would happen to either her fellow Skair or the Starborn was of no interest to her whatsoever. If it occurred to her to wonder why it should take six guards to escort her to the Princess, it was no more than a fleeting puzzlement. She had won. Thaskan would be freed.

Lidan was watching the Emperor-Elect. She had been surprised by how relatively young he was, and how open and pleasant he seemed; though she had not for a moment made the mistake of thinking that any of these factors lessened his potential for evil. Seated at his ease on the Horned Throne, elegantly clad in deep green robes bordered with gold, he did not look like the monster he must be to have done what he had. In different circumstances she might well have thought him noble. That in itself made him deeply dangerous. As the double doors swung shut behind Riyeth she saw the unexplained glimmer in his eyes deepen into an unholy amusement. He threw back his head and laughed. The gems set into the broad gold collar around his neck glittered in the flaring torchlight.

Brendan did not understand the reasons for the Venel's evident entertainment any more than Lidan did, and Stiv'aran's high-pitched laughter grated on his ears. His visceral dislike for the Venelai had returned with all and more of its original force. But for the fact that they were surrounded by at least twenty soldiers and there was not a hope of his succeeding, he would have been acutely tempted to at least try to wipe the smile off Stiv'aran's face.
"Ah, my lack of proper respect!" The Emperor-Elect sobered presently. "Well, she'll have what she wanted: much joy may she have of the bargain! In the meantime, Lidan – if that's truly your name – I regret that it won't be possible to invite you to eat. You'll understand that I can't take the risk of untying you. In the meantime, you'll be taken to a place of safety, and kept there until I have time to deal with you." He signalled to the guards.

Bound or not, at this Lidan went into a fresh frenzy of struggling against the ropes that were now cruelly tight around her wrists and paws. The skin beneath them was already raw, but she did not even feel the agony as she reared up on her hind legs, wrenching at her bonds with every atom of her strength. The only result was that one good shove was enough to send her crashing sideways, unable to save herself. Brendan leapt to her, disregarding the spears and swords, but there was nothing he could do. She stared up at him in utter despair, not even able to say a word of warning or farewell. They seized him bodily and wrenched him away from her, and dragged her out of the hall.

He had never realised quite how dependent he had become on her presence, her protection. It was like watching his oxygen supply being carried away. Panic almost stopped his breath. He struggled madly in the guards' grasp, panting every obscenity in his vocabulary, but he was totally unable to free himself. He did not notice the watching Stiv'aran smile as his suspicion that the Otherworlder was basically powerless was confirmed. Bruised, battered and despairing, Brendan could do nothing but watch as his only friend and defender was dragged away, and the double doors crashed shut behind her. Then, at a gesture from his enemy, he was released to stand upright, waiting tensely for the cruelty to start.

"So. The complications are now removed," said Stiv'aran tranquilly. "Will you eat with me?"

He gestured to one side, where a generous table was set.

The suggestion threw Brendan completely out of his stride. He stared at his captor, face drawn with fear and suspicion. He had been braced for anything including torture, but not for being invited to dinner. It was extremely tempting: there had not been time on the journey for set meals, and they had had to return to foraging as they went, which was enough to keep them going but hardly satisfactory. The prospect of at last being able to sit down, rest and eat was dreadfully hard to resist, especially now that the smell of roast meat drifted enticingly to him. Saliva ran in his mouth. What could he achieve by unnecessarily antagonising his captor? What had he to lose by accepting a meal?

"No," he said somehow. "I'm not hungry." The Emperor-Elect gave him such a piercing look that he must surely be able to hear his captive's belly growling. Brendan stood as straight and stubborn as he could, and returned it.

"A pity," Stiv'aran commented at last, and leaving the throne, walked over to the table, sat down at it, and began eating. Brendan gave him a look that he hoped conveyed indifference before returning his gaze to the empty Throne. It was a beautiful piece of craftsmanship, carved out of a solid piece of what looked like yellow marble. The back of it rose to a peak, intricately carved, from which rose two horns like a crescent moon. These were of pure gold. The cushioned seat of it was of gold tissue. More gold glimmered on the footstool beside it, and on the smaller and far less impressive Empress's chair on a lower part of the dais.

"You're admiring my throne?" inquired Stiv'aran conversationally.

"It's not yours yet," said Brendan, who had gathered as much from the Skaira.

The Emperor-Elect stiffened momentarily, then relaxed again. Why allow the Other- worlder to provoke him? "No," he agreed easily, "but it soon will be." He picked up a roast fowl and ripped off a plump leg, making Brendan wonder irreverently if for a Venel to eat poultry wasn't close to cannibalism. If it was, Stiv'aran seemed not to care. He ate the flesh with every evidence of enjoyment, and tore open a fragrant loaf. Brendan's stomach grumbled dismally but his mouth remained obstinately shut. He couldn't believe that he was being asked to dine out of kindness, and having managed to refuse, pride helped him to stick to it. There had to be some ulterior motive for the offer, and he wasn't going to be bribed by food, no matter how hungry he might be. He stood silent while Stiv'aran ate, and did not even look across at the table, though he was aware of the glances the other cast in his direction. His guards did not move, nor did they relax their vigilance. The meal seemed to take a very long time. Initiating a conversation would only betray his own fear, and increase the risk of giving away incriminating information. It was best on all counts to say nothing. He stood completely still, trying to maintain as calm a face as possible, and to prevent his thoughts from straying back to the Earth he would never see again. If he shut his eyes he could see it with agonising clarity, his home in Connemara facing the vast Atlantic and the setting sun: the front garden hedged with fuchsias which dripped red beauty all late summer, the conservatory he'd had built on to the upper floor so that he could sit and watch the sunsets when he was at home between tours. He could even smell the wind off the sea, the purity of it mingled with salt and seaweed, and carried on it the sound of the eternal waves pounding on the white sand beaches. Home. He dared not think about his family: it was not bearable.

The waiting passed somehow. At last Stiv'aran pushed back his chair and rose. He strolled across and circled Brendan slowly, examining him in minute detail. He was trying to catch his prisoner's eye, brilliant gold clawing at hazel. Brendan went on staring through him, trying not to be intimidated by the sheer height and strength of the man. "Why have you come here?" he asked presently, still circling. His footfalls were almost soundless on the tiles, for all his size.

"Because I was brought."

"Brought from where?"

"From where I was born."

"And where were you born?"

"Where my parents were living at the time."

"Why are you being so unco-operative?"

"Because you've no right to ask me questions."

"I control this world. At one word from me you'll die; possibly very unpleasantly. And you say I have no rights?" If he was angry he didn't show it. The voice remained even. Nevertheless the power was there, the threat. The inhuman cruelty.

Brendan's mouth was dry, but he answered steadily enough, "You've rights over your own people. I'm not one of them. You can kill me if you like, but you'll not make me crawl to you."

"Are you a very brave man or a fool, I wonder?" mused Stiv'aran. "No matter. Perhaps you may decide to be informative later if it'll spare your four-legged friend unpleasantness. For now, I've other matters to attend to, so I'll have to ask you to excuse me for a while. I don't suppose you'll give me your word not to try to escape? No, I thought not. In that case you'll just have to be kept safe for me too." He nodded to the chief guard, and eight of them formed a hollow square around their prisoner and marched him out of the Throne Room. It was useless to resist, so Brendan walked quietly in their midst down the maze of corridors. He was eventually left in a surprisingly comfortable room, which while windowless had a large candle-lamp on a high shelf, illuminating a bed and a small table which were the only pieces of furniture. Both were solidly fixed in place, but although the bed was of heavy dark wood it was well supplied with blankets and a pillow, and there was a covered pail at one end that was obviously for body wastes. Another shelf under the table even had a couple of books on it, but as with those in Lidan's hut, the text was completely illegible to Brendan, though he looked through them with interest, noting that these too were hand-written and in places beautifully illustrated with abstract designs. Perhaps half an hour after he had been left there the door was unlocked and what appeared to be a servant entered, shadowed by a guard, bringing several plates of food which were left on the table. Defiance was one thing, stupidity another. After sampling the various dishes cautiously (not that he thought it likely he would be poisoned, at least not until he had given up a lot more information), he made the best meal he had had since leaving Kanehar's house. He had also been left a beaker of wine, but this was very strong, and he did not drink it. Although the chances were it would be safe enough, there was every possibility that the Venelai had expertise with drugs, and that thick sweet taste could hide a great deal. In any case, he was not about to risk it.

When he had finished eating he lay down. He had thought himself so tired by now that sleep would come readily, despite the aches and pains from where Riyeth had derived evident amusement from bringing him crashing to the pavement, but he found himself thinking instead of where Lidan was. It was unlikely that she was housed in such comfort: and it was immaterial what kind of room they had put her in, if they had not untied her. Would he be able to purchase better treatment for her if he co-operated? And would she want him to do it? He thought not on both counts, but the difference between his circumstances and hers made him miserably restless. Finally, a long-forgotten habit reasserted itself. Feeling strangely foolish, he got out of bed and knelt down beside it. He couldn't help Lidan, but he could pray for her; and he had always been taught that prayer was never wasted.

29

It had been a long wait, longer than he had expected; but the end had come at last. In his present suffering, Keri'khai could even welcome it. Several times he had summoned enough courage to try to move. Twice the pain of the attempt had sent him into a dead faint; and even when he retained consciousness, he simply had not been able to find any way of raising himself from the ground. There was no more he could do except wait to die, of exposure or as the victim of some predator. In far too much pain to sleep, he had simply lain where he was and waited. It seemed that half the night passed before he saw his dozing stag's head come up sharply, the large ears swivelling and the nostrils flaring. A couple of moments later the animal rose to its hooves with a nervous snort, nuzzling him for reassurance. It needed the keenest of ears to detect the approaching footfalls among the greenery. Too soft and stealthy for another stag, they were almost certainly those of a large meat-eater on the prowl. Keri'khai was not afraid of death, he had seen it too often, and it was the only mercy for which he hoped now. He was bitter with his failure to keep faith with his companions, or to help Teho'evan, and with the knowledge that he would never see his family again on this side of the Endless Ocean. He had failed them all, and the sooner he laid down the insupportable burden the better.

The undergrowth a couple of feet away from him rustled. He could hear the soft breaths now, and the breeze must surely be taking his scent that way. Whatever it was, it could not fail to be aware of him. It had two potential victims, and the larger of the two was poised, trembling, to bolt. Any intelligent predator would take the injured one that could make the least resistance. At any second now it would pounce, and there would be an end. He did not open his eyes; it was one thing to know that his death was within seconds, another to watch it coming for him when he could see his family behind his eyelids instead – he hoped that his failure would not be held against them at Vanreil. But for the arrival of the hostile Skair, he thought he might have had a fighting chance of at least getting Lidan and Kelti to the Temple, but once she was on the scene all their chances had gone. Only the Shining One knew what had happened to his companions since. They were probably already dead.

Why was the predator hesitating? Was it afraid he might be shamming injury? He didn't have to fake a groan: all he had to do was release one. That should do the trick.

The darker shadow among the shadows moved suddenly. Shieih receive me, he thought, and tensed for the rush.

"How are you hurt?" asked the voice of a Skair. "Do not be afraid: I am a Healer."

About half an hour later he was sitting propped against a tree trunk, his upper arms firmly strapped to his torso with strips torn from his stag's saddle blanket. The remainder of this was wrapped around him while his body temperature recovered – fortunately the night had been a relatively mild one, and the chill of exposure had not bitten too deeply. Kanehar had had to treat him without any anaesthetic relief, and several times during the process of manoeuvring his bones back into their sockets he had lost consciousness again. It was done now, but he would have to remain almost immobile for a long time while the swelling and bruising took their course. It was not to be expected that the replacement would end the pain, but it was less than half of what it had been; and he was able to give his rescuer a reasonable account of what had happened.

Nobody, least of all herself, would ever have imagined that Kanehar would have been able to keep up with Riyeth on the journey from Vanreil. She had even bettered her enemy's time, in fact: another half day and she might well have caught up with her. Neither of them had stopped to sleep or eat. Both were driven by rage. Riyeth's innate strength was far less than the Healer's, but the force of her obsession lent her far greater than ordinary stamina. For both of them, equally hungry and both low in blood-reserves, the journey had been gruelling.

Even if she had not known Riyeth's destination, it would almost have been possible to track her by the trail of corpses she had left. Wherever possible she had killed the Venel soldiers patrolling the woods: there was even a suspicion in the Healer's mind that she had actually fed on one of them. The teeth-marks on the body had been those of a large feline, though heavy rain had washed away the scents that would have confirmed it, one way or another. Admittedly there were other feline predators abroad that would not have hesitated to take advantage of the corpse callously left lying in the ditch with his neck broken, but whatever had been at it had deliberately sucked the blood out of it and eaten relatively little of the flesh. This would be strange behaviour for an ordinary animal; it would be perfectly sensible behaviour in a Skair wanting to take on board the maximum nourishment in the shortest possible time without jeopardising her speed. Nevertheless it was an unspoken law that Skaira did not eat the flesh of the other two races. In ordinary circumstances it would have been unthinkable – but who would ever have thought that one Skair would murder another for information forbidden to her? Half the world seemed to have run mad. Keri'khai was the first of her victims Riyeth had left breathing, and it had not been out of kindness. Kanehar herself had had a couple of narrow escapes from discovery, but had not had to resort to killing; that she reserved for Riyeth herself. Now she had not only Kelti and Lidan to safeguard, but Hargen to avenge; and appalled as she had been by Hargen's murder, what had been done to Keri'khai was almost worse. The Healer had known his identity as soon as she caught his scent – it had been strong on his wife's clothing, and she had caught traces of it along with Lidan's and Brendan's as she tracked them. In view of the fact that he had been helping one of her sisters, whether or not she approved the course they had been pursuing, the deliberate cruelty Riyeth had shown towards him was sickening. It was no longer a question in Kanehar's mind of whether Riyeth was justified – the question now was whether she was sane. And if, as it seemed, she was not, then putting her out of her suffering was the only course possible. Those who had failed to finish her off at Weruavwe had done her no kindness.

Kanehar looked across at the city, a dark hunched shape pierced here and there by small lighted windows, and sighed. No question but that Lidan and Kelti were captive in it by now. If it had been likely that her following them into captivity would have helped, she would willingly have done it; but there seemed small sense in surrendering her freedom for no visible gain. While she was out here, assuming she could avoid capture in the meantime, at least she still had the capacity to act if it were called for. And in the meantime she could care for Keri'khai, who had deserved considerably better from Skaira than he had received thus far. Many of her sisters had wanted to come with her, but she had refused the offers: it was a mad venture at best, and every hand might soon be needed to defend the Temple Complex.

"You say that this – Riyeth – killed the Skair who was with my wife?" Keri'khai's voice jerked her from her dark reverie.

"Yes. But the women were unhurt," said Kanehar quickly. "They reached the Complex safely, and Hargen lived long enough to commit them to our care. I have the First Priestess's word that they will be regarded as guests, as Hargen had asked. While there is safety among us, they are assured of it."

"I'm sorry about Hargen. I wish I'd had the chance to thank her. The world's worse off without her."

"According to the will of the Goddess," sighed the Healer.

The soldier raised his head and looked at her. Many a time he had wondered, on the march or around the campfire, about the nature of the love that their gods supposedly bore to their world. In ordinary circumstances he would never have dared to question one of the Daughters of the Stars on the subject; but the circumstances were so very far from ordinary, and the Skair seemed approachable. The bitterness he could not contain welled into his voice as he asked, almost accused, "You honestly believe that all this suffering's according to Her will?"

"I think that to permit a thing to happen is not the same as to want it to happen," replied Kanehar evenly. "If Shieih wills that we are free to act, then we must be free to do even what does not please Her. There is no freedom without choices, and by the nature of things some choices must be evil. I did not say 'according to the *pleasure* of the Goddess'."

"If She dislikes it so much, why doesn't She act?" he burst out. "Why's this being allowed to happen? If She's all-powerful – all-caring – by the One! If She cares at all! – why doesn't She strike down that son of offal in the Palace? He deserves damnation on a dozen counts! And the gods do nothing!"

"I would not say that they had done nothing. You have met Kelti."

"Kelti -! What use is he? Oh, I liked him, insofar as I knew him! But we need an avenger! You don't need me to tell you what crimes Stiv'aran's committed! He earned death a score of times just for what he had done at Weruavwe! And what about all the others, the Manyei, the Emperor, the royal children, the junior queens – don't their deaths count for anything?"

"Shieih has the tally," said Kanehar steadily. "And what Kelti can or will do is hidden from all of us as yet. Perhaps even from himself."

He exhaled loudly, and was silent. The Healer came over to him and checked that the bandaging had not come loose. If they had been back at Vanreil there were treatments available to her there which she could have used to relieve the pain and reduce the swelling, but here there was nothing she could do but keep the disturbance of it to a minimum. An unwary movement could put a joint that had been dislocated back out again, and if he was to regain full use of it for the future he was just going to have to be very patient for a while. "'The song is not over until the Singer falls silent'," she quoted softly. "There may yet be work for us to do. Be patient."

For a long while he said nothing. Then, his voice completely neutral in the dark, "Do you honestly believe we can still win?"
"I believe that we are not abandoned, and never will be, no matter how dark the world may seem. Whether that is the same thing, I do not know. We are all between the paws of the Goddess."
"That's more comfort to you than to me."
"Who do you think shaped you in the egg? Who loved the thought of you before the world circled the sun? Do not spurn the Goddess, Keri'khai. She is the Mother of all of us, not only of Skaira. Now, I am going to help you to lie down. You should try to rest, if you can not sleep." And she did so with calm competence, settling him down on a bed of greenery. She was still not entirely happy with his temperature, but she had nothing else to wrap him with. So, having seen him lying as easy as was possible in the circumstances, she settled down close beside him, where the heat of her body could penetrate the thick wool of the blanket and permeate it. Her face she kept turned steadily towards Thervanil. If she could not enter it, she could keep vigil over it. The Goddess knew that there were those within in need of prayer.

Time passed. The night was very quiet. Overhead the stars wheeled. Keri'khai drowsed a little. The lamps in the windows of Thervanil were extinguished one by one, giving way to darkness, and the silent Skair noted the passage of detachments of soldiers returning to their base within the city. None came close to where she lay; who would suspect that an enemy would be so near to the walls? She wondered what Kelti was doing, and her heart ached for him.

* * *

Stiv'aran strode easily back down the corridor, his bodyguards keeping pace but not impinging on his consciousness in any way. It was his custom to visit Mia'naan every night; chiefly to see that the egg was being well cared for, but secondarily to check on her progress after the delivery. This was not out of affection – to resume sexual relations too early could endanger a woman's capacity to bear children in the future, and he fully intended to breed from her as a junior queen. Nevertheless he was impatient for the time when he could bed her again: several times the proximity of her had roused him to the point where he had had to relieve his desire with one of her attendants. Now that she was no longer burdened by pregnancy, he would no longer be restricted by the inconvenient consideration of the welfare of the egg.

She had not had much to say this evening – not that she was ever really talkative; but somehow they had achieved a strange relationship quite unlike any he had ever known with anyone else. Liking was no part of it, that could not be expected, but there was an odd savage honesty between them. He was under no illusions; if ever she got hold of a knife, she would plant it between his ribs without a qualm. But the force that had taken him over could only warp what he had been, not change it. During their encounters, she had begun to see something, some twisted remnant, of what her dead husband had seen; and whilst it had done nothing to lessen her loathing, it had filled her with regret for what might have been. He felt the change in her without understanding it. It did not affect his plans materially: it would still be far too risky to take her as his Empress. But he had some hopes that eventually he would be able to reach some kind of understanding with her which would allow him to use her intelligence as the asset her previous husband had found it to be. That was for the future, however, and would have to wait until the egg had hatched; it was unlikely that if he were forced to kill the hatchling she would ever forgive him sufficiently to co-operate over anything. That would be a pity, but it could not be helped. Now he had one last call to make – to the Great Temple, to pass on the news of what he had seen and learned this evening.

They passed through the streets without incident, and entered the courtyard of the Temple. As he had ordered, this was heavily guarded, and they were challenged at once. The captain of the guard was he who had taken Riyeth from the Throne Room earlier on. Stiv'aran recognised him immediately, and gestured to him to accompany them for a moment.

"Was all well with our new guest?" he inquired blandly as they walked onward.

"Yes, Great Lord, until she discovered the truth," replied his subordinate.

"And she hadn't had any suspicion?"

"Apparently not. She was – upset." The captain was a master of understatement. Riyeth had been escorted to the Temple, and taken to where what remained of Thaskan was lying. She had initially thought that the smell was from the Venel to whom the Princess was chained in the foetid darkness. That had enraged her enough. When it dawned on her that the man was alive – if badly injured – but Thaskan was dead and rotting, the soldiers thought she would collapse. They had prudently not gone into the cell with her. As the first tremor of realisation went through her they had slammed the door shut and bolted it. Hardened though they all were, nobody wanted to witness the disintegration of the Skair as she discovered the magnitude of her folly. They had left her to it, sparing a grudging shred of pity for the probable fate of the officer left sharing the cell with her.

Stiv'aran smiled slightly. It would be unfortunate if Riyeth did make an end of Teho'evan; he had planned something far more lingering. Nevertheless, he was reasonably certain that the distraught Skair would make the death excruciating enough. She was of no further interest to him: the door to the cell would stay locked for the rest of eternity. All three of them could rot together.

The corridors of the Temple were quiet. He had half expected to hear distant screaming even now, but there was no sound. Nothing distracted him from his goal, and soon he was there, bowing before the Stone. He did not have to speak; what he knew was open to examination as soon as he was in its presence. Riyeth had dragged the whole tale out of Hargen's brain, and had spoken briefly and with disgust of the method used to bring the Otherworlder to Kerriel. It had not had much significance for Stiv'aran, apart from affording him a certain amount of salacious curiosity. It was of the greatest significance to Esdiol, however. A Shapechanger! It opened up astounding possibilities. Perhaps Thaskan's death was not the blow it might have been after all! And the Otherworlder was still alive, and well cared for? Yes, it seemed so. Well, well! And the Shapechanger was young, and healthy? That too! The silent voice was almost crowing with triumph. This pitiful ploy was about to backfire with terrible consequences. They had brought an Otherworlder to save this world, but he could be used as a stepping-stone to his own!

Stiv'aran listened to the orders. It would not have occurred to him to disobey any of them. In another age, another life, they would have made him shudder. Now he did not even blink.

*   *   *

In a bare room partly below ground in the Temple, that had once upon a time held sacks of grain and still held musty traces of it in the air, Lidan lay sleepless on the cold floor, trying to find some shred of hope in the situation. Despair clawed at her, for all she fought against it. The one small fact that both bewildered and encouraged her was that although the cart had been searched quite thoroughly when she and Kelti were no longer in it, Irvathil had not been found. Uisge had jumped out after her master, and tried to follow, but a needlessly vicious kick had sent the animal yelping away. She had last been seen crouching beside the door, on guard over the nuluoi Kelti had brought with him from the village. Could Irvathil be secreted somewhere in the Starborn's clothing? It was too big to fit into a pocket, even if the garment had had one. Surely it was not lost! She was certain that Kelti had had it in his possession. He knew how precious it was – he could not have lost it, he could not! But where could it be? Did he have it? And if so, could he make sure it remained safe? By the Goddess, he could be dead by now. If that was so, did it matter what became of Irvathil, or of her for that matter? She had failed – failed – failed!

30

"You want *what?*" The ex-Empress Mia'naan raised her head and looked in disbelief at her visitor. He repeated the demand, rather shortly. He was not used to having his commands questioned, and couldn't see that it was such an out of the ordinary request. By the One, the Women's Quarters must be knee-deep in such things!

"I take it you don't want me to get up and select something suitable?" she asked with more than a little irony, caressing the smooth pearly surface of the egg around which she was curled. She had tried extremely hard not to feel anything for the child inside it, but she was not made of metal, and love had crept up on her almost unawares. Now she spent almost every waking moment in prayer that the child might be a girl, so that it would not have to die before taking its first glance at the sunshine.

It was normal for a brooding mother to have plenty of company, largely to relieve the boredom, and she gestured languidly for one of her attendants to open the chests along one wall. As the girl passed him, Stiv'aran automatically ran a hand over her body, and Mia'naan was hard put to it not to smile, if a little bitterly. Why on Kerriel did he want seductive clothing? She'd seen more than enough of his sexual capacity: he had no need whatsoever of titillation to stimulate his appetites. After a moment he stood up and walked over to where the girl was kneeling, her arms delving into the carefully folded clothes to be brought out for his inspection. He pulled her upright, pivoted her and laid her down on her back. Nothing was said. Mia'naan watched with mild distaste, thankful that her responsibility for the brooding of her precious egg protected her from being the target on this occasion. After the first time this had happened, she had exerted what very little authority she had left to ensure that no woman in oestrus should be in attendance on her: his current victim would take no harm of Stiv'aran's passing lust, other than a few aches. They had all learned by now that their soon-to-be Emperor paid no attention whatsoever to whether a woman wanted him or not. The only danger was in resistance – the right of refusal did not apply where he was concerned. One woman who had been too stupid to understand that had soon learned the folly of her conduct: she had spent the night in his room and the remainder of her short life in the barracks. Though nobody had said as much to Mia'naan, rumour had it that a brusquely kind officer had arranged the cremation so swiftly that no member of her family had had a chance to view the body afterwards. Stiv'aran did not accept defiance from anyone.

He finished with the girl, and turned back to the clothes. He lifted them out one by one, putting them neatly on the floor after examining them. The ex-Empress watched with growing perplexity. There seemed something beyond the normal in the intensity with which he was searching for whatever he wanted. Had he chosen his Empress already? Was he looking for a bridal gift? Impossible. Granted that most men had little real understanding of the way to please a woman, but Stiv'aran could not possibly imagine that he would do other than mortally insult his bride by giving her another woman's clothes! With the riches available to him, could he not afford to deck out his chosen Empress in garments that would be the envy of every woman in the world?

Presently, after rejecting many that Mia'naan would have personally chosen as some of the best pieces she owned, he straightened up. He held the chosen article between his hands, so gently that it might almost have been alive. It was very plain and sheer, the shimmering white fabric so fine that the light shone through it. It had come from very far away, and had been among the gifts Sevi'nke had given her at their wedding. She had never seen anything else made of anything near as delicate, and had never worn it. Somehow it had seemed too fragile, too precious to be risked. Now, seeing it in Stiv'aran's hands, she bit back a protest. He would not heed her anyway.

"You'll get it back," he said quietly, almost as if he had heard what she had not said. "If it's damaged in any way, I'll find you another."

She lifted an eyebrow. A disdainful retort sprang to her tongue, but she restrained it for no reason she could have explained, except that it had not been something she would have expected him to say. As he knelt looking down at the garment, there was something quite inexplicable about him: if it had not been impossible, she would have called it sadness.

He stood up, and the moment passed. Without another word he strode out of the room, not giving a second glance to any of them. As the door closed behind him a soft susurration of speculation broke out. Mia'naan did not join in it. She watched the girl he had just taken, who lay motionless where he had left her, keening quietly. It was an open secret that she had courted Stiv'aran's glances even before the world had tilted on its axis: it was not the rape that distressed her, but the way he had ignored her not only after but even during it. A kind word or even a gentle touch afterwards would have amended all, and he had not said a single thing to her throughout. Who could account for the heart? It would seem that even Stiv'aran was capable of inspiring love.

* * *

Lidan had finally managed to struggle upright. The fact that her hind paws were tied together made it impossible to lie on her stomach in comfort, but she had achieved a kind of almost bearable compromise by resting with her hind paws slightly to one side while her forequarters lay square. The pain in her shoulders and arms was inescapable, and the pressure of the rope around her now badly swollen wrists had almost robbed her hands of feeling. Ordinary sleep was out of the question, but she had been able to snatch a couple of hours of hunting-sleep, forcing her brain to shut down in spite of her suffering; common sense dictated that it was her duty to do whatever she could to maintain her own physical condition. The remainder of the time had passed in prayer. Over and over again she had beseeched Shieih to send aid, mentally hurling her prayers into the unresponsive night. Imprisoned in the Great Temple, she could not have used sorcery even if she had been able to speak; in that respect it would have been quite safe to remove the gag. Perhaps her captors didn't know that, or perhaps they didn't care. At any rate it was still there, cutting into the soft flesh of her mouth. She did not expect to be given food or water. If Thaskan was being starved she could expect the same treatment.

She lay now in an attitude of despair, her shoulders slumped. Her head hung low, its fair hair matted with sweat and blood from cuts that the beating in the courtyard had opened up. High above her a tiny window gave a view of the wheeling stars, but she did not look up at it. If she had done, the sight would have afforded her no comfort.

She wondered if Thaskan was being held nearby. It would not have helped if she had had any powers of telepathy; even those would be ineffective here. The gag would prevent her from making any recognisable sound – she could force a muffled roar past it, but what would that achieve? It would hardly comfort the Princess to discover that one of her subjects was in the same desperate predicament as herself. And where was Riyeth now? Stiv'aran's laughter had not boded well for the bargain she had struck. That there was treachery in it somewhere was easy to guess. What form it had taken was a mystery, but the chances were that Riyeth had not had the victory of which she had seemed so certain when she left the Throne Room.

But most urgent of all was the question of what was happening to Kelti. Lidan's heart was wrung with guilt at her failure to protect him, and dread at what might have happened to him since. She had gone over and over her actions, torturing herself with trying to guess where she had gone wrong. Events had proved that she had not done ill to trust Keri'khai: unless he had enacted an extremely realistic pretence of trying to save them from Riyeth, he had done his best to keep faith. It had not been his fault that the attempt was hopeless. Should she have waited for Hargen to come back? It might have been wise; but there had been the time factor, the time that was ebbing away for Thaskan and Teho'evan. Everything had seemed inevitable. And this was where it had led them, to captivity and death. Kelti would never go back to his world now. Horror after horror rose before her mind's eye; she relived over and over again the sight of Riyeth bringing him crashing down, baring her jaws across his face and so evidently relishing the thought of closing them. If he should fall into her claws again, now that his usefulness as a bargaining counter was over… Lidan writhed in her bonds at the thought. The Goddess send that Stiv'aran might think him so slight a threat that he might be killed at once, and with as little suffering as possible!

The dawn found her silently weeping. Her own fate would have been unimportant if she could have secured his. Even if she could have questioned the guards outside her room, it was unlikely they would tell her what had happened to him. If they had been dealing with a simple brigand, she would have been far less afraid; but the man whom they had faced in the Throne Room was subtle and complex. Who could guess at his motives? How could anyone tell what he would do or cause to be done to an alien whom he saw as a possible threat to his plans? For what it mattered, she was under no illusions about what lay in wait for her. Assuming that he had no more sinister intentions than removing one more minor threat from the game, she would probably be left here to die. Why should he offer her the mercy of a quick death? She had conspired against him. Probably, when he had leisure, he would have her questioned about the nature of that conspiracy. That would involve torture. Venel law allowed torture, under specific conditions and within degrees – but the likelihood of those limitations being observed in her case was remote. The first condition was the presence of a skilled Healer, who had the authority to halt any action likely to cause permanent damage; and it was beyond the bounds of imagination that Stiv'aran would bother to have his victim's welfare monitored by anybody. She would suffer the torments of the damned before he would believe – if he ever did believe – that she had been acting alone. Once that was done with, assuming she survived it, he would have no further use for her, no reason to keep her alive. It would take days for her to starve; though blood-deprivation would take her more swiftly than mere hunger. Thirst might also hasten the process. The prospect of the long-drawn-out end, never knowing until she crossed the Endless Ocean what had become of her responsibility, her friend, was more than she could bear. Nevertheless, it seemed that she must face it. Even if Hargen came now, she could not storm Thervanil. "Forgive me!" she cried out, though nothing but garbled sounds emerged through the gag. The tears trickled down her nose. "Kelti, Kelti, forgive me!"

She was so deep in misery that she did not hear the door quietly opening. It was the vibration of a footstep inside the room that alerted her. Her head jerked around. Stiv'aran stood there, looking down at her with an expression she found hard to interpret. He didn't speak, but gestured to the soldiers behind him. They came past him, and tied a new rope shackle around her wrists; it was still not possible for her to bring her hands forward, but when the original was cut (and cut quite carefully too), it allowed her arms to part and fall almost level with her sides. Astonishingly, they even removed the pieces still remaining around her wrists. The relief and the pain of movement were so great she had to bite the gag savagely to keep from crying out; the pressure of blood returning into her hands sent them into muscular spasms that brought the fingerclaws flashing into the weak light. Then they lifted her up – even more to her surprise, handling her rather more gently than those of the previous day had done. Similar shackles were also fitted to her paws, allowing her to stand foursquare, though a sturdy link was added joining fore to hind so that she could only move forward or backwards in very small steps.

It would have been too much to hope for that the gag would be removed, and it was not. At that moment, however, the lessening of the agony in her extremities was enough to be grateful for. She was allowed to stand, trying to still the shaking as blood and feeling ran back into her cramped limbs. The Emperor-Elect looked at her, and she looked back at him. The great amber eyes silently pleaded with him to tell her what he had done to Kelti.

"Take her," he said evenly. And as soon as she was capable of putting one paw in front of another without falling, she was partly pushed, partly pulled out of the room, walking because it was better than being dragged. A couple of times she stumbled, but they steadied her gently enough. They took her at the best pace she could contrive, always aware of Stiv'aran walking silently in the rear. A couple of hundred yards down the corridor they turned right and went through a double door. They were now in what she recognised with astonishment as a bathing room: for the priests of Aiyeh as well as for the devotees of Shieih, cleansing was a necessary part of sacred ritual. It was a light, lovely room, panelled and floored in pale wood. There were steps leading down into a large, sunken marble bath, filled with water scented with herbs. To ordinary nostrils the scent would not have been unpleasant. But to Lidan, the perfume raised her hackles with the first breath. All Skaira had some knowledge of herb-lore. Many were used in healing, many had their part in ceremony; and some were avoided for good reason. This water contained the essence of at least some of these last. The smell of it had bitter undertones.

It did not need anyone to tell her that she had been brought here to be washed in it. She braced her paws and resisted ferociously, with all the strength she still had, as her guards tried to propel her forwards. There could be no good reason for immersing her in that water. Resistance was futile, however: they simply lifted her up, carried her forward and threw her in.

Fortunately she landed feet-down, and was agile enough to keep upright even with her restricted movements. Some of the water went into her mouth, and she spat it out as best she could. To her outrage, two of the guards joined her in the bath and began washing her, ignoring her furious attempts to shoulder them away. Even the thick fluid with which they cleaned her hair stank of the rank herb-smell. It smarted in her cuts and grazes, made her eyes sting; there was nothing in it of the holy perfumes the priest-kind would normally use for ritual cleansing. Bound and weary though she was, she made life very difficult for the two guards sharing the bath with her; and they were probably extremely grateful when at last they were able to drag her up the steps to the slightly sloping slab on the far side, pour fresh water over her and pronounce her clean. She was thankful to be done with the indignity, but aware that she now reeked (at least to a Skair's nose) of herbs associated with darkness. Even the weight of water could not flatten the hairs of her hackles as she stood dripping.

Stiv'aran had silently watched the entire process. He now ordered that she be dried, and towels were produced. Skaira never dried themselves after bathing, and the novel experience was not pleasant. Finally she was pronounced satisfactory, and she stood waiting for the next development. The less cruel (but equally effective) shackles might or might not have been put on her out of kindness, but whoever had prepared that bath had known very well what they were doing. She didn't like the feel of this at all.

Still without a word, she was escorted out of the bathing room and down more corridors. Eventually they reached another, smaller room, which contained nothing but a table. On this stood an alabaster goblet of wine. As she stood looking at it, one of the guards produced a knife. She would not give him the satisfaction of seeing her flinch as he brought it close to her face, but it took some effort to remain expressionless as he took hold of the rope around her head. Each of the relatively small movements as the blade sawed at the gag dragged the rope cruelly into the broken flesh of her mouth. Regard for the safety of his hands in the proximity of those teeth made the soldier wrench the rope away to snap the remaining strands, rather than risk cutting it completely. The pain of the action on her mouth made her senses swim, but a couple of moments later, with indescribable relief, she was able to spit out the cloth and close her aching jaw.

Stiv'aran came around from behind her and picked up the goblet. "You will now drink this," he said levelly.

She could not answer for a few seconds, until she had got back control of her mouth. Even then the words emerged slowly and clumsily. "I will not."

He nodded, as if he had expected nothing else. "So be it. Then your Starborn friend will die."
"He will die anyway. You will not spare his life."
"True. Perhaps I should have said he'll die – slowly. In agony. Knowing – for believe me I'll tell him – that you could have saved him every moment of it, and you wouldn't."
"You would not do it." Knowing that he would, and willingly.
"You don't believe that. If you refuse, he'll end by screaming to be allowed to die. And you'll watch every minute of it." He looked reflectively into the gleaming red heart of the wine. "He's a brave man. And too strong to die easily. He'll pay a dreadful price for your obstinacy."

There was a long, terrible silence.

"Give me the wine," she said almost inaudibly.

At least he had the grace not to smile as he brought it to her lips. She smelled it carefully, expecting some kind of slow poison. To her surprise, there was no trace of anything lethal in it. Kanehar would have recognised some of the ingredients, but they held no significance for Lidan: they did not even smell wrong as the bathing water had.

Still, whatever its effects, what choice did she have? Stiv'aran would have no hesitation in having Kelti tortured to death. Perhaps her acquiescence could buy him a merciful end – she had no alternative but to hope so. She drank the wine, every drop of it. No question but that it was drugged, she could taste the strangeness, but her throat went on moving steadily. As the Emperor-Elect removed the empty goblet from her mouth, she caught his gaze with her own: "Now have mercy on him."
"I don't intend any harm to him. He's a part of my plans. Just as you are." Before she had time to begin worrying over his words, the guards moved forward again, and took her from the room. She went submissively, accepting whatever fate held for her now. The drug was quick acting: her senses were beginning to spin already. And yet it was not an unpleasant sensation. Her skin prickled slightly, and felt warm. Her pulse was speeding up. If she had been able to think clearly, she felt that she might have been able to remember when she had felt like this once before; but the memory slid away from her grasp. She was almost surprised when the great doors appeared in front of her. In another life she might have been afraid, but a surge of anticipation filled her. *"Bren-dan,"* she said dreamily, and walked forward into the darkness.

31

Brendan awoke with a jerk. He sat up sharply and looked around, for a couple of moments too muzzy with sleep to be able to remember where he was. Since coming to Kerriel he had had to become used to sleeping on the ground, but it did not make for refreshing rest even so. His prayers finished, he had crawled back into bed – a real bed, with a padded mattress! – and fallen into fathomless oblivion. His body clock suggested that he must have slept for something like twelve hours, possibly longer. That in itself was unlike him, and was eloquent testimony to how exhausted he had been. Apart from the fact that he had stiffened up slightly from Riyeth's unnecessarily forceful treatment of him the previous day, and had the bruises to show for it, the long rest had done much to restore him physically. He sat up on the edge of the bed, smoothing his rumpled hair. He felt considerably better now as his brain cleared, though the remembrance of other events of the previous day brought a small surge of adrenaline into his bloodstream, and his heart contracted a little. The fact that thus far he had been treated reasonably well was not all that reassuring. He had no illusions about what Stiv'aran was capable of if crossed. And there was still the whatever-it-was – Esdiol – to be dealt with. If indeed such a person, such a force, existed at all. His twentieth-century-Earth mentality was still sceptical about this, but what had twentieth-century-Earth to do with what had happened to him?

His room had had a visitor whilst he slept, for a bowl of water and a folded towel stood on the table, while the remains of his supper had been cleared away, and replaced with what was undoubtedly meant for his breakfast. After twelve hours' sleep he was ready for it, and after relieving himself and washing his face and hands, he attacked the food with gusto. The condemned man always ate a hearty breakfast. He'd always thought that in such circumstances he wouldn't have any appetite anyway, but now found that this was not the case: if this was going to be his last meal he was bloody well going to enjoy it. A pity it couldn't have included a couple of rashers of bacon and an egg or so, but that being out of the question, he made the most of what he'd been given. It had been some days since he'd last missed a cup of coffee, but he thought rather wistfully of one now. Strange, how he hadn't had the faintest inkling that the half-cup he'd thrown down his throat during the warm-up at the King's Hall Arena might be the last he'd ever taste. Somehow it felt that he ought to have known…

The guards outside the room must have been checking on him periodically through the slots in the door, for shortly after he had finished and lain back down again, the door opened. Four soldiers stood there. They were as anonymous as all the others, in their heavy bronze armour and helmets; and though their swords were not drawn, he received the distinct impression that they were ready to counter any resistance with whatever force should be necessary.

"The Great Lord sends his greetings," said one formally. "You must accompany us."

"Any chance of telling me where?" inquired Brendan, not moving.

"As the Great Lord has ordered," was the flat reply. He hesitated, shrugged and stood up. Four on to one was not good odds anyway. Holding his head high, though his heart had begun to beat rather fast, he walked out among them. It felt like late morning, though there were no windows through which he could see whether the sun was shining. This building must be absolutely enormous, there was a perfect maze of corridors; he'd been too tired last night to keep track of where he had been taken, so he had no way of knowing now if they were retracing his steps. The room into which they presently escorted him certainly was not the Throne Room, however. It was bright and airy, and the chief feature of it was an enormous sunken bath, of such a size that it would literally be possible to swim several strokes in it. The sight immediately reminded him that he had had only one opportunity to wash properly since coming to Kerriel (his venture into the subterranean waterfall in the Shrine had been more ritual than practical), and although his scruffy, unwashed state was far from being the most pressing of his worries, he would be extremely glad to remedy the situation. The chief of his guards gestured, and he needed no second invitation. Stripping off his dreadful garment, which was by now almost in rags, he ran forward and plunged into the pool without even pausing to check the temperature of the water. Fortunately it was pleasantly warm, and even faintly herb-scented. He surfaced, blowing, indescribably glad to feel the accumulation of dirt and sweat falling off him. There was a shallow bowl to one side of it, and it took only a moment to establish that it contained some of the thick, slightly grainy fluid that Kanehar had given him to use as soap. It didn't lather up like soap on Earth did, but it did the job well enough, and he got out of the bath for a moment and gratefully slapped handfuls of it on to his hair and body. It too was quite strongly scented, unlike the type Kanehar had used. He didn't care much for the perfume, but he was too delighted at the prospect of being clean to refuse to use it. It smarted a little when it came into contact with the half-healed cut on his shoulder, but that was a small price to pay for cleanliness. A strong swimmer, he jumped back into the water and rolled in it like a seal, uncaring what his audience thought of him.

He was still enjoying himself getting clean when he became aware that he was no longer alone in the bath. The discovery startled him instantly into defensiveness; he splashed to the side and turned, dashing the water out of his eyes. The four guards were still where he had left them, near the door. There were two total strangers naked in the bath with him, and to his shock he realised that they were both female: they were slimmer than the males, and their long slender heads were so alike they could have been twins. They advanced on him rather nervously, the almost yellow eyes bright with interest. On Earth it was the sort of surprise the average red-blooded male fantasised about. Here it was by no means such an undiluted thrill. For one thing, their bodies didn't much resemble a human woman's: most noticeably, as he had already seen, they had no substantial breasts, as they did not suckle their young. The shifting water obscured some of the view of their lower parts, though the brief glance he couldn't resist taking suggested that they had no body hair.

He wasn't having any of it. "Thanks, but no thanks," he said shortly. With a mixture of embarrassment, distaste and annoyance he hoisted himself out of the water and looked around for a towel to cover himself with. It might have been a long time since he'd had sex – longer than he was used to going these days – but he wasn't going down that road. If this was Stiv'aran's idea of a treat, he was barking up the wrong tree altogether.

There were towels laid ready, and he found rather to his surprise that though he had seen nobody near it, his old tattered clothing had disappeared. In its place was a set of clean Venel garments, a black tunic whose sleeves reached his elbows whilst its hemline was a few inches below his knees, and a warm cloak of dark red wool that fastened across his throat with a clasp of what looked like bronze. The tunic should have had a belt, but his captors would not trust him with something that could be used as a weapon, however primitive; and in any case, it was a reasonably good fit even without one. At some point, somebody had taken stock of him with remarkable accuracy – even his makeshift moccasins had been replaced by a pair of well-fitting soft leather calf-length boots, such as the Venelai themselves wore. He dried himself hurriedly, turning his shoulder and casting a snapping glance over it to ward off a tentative attempt by one of the women to attempt to help him. To his relief, they both seemed to take the hint after that. They left reluctantly by another door, not without many a backward look at him, and he was able to get dressed without having to worry about them any longer. The clothes felt odd, but he suspected that they suited him; dark colours usually did. And it was undoubtedly pleasant to be clean again, and wearing well-made clothing, no matter how unfamiliar. Lidan had done her best, but she was no needlewoman, and the boiler suit had been close to the end of its useful life. Brendan towelled his hair dry, and rubbed a considering hand across the young beard that by now covered the lower half of his face. It was doubtful whether any of his captors would trust him with anything he could use as a razor!
"Have you finished? Was everything satisfactory?" asked the guard.
"Yes and yes, apart from the company." So he wasn't being the gracious guest, but he didn't feel like apologising; the arrival of the women had spoiled what had started off as a pleasant morning. He felt oddly soiled, though he was aware that the gesture had (probably) been made in good faith. It might be the Venel custom to make love in front of an audience, but he wasn't going to provide the floor-show today.

Still, allowing the incident to unsettle him was probably playing into Stiv'aran's talons. He shrugged off the distaste, and followed the guards out of the room. With a bit of luck he was going to be taken to see his captor, and find out what had happened to Lidan.

He was right on the first count; Stiv'aran was waiting for him in the Throne Room. The Emperor-Elect was dressed royally this morning, in red and gold. He sat easily in the Horned Throne, looking very much as though he belonged there. The guards marched the prisoner to the foot of the dais and knelt, ordering him harshly to kneel also. He made no reply. Neither did he kneel. He wouldn't kneel to the Taoiseach, and he wasn't kneeling to Stiv'aran. The Venel surveyed him thoughtfully.
"Where's Lidan?" asked Brendan without preamble.
"She's not far from here. You have my assurance that she's being well treated."
"If I'd your assurance it was raining I'd still look out of the window. I want to see her for myself."
"You'll see her in due course. In the meantime you're my guest. If there's anything you want you only have to name it."

"Except my freedom," he replied tersely.
"When you've done me one small – favour – you can walk out of here with my blessing. You have my promise on it."
Brendan frowned. This wasn't turning out at all as he'd expected. He hadn't had nearly enough of an acquaintance with Venelai to read their faces with anything like certainty, but Stiv'aran seemed completely sincere.
"What about Lidan?" he demanded.
"She'll be released unharmed, just like you. If she wants to go with you I'll let her. That'll be up to her."
He stared into the golden eyes, trying vainly to reach what was behind the answer. It sounded honest enough, and strangely enough he got the feeling that Stiv'aran was naturally honest, but he sensed an evasion.
"You'll let her go? Just like that?"
"If she wants to leave with you, she'll be allowed to do it. I'll do nothing to hinder either of you. I'll take oath on anything you choose, if you won't take my word."
It couldn't be put much plainer, but to Brendan it still didn't quite ring true. After all the agony, he and Lidan were just going to be allowed to walk away, unhurt? It was too good to believe, and he didn't believe a word of it. Nevertheless, it was obvious enough that for whatever reasons, Stiv'aran was trying to reassure him.
"So what's the favour?" he asked. That had to be the catch; and the Emperor-Elect's eyes immediately became veiled.
"Nothing unpleasant. You'll find out presently. There are certain …preparations… to make first. In the meantime, you're free of the Palace."
"Except the exits."
"Except the exits," he agreed. He rose.
"Wait a minute," said Brendan, remembering just in time: if he could have anything he wanted, there was one thing he'd almost forgotten. "When they brought me here there was an animal with me – a pet – I don't know what you call them. I want it back."
"I'd heard about it." It was his business to know every detail, and his subordinates had learned it the hard way. "They'll find it and bring it to you." And without more words he left the dais and quitted the room by another door. There was something going on elsewhere that required his personal supervision, and he wanted nothing to go wrong; not that he could imagine what could possibly go wrong. The power resident in the Skair was nowhere near as great as that which had belonged to Thaskan, but it would still take some time to subdue. In between whiles she was being given further doses of the drugged wine, which would have a cumulative effect. By the time the light began to wane she should be both compliant and eager. With the addition of the last detail – the ace up his sleeve, so to speak – the pieces of the plan should fall exactly into place. He despatched an underling immediately to find the animal that the Starborn wanted. If such a small favour could help to keep him quiescent until sundown, it would do no harm to oblige him.

For want of anything better to do while he waited, Brendan sat down on the dais and began his warm-up exercises. He never tired of the sense of suppleness and control, the spreading warmth as each set of muscles was worked on. Ignoring the watching guards, he finished the exercises and stood up to rehearse one or two of the more complex parts of his routine. The dais was polished smooth, and his boots were surprisingly supple. The hypnotic rhythm echoed in his head as his feet began the flying steps; he lost himself briefly in the unheard music, shadow-dancing opposite an unseen Adrian. The watching guards' initial unease at this unaccountable behaviour swiftly intensified into near panic. Even in these circumstances, his blazing talent drew for them the invisible other sharing the dais with him, and they had no way of knowing the significance of these mysterious actions. It might well be some kind of sorcery, and there was no priest nearby to protect them from whatever power the stranger might be summoning up. His whole demeanour told them that he at least could actually see someone – or some *thing* – immediately in front of him. He never knew how close he came to being attacked in terrified self-defence by his guards before the opening and closing of a door jerked him back to unwelcome reality. A she-Venel he had not seen before had come in, and under one arm she was carrying Uisge. The animal began to wriggle and vocalise as soon as she sighted him; the thin tail wagged furiously. The noise level would probably have been greater but for the fact that the instrument he still thought of as a flute was still clamped between the jaws.

Brendan laughed, and stopped. Unaware that at least a part of his guards' awareness now remained fearfully concentrated on the part of the dais that was (apparently) empty, he stepped down from it and walked to meet the woman. She was quite young and slim, perhaps six feet tall, clad in a long tunic and wrap of yellow cloth, embroidered with gold; he took the time to study her, trying to appraise her looks from a Venel's point of view. Her feet were encased in sandals whose straps were gold thread; giving him the first good look at what her people's feet looked like. Although longer than a human foot, with the lower half more strongly defined as having three bones that ended in clawed, birdlike toes, they were not scaled, as he would have expected. She moved with great grace, which was in marked contrast to the heavy deliberation that had characterised all of the males he had encountered so far. Quite possibly she was pretty, with that long neck. The shape of the head was longer, the beak far less aggressive than that of the male, and the eyes less deep-set and piercing. The creamy feathers on it grew all down her neck before going wispy in the hollow of her throat, where they gave way to smooth pale flesh. She looked so appraisingly at him before handing over her cooing burden that he paused in the act of taking Uisge from her and raised a rather sardonic eyebrow. "Don't worry, I'm not hungry at the moment."

The slender head dipped, but the eyes had what was surely a twinkle of mischief. "I couldn't resist the chance to get close to you. The Empress wants a complete report."

The other eyebrow climbed. "Oh, she does, does she? Just how complete would she like it?"

Now there was no mistaking the sideways glance. "They've already learned in the Women's Quarters that you have the means to satisfy a woman. It's not every day that a Starborn comes to the palace. Of course the Empress would want to know of him."

"I see," he said drily, taking the nuluoi and fending off Uisge's enthusiastic attempts to lick his face. "And was it the Empress's idea to send me company in the bath this morning?"

"No, but it was natural that we'd be interested in what happened. And what didn't."

He was now torn between thankfulness that he hadn't given what he interpreted as a harem food for the most intimate gossip, and indignation that his refusal to do so might have been taken as a slur on his virility.

"I prefer to choose my own lovers," he said a little coolly. "I'm sure the ladies were charming, but that's just the way I play it."

"It'll be a relief to them to hear it. And the Empress will be *most* interested to hear of you." Her eyes gleamed at him from under the long lashes. One of the guards growled, and she shot him a look of mingled defiance and mischief. She had quite deliberately used Mia'naan's now obsolete title, knowing that the guard had no power to reprove her. 'Minx,' thought Brendan, recognising that the girl was pushing her luck though not understanding in what way. And then, by way of joining in the provocation, he asked, "Wouldn't she prefer a personal viewing?"

"It wouldn't be possible. She's brooding the Heir, and she can't leave the egg for any reason, for fear it would cool." Leaving aside the fact that Mia'naan was not allowed to leave the room anyway, and had not been since Stiv'aran's coup.

An idle idea came to him. Stiv'aran had said he was free of the Palace, hadn't he? "So can't I go to her?"

She looked startled. It would have been unheard-of for an ordinary visitor to ask to visit the Women's Quarters; nobody would even have thought of asking to do so. "I don't know if it would be allowed."

He grinned; the thought of annoying Stiv'aran appealed to him. "You can blame me, it was my idea. I'd like to meet the Empress. I've never met one before."

She turned and looked at the guards, who looked relieved but uncertain. They would not be sorry to leave the Throne Room to whatever might or might not now be lurking on the dais, but the suggestion that the Otherworlder be taken to visit Mia'naan was not one for which they had been prepared. They had heard the Emperor-Elect give him the freedom of the Palace, and Stiv'aran had a short way with subordinates who did not obey his orders to the letter. The Women's Quarters were undeniably in the Palace. They could be reached without leaving the main building at any point. That said, whoever would have expected the prisoner to have the effrontery to want to visit the ex-Empress? Uncertain glances were exchanged.

For a moment, reading their hesitation, she too hesitated; but she was a warm-hearted creature, and could sympathise with the degree of Mia'naan's boredom. A visit from the Starborn would surely be of the deepest interest to her. "Come on then, if you want to."

'Why not?' he thought. The cloak had a deep inside pocket, and he slipped the nuluoi casually into it. A corner of his mind noted that the wood was wet and extremely cold, as if it had been dropped in a puddle; it must be raining outside, although Uisge's coat was quite dry. He put the animal – his mind insisted on terming her a dog – down on the floor, where she trotted happily beside him as he followed the Empress's handmaid. Looking down at her, he toyed with the idea of asking the unknown Empress if she could find the unfortunate beast a home if anything happened to him. Having evidently lost one master, she was clinging to him like a burr: and how did you explain to an animal that it had picked another loser?

A few minutes later he was being introduced to Mia'naan. She was in the customary pose of a brooding mother, lying on one side wrapped closely around the egg. The back of her body was protected from draughts by heaped cushions. More supported her neck and head. The rest of her was swathed loosely in a fine gown of a silvery grey fabric; her feathers were almost the same colour, a setting that made the wide golden eyes startlingly luminous. He wouldn't have needed to be told that she was of rank. Even at the relative disadvantage of being unable to rise, she radiated authority. There were other women in the room – quite a number of them, in fact – but she would command interest and respect in any gathering. He wasn't sure of the correct courtesies, but he didn't mind being suitably polite to her, as long as nobody demanded that he kneel. His gaze strayed curiously to the egg. The shell was pale blue, with a faint nacreous sheen. It was larger than he would have expected; if it had not been flaccid until exposed to air, it would have been far too large for her pelvic girdle to allow it through. The ex-Empress surveyed him with equal curiosity as her handmaid folded up decorously on the cushions at one end of the couch.

"You're most welcome," she said courteously. "I trust that you've been made comfortable."

"Your husband's done his best to make me feel so. Though I'd have been more grateful if my friend had been treated as well as I have."

"My husband is dead," she said, not unkindly. "I don't think you understand my situation. Stiv'aran's no relation to me, yet. He had my husband assassinated and all his other children murdered, and now he's waiting for this egg to hatch. If the hatchling's a female, he'll marry her and become Emperor. If it's a male, he'll kill him and become Emperor that way. That's what I'm here for: to ensure my egg hatches safely, so that a usurper can make the choice of killing my child or allowing it to live in order to legitimise his claim to the Horned Throne."

He was appalled by the calm recital, and almost more so by the matter-of-fact tone of her voice. For an instant he almost recoiled from her, until he realised that she had channelled all the bitterness at her fate into incalculable hatred for the cause of it. The tone was unemotional, but the words vibrated with scorn. She gestured him closer, and warily he approached her. At another gesture her women drew back out of immediate earshot, all but the one who had brought Uisge to him, who was evidently trusted enough to be allowed to remain.

"I don't expect you to trust me," she said in a low voice, "but believe me, I have no reason to lie on Stiv'aran's behalf. I'm not asking why you're here. I may have hopes, but I won't burden you with them. I only want to warn you of one thing: don't trust Stiv'aran. He's capable of anything, and if he's treating you well it isn't out of kindness."

"That's pretty well what I thought," he answered, though his throat had gone dry. What harm could there be in admitting that much?

“And one other thing.” She beckoned him even closer, until involuntarily he went down on one knee beside her. Her voice was now hardly more than a breath. “I can’t help you in any way. I’m not even sure I believe in prayer any more. But take this for good luck.”

Fortunately the angle of his body concealed the small gesture as she slipped something into his hand. After the briefest of glances, and with the minimum of betraying movement, he slid it into the pocket along with the flute. In his world it would have been a ‘corn-dolly’ – he had no idea of its significance in this world, but the shape could not help but make his heart jump. To return thanks would have been to prolong the moment into something that might cause suspicion, and he stood up and stepped back. “Thank you for telling me,” he said tonelessly. “I hope you’re right, and it’s a girl.”

A wave of her hand dismissed him as of no further significance. He shrugged, and turned away. The watching women whispered to see them so uninterested in each other. The guards had not invited themselves into the room – he had been given the freedom of the Palace, but they doubted whether that extended to them – but they had watched carefully from the door, ready to intervene at once if necessary, and were relieved that the visit had been short and uneventful. After his inexplicable lack of interest in the beautiful companions provided for him earlier, they had not felt it likely that the Starborn would be overcome by the sight of so much alluring female flesh now. However, there was no telling how his kind behaved towards their women; and there was the safety of the egg to consider above everything. He had got closer to it than Stiv’aran would probably have preferred, but they could truthfully report that he had not shown more curiosity than was proper, and certainly not even tried to touch it.

For the remainder of the morning, Brendan wandered where he would around the Palace, trailed by his guards, whom he had begun to find distinctly tiresome. Nobody prevented him from entering any room he wished, but though there were evidently orders in effect that his arrival should not disrupt the daily routine of the Palace, the horrified fascination with which he was covertly studied on every side was at first amusing and then slowly began to grow painful. Part way through the afternoon they took him back to his room, where he found another meal waiting. He ate that too, though again he did not drink the wine, but asked for water, which was brought. Although Brendan offered her titbits of anything he thought an animal likely to fancy, Uisge accepted none of them; all through the journey the ‘dog’ had foraged for herself, and it seemed that she must have done so while she waited for a chance to rejoin him. Or perhaps, he speculated idly, some kind soul around the Palace had fed her. Lidan had said that the creatures were kept for rodent control, and he supposed that she must have gone hunting and kept herself fed on these while he slept, for he had never seen her eating. After finishing his meal he indulged in a brief flare of rebellion, demanding to be shaved. It took some explaining to make his guards understand what he meant, and when they finally understood they were so appalled by the idea of a naked blade being allowed anywhere near him that they insisted on asking Stiv’aran’s permission before they co-operated. Finally an underling appeared with a bowl of soap and a scalpel, much the same as Kanehar had given him, and on condition that the prisoner directed operations with his hands and feet tied to the bedstead – Stiv'aran was taking no chances – the required service was performed. Considering that the unfortunate servant was evidently terrified, either by the proximity of the Starborn or by the threat of the Emperor-elect's wrath should his hand slip with the blade, it was done remarkably tidily, and Brendan smoothed his released hands over his clean face and felt better for it. Then he lay down on the bed. He had no appetite left for being a walking wonder, and besides, a kind of fatalism had laid hold of him, allowing him to push all the crowding fears to the back of his mind. He'd come here of his own free will, and there was still something waiting for him to face. It would be best on all counts if he was well rested; nothing was done better for a tired mind or a tired body. Uisge jumped up on to the bed and curled up beside him; he patted her head, and smiled. Someone would be sure to wake him if there was anything interesting going on – in the meantime, he was going to take a nap, and he hoped his guards would be excruciatingly bored watching him do it.

He yawned, snuggled his head down into the pillow, and went to sleep.

32

When he woke again, Brendan knew instantly that this was it. Stiv'aran was in the room with him, and there were far more guards, some also in the room and more in the corridor. The Emperor-Elect was now wearing half-armour, and looked formidable in it. Whatever was going to be asked of the prisoner, or done to him, they were taking no chances of his walking away from it. Or, more probably, of his being rescued from it.

Not bothering to speak – what was there to say? – he sat up. Uisge jumped up with him, cooing, and he hugged her briefly. A pity she probably didn't understand the 'Stay' command: he had a sick feeling she wasn't going to like what was coming next. If he couldn't make her stay behind (and a glance around revealed nothing he could use to tie her up with), she'd just have to take her chances. Perhaps she'd be too insignificant to be hurt, as long as he co-operated. He knew perfectly well that nothing whatsoever would be too insignificant to be hurt if he should suddenly happen to need coercion.

They walked him briskly through the Palace. It appeared to be deserted. The light had changed significantly; dimness advanced down the corridors. Very shortly the torches would be lit.

A sharp turn brought them to the outer doors, which were swung open immediately. Brendan blinked in the sudden rush of fresh air. Outside in the courtyard, saddled stags were waiting. He recognised his own, tied by ropes to the reins of two others. So he was to be allowed to ride wherever they were going, but they still weren't taking any chances. As the squadron reached the saddles, they drew their swords. He mounted his own beast, scorning the helping hand that was offered. Unseen by him, the officer behind him shot Stiv'aran a glance that suggested tying the prisoner's ankles together under his mount's belly. The Emperor-Elect studied Brendan for a moment, then shook his head imperceptibly and moved away. The officer stepped back and allowed his soldiers to close ranks around the prisoner. Moments later Stiv'aran rode to the front, mounted on a stag that even Brendan's inexperienced eye could see was an exceptionally fine animal, with a glossy coat so dark it was almost black, and a huge spread of antlers.

The outer gates opened. They clattered out into the streets of the city, which were also emptier than he would have expected. The few passers-by cast them scared glances. Above them the sky was stained with the ominous flush of a stormy evening, the setting sun hidden by banks of broken cloud. As they rode down the street at a quick trot, Brendan's hands tightened on the reins – but the scabbard beside his knee was empty, and the ropes securing his mount's head were strong and well fastened. He hadn't a hope in Hell of getting away; and if by some crazy chance he managed it, to where would he run? He might as well just go along with it. At least they hadn't forced on him the indignity of riding with his hands tied.

The journey was relatively short. In less than fifteen minutes they pulled up in front of another gated wall; and beyond this rose the unmistakable shape of the tower Brendan had so briefly glimpsed in the depths of the Star Pool on Sikkthi. His heart jumped into his mouth. He'd thought himself prepared for it, as far as any man could be, but the realisation that *this is it* smashed into his fragile defences like a cannonball. He stared around wildly at the clean daylight, wanting to take it with him. This couldn't be happening. It was simply not possible that it was going to end here. This was the sort of way people died, and he wanted to die with the Atlantic sounding in his ears and his own folk around him…

It was faintly surprising the way his body went on working so efficiently when he was no longer consciously giving it orders. He dismounted lightly enough, and stood waiting to be told what to do. It was probably a compliment of sorts that he was surrounded by soldiers six-deep, but it reinforced the impression that there was something really terrible waiting for him, no matter what Stiv'aran had said. Uisge had followed him, pattering at the stag's hind hooves, but now that he looked around to make sure she'd got here safely, she was nowhere to be seen. He was grateful for it, even though she was sure to be distressed by being parted from him: at least she'd be spared exposure to whatever he was going to be taken to. And perhaps somewhere in the city there would be someone better able to offer her a kind home and a future.

The gates swung open; there were more soldiers within. For a Temple, the place was manned like a fortress. Despite his fear as he was escorted inside, Brendan couldn't help appreciating the beauty of the architecture. The courtyard was ringed with arches whose pillars and capitals were of carved marble, and the artistry of the carving was breathtaking. Each pillar was a column of frozen plant life, twining and budding and blossoming as if some freak of nature had turned a score of prize exhibits from this world's equivalent of the Chelsea Flower Show into stone to preserve them for posterity. The same work framed the double doors, of wood panelled with engraved gold, and the great windows set into the stonework. It was a single-storey building, with the tower rising from the centre of it. Now that he was this close, he could see that the tower was pierced with tall windows, from the pattern of them following the course of a spiral staircase within. It was indeed a beautiful place, reminding him of the elegance of parts of Florence or Vienna. Somehow that made it all the more horrible, that something so beautiful outside should contain something so awful inside, like the soft golden fur of a ripe peach hiding corruption instead of a stone. A corner of his mind noticed that though the honey-coloured stone of the buildings was meticulously pure, the stones of the courtyard were strangely mottled; but he didn't recognise the light-coloured stains as blood.

Stiv'aran materialised beside him. "If you're ready?"

"As ready as I'll ever be." He set his teeth. Ten soldiers escorted them through the doors. The inside of the building reminded him vividly of a church, airy and echoing. Its floors were of the same yellow marble as the Horned Throne, the walls frescoed with exquisite paintings of stylised plant life. Immediately behind the doors two side corridors opened off from the main one, but they were deserted and dim. The one ahead led directly to the core of the building. The twelve of them walked straight up it, and stopped in front of another pair of double doors, beautiful things of intricately carved wood inlaid with gold, though Brendan was in no state by now to appreciate the craftsmanship that must have gone into the making of them. There was no mistaking where he was standing. The tower must rise almost directly in front of them now, above the heart and core of the Great

Temple. Right behind these doors. As two of the escort moved to the huge gold handles to draw them wide, Brendan crossed himself, not caring if anyone saw the movement. 'Deliver us from evil'… He wanted to pray, but his brain was so paralysed with fear that he couldn't remember any words: God would just have to understand.

Inside the room was total darkness. Not even the open doors admitted any light. For one appalled moment his feet literally refused to move. His heart was thumping in his chest as if trying to burst his ribs asunder, and sweat ran down the back of his neck. But Stiv'aran was beckoning him forward, and there were naked swords behind him. It was walk or be driven. Pride would have to serve instead of courage; he walked. One pace, two, three, four… ten paces and the doors slammed shut behind him. Even the slam sounded muffled, as if the darkness was something solid, a curtain cutting him off from any hope of escape or rescue. Around him the blackness and the silence were absolute. He felt a scream of terror building up inside him, and fought it down. There was no way of telling where Stiv'aran was, if he was still here at all. The air was stale, and he breathed with difficulty – or was it just his own panic?

Time had come to a standstill. He never knew how many seconds or minutes or hours had passed before he heard the voice; and it was not Stiv'aran's voice. He did not even know if he heard it in the same way as ordinary sound. It had no quality that he could possibly have described.

"You are welcome, Starborn Kelti. Or would you prefer that I call you Brendan Doyle?"

His heart almost stopped. Nobody on this planet knew his real name. No one except Lidan. Even Kanehar and Hargen had not been told. 'There is power in names'. What had they done to her, to make her tell?

"She has not been injured in any way. And despite what you fear, I have no wish to injure you either. It is up to you."

He swallowed. In the pit of his terror, a desperate thread of hope came into being, and he fought it down in vain. "In what way, up to me?" He trusted no one and believed nothing, but that obstinate craving for survival put the words in his mouth whether he would or no.

"I require a service of you. A small service. Nothing you will find unpleasant. And if you oblige me, you will find that I can be generous. Your life will be the first and smallest of the rewards."

"Rewards?" Could there, somehow, be a way through this nightmare? He did not believe, he must not believe – but what harm was there in listening?

"Do not the men of Earth desire the same things as those of Kerriel? Wealth – power – their choice of females? All will be yours, if you are wise. I am certain that you understand the alternative."

The temptation dragged ferociously at him. 'I will give you sovereignty over all the kingdoms of the Earth'… who wouldn't be tempted? And he wanted to live, with a savage intensity that he would never have guessed at until his grasp on life was in this mortal danger. To simply let go, to surrender it, like CúChulainn on the Plain of Murthemney… 'To destroy you would destroy him, and he knows it'…

He sucked air into his lungs, and straightened up. He'd done a parachute jump once, and he felt now just the way he had done then, poised on the edge of the dizzying drop. And this time there was nothing strapped to his back; nothing

to hold on to but the hope that Lidan had known what she was talking about. He stepped into space.
"My soul belongs to the Lord my God, and you can go to Hell where you belong," he said clearly into the darkness. He'd spoken in Gaelic, but the message was clear in any language. There was no more to add. He waited for the cataclysm.

It did not come. The darkness shivered with what felt disconcertingly like laughter. Then, in front of him, it parted.

She was standing with her head slightly forward, looking at him from under her lashes with a mixture of innocence and invitation. The silky garment reached just to the middle of her long, slender thighs; it covered her body like a semi-transparent shimmering skin, sensuously outlining her breasts. A silver chain glimmered around one slim ankle. She moved a step towards him, rotating her hips with a gentle and incredibly erotic grace. He saw and did not see that around her forehead was a circlet of silver, a diamond of unbelievable purity set in the centre of it. The radiance from it glinted on every curve and accentuated every hollow, gleamed on the moist redness of her mouth. He had never seen any woman so beautiful, nor ever wanted one so much. His capacity for rational thought had been destroyed. None of the Skaira had thought to explain what had been the most precious relic stolen from the Shrine on Vanreil, the crown not made by mortal hands, its lodestone reflecting its own unearthly light eternally among its millions of facets. Nobody had warned him, nothing could have protected him from the magic of Genshenna the Star of Heaven, bestowing on the wearer beauty beyond that of mortals.
"All men may make one mistake," the voice said slyly. "I am not unforgiving. I spoke of rewards: perhaps you did not understand the form these could take. She is yours, Brendan Doyle. Take her."

Any remnant of defiance, of distrust, of resistance had been blasted away from him. He only thought of one thing now, and it was within his grasp. He stepped forward, took hold of the neck of the garment, and ripped it apart.

*   *   *

Kanehar had been obliged to spend a large part of the day sleeping; the stresses and strains of the journey from Vanreil had taken their toll. The forest had remained quiet, and Keri'khai had kept watch on the city, though that too had seemed peaceful enough. Towards evening the Skair woke, and decided that she had better set about getting them both some supper: the lieutenant's stag might be able to manage on grass, but they needed something rather more substantial. He had been able to break his fast at dawn with some dried meat and fruit he had had packed in a roll strapped behind his saddle, but there had not been much left and she knew that he must be ravenous by now. (He had politely offered her a share, but she had refused, knowing that the cooked meat would make her stomach sour.) She remembered that she'd come past a sizeable stream not far back, and noted the abundance of fruiting trees along its bank. They would suffice for

Keri'khai for the moment. She was reaching the stage where it was becoming imperative that she kill, and it was possible that she might find some small animal in the same area. Leaving her patient was a risk, but she judged it a relatively small one. Risk or not, they both had to eat; the journey here had drained her reserves completely, and all of her stomachs were snarling. Hunger she could bear, but blood deprivation would presently begin to affect her reflexes, cloud her mental processes and begin the slow deterioration of her body systems that unchecked would lead to death. She couldn't take the smallest risk of losing any of her mental or physical capabilities, not with so much at stake. With his upper arms immobilised the Venel had very little capacity to defend himself, but she had fetched his sword and laid it across his lap so that he was not completely unarmed. She assured him that she would not be gone for very long, nor be out of earshot if he should call for help – it would be a swift kill or nothing, she could not afford the time to lie in wait.

Quickly she padded back through the quiet woods. She could smell the water clearly. First a drink – she was very thirsty – and then she would gather fruit. Perhaps she might startle some small animal out of hiding among the bushes. She did not need great quantities of blood, she could fill up with fruit, but it would certainly be well if the Goddess sent her a kill of some sort.

Reaching the bank of the stream where it widened to a pool, she glanced down – and froze. Almost under the bank was a large fish, its tail moving gently to keep it stationary in the current. By the Goddess! She had not hoped for luck like this!

Infinitesimally she shifted her stance. Her knees bent stealthily, bringing her heights low without altering the outline she must present from beneath the water. Eventually she stopped, waited, waited…

And struck. The force of the strike hurled her entire weight into the water, but the bared claws of her right forepaw sank into the plump flesh of the fish even as it tensed to flee. Rolling upright, completely indifferent to the soaking, she hissed in triumph: she would eat well!

The colossal splash cleared, the water quietened. Regaining her paws, she reached down to take the wriggling fish in her hands and free her paw so that she could wade out of the water. As her hands thrust into the water, ripples spread out from her flesh. Ripples that began shimmering with colour. She became perfectly still. Though her hand had closed around it, the fish was forgotten. The colours spread, deepened, brightened. The brilliance beat upwards, illuminating her intent face and the undersides of the leaning trees. There was no sound except the murmur of the water spilling over the rapids a little way upstream, but Kanehar's ears were swivelled to listen raptly to her instructions.

Abruptly she exploded forwards, the forgotten fish still clutched in her hand. Stealth and fruit equally forgotten, she leaped up the bank and hurtled back to the clearing. Hearing her coming in such haste, Keri'khai sat up, ignoring the pain it cost him to close his hand on the hilt of the sword she'd left with him.

Throwing the fish down in the grass, she flung herself at the astonished Venel. "Your captain! Find him!" she snarled. Her hands closed on either side of his head. "You know him! Find him! Now!"

33

Teho'evan stirred. He had gone past the need for food, but thirst was torture. As well as his arm, several of his ribs were broken, and each breath hurt him. Chained to the Skair he had killed, he had nothing to hope for but that he might die of his untreated injuries before Stiv'aran's promised revenge could be carried out, but he was young and strong. It was not likely. His future was not so much bleak as bloody and short. And for all that, he still thought himself fortunate in comparison to the third occupant of the cell.

He had woken from dark dreams to see her come in. He had been too bewildered at first to understand, but the changing expressions on her face as her eyes adjusted to the gloom had been appallingly easy to read. As the door was slammed shut behind her she had fallen forward, burying her face in the cold damp fur of Thaskan's withers. He had expected a scream, but what emerged was almost worse. A soul wailing on its way to damnation would have made a sound like that.

For a very long time she had not moved. Even in the dimness he could see tremor after tremor going through her body, though she made no further sound. He could only imagine what was passing in her mind, but he knew clearly that his own danger was very real. Should she require a victim on whom to avenge her Princess, he was it. She was unlikely to care that he had killed Thaskan for the purest of motives, even if she gave him enough time to explain, or indeed if it mattered to her whether he had had anything to do with it at all. He reflected wryly that it might well be that Stiv'aran was going to be cheated of his revenge after all; or perhaps the Emperor-Elect had seen some twisted poetic justice in the possibility.

When she had finally sat up again, however, she had not attacked him. She had begun talking, whether to him or to Thaskan or even to herself he found it hard to tell. It was not ordinary conversation, sometimes she even lapsed into what he supposed to be the Old Speech, but scraps of sentences and phrases like bleeding made audible. His heart wrung with pity. The night passed slowly, and she kept on talking; though sometimes she fell silent for a while, as if listening for an answer that never came. Now she was speaking to someone who was not even there, asking forgiveness. He hated to hear it; it was not right for him to listen to another creature's soul collapsing. This was for Shieih's ears, not for his.

When dawn came, the periods of quiet became longer. He still believed that sooner or later this phase would break into violence and he would die. Sometimes she wept, the tears trickling down her face as if she did not even know that she was crying. Nobody came to bring her food; evidently they were both to be left to die. He wanted to console her, but didn't know if she even heard his extremely tentative attempts to answer the few pieces of speech that might have been aimed vaguely in his direction.

The day crept past. Sometimes he drifted into a doze in spite of his suffering, but she gave no indication that she knew he existed, let alone cared what he did. At one point he woke to see her trying to comb Thaskan's cropped hair with her fingerclaws; the tears were falling again. More than ever he felt an intruder, and buried his head in the angle of his elbow to shut out the sight. He must have slept again, for when he raised his head she had moved back and was sitting against the door, moaning softly as if in indescribable torment. Her eyes were closed. The bar of light beneath the door shone redly on her fur. It was evening again.

It came to him like a sudden pain, blossoming in the core of his skull. Forgetting for a moment the severity of his injuries, he tried awkwardly to sit up, pressing a hand to his head. He had never felt anything like it. Had he sustained some internal damage during the beating, that was only now manifesting itself? It was not impossible: he had seen men die unexpectedly days after apparently surviving a blow to the head without ill effects. Such a strange feeling – not like pain after all, though it was intensely unpleasant. Almost, if such a thing was not absurd, it was like a voice, telling him to do something…

Dizzy with weakness and confusion, he tried to ignore it. It would not be ignored. The voice became yet more imperative. The order was repeated, senseless as it was. He couldn't make it go away. Perhaps the injury caused such effects as the damage spread. What difference did it make? He might as well obey. The Skair was going to kill him sooner or later anyway…

Trying to cradle his broken arm as much as possible from the jolting, he shuffled sideways and climbed reluctantly and unsteadily over Thaskan. His breathing was ragged with pain, and the chains clinked as he moved, but the other Skair did not even glance at him. Not until he was right beside her did the amber eyes open. They fastened on him then, glaring. Even in the gloom he could see her lips writhing back to expose the formidable teeth. He braced himself, and thrust out his uninjured arm to flatten his palm against her head.

Power surged through the contact. She screamed and lashed out at nothing. He could hear the unknown voice battering at the half-destroyed intelligence in her skull. The brain was crumpled with shock and remorse, but the power was still there, an untapped well that the events of the past hours had passed by. *"Use it! Use it! FIND HER!"*

* * *

Stiv'aran shivered. The air in the Shrine was bitterly cold: how was it that he had never noticed it before?

Everything was going according to plan. He had only to wait and watch. Somehow the scene before him was not as erotic as he might have expected, although the unfailing radiance of Genshenna made the twining bodies into a sculpture of molten silver. For all his puny attempt at defiance, the Starborn had not been proof against his own treacherous body. Now he would do the will of… of…

What did it matter? He would do what he had been brought here to do. After that it hardly mattered what happened to him. He could go where he wished and do what he would, it would make no difference. The cataclysm he would have unleashed would be completely unstoppable.

The Emperor-Elect shivered again. His robes were not proof against this savage chill. He looked down and saw the cloak that the Starborn had discarded. It lay on the marble like a pool of blood, but it was thick and warm. It would do no harm to wrap it around himself while he waited.

He bent down – and stopped in disgust. From the deep pocket sewn on to the inside of the cloak a small object had spilled out. The crown of little white flowers shimmered in the gloom. Whoever made it had been incredibly skilled and patient: there were even tiny contours that suggested a face framed by the white flowers and the long, rippling hair. Two minute gold beads completed the illusion, staring accusingly at the darkness. How could this have come here? He would have to get rid of it, and at once. Tear it up, shred it into pieces, anything to rid himself of the strange and unwelcome feelings the sight of it stirred. Completing the movement, he closed his talons around it.

Instantaneously everything changed. An inanimate object, incapable of being influenced by anything in its surroundings, it had been made in a shape that made it a ready channel for sorcery. Lidan had spoken truly when she said that Skaira were powerless within the confines of the Great Temple, but there was no bar against their power being used and directed by a consenting male. Beyond the city walls, Kanehar and Keri'khai stared sightlessly into each other's eyes, their united consciousness aware of nothing but the struggle to control the half-crippled officer and almost broken Skair within the city. Even now Riyeth barely understood what was happening, but some shred of awareness in her caught at the suggestion of avenging Thaskan. Screaming, she hurled all of herself that was still alive into the fray. The Power flooded up Stiv'aran's arm, exploded in his brain. The linked sources were just enough to break the residual grip that held him now, and he staggered backwards and crashed into the altar. As the true situation burst into his consciousness, he stared in utter horror at what was happening in front of him. He had been in the heart of the Darkness, and he knew – he *knew...*

Esdiol had instantly recognised the possibilities inherent in the meeting of two different life forms. The meteor had been his key to Kerriel. The Starborn could be his key to Earth. Brendan himself was safe from harm, as Lidan had known; but Brendan's *offspring...* that was another matter completely. Protected by no Earth spells, fathered during an act of free will... Lidan, as a Skair, had a completely alien physiology to his; her reproductive process did not require the intervention of a male. But she contained the egg that in due course would ripen to become her daughter. Genetic manipulation on this scale was not possible to Esdiol at a remove. To effect a change so comprehensive, he had to literally enter the egg, and control the fusion of it and the sperm to produce the end result he wanted: a body he had created, a host for himself, containing genetic material of both Kerriel and Earth. As a creature of both, he would be free of both. And they would both be destroyed within a single generation.

He had to be stopped. And there was very little time, perhaps only seconds, before the Starborn reached his climax.

Moving like a drunkard in a dream, Stiv'aran turned around to the altar. A weaker soul would have collapsed beneath the weight of guilt that rose up to overwhelm him: *betrayer, murderer, usurper, infanticide!*, but there was no time for that now. A lifetime's hard lessons in necessity told him that what was required now was action, not remorse; if the Good God permitted, there would be all eternity in which to pay for the unspeakable things he had done. He reached out towards the Stone, the accursed thing that had begun everything. His talons closed around it, but the cold sent him staggering backwards. He couldn't hold it; it would kill him. He dragged the cloak up off the floor and threw it over the Stone. That helped, a little, though in such proximity its renewed assault on him made his senses spin. With an effort, he could lift it. But the Starborn…

Brendan was in another world, one of heat and softness and hardness and the fiery craving in the pit of his belly. She rolled him over and sat up, grinding her pelvis down until the sensation became too much to bear. In another minute he was going to explode. He pulled her down and got on top of her again, pinning her down for the last exquisite, agonised seconds he could hold it. And suddenly there was something happening, an ugly, clumsy hand fumbling across her face. In a rush of wild fury, he jerked up and screamed something – there were no words in it, he was past speech, but it echoed around the room like the bellow of a wounded animal. The hand jerked upwards, and the thumb hooked under the coruscating stone on her forehead. Next instant Genshenna was gone, rolling across the floor, the light from it whirling crazily in the darkness; and suddenly there was darkness everywhere, deepest of all in the eyes a bare eight inches away from his own. The sorcerous radiance removed, the change was stunning. He was able to think again, but it did not take thought to bring him rearing upright away from her – God Almighty, was it a her, was it human at all?, and slamming aside the arms that reached to draw him back to damnation. The simple construction of male and female human bodies meant that he was far stronger than she was (*in all that matters I was a human*), and she was dashed back against the floor as he leaped to his feet. He turned to run, but there was nowhere to run to; the darkness pressed in on every side. A hand groped for his ankle, and he snarled like an animal in a cage. Her free hand was reaching for the coronet that had rolled to a halt on the floor, the light still beating out of it to cast a strange wavering radiance up the wall; she had only to put it on again for him to be as enmeshed and helpless as before. Then, out of nowhere, there was Uisge, luminous silver in the blackness: a shape that changed and swelled in his unbelieving gaze until its head swung level and higher than his own, the huge spread of antlers flashing in the gloom. There was no saddle, but the shoulders were ready, and he needed no urging; he caught hold of a handful of the shimmering hair and vaulted astride. The stag swung around, and pushed forward a pace. Suddenly Stiv'aran was there, at Brendan's knee: his face hardly recognisable from the conflict of powers tearing his brain asunder, he thrust something heavy wrapped in cloth onto his lap. "Take it – " he croaked. "Go!"

Brendan needed no second bidding. His heels dug savagely into his mount's sides, and the animal sprang forward. The Venel stumbled alongside, and then the doors appeared in the darkness, made visible only by the stag's pale radiance reflected in the inlaid gold. Dreadful sorcery kept them shut. Uisge plunged to a halt, snorting, and Stiv'aran staggered out in front of them. There would be a terrible price to pay for opening those doors; and he had only one coin to offer. Drawing the deep breath that he knew would be his last, he put both hands on the golden panels, and pushed.

Light and darkness exploded. Stiv'aran pitched dying on to his face, and Uisge jumped lightly over him, out into the corridor. Brendan braced himself ready for the rush towards the outer doors, but what happened next almost threw him bodily off the stag's back. Uisge leaped, not forward but upward, like spray flung from a fountain. The ornate wooden ceiling and the tiled roof above it burst soundlessly outwards as if struck by a shock wave, and they were out, incredibly out and free, climbing the sky as if galloping up the arch of a rainbow.

His brain reeling, Brendan stared down at the diminishing city. Activity boiled around the Temple. A figure raced from the outer doors, and grasped at the rein of a magnificent stag with a coat so dark it was almost black. The hunt was on.

"Who are you? What are you?" he shouted above the rush of the wind. The dark markings like rainwater rings on a pool shimmered across the silken hide between his knees. For an instant he mocked himself for expecting an answer from an animal; but what kind of animal could this be? And sure enough, there was an answer, silvery and disembodied in his head. *"I do not have a name. I am what I am."*

Dizzy with shock, he crouched lower on the broad back. His face was close to the furry neck, and the flick of the hairs whipping in the wind touched his skin like minute cool stroking fingers. Oddly enough, he felt no fear of falling, even though he hadn't even a saddle to provide a sense of security.

"Why did you rescue me?"

"You called me beautiful, and wished to stay with me always. No one has ever said such a thing before. So I did not want you to go into danger alone."

When on earth-? His mind raced, and stopped in disbelief. It wasn't possible!

"You're a *lake?*"

*"I am **of** the lake. It is I who answers questions. Did you think that water could hear or answer?"*

"I never thought about it," he confessed. "We don't have any magic where I come from."

"What a dull world you live in."

"It has its good points." He glanced back over his shoulder. It was a good job he had a head for heights, but even so his stomach lurched at the altitude they had achieved. And behind them, still some way back but gaining, was the black stag. His heart contracted with fear. He couldn't, he wouldn't be caught again; but where in the world was safety to be found from that horror? 'Lidan', he thought in anguish. They had trapped him with her like a wasp to a jam pot, and he'd just walked straight into it.

"Do not blame yourself. There is no mortal on this world or on yours who could have resisted Genshenna the Beautiful." Uisge – or whatever he should properly call it – could evidently read his thoughts. *"And do not fear. You have all that you need to defeat the Dark One."*

"But I haven't!" he cried in desperation. "I had a knife – Irvathil – and I had to leave it in the hay in the cart! They've got it!"

"Did I not bring you a gift?"

"That wasn't a knife, it was an instrument! A musical instrument!"

"Did you not notice something strange when you pocketed it?"

Strange? It had been wet and cold-

Wet. From immersion in water. Cold. From sorcery, as his hand had been when he dreamwalked in Kanehar's house. The cloth on his lap was his cloak, bundled around something. Another something, rather lighter, tapped against his right shin as a trailing fold of the fabric whipped in the wind of their going. He leaned forward and groped for it, and his hand closed around a wooden case, hanging perilously half-out of the pocket, thousands of feet above the forest.

"It was necessary to keep it hidden, even from you. If you had known, you would not have been able to disguise your knowledge. I am sorry you were never able to play the nuluoi, but one of the grooms is fond of music. He will probably play it better than you would."

"Hell's bells!" He clutched the case, hardly able to believe his eyes. A shred of hope was reborn, though it still battled with fear as he looked back again. Their flight had levelled off. The black stag was much closer. He dared not look at the face of the rider; it would have been more than he could bear. "He's going to catch us!"

"He believes so."

'He's not the only one,' thought Brendan desperately. Looking down, he could see the range of mountains that contained Vanreil coming swiftly nearer. The lake on Sikkthi gleamed like a mirror, reflecting the darkening sky: was Uisge going home? Was there some power in the water that could resist Esdiol?

"I am taking you where you must go. Do not be afraid."

Moments later he heard the first sound of the breathing. For all that the hooves were pounding air, the legs were still working like pistons, and the lungs laboured in the thin air of altitude. Uisge was running in eerie silence, but the black stag was a mortal animal, and hard-ridden. A swift glance over his shoulder showed that barely ten lengths separated them now. The endless seconds flowed past; he did not want to look back again but the breathing was growing louder and louder. The distance had halved again. He gripped the wooden case, nerving himself to loose the catch: if it came to the crunch, he wasn't going to be caught without a fight. However dreadful the pain of taking the weapon into his hand might be, it would still be preferable to surrendering to the fate that awaited him otherwise.

"Farewell, Kelti!"

He did not understand the words for a split second; then as he realised with a stab of pure horror what they meant, he grasped frantically for the ruff of hair above the shoulders. It was too late. Uisge had twisted in mid-air, rolling with the fluid violence of a bucking bronco, and Brendan was falling to his death. There was no way he could survive the impact from this height, even if he landed in water; and there was no water underneath him. There was only the barren shoulder of one of the mountains, with the woodland crowding around its foot: and threaded between them a black crack that widened like ravening jaws as he hurtled towards it.

Geirion!

He was completely helpless. He fell like a stone, with the wind roaring in his ears and the cloak snapping like machine-gun fire with the speed. The thing Stiv'aran had pushed on to his lap was still wound up in it, and as he was quite incapable of pushing it away, both of them fell together. The wooden case was still clutched in one hand, but of what use was that going to be when he would be pulverised by the impact?

Nearer and nearer sped the forest; wider and wider yawned Geirion. He twisted madly, trying to control the angle of his fall to miss that dreadful mouth, but there was no time. He had been rescued from one hell to be thrown into another, and for all his attempts to put up a last prayer; the syllables broke on a scream as the blackness swallowed him.

34

Suddenly the air rush stopped, as totally and abruptly as though someone had slammed a door between himself and a gigantic fan. He had been waiting, rigid with horror, for the unimaginable second when he would hit the ground; and he had not felt anything. It was perfectly dark and quiet, and he lay for some moments in a total daze. Was he dead? He *must* be dead. He wasn't falling any more. Well, that had been less painful than he'd expected; his head must have hit the rock floor and been pulped before his brain could even register the fact he'd reached the bottom. With a mixture of immense relief and morbid curiosity, he lifted his head slightly and put a hand tentatively to his chest, more than half expecting not to feel anything at all. It felt startlingly normal. Did a spirit have a body, then? It must have; he undoubtedly felt just the same way he had when he'd been alive.

This was all a bit peculiar. Shouldn't he be in Heaven or (more probably) Purgatory or (God forbid!) Hell? Any of those should have felt a bit different to this. Sort of... *busier.* Would they, could they be this quiet? He frowned. Would the floor of the spirit world feel like cold dry stone? He was still breathing, too, and there was a twinge from the cut on his shoulder as he shifted experimentally. This couldn't be right. There was no way he could have survived that fall. And besides – memory stirred – if this was Geirion he was at the bottom of, where was that nightmarish reaction he'd experienced before? He blinked, dazed, into the darkness. The air was cold, still and clean, and smelled faintly of moss. Wouldn't an ordinary gorge have something at the bottom of it – water at least, or the accumulated debris of ages that the wind had swept into it from the forest above? He'd have to get up and explore. There must be some reason why Uisge had brought him here. Perhaps there was something he was meant to find...

He experienced a moment's panic when a tentative attempt to sit up was hindered by something he couldn't see; but his groping fingers identified the culprit as his cloak, partly wrapped around him and pinned down under the whatever-it-was that Stiv'aran had handed to him, now lying almost in the crook of his arm. It was at this point that the total impossibility of his having survived a fall from such a height struck him. This was crazy! He *couldn't* be still alive! It just wasn't possible!

"Oh yes, you are alive," said a cold voice. "I still need you, and I shall have you. With or without your co-operation. You scorned the pleasurable way: so be it. You will come to me in agony and despair, but you will come to me just the same."

His heart jumped into his throat. Just in front of him a dull green glow ignited in the blackness, and there she was: no longer beautiful, no longer irresistible, just a parody of a memory he hated someone for having the cunning and the cruelty to sully. She had not troubled to bring Genshenna; the time for deception was over. The human would be made obedient – one way or another. For all that he now recognised wretchedly that part of the fatal attraction she had exercised over him was the sight of a human face after so long, now her humanity was the worst part of everything.

"You wish to live," she said. "Give me what is mine and I shall spare you to worship me."

"Nothing of me is yours," he snarled. "You've had all of me you're getting, and you can go to Hell!"
"I could take your mind if I so wished, and you would be powerless to stop me," she replied, smiling terribly. -"Do you think that anything you are is capable of resisting me? But first, give me the thing that the traitor Stiv'aran gave to you in the Temple."
"You mean this?" He moved aside a fold of the cloth, and looked in surprise at what it revealed. A large, plain chunk of rock, pitted and blackened by heat. No wonder it had been heavy. Was that all? A second and swifter glance showed him the greedy gaze fastened on it. It was precious, then, whatever it was. An idea germinated. "You can have it – in return for letting me go."
The face was completely expressionless. The eyes examined him. "It is a bargain. Give it to me."

His heart beating wildly, he got up slowly and picked up the bundle, folding and arranging the cloth with great care. Even through several thicknesses of the wool he could feel the dreadful cold beating out of the stone: it would occasion no surprise that he should be careful not to be burned by the vicious chill whilst handling it. He took a couple of steps forward, and she came to meet him, reaching for it eagerly. The eyes were bright and confident. He could read that expression like a book: if the Starborn was fool enough to believe that bargains were for keeping, that folly would be his last.

An instant before her hands closed on it, he acted. He'd taken care to drape the cloak so that it would allow his arm to pivot freely. His hand whirled back and over, the stone becoming a deadly weapon. *In all that matters I was a human*: her reflexes were fast, but the first instant of horrified disbelief held her paralysed for just half a second too long. If the meteor had struck on her temple, as he'd intended, it would probably have killed her outright. As it was, it scoured down the side of her face and slammed into her shoulder. She fell to one knee with an inhuman scream of fury, and when she leaped up again she was holding something that had been lying on the floor between them. Shards of wood fell away from it, the fragments of an ancient case that had not been proof against the shattering impact. The shock and incredulity of the first pain Esdiol had ever been made to feel had sent him so crazed with rage that he discarded every idea of keeping the Starborn intact. His life might be sacrosanct, but there were untold degrees of suffering short of the end. The miserable mortal would pay, and pay with his skin – now!

Springing forward as Brendan backed off cursing his failure, she tore the dagger from the sheath.

Even Princess Tharien who had brought the weapon to her world could have had no true conception of the power contained within it. Metal of an older world than hers, wound about with sorcery from the deeps of time, it sprang from the leather scabbard like a living thing. Vivid, unearthly blue flame ignited along the narrow, leaf-shaped blade, and staring in disbelief at it, Esdiol recognised too late the nature of the force he had released. Nothing less powerful than the deep spells of Geirion could have hidden from him the nature of the thing that the Otherworlder had carried with him. Irvathil the Avenger, concealed in a humble wooden case and a shabby old sheath, was a weapon against which even he was helpless. The light leaped outward from the blade in a great silent explosion, illuminating the gorge like a magnesium flare. Brendan's wild glance around took in the walls of damp stone rearing on either side of him. Instead of being smooth as he would somehow have expected, they were sculpted, probably by the action of wind and water down the centuries; it would not be hard to make the lumps and hollows look like creatures, vast shapes half-embedded in the stone like the faces of the American Presidents on Mount Rushmore… Perhaps that was where the old story Lidan had told him had originated – perhaps somebody, at some point in time, had come down here for some reason and seen the shapes by torchlight; the more one looked at them, the more realistic they became. In fact – in fact…

If he'd thought about it at all, he would have thought himself inured to shock by now. Nevertheless, an appalled moan broke from him, though he never knew it. There was no mistaking it. One of the shapes had *moved...*

They broke free from the stone slowly, with ponderous, inexorable movements. Bits of rock snapped off and pattered down to the floor. A huge stone head moved. Its eyes opened. They reflected the unearthly blue glare that was still beating from Irvathil's blade. The air was growing hot, without a visible heat source.

Esdiol screamed.

In the same instant, the gorge was battered by a soundless shriek that drove Brendan to his knees, vainly shielding his ears:

'At last! AT LAST!'

From nowhere came the gale, a scorching, howling tempest of wind that clawed and buffeted at him. No ordinary storm this, however. It was an explosion of pure hatred, the harvest of uncounted centuries of waiting and dreaming of vengeance. The air was black and choking with it as the moment for repayment opened out. The indescribable violence of it pinned him to the floor, struggling desperately, blindly to burrow and escape it, helpless as an earthworm trapped and vulnerable on the stone.

Just in front of him, Esdiol screamed again. He understood too late that his greed had betrayed him. Joined with a mortal, he was himself no more than a mortal. The creatures he had deceived and used all those uncounted years ago tore themselves free of the rock and lurched forward. Snatching a chance to peep over his shielding arm, Brendan saw them only by glimpses. Enormous things, the darkness of their stone hides obscuring the details of their form, except where the light glanced off long curving claws, a narrow, deeply ridged forehead, teeth like glittering needles in the parting jaws…

The Skair flung Irvathil down, and in a frenzy of terror Esdiol tore himself loose. Turning his head, face still partly protected against the gale, Brendan saw the green glow eddying out of her, and when she cried out her voice was her own again. Her body twisted and changed, fluid and horrible and incredible to watch. It was very fast: mere seconds elapsed before she was a Skair again. Esdiol, now visible by the light of his own sorcerous nature, was a shape that might haunt fevered dreams. There was something horribly close to humanity in the hunched, shifting, sinuous shape, but the details of the face were hard to define, blurred like an image whose wax has melted. The eyes that glared from it were like a gateway into the Pit.

There was only one possible escape route for him now, and he took it. A gap appeared in the rocky wall, a pathway to his own world and safety. Returned to his own immortal form, he would have been beyond hurt by any mortal creature, but the sorcery of Irvathil at work in the deeps of Geirion made the three ancient creatures incalculably powerful. He leaped for the gap with a long bound that was utterly inhuman but curiously, dreadfully graceful. Desperation made him unbelievably swift. In an instant he was through, but even before Brendan could draw breath for a yell of fury, Lidan darted forward and picked up the blazing knife. Three slashes drew blue fire on the air, slicing open the gateway that had already begun to close. Then, incredibly, she picked up the meteor and drove the blade into it as easily as though it had been a rotten fruit.

For one instant she held it high, the focus of six great eyes. Then with a movement that almost flung her headlong, she hurled it into the gap. Dimensions shuddered and dissolved. With a concerted, vast cry that had in it an awful echo of the garynon's crazed shriek of triumph, the three creatures flung themselves after it. The gateway swallowed them and crashed shut. A great silent flash of blue fire came back, and a far-off wail of unutterable anguish; and then there was silence.

The quiet gorge was now filled with a faint luminosity, though there was no visible source for it. Brendan got to his knees and staggered upright. Lidan stumbled towards him. The leonine face had never been so eloquent or so dear. They met with bruising force, and hugged each other, both their faces wet.

He almost jerked back with shock as he felt her body begin to shudder. Surely it was over? But it seemed not, for the twisting accelerated. Her eyes held his, trying to communicate. Incredulously he saw her shape changing again; and then he understood.

"Lidan. *Lidan…*" He pulled her closer than before, burying his face in the side of her neck. The last shreds of horror were swallowed in the uprush of joy. Her inhumanity no longer mattered to him; finally he was able to accept her on equal terms, as lover and friend. He drew her down, and the stone floor was green and springy turf amid the bracken and the spreading bell-heather. Her eyes opened wide on his beautiful world, reflecting the wide sky where the cirrus clouds were pastel feathers stroked by the breeze from the vast Atlantic that spread out into the west, reflecting the pearl-shell colours of the sunset. Time stood still as they rediscovered the delight that two bodies can give one another, given new and wonderful depth by the acceptance and love that now replaced subterfuge on her side and casual lust on his. Now not just their bodies but their souls met, and when at last neither of them was able to contain it, the explosion was simultaneous. His deep masculine voice and her lighter feminine one echoed through the now empty and peaceful gorge, and when she opened her eyes again, over his shoulder she saw the first pale streaks of daylight. Far above, the new day was beginning. They lay entwined, utterly at peace, not even aware of the hardness of the stone floor on which they lay. Out of nowhere the thought came into his head: '*Now* I can go home!' and for a moment he didn't know whether to cheer or cry.

"You have done well, Starborn Kelti. Or Brendan Doyle, as you must be from now on."

"Mother Shieih," murmured Lidan dreamily. She did not move; was she not warm with the aftermath of honouring the Goddess?

"I'm delighted to meet you at last." He was too sleepy and relaxed to worry about Her. "I wish I could say it's been a pleasure, but it's certainly been an experience."

"You were equal to the task. Now we are in your debt. You deserve reward."

"I just had one." He kissed his companion's forehead gently.

"You are Dancer-born, a talent that Skaira hold sacred. If you so desire, I will make you the greatest dancer your world has ever seen. It would be small recompense for what you have done for my world."

He considered. It was certainly tempting. To be the best – to be a legend in his own right; to go down in the record books… He shook his head. If he was going to be the best, he wanted to do it on his own. "Don't think I'm not grateful. I am. But I don't want anything. Just to go home." It hurt to say it, but it was time. As wonderful as it was to lie here, he was hungry for the sights and sounds of his own world and his own friends, an English breakfast and a good cup of coffee (make that a dozen cups), and even Adrian in a tantrum over a sequence of steps that didn't look right. "I have to go," he whispered to Lidan. "Give my love to Kanehar and Hargen."

"Could you not give it to them yourself?" she asked, though she already knew the answer. The Singer had fallen silent, and the song was over.

"He has work to do, my Daughter, and so have you. You must now know that Thaskan has crossed the Endless Ocean. You are descended from Princess Tharien, and on your shoulders rests the task of healing your people and helping to restore your world."

"On mine?" Shock and apprehension showed for a few moments on her face, to be replaced by a grave acceptance. "Thaskan dead… there is no choice, then. It is my duty."

"Thaskan among others." The voice was very gentle. *"It is best that I should tell you the whole. Hargen too has come to me, and Riyeth will follow very soon. She has made amends for what she did amiss. Think of her gently. She had her part to play."*

"Hargen too?" They both moved suddenly, involuntarily, with shock and grief. A frown etched itself on Brendan's forehead, and he shook his head slowly.

"Hargen's name will be written in the songs that Kerriel will sing for ever. Your part now is to be the one who brings renewal. Lidan is no royal name. Thanaih I name you, the Royal Healer, and when you return to your own place and your own form, you will bear the colouring of the Royal House. Many await your help, though Kanehar has entered Thervanil and begun to restore order there in my name. Have no fear, I shall be with you in all things, and the worst will be past when your daughter mounts the Divan Throne. Do not grieve. You will have your reminder of Kelti."

They both looked up at that, startled; Lidan's face held dawning, half-fearful hope.

"The Dark One damaged your egg for his own purposes, but there is nothing that can not be turned to good by the Uncreated. You will bear a daughter to be proud of, and no-one but you will know the truth."

"I don't believe it." His brain reeled. Was it possible?

"Not only possible, but already accomplished."

"I'll never see her!"

"There is no such word as never. All worlds touch the Endless Ocean, and she and her mother will wait for you beyond it."

"Oh, Christ." He was crying, though he could never have said for what reasons: for joy and relief and regret inextricably mingled, for loss and gain and bewilderment. He held Lidan close with astonished reverence, and turned to look up for the last time at the sky of Kerriel. There were tiles on it. There were tiles on the wall in front of him too, and a glass door behind him. He and Lidan were standing locked together as though welded, and water dripped off them both. The smell of shower gel filled his nostrils.

"I can not bear to lose you," she whispered. "I am not strong enough."

"You haven't, and you are." He kissed her nose. "You heard what Shieih said – Thanaih." It wasn't something he was going to forget in a hurry. He touched her belly gently. His daughter. He had never seen a baby Skair, but he could imagine her. For a moment he found himself wishing that he could go back to Kerriel some day, to see it as it should be, and his daughter in her place there; but he knew without having to be told that there is never any going back.

"I know. I shall look after her for you." She grimaced. "By the One! I am of royal blood, and our daughter will be the Princess! To think I had hoped to return to my hut in peace when all was over – I think there is small chance of that now! How shall I manage?"

"You'll manage the way you managed to look after me." He gave her his infectious grin. –"And don't forget to tell her how handsome her daddy was. Have you decided on a name for her yet?"

"We do not name our daughters. It is revealed to us during the *ka'uere,* the travail. No doubt but Shieih will have something appropriate in mind." Her face softened. "As for speaking of her father – I may tell her, but I had better not tell anyone else! Sky and stars! That would set them all by the tail!" He'd succeeded; she was smiling again. He thought she had never looked lovelier. "I must go, dear Kelti. There is much to do on Kerriel, many wounds to bind. There will be work for many years to put right what was damaged or destroyed by the Evil One, but thanks to you we have hope for the future."

"You did help a little bit, you know." He gave her a last hug. "Now you'd better go, or I'll start honouring the Goddess with you all over again."

"Kelti!" She'd gone pink again. "You have a wicked tongue!"

"I thought you liked it," he replied, arching a suggestive eyebrow. She slapped him and laughed. Then, before either of them could waver, she stepped backwards. The wall dissolved. They made their farewells with their eyes. The darkness of between-worlds enveloped her.

"I wish he could have had some reward," she said aloud.

"He has his reward," replied Shieih enigmatically; and the Shrine of Vanreil came into being around her. In the light of the candles her brilliant white fur and blonde hair gleamed.

The Duty Priestess shrieked.

35

"What happened? What should we do now?" Keri'khai's voice battered insistently at Kanehar's exhaustion.

"Mother Shieih!" The Skair groaned. She hardly had the strength to raise her head. "Did you not understand, Son of the Sun?"

"Would I be asking if I had?"

She stifled a malediction. The snapping of the link that held her and the other three to Stiv'aran had been traumatic, for she had had to pull them all back from the path that the Emperor-Elect had taken. Even if she had been prepared for it, it would have been difficult: suddenly to be confronted with the reality of the Endless Ocean opening before them all had been a hideous shock. Her task had been to break Esdiol's hold on Stiv'aran's mind and keep it from being renewed: the intensity of concentration this had demanded had not allowed her any awareness of what the Venel lord was actually doing. To find herself and the others mind-linked to a suicide was perhaps the most dangerous situation telepathy could involve, and the effort it had taken to tear loose in time had left her lying flat on the greensward, feeling as though she had been run over by a herd of saddlebeasts.

Nevertheless, she still did not know what actually *had* happened. She had followed the Goddess's instructions, and hoped that together the four of them had done what was necessary; but she had no inkling of what the situation in Thervanil was now. Assuredly the evil Emperor-Elect had met the fate he deserved, but what had happened to Lidan and Kelti? She made the effort to sit up. The light was dying swiftly out of the sky. Some time had passed since Stiv'aran's death; the city was quiet, but at some very deep level of awareness she knew that the quietness was deceptive. Above them the air was strangely misty, and there was an odd strong smell of deep water all around.

"I do not like this," she said uneasily.

"What's wrong?" Keri'khai sat back and looked around sharply. "Have we been found?"

"No. It is – I think it is – *get down!"*

Regardless for once of any risk to his injured arms, she threw herself at him and flung both of them flat beside the tree. Before he could even gasp, the whole forest bent sideways before a blast of air that plucked leaves and blossoms wholesale from every twig, tore branches from trees and even uprooted saplings as it screamed westward towards the city.

It did not last long, perhaps a few minutes, but while it lasted it was terrifying in its intensity. For no reason he could have explained, for he was used to all weathers, Keri'khai was deeply grateful for Kanehar's proximity; afterwards he was faintly embarrassed to recall that he'd huddled into shelter underneath her like a hatchling, not even feeling the pain of his strained shoulder joints. The air all around was unnaturally hot, filled with flying debris that stung the skin; they both kept their heads down, protecting their faces.

Presently the turbulence lessened and died. The Skair raised her head cautiously, brushing back the long hair that had been whirled into a russet tangle it would take many hours of brushing and combing to restore to its customary order.

She knew that that gale had been something quite different to anything that ordinary weather patterns could produce: every nerve of her body had shrieked with the recognition of deep sorcery.

The world was ordinary again. The strange smell of water had gone, blown away on the wings of the gale. Above her the air was clear and clean, and the clouds had gone too. The vast pulsating spiral of stars that her people called the Great Dance hung motionless against the deep blue of infinity, surrounded by a thousand other pinpricks of light that pulsed as though with some unfathomable joy.

"It is over," she breathed. "Great Goddess, it is *over!"* He heard her draw in a great breath that broke on a sob. Hope surged up in him, half-suffocated by the fear that he might be misunderstanding her, but she leaped up from him and reared up to bare her wrists in an almost frenzied salute to the heavens. Incredulously he saw that she was almost dancing on hind-legs, tiredness and dignity alike forgotten as she shouted aloud in the Old Speech. That in itself, her abandonment of wariness and fear, told him that he had not misunderstood. Tension broke in him like a snapping bowstring and he flopped back on to the grass. Tears he had not shed for many years pricked at his eyes.

"Kelti," he murmured. "You have saved us all. The Goddess be praised!"

"Rehi!" Kanehar cried assent, plunging back on to all fours. "Now we have work to do. Your commander still lives! Do you not want to find him?"

"By the One! I knew I came here for something!" He laughed aloud – it was so easy to laugh over anything and nothing now. "We must fill Kelti's lap with gold for this night's work!"

Kanehar looked suddenly thoughtful. "It is in my heart that we may not find Kelti in Thervanil," she said slowly. "I think he has fulfilled his destiny here."

"So soon?"

"The One who brought him will take him home." She stared up at the stars. "Somewhere out there. Somewhere his heart belongs."

"'Every stag wants his own stable'," he quoted wryly. "And if you can help me up, I'd like to get back to my stable eventually!"

* * *

Teho'evan blinked into the sudden light of the opening door. For a long moment he was too dazzled to know who came with torches; there were at least five figures outside, and surely one of them was a Skair? Three of them advanced into the room, and as his eyes adjusted he knew two of them. Keri'khai bent over him, and reflected light glinted on the keys in his hand. Not even the renewed pain to his injured shoulders could prevent him from taking the satisfaction of unlocking his Commander's manacles personally, though all else he must leave to his subordinate. The Skair had checked briefly at what she saw.

"Thaskan," she said sadly, after a pause. "I feared that this might have happened." She touched the other Skair, now slumped over the Princess's body. "Riyeth!"

There was no reply. Nor, it seemed, did she truly expect one. She straightened up and stepped carefully over her two sisters to crouch beside Teho'evan. "There will be a time and a place to attend to those, who are beyond any skills of mine. For now, my duty is to the living. Lay him back carefully, I must examine him." The second soldier gently eased him flat on the floor and put a folded cloth under his head.

"She's a Healer," the lieutenant reassured his senior officer. "Sir, we've won – we've won!"

"*She* didn't," Teho'evan said dully, looking sideways at Riyeth. "I don't understand. She wasn't hurt!"

"She was hurt in a way for which there is no healing this side of the Endless Ocean," answered Kanehar, feeling gently at his broken arm. "She will not come back."

"Then it's not fair!"

"No, it is not fair. Life is not fair, warlord. You above all others should know that. Are there not orphans and widows left bereft when you wage war? Nevertheless we could not have succeeded without her, and I think she would not grudge the cost." She ripped his tunic and began checking his ribs, then his legs. "Well, it will be a while and a while before you are fit for the war-trail again, but I think you not beyond salvaging."

"Stiv'aran's dead, isn't he?" he said suddenly. "What actually happened?"

She looked down at him with a flicker of humour. "What happened? I wonder if we will ever truly know! Some of it your lieutenant here can tell you, when I have you properly washed and treated. The rest I think is the Goddess's secret, to be revealed if and when She chooses. But yes, the Emperor-Elect is dead. These men behind us are from your squadron, and they say the Empress is safe. We have despatched trustworthy officers to take control in the Palace and release her. Now whatever hatches from her egg will inherit the Horned Throne after all."

"The Palace won't be any problem," Keri'khai put in. "Half the people here are just waiting to be told what to do. With Stiv'aran gone, they're leaderless – and most of them are just relieved to have somebody take charge."

"Let's hope the egg has a boy inside it." Teho'evan managed an echo of her half-smile.- "Otherwise there'll be Tharnil to pay fending off all the suitors as soon as the Heiress comes of age."

At that Kanehar did laugh. "A throne to inherit and all this to put to rights? And you think the Good Goddess so small of heart that she might add warfare over a princess to the grief? I think you need have small worry there. I would wager a gold armlet against a broken waterpot that when Mia'naan's egg hatches there will be a little prince kicking in the shards!" She signed to another of the soldiers to come forward. "But first, Son of the Sun, I am going to have you taken out of here to somewhere I can look after you properly."

The Epilogue

There were towels warming on the radiator, and Brendan got out of the shower cubicle and dried himself slowly, staring at nothing. Even now, it would have been so easy to believe he'd imagined it all. When he was finished, he walked back into the bedroom, and stood for a while, looking around at the marvels he had always taken so much for granted. He picked up his watch from the bedside table and put it on, lifting it to his ear to listen as if for the first time to the tiny silvery sounds of its movement. The table-lamp was still on. The moon had advanced a little: the broad bar of its light was now on the carpet. He stepped to the bed, and rested his fingers lightly on the crumpled sheets; then he knelt, and stayed there for several minutes, breathing the lost scent of her.

For all that he had wanted so desperately to come back, for all that this world was his home and everything he had ever known and loved was here, he was suddenly torn by an agonising sense of loss and loneliness. The rest of his life stretched out in front of him, a featureless waste of meaningless encounters in hotel rooms. Was he always to look into one pretty face after another, hungering vainly for the eyes that looked back into his with an intensity that belonged to no other in the world? His fingers tightened on the sheets, clenching into fists. He couldn't stay in this room tonight. Turning away to the bedside table, he picked up the phone and spoke briefly. The whims of an important member of their entourage had to be indulged; finding him alternative quarters wouldn't be a problem. Meanwhile, it would be senseless for him to linger here, tormenting himself with memories. He'd get dressed again, go downstairs and see if at this hour they could fix him a sandwich – and he was definitely going to have at least six cups of coffee. For a moment he savoured the possibility of ringing his family, but though he touched the phone again, largely just for the pleasure of its familiarity, he didn't lift the receiver. A call at this hour would only alarm them, and what could he say? Just to know that he could do it was enough. He'd ring them in the morning. Well, later in the morning – it was now well past midnight.

Luxuriating in the sheer *normality* of it all, he got into clean clothing – even the button and zip on his jeans were a novelty after all this time – then left the room and sauntered towards the stairs. For all that he'd seen so many, had become jaded by the succession of hotels that his nomadic existence had made into part of the background, he looked around him now at this one with something close to euphoria. Even the buttons in the lift were something to be gazed at with gratitude. He reached the foyer just as a good number of his colleagues walked in fresh from the celebration, and he was immediately barraged with vulgarities.

"What, got rid of her already? Come and have a drink then, you randy bogtrotter," shouted Adrian, who had a flower stuck behind one ear and a giggling girl in either arm. "Was she good?"

"Out of this world," replied Brendan, grinning.

"And you only shagged her once?" demanded Kieran in mock disgust. "And I bet you never took her phone number. You should've introduced her to me, and I'd have shown her what a real man's made of."

"She wanted a stallion, not a donkey."

They sparred cheerfully as they crowded into the bar with the rest of the gang. Normality folded itself back around Brendan like warm wings as he sat back in a big leather easy chair, though it couldn't quite warm away the lingering chill of loss inside him. Now even the glass in his hand was worth a second look, with the light glittering in the facets of it, and glowing in the tawny heart of the Irish whiskey inside. (*Uisge beatha,* he thought reminiscently as the first rush of fire went down his throat, and he lifted his glass slightly in a silent, private salute.) He was just about to settle down to enjoy the rest of it when a movement a couple of tables away caught his idly roaming gaze. He stiffened.

A brunette, in a white blouse and a long black skirt, with a loose leather jacket. She was sitting alone, and had just finished her drink. As he watched, she dropped something in the ashtray and reached for her handbag.

He put his drink down so hastily that the golden spirit slopped out of the glass. It wasn't possible! She looked around the room. Brown eyes, but they held no strangeness, only sadness. He was suddenly certain she'd come to meet someone who hadn't shown up. It hadn't struck him before to wonder why Lidan's human form had been so surprisingly unlike her own as a Skair: even her hair colour had been different. The suspicion crystallised into certainty that she had been a pointer to his future when their paths diverged again, as diverge they must when their joint destiny had been fulfilled.

"Shieih, you cunning, devious bitch," he said under his breath.

"I shall take that as a compliment. Farewell, Kelti. Be kind to her."

Kieran looked at him in surprise as he stood up. Following the direction of his now intent stare, he swore: "You dirty bleeder, don't you ever give up?"

"I've a feeling I may be about to," replied Brendan enigmatically as he walked away. She too had stood up, settling the strap of the handbag over her shoulder. As he drew level with her, he looked down into the ashtray. A ring: a miserable little gewgaw like something out of a Christmas cracker. He'd buy her a solitaire the size of a plum stone, and they'd have handsome children and laugh a lot in bed. 'You stupid bastard,' he thought to whatever fool had let her go. 'You dropped, I caught!'

She looked up in surprise to find him beside her. There was a scattering of freckles on her cheekbones, just where Lidan's whiskers had been. He took in the faint frown line between the slightly arching eyebrows, the gathering tears she blinked away from the gaze of a stranger. *Be kind to her.* She'd been hurt: he mustn't take advantage. His body was quiet, but he felt suddenly fiercely protective. He wanted to put his arms around her, but it would take time for her to discover what he already knew.

The watching dancers saw him speak gently to her. There was a hint of the devastating smile; he knew exactly how to be irresistible. With a mixture of awe and resignation they watched the two of them sit down together; but even they were taken aback when a few moments later her hands and his were clasped on the table.

"Oh, quick work, Bren!" Martin chalked a score on an imaginary board, and guffawed. Neither he nor any of his fellows recognised her; none of them ever even noticed that the details of their friend's earlier conquest had been totally erased from their minds. "Two in a row! Did you ever know such a horny sod?"

"And they call me a womaniser!" grinned Adrian. "I could take lessons from that one!"
"Doesn't he *ever* get his face slapped?" asked Sean rhetorically; they'd never seen it happen yet. "How does he do it?"
"And where does he get the bloody energy from?" demanded Kevin, yawning. "Doesn't he need any sleep?"
Kieran had been watching the scene with an unaccustomed thoughtfulness. He'd seen Brendan in action often enough; holding hands was nothing to write home about. It should have been just one move in another seduction. And yet he looked at the intent dark face bent towards her; and was it just imagination…? He picked up the forgotten whiskey, intending to take it over and play his friend up a little. He laughed. "Practice, kiddies. And generally speaking, you could just say he's a luckier sod than most!"

The Author

Bernadette Danaher was born and still lives in Birmingham with her husband and two children. *The Annunciation of the Starborn* is her first novel